THE BIG BOOK OF Favorite Horse Stories

Twenty-Five Outstanding Stories by Distinguished Authors

Foreword and Illustrations by Sam Savitt

Edited by P.C. Braun

Platt & Munk, Publishers/New York
A Division of Grosset & Dunlap

Published simultaneously in Canada. Printed in the U.S.A.
Library of Congress Catalog Card Number: 65-15196
ISBN 0-448-42641-2

1989 Printing

ACKNOWLEDGMENTS

For their courtesy in extending permission to reprint certain copyrighted material, grateful acknowledgment is made to the following authors, representatives, and publishing houses:

BETTER READING FOUNDATION, INC.: "The Winning of Dark Boy" by Josephine Noyes Felts; from *Calling All Girls* magazine; copyright 1945 by Parents' Institute.

WILLIAM BLACKWOOD & SONS LIMITED, Edinburgh, Scotland: "Beast of God" by Cecilia Dabrowska; copyright © Cecilia Dabrowska; first appeared in *Blackwood's* magazine, April, 1963.

LURTON BLASSINGAME: "The Black Horse" by Jim Kjelgaard; copyright 1939 by Crowell-Collier.

BOYS' LIFE and IRVING CRUMP: "Two-bits of Traffic C" by Irving Crump; from *Boys' Life*, published by the Boy Scouts of America; first appeared in the August, 1935 issue.

DOUBLEDAY & COMPANY, INC.: "Coaly-bay, the Outlaw Horse" from *Wild Animal Ways* by Ernest Thompson Seton; copyright 1916 by Ernest Thompson Seton. "Trapped" from *Vicki and the Black Horse* by Sam Savitt; copyright 1964 by Sam Savitt.

E. P. DUTTON & CO., INC. and THE ROYAL SOCIETY FOR THE PROTECTION OF BIRDS and THE SOCIETY OF AUTHORS: "Cristiano: A Horse" from *The Book of a Naturalist* by W. H. Hudson.

NINA AMES FREY: "Waif of the Jungle," selections from *The River Horse* by Nina Ames Frey, published by William R. Scott, Inc.; copyright 1953 by Nina Ames Frey.

HARCOURT, BRACE & WORLD, INC.: "First Day Finish" from *The Friendly Persuasion* by Jessamyn West; copyright 1944 by Jessamyn West. "The Summer of the Beautiful White Horse" from *My Name Is Aram* by William Saroyan; copyright 1937, 1938, 1939, 1940 by William Saroyan.

Acknowledgments continued

JUDSON PRESS: "Night Star" and "Indian Fighter" by Stephen Holt; copyright 1947 *Teens* and 1944 The Judson Press, respectively. "Flame" by Willis Lindquist; copyright 1949 *Teens.*

GLADYS FRANCIS LEWIS: "The Black Stallion and the Red Mare" by Gladys Francis Lewis, published by the Copp Clark Publishing Co., Ltd.; Gladys Francis Lewis, copyright owner.

THE MACMILLAN COMPANY: "The First Race" from *High Courage* by C. W. Anderson; copyright 1941 by The Macmillan Company.

RAND MCNALLY & COMPANY: "Before Misty" from *Misty of Chincoteague* by Marguerite Henry; copyright 1947 by Rand McNally & Company, publishers.

PAUL R. REYNOLDS, INC.: "My Friend Flicka" by Mary O'Hara; copyright 1941 by Mary O'Hara.

SCHOLASTIC MAGAZINES, INC.: "Easy Does It!" by Robert L. McGrath; copyright 1955 by Scholastic Magazines, Inc.

CHARLES SCRIBNER'S SONS: "The Seeing Eye" from *Horses I Have Known* by Will James; copyright 1940 by Will James.

STORY PARADE, INC.: "The Royal Greens" by Russell Gordon Carter; copyright 1940 by Story Parade, Inc.

UNITED NATIONS WORLD, INC. and WORLD EVENTS MAGAZINE, INC.: "The Horse of the Sword" by Manuel Buaken; appeared in *Asia Magazine,* August, 1943.

THE VIKING PRESS, INC.: "The Gift" from *The Red Pony* by John Steinbeck; copyright 1933, 1961 by John Steinbeck.

ANNA-KATHARINA WYLER-SALTEN: "An Imperial Performance" from *Florian, the Emperor's Stallion* by Felix Salten; copyright by Anna-Katharina Wyler-Salten, Zurich, Switzerland.

Contents

CONTENTS

Foreword

BY SAM SAVITT

IT'S no secret that I love horses—all horses, and have, ever since I can remember.

To me they are action, strength, rhythm, beauty, all rolled into one superb creature—a "beast of God" as one author so aptly puts it. I have spent many years with horses, and devoted much time and energy to the study of these magnificent animals. I have written about them and illustrated them. I have raised them, schooled them, shown them, and galloped cross country on them to the music of the hounds and the thrilling sound of the hunting horn. I've had my falls, too, plenty of them. But I've also experienced a deep thrill of pride and pleasure as I leaned my elbows on a barway rail and watched my own horse move freely across a green meadow, his dark coat shimmering in the brilliant sunlight.

There is nothing quite so fine, to my mind, as seeing a spirited horse galloping and wheeling across a field. I decided this when I was still a boy, when owning a horse seemed a remote and impossible dream.

Since that time, I have taught a good many people to ride. And the point I stress to all my pupils is that, to handle any horse skillfully, one must first understand him, be aware of his way of thinking and acting.

What is this unique horse being? What is he like?

He is, in some ways, a paradox of nature. Because of his size it is difficult to realize that he is a timid creature, quick to fright and flight. Yet he can be taught to gallop into the thick of artillery fire, ford a flooded river, endure head-on collisions of the polo field, face a maddened steer, or jump a course of the most formidable obstacles you've ever seen. He has a simple one-track mind, but he possesses a terrific memory, like Cristiano, or Two-bits in "Two-bits of Traffic C."

A horse is, actually, a reasonable creature. He responds to firm, kind, consistent treatment and is taught to do things by extreme patience and repetition. He can and should be punished for disobedience, but never in anger and never, of course, painfully. A horse, like most animals, will respond more to rewards for good performance than to blows for misbehavior. The carrot is mightier than the whip, as C. W. Anderson's story of Bobcat illustrates. Almost any horse will shy if surprised, and almost any horse likes to be "reasoned with" and talked to. As Billy Buck told Jody in "The Gift," "A horse never kicked up a fuss if someone he liked explained things to him."

In this way and in other ways too, horses are a lot like people. Some are bold and fearless, some extremely timid. There are the standoffish kind, and the friendly and affectionate ones. There are even a few like Coaly-bay, who make up their minds to accomplish something and scheme to that end until they succeed. But whatever their individual characteristics, they remain horses, who think and act like horses.

In the stories I've mentioned so far and in most of the stories in this anthology, I have been impressed with one thing: the authors write about real horses, and not creatures somehow endowed with human characteristics; their horses have horse sense, not human intelligence. The great westerner Will James never had to humanize the horses in his wonderful stories, of which "The Seeing Eye" is a shining example. Mary O'Hara's Flicka is all horse, satin skin and flying mane—big as life. The red pony and all that happens to him is real, as poignantly real as the joy and anguish of the boy Jody for his little foal. And not only the horses, but the stories themselves have the quality of reality. They deal not just with the good and the beautiful, but also with the unpleasant things that are as much a part of life.

There is, it's true, one story in which a horse is endowed with human characteristics: "Black Beauty," that favorite of generations of readers. Certainly Black Beauty talks and thinks like a human about his horse's life. But I believe that Anna Sewell, who loved horses, wrote as she did deliberately. She wanted to dramatize the plight of horses in a time when too many people thought of them only as machines of work. Her main point, that horses are feeling animals, often sorely abused and ignorantly handled, comes across just as eloquently today.

Every story in this collection reached me in a different way with its own particular impact. Saroyan's "The Summer of the Beautiful White Horse" has a whimsical nostalgia that recalls to me a summer when I was a boy, and the brown horse my friend and I rode double all over the Pennsylvania countryside. Edgar Allan Poe's "Metzengerstein" chilled me with an eeriness that only Poe can impart. And Jim Kjelgaard's "The Black Horse" bound me to that crippled boy who was so determined to catch him. "The Beast of God" and "The Royal Greens" sat me on the edge of my seat, and I don't think I'll ever forget the touching tale of "The Black Stallion and the Red Mare."

All of these stories I relished, and when I finished I knew I had been brought closer to the animals I love best, and that somehow my life was made richer and fuller by the experience—as I hope yours will be, too.

North Salem, New York
January, 1965

THE BIG BOOK OF FAVORITE HORSE STORIES

The bonds of devotion

The Black Stallion and the Red Mare

BY GLADYS FRANCIS LEWIS

AT first Donald lay still. Scarcely a muscle moved. The boulders and the low shrubs screened him from view. Excitement held him motionless. His hands gripped the short grass and his toes dug into the dry earth. Cautiously he raised himself on his elbows and gazed at the scene below him.

There, in his father's unfenced hay flats, was the outlaw band of wild horses. They were grazing quietly on the rich grass. Some drank from the small hillside stream. Donald tried to count them, but they suddenly began moving about and he could not get beyond twenty. He thought there might be two hundred.

Donald knew a good deal about that band of horses, but he had never had the good luck to see them. They were known over many hundreds of square miles. They had roamed at will over the grain fields and they had led away many a domestic horse to the wild life. Once in that band, a horse was lost to the farm.

There in the flats was the great black stallion, the hero or the villain of a hundred tales. Over the far-flung prairie and grasslands there was scarcely a boy who had not dreamed of wild rides with the great body of the stallion beneath him, bearing him clean through the air with the sharp speed of lightning.

There was the stallion now, moving among the horses with the sureness and ease of a master. As he moved about, teasingly kicking here and nipping there, a restlessness, as of a danger sensed, stirred through the band. The stallion cut to the outside of the group. At a full gallop he snaked around the wide circle, roughly bunching the mares and colts into the smaller circle of an invisible corral.

He was a magnificent creature, huge and proudly built. Donald saw the gloss of the black coat and the great curving muscles of the strong legs, the massive hoofs, the powerful arch of the neck, the proud crest of the head. Donald imagined he could see the flash of black, intelligent eyes. Surely a nobler creature never roamed the plains!

Off-wind from the herd, a red mare came out from the fold of the low hills opposite. She stood motionless a moment, her graceful head held high. Then she nickered. The black stallion drew up short in his herding, nickered eagerly, then bolted off in the direction of the mare. She stood waiting until he had almost reached her; then they galloped back to the herd together.

The shadows crept across the hay flats and the evening stillness settled down. A bird sang sleepily on one note. Donald suddenly became aware of the monotonous song and stirred from his intent watching. He must tell his father and help send news around the countryside. He was still intensely excited as he crept back from the brow of the hill and hurried home. All the time his mind was busy and his heart was bursting.

Donald knew that three hundred years ago the Spaniards had brought horses to Mexico. Descendants of these horses had wandered into the Great Plains. These horses he now was watching were of that Spanish strain. Thousands of them roamed the cattle lands north to the American boundary. This band now grazed wild over these park lands here in Canada—four hundred and fifty miles north of the boundary.

His father and the farmers for many miles around had determined to round up the horses and make an end of the roving band. As a farmer's son, Donald knew that this was necessary and right. But a certain respect for the band and the fierce loyalty that he felt toward all wild, free creatures made him wish in his heart that they might never be caught, never be broken and tamed. He, who was so full of sympathy for the horses, must be traitor to them!

There had been conflicts in his heart before, but never had there been such a warring of two strong loyalties. He saw himself for the first time as a person of importance because he, Donald Turner, had the power to affect the lives of others. This power, because it could help or harm others, he knew he must use wisely.

When he stood before his father half an hour later, he did not blurt out his news. It was too important for that. But his voice and his eyes were tense with excitement. "That band of wild horses is in the hay hollow, west of the homestead quarter," he said. "There must be close to two hundred."

His father was aware of the boy's deep excitement. At Donald's first words he stopped his milking, his hands resting on the rim of the pail as he looked up.

"Good lad, Donald!" he said, quietly enough. "Get your supper and we'll ride to Smith's and Duncan's to start the word around. Tell Mother to pack lunches for tomorrow. We'll start at sunup." He turned to his milking again.

The other men were in the yard shortly after daylight.

Donald afterward wondered how long it would have taken ranch hands to round up the band of horses. These farmers knew horses, but not how to round up large numbers of them as the men of the ranch country knew so well. The farmers learned a good deal in the next two weeks.

Twenty men started out after the band as it thundered out of the hay flats, through the hills and over the country. The dust rose in clouds as their pounding hoofs dug the dry earth. The herd sped before the pursuers with the effortless speed of the wind. The black stallion led or drove his band and kept them well together. That first day only the young colts were taken.

At sunset the riders unsaddled and staked their horses by a poplar thicket, ate their stale lunches and lay down to sleep under the stars. Their horses cropped the short grass and drank from the stream. Some slept standing; others lay down.

At dawn the herd was spied moving westward. With the coming of night, they, too, had rested. For a mile or more they now sped along the rim of a knoll, swift as bronchos pulled in off the range after a winter out. The black stallion was a hundred feet ahead, running with a tireless, easy swing, his mane and tail streaming and his body stretched level as it cut through the morning mists. Close at his side, but half a length behind him, ran the red mare. The band streamed after.

After the first day's chase and the night under the stars, Donald had ridden back home. Not that he had wanted to go back. He would have given everything that he owned to have gone on with the men. But there were horses and cattle and chores to attend to at home, and there was school.

The roundup continued. Each day saw the capture of more and more horses. As the men doubled back on their course, they began to see that the wild horses traveled in a great circle, coming back again and again over the same ground, stopping at the same watering holes and feeding in the same rich grass flats. Once this course became clear, fresh riders and mounts in relays were posted along the way, while others drove on from behind. The wild band had still to press on with little chance for rest and feeding. The strain of the pursuit took away their desire for food, but they had a burning thirst and the black stallion would never let them drink their fill before he drove them on. Fatigue grew on them.

As the roundup continued, the whole countryside stirred with excitement. At every town where there was a grain elevator along the railroad, people repeated the latest news of the chase. On the farms the hay went unmown or unraked, and the plows rested still in the last furrow of the summer fallow. At school the children played roundup at recess. Donald, at his desk, saw the printed pages of his books, but his mind was miles away, running with the now almost exhausted wild horses.

Near the end of the second week of the chase, Donald's father rode into the yard. Donald dropped the wood he was carrying to the house and ran to meet his father.

"Dad, they haven't got the black stallion and the red mare, have they?" Donald could scarcely wait for his father's slow reply.

"No, Donald, lad," he said. "Though those two are the only horses still free. They're back in the flats. We'll get them tomorrow."

Donald felt both relief and fear.

In the yellow lamplight of the supper table his father told of the long days of riding, of the farms where he had eaten and rested, and of the adventures of each day.

"That was a gallant band, lad!" he said. "Never shall we see their equal! Those two that are left are a pair of great horses. Most wild horses show a weakening in the strain and grow up with little wind or muscle. But these two are sound of wind and their muscles are like steel. Besides that, they have intelligence. They would have been taken long ago but for that."

No one spoke. Donald felt that his father was on his side, the side of the horses. After a long pause, Mr. Turner continued.

"With his brains and his strength, that stallion could have got away in the very beginning. He could have got away a dozen times and would now be free south of the border. But that was his band. He stayed by them and he tried to get them to safety. This week, when his band had been rounded up, he stuck by that red mare. She is swift but she can't match his speed. It's curious the way they keep together! He stops and nickers. She nickers in reply and comes close to him, her nose touching his flank. They stand a moment. Then they are away again, she running beside him but not quite neck to neck. Day after day it is the same. They are no ordinary horseflesh, those two, lad!"

There was a lump in Donald's throat. He knew what his father meant. Those horses seemed to stand for something bigger and greater than himself. There were other things that made him feel the same—the first full-throated song of the meadow lark in the spring, ripe golden fields of wheat with the breeze rippling it in waves, the sun setting over the rim of the world in a blaze of rose and gold, the sun rising again in the quiet east, the smile in the blue depths of his mother's eyes, the still whiteness of the snowbound plains, the story of Columbus dauntlessly sailing off into unknown seas.

These things were part of a hidden, exciting world. The boy belonged to these things in some strange way. He caught only glimpses of that hidden world, but those glimpses were tantalizing. Something deep within him leaped up in joy.

That night Donald dreamed of horses nickering to him, but when he tried to find them, they were no longer there. Then he dreamed that he was riding the great black stallion, riding over a far-flung range, riding along a hilltop road with the world spread below him on every side. He felt the powerful body of the horse beneath him. He felt the smooth curves of the mighty muscles. Horse and rider seemed as one.

A cold dawn shattered his glorious dream ride. With his father he joined the other horsemen. From the crest of the slope from which Donald had first seen them, the pair of horses was sighted. They were dark moving shadows in the gray mists of the morning.

They had just finished drinking deep from the stream. Not for two weeks had the men seen the horses drink like that. Thirsty as they were, they had taken but one drink at each water hole. This last morning they were jaded and spent; they had thrown caution to the winds.

At the first suspicion of close danger, they stood still, heads and tails erect. Then they dashed toward the protecting hills. There the way forked.

It was then Donald saw happen the strange thing his father had described. At the fork the stallion halted and nickered. The mare answered and came close. She touched his flank with her head. Then they bounded off and disappeared in the path that led northwest to the rougher country where the chase had not led before.

Along the way the horses had been expected to take, grain-fed horses had been stationed. These had now to move over northwest. But the men were in no hurry today. They were sure of the take before nightfall. The sun was low in the west when two riders spurred their mounts for the close-in. The stallion and the mare were not a hundred yards ahead. They were dead spent. Their glossy coats were flecked with dark foam. Fatigue showed in every line of their bodies. Their gallant spirits no longer could drive their spent bodies. The stallion called to the mare. He heard her answer behind him. He slowed down, turning wildly in every direction. She came up to him, her head drooped on his flank and rested there. In a last wild defiance, the stallion tossed his magnificent head and drew strength for a last mighty effort. Too late!

The smooth coils of a rope tightened around his feet. He was down, down and helpless. He saw the mare fall as the rope slipped over her body and drew tight around her legs. It maddened him. He struggled wildly to be free. The taut rope held. The stallion was conquered. In that last struggle something went out of him. Broken was his body and broken was his spirit. Never again would he roam the plains, proud and free, the monarch of his herd.

Donald saw it all. He felt it all. His hands gripped the pommel of the saddle and his knees pressed hard against his pony's side. Tears blinded his eyes, and from his throat came the sound of a single sob. It was as if he himself were being broken and tied.

The sun dipped below the rim of the plains. The day was gone; the chase was ended. The men stood about smoking and talking in groups of twos and threes, examining the two roped horses. Donald's father knelt close to the mare, watching her intently. Donald watched him. His father remained quiet for a moment, one knee still resting on the ground, in his hand his unsmoked pipe. Donald waited for his father to speak. At last the words came.

"Boys," he said, without looking up, and with measured words, "do you know, this mare is blind—stone blind!"

A week later, Donald and his father stood watching those two horses in the Turner corral. They were not the same spirited creatures, but they were still magnificent horses.

"I figured," his father said, turning to the boy, "that they had won the right to stay together. I've brought them home for you. They are yours, lad. I know you will be good to them."

GLADYS FRANCIS LEWIS first heard the story of "The Black Stallion and the Red Mare" as a 12-year old girl, when her family moved from Ontario to the prairie city of Saskatoon, Saskatchewan. During a roundup of a band of wild horses which were damaging their grain fields, the neighboring prairie farmers tumbled onto the secret of the devoted black stallion and the red mare. It made a deep impression on the young girl. For over thirty years, during which Mrs. Lewis graduated from the University, taught school, married and raised a daughter, the idea stayed with her. Finally, in 1946, she wrote it down. It was her first writing attempt and so successful that she has kept on writing ever since, producing children's stories and a historical novel. Although Mrs. Lewis and her editor-husband are both Canadians they have roots in America through their colonial ancestors.

Of the thousands of readers who have been deeply moved by the story of the stallion and his mare, few know their real-life ending: the two horses finished out their days completely tamed, and surrounded by adoring children who rode the horse-drawn school "bus" it was the job of the pair to pull!

Victory in defeat

The First Race

BY C. W. ANDERSON

PATSY turned over drowsily, then suddenly sat up listening. The sound of driving rain beat against the windows. She leaped out of bed and hurried to look out. In the thin watery light of early dawn she could see puddles standing everywhere. Early fall leaves lay sodden on the graveled walks. She groaned as she crawled back into bed. This was the great day she and Holley had been waiting for so eagerly—Bobcat's first start in a race. Now the going would be deep and treacherous; even willing jumpers would be falling or refusing. What chance would she have with as uncertain and temperamental a horse as Bobcat? She tossed and turned from side to side trying to go to sleep again, but her mind was too active. She wouldn't scratch the horse, not after all the chaffing she had taken since the entry lists had appeared in the program. But wasn't the rain stopping? As she sat up to listen, the lull was followed by a downpour that sounded like surf against the house.

A little later a dripping, woebegone figure in a streaming raincoat hurried into the stable. Holley was not in sight, but the smell of coffee led her to his room.

"Morning, Miss Patsy. My, but you're wet," said Holley

"Take off your coat and sit next to the stove an' dry yourself. Won't offer you any coffee—it's strong enough to knock you down. Myself, I sort of need something to wake me up mornings."

"Oh, Holley! What shall we do?" Patsy was almost in tears.

"Do? Why, we'll prob'ly win ourselves a race," answered Holley, pouring out another cup of coffee that was black as night.

"But all this rain, Holley. The course will be terrible. And you know how Bobcat is."

"I know he's the fastest horse in the race, an' the most powerful an' the best jumper. It's raining all over the course, honey, an' it's going to be just as deep an' slippery where the other horses jump as where Bobcat does. Don't forget that."

"But, Holley, I wanted things perfect so he'd do his best."

"Listen, honey. I don't mind a horse that's choosy because he's headstrong an' independent. But a horse that quits just because the going is tough ain't worth his salt. If I thought our horse was like that I wouldn't have let you get so high on him. But I think Bobcat's a fighter an' I b'lieve the tougher things are the better he'll be. You've never seen him refuse a real big fence, have you? That's the kind that stops a fainthearted horse. But he never even picks the lowest part of a jump—he's too proud for that. Course, it's too bad that it ain't a nice day so more people would see him win. Prob'ly the wet'll make the curl come out of your hair, too, but I don't think it'll tarnish the cup before you get it home."

"Holley, you're a darling. I feel better already. You're sure you aren't saying this just to cheer me up?"

"Now listen, honey; listen carefully. Today we got to find out things about our horse. If he ain't got plenty of heart an' stay we better know it now. Maybe we won't win the race—lots of things can happen, an' he's green an' willful—but I want to see him make his mistakes the right way. There are too many that look like champs when they have things their own way. They can run like stake horses in the workouts an' then quit cold when another colt looks them in the eye in a race. They call that kind 'morning-glories' around the tracks. We don't want to waste any time training that sort. Whether Bobcat is running first or last I want to see him fighting—coming into the last fence.

"I ain't worrying much about Bobcat. Orneriness is usually courage that's got twisted, somehow. All you got to do is straighten it out. You better get a good breakfast so you can stay on. From the way Bobcat has been acting this morning I think you're going to have a running horse under you. Yes, I sure do."

"Keep the red flags to your left," called the starter.

The rain was now a steady drizzle, and the flag the starter held in his hand hung limp in damp heavy folds. There was a little crowding, several horses were impatient, and Bobcat on the outside snorted, swerved and lunged every time another horse moved forward. Patsy sat him closely, pale and tense, trying to quiet him and glowing inwardly at his eagerness.

Despite the miserable day a good-sized crowd was out. Colored umbrellas spotted the soft green landscape like colorful mushrooms and made a gay accent against the clusters of wet raincoats. Many of Patsy's friends and acquaintances were present, and in spite of occasional good-natured banter she had been warmed by the many wishes of good luck that she had received. When Holley had pulled the blanket from Bobcat she heard enough exclamations from seasoned horsemen to know that they also felt that Bobcat was the fittest horse in the field. At no time since they left the stable had he shown anything but impatience and eager excitement. Holley was obviously pleased and as she neared the course Patsy's heart rose to feel that her mount responded so completely to her own eagerness. Holley carried a bucket in his hand in which were twenty carrots covered by a cloth.

"I'll give him a look at them before the race, just for luck. It won't do any harm, though I feel you're more apt to need some four-wheel brakes to keep him from going around the course twice."

A blaze-faced bay horse broke up the start again, carrying Bobcat and two others with him, and the starter called them back impatiently. They lined up again, and as Patsy swung Bobcat around, the flag dropped and in a churning of hoofs they were off to a good start. The bay showed in front as they came to the first fence, but Bobcat was almost even as they rose to it. Despite the soft turf Bobcat jumped as always, big and bold, and in a few strides he was in front and drawing away. Patsy crouched forward and looked for the next fence through the gray drizzle. Here was the test. Would he keep to the job, now that he was in front, or would he refuse or run out at the next fence? If there had been a horse in front she would have had no fears. She glanced over her shoulder and saw that already the field was strung out and that the bay, who was nearest, was four lengths back.

There was the next fence—six panels of chestnut post and rails between the flags—and she took a steady hold on her horse and headed for the center panel, felt him gather himself and rise like something propelled by huge springs. The surging power of his stride as he drove on made her feel like singing.

"Bobcat," she cried, "oh, Bobcat, you're wonderful!"

The big horse pricked his ears and raced for the next fence.

He was now settled into a powerful rhythmic stride that ate up the distance; she knew he had another notch that he could let out—maybe two—and, even so, he led by ten lengths. Now Patsy was being repaid for all the weeks and months of patience. Now he was going as she had dreamed he would, as she and Holley had known he could. Through her reins, through her whole body, she felt the willingness and spirit of the big horse under her.

In a slight dip stood the next fence, the biggest on the course. Bobcat had often jumped it at this speed, but not in such soft, treacherous footing. Patsy took a strong pull, hoping to slow him a trifle; but she felt at once that there was nothing to do but to let the big horse take it in his own way. The fence loomed large, solid and threatening; surely he was coming into it too far away. She felt the swelling muscles in his shoulder and then she was looking down at the fence from what seemed a great height.

"Bobcat, you're grand!" she whispered over and over.

The course swung slightly left and up a slope, and glancing back, Patsy caught a glimpse of a horse down and another refusing. Five were over, but the nearest was twenty lengths away. Nothing but bad luck could stop them now. She had no more fear of Bobcat's refusing; his excitement and spirit of competition were as great as her own. She had been afraid that he might go at such speed that he would have nothing left for the finish, but he was well within himself and still was increasing his lead with every fence. They were now halfway around the course and he was moving as powerfully and jumping as big as ever.

Here was the eleventh fence, and she saw a friend of her father, on his gray hunter, acting as a patrol judge. He raised his hand slightly and gave her a wide unjudicial smile as Bobcat cleared the fence with six inches to spare.

"Nine more fences, Bobcat. Just nine more, honey, and we're in." She crouched lower and looked across the meadow.

The crowds were only a varicolored pattern on the misty green expanse. Holley was probably cheering, perhaps some of the others, too; but Bobcat's hoofs on the wet turf and the wind in her ears made it impossible to hear.

"Nobody's laughing at us now, Bobcat," cried Patsy, and the big horse's ears moved slightly. In spite of the hunting cap pulled low, her hair was flying in wet tendrils. Her eyes were bright with excitement and she crooned as Bobcat's mane whipped in front of her. "A few more, Bobcat. Just a few more, baby. Easy now . . . easy. Nobody near us. Oh, you're great, honey; you're wonderful! Easy on the turn, now. Not too fast on the turn."

A hundred yards ahead she saw Jack Randolph, his arm in a sling, sitting his hunter beside the seventeenth fence. He was the one who first called her Patsy Buck.

"Make this a good one, Bobcat," she cried. "Make this an extra-good one. Let's show him how a real horse jumps."

The big horse let out another notch suddenly and Patsy began pulling desperately on the left rein.

"Not so fast, boy, not so fast—you're going too wide."

The turn was sharp and their speed was too great; wider and wider they went. The flags swung away to her left and as Bobcat rose to the fence she saw with a sinking feeling that they were thirty yards off the course. Now they were done for; they'd be disqualified. Bobcat was roaring down the field, and she gradually swung him back onto the course. Looking back, Patsy saw that in spite of having lost much distance in going so wide they still were leading by a big margin.

"We won't get the cup, Bobcat," she whispered, "but we'll show them who's who. What's a little old cup? We'll win plenty of them. Nothing can stop us now."

Straight through the flags flashed the big chestnut as he cleared the last jump and crossed the finish line thirty lengths in front. The finish judge rode up as Patsy brought Bobcat back.

"I'm sorry, but you're disqualified for cutting the flags at the seventeenth fence," he said.

"Yes, I know," answered Patsy, eyes alight and a smile on her lips as she stroked Bobcat's neck. "Wasn't he wonderful?"

"We can't give you the cup, you know," he added.

"I know." And the smile grew. "Oh, I'm so happy!" she cried, glowing with excitement.

"It's too bad, Miss Allison. He ran a great race. The turn is pretty sharp in this sort of going, and you took it too fast."

"Yes, I know. It was my fault. He did everything perfectly."

The judge looked at the flushed, happy face and rode off shaking his head. People gathered around and offered condolences, but Patsy scarcely heard them. She was looking for Holley. When he appeared she saw that he understood. He was grinning from ear to ear. He stroked Bobcat as he spoke to Patsy.

"We're in, Miss Patsy. That was grand. I'm proud of you both."

"You don't mind about the cup, Holley?"

"Oh, that!" said Holley. "Come spring an' we won't have room for a little cup like that."

CLARENCE WILLIAM ANDERSON came to writing about horses through illustrating them. As a young boy in Nebraska he never tired of watching the ranch horses, and used to sketch them for his own pleasure. He studied at the Chicago Art Institute and soon became widely recognized as a horse artist. He has a rare talent for capturing the spirit and character of horses in black and white, and his etchings and lithographs are prized by horse lovers and art collectors. They have been displayed in museums throughout the country.

From illustrating other authors' books about horses, Anderson began in the mid-thirties to write and illustrate his own books. Since then, he has produced a number of well known stories for young children as well as for horse lovers of all ages. One of his best is *High Courage,* the book from which "The First Race" was taken.

Mr. Anderson now lives in New Hampshire and is a member of the American Society of Etchers.

Love is powerful medicine

My Friend Flicka

BY MARY O'HARA

REPORT cards for the second semester were sent out soon after school closed in mid-June.

Kennie's was a shock to the whole family.

"If I could have a colt all for my own," said Kennie, "I might do better."

Rob McLaughlin glared at his son. "Just as a matter of curiosity," he said, "how do you go about it to get a *zero* in an examination? Forty in arithmetic; seventeen in history! But a *zero?* Just as one man to another, what goes on in your head?"

"Yes, tell us how you do it, Ken," chirped Howard.

"Eat your breakfast, Howard," snapped his mother.

Kennie's blond head bent over his plate until his face was almost hidden. His cheeks burned.

McLaughlin finished his coffee and pushed his chair back. "You'll do an hour a day on your lessons all through the summer."

Nell McLaughlin saw Kennie wince as if something had actually hurt him.

Lessons and study in the summertime, when the long winter was just over and there weren't hours enough in the day for all the things he wanted to do!

Kennie took things hard. His eyes turned to the wide-open window with a look almost of despair.

The hill opposite the house, covered with arrow-straight jack pines, was sharply etched in the thin air of the eight-thousand-foot altitude. Where it fell away, vivid green grass ran up to meet it; and over range and upland poured the strong Wyoming sunlight that stung everything into burning color. A big jack rabbit sat under one of the pines, waving his long ears back and forth.

Ken had to look at his plate and blink back tears before he could turn to his father and say carelessly, "Can I help you in the corral with the horses this morning, Dad?"

"You'll do your study every morning before you do anything else." And McLaughlin's scarred boots and heavy spurs clattered across the kitchen floor. "I'm disgusted with you. Come. Howard."

Howard strode after his father, nobly refraining from looking at Kennie.

"Help me with the dishes, Kennie," said Nell McLaughlin as she rose, tied on a big apron, and began to clear the table.

Kennie looked at her in despair. She poured steaming water into the dishpan and sent him for the soap powder.

"If I could have a colt," he muttered again.

"Now get busy with that dish towel, Ken. It's eight o'clock. You can study till nine and then go up to the corral. They'll still be there."

At supper that night Kennie said, "But Dad, Howard had a colt all of his own when he was only eight. And he trained it and schooled it all himself; and now he's eleven, and Highboy is three, and he's riding him. I'm nine now and even if you did give me a colt now I couldn't catch up to Howard because I couldn't ride it till it was a three-year-old and then I'd be twelve."

Nell laughed. "Nothing wrong with that arithmetic."

But Rob said, "Howard never gets less than seventy-five average at school, and hasn't disgraced himself and his family by getting more demerits than any other boy in his class."

Kennie didn't answer. He couldn't figure it out. He tried hard; he spent hours poring over his books. That was supposed to get you good marks, but it never did. Everyone said he was bright. Why was it that when he studied he didn't learn? He had a vague feeling that perhaps he looked out the window too much, or looked through the walls to see clouds and sky and hills and wonder what was happening out there. Sometimes it wasn't even a wonder, but just a pleasant drifting feeling of nothing at all, as if nothing mattered, as if there was always plenty of time, as if the lessons would get done of themselves. And then the bell would ring, and study period was over.

If he had a colt . . .

When the boys had gone to bed that night Nell McLaughlin sat down with her overflowing mending basket and glanced at her husband.

He was at his desk as usual, working on account books and inventories.

Nell threaded a darning needle and thought, "It's either that whacking big bill from the vet for the mare that died or the last half of the tax bill."

It didn't seem just the auspicious moment to plead Kennie's cause. But then, these days, there was always a line between Rob's eyes and a harsh note in his voice.

"Rob," she began.

He flung down his pencil and turned around.

"Damn that law!" he exclaimed.

"What law?"

"The state law that puts high taxes on pedigreed stock. I'll have to do as the rest of 'em do—drop the papers."

"Drop the papers! But you'll never get decent prices if you don't have registered horses."

"I don't get decent prices now."

"But you will someday if you don't drop the papers."

"Maybe." He bent again over the desk.

Rob, thought Nell, was a lot like Kennie himself. He set his heart. Oh, how stubbornly he set his heart on just some one thing he wanted above everything else. He had set his heart on horses and ranching way back when he had been a crack rider at West Point; and he had resigned and thrown away his army career just for the horses. Well, he'd got what he wanted. . . .

She drew a deep breath, snipped her thread, laid down the sock, and again looked across at her husband as she unrolled another length of darning cotton.

To get what you want is one thing, she was thinking. The three-thousand-acre ranch and the hundred head of horses. But to make it pay—for a dozen or more years they had been trying to make it pay. People said ranching hadn't paid since the beef barons ran their herds on public land; people said the only prosperous ranchers in Wyoming were the dude ranchers; people said . . .

But suddenly she gave her head a little rebellious, gallant shake. Rob would always be fighting and struggling against something, like Kennie; perhaps like herself, too. Even those first years when there was no water piped into the house, when every day brought a new difficulty or danger, how she had loved it! How she still loved it!

She ran the darning ball into the toe of a sock, Kennie's sock. The length of it gave her a shock. Yes, the boys were growing up fast, and now Kennie—Kennie and the colt . . .

After a while she said, "Give Kennie a colt, Rob."

"He doesn't deserve it." The answer was short. Rob pushed away his papers and took out his pipe.

"Howard's too far ahead of him, older and bigger and quicker, and his wits about him, and——"

"Ken doesn't half try, doesn't stick at anything."

She put down her sewing. "He's crazy for a colt of his own. He hasn't had another idea in his head since you gave Highboy to Howard."

"I don't believe in bribing children to do their duty."

"Not a bribe." She hesitated.

"No? What would you call it?"

She tried to think it out. "I just have the feeling Ken isn't going to pull anything off, and"—her eyes sought Rob's—"it's time he did. It isn't the school marks alone, but I just don't want things to go on any longer with Ken never coming out at the right end of anything."

"I'm beginning to think he's just dumb."

"He's not dumb. Maybe a little thing like this—if he had a colt of his own, trained him, rode him——"

Rob interrupted. "But it isn't a little thing, nor an easy thing, to break and school a colt the way Howard has schooled Highboy. I'm not going to have a good horse spoiled by Ken's careless ways. He goes woolgathering. He never knows what he's doing."

"But he'd *love* a colt of his own, Rob. If he could do it, it might make a big difference in him."

"*If* he could do it! But that's a big if."

At breakfast next morning Kennie's father said to him, "When you've done your study come out to the barn. I'm going in the car up to section twenty-one this morning to look over the brood mares. You can go with me."

"Can I go, too, Dad?" cried Howard.

McLaughlin frowned at Howard. "You turned Highboy out last evening with dirty legs."

Howard wriggled. "I groomed him——"

"Yes, down to his knees."

"He kicks."

"And whose fault is that? You don't get on his back again until I see his legs clean."

The two boys eyed each other, Kennie secretly triumphant and Howard chagrined. McLaughlin turned at the door, "And, Ken, a week from today I'll give you a colt. Between now and then you can decide what one you want."

Kennie shot out of his chair and stared at his father. "A—a spring colt, Dad, or a yearling?"

McLaughlin was somewhat taken aback, but his wife concealed a smile. If Kennie got a yearling colt he would be even up with Howard.

"A yearling colt, your father means, Ken," she said smoothly. "Now hurry with your lessons. Howard will wipe."

Kennie found himself the most important personage on the ranch. Prestige lifted his head, gave him an inch more of height and a bold stare, and made him feel different all the way through. Even Gus and Tim Murphy, the ranch hands, were more interested in Kennie's choice of a colt than anything else.

Howard was fidgety with suspense. "Who'll you pick, Ken? Say—pick Doughboy, why don't you? Then when he grows up he'll be sort of twins with mine, in his name anyway. Doughboy, Highboy, see?"

The boys were sitting on the worn wooden step of the door which led from the tack room into the corral, busy with rags and polish, shining their bridles.

Ken looked at his brother with scorn. Doughboy would never have half of Highboy's speed.

"Lassie, then," suggested Howard. "She's black as ink, like mine. And she'll be fast——"

"Dad says Lassie'll never go over fifteen hands."

Nell McLaughlin saw the change in Kennie, and her hopes rose. He went to his books in the morning with determination and really studied. A new alertness took the place of the day-dreaming. Examples in arithmetic were neatly written out, and as she passed his door before breakfast she often heard the monotonous drone of his voice as he read his American history aloud.

Each night, when he kissed her, he flung his arms around her and held her fiercely for a moment, then, with a winsome and blissful smile into her eyes, turned away to bed.

He spent days inspecting the different bands of horses and colts. He sat for hours on the corral fence, very important, chewing straws. He rode off on one of the ponies for half the day, wandering through the mile-square pastures that ran down toward the Colorado border.

And when the week was up he announced his decision. "I'll take that yearling filly of Rocket's. The sorrel with the cream tail and mane."

His father looked at him in surprise. "The one that got tangled in the barbed wire? That's never been named?"

In a second all Kennie's new pride was gone. He hung his head defensively. "Yes."

"You've made a bad choice, son. You couldn't have picked a worse."

"She's fast, Dad. And Rocket's fast——"

"It's the worst line of horses I've got. There's never one amongst them with real sense. The mares are hellions and the stallions outlaws; they're untamable."

"I'll tame her."

Rob guffawed. "Not I, nor anyone, has ever been able to really tame any one of them."

Kennie's chest heaved.

"Better change your mind, Ken. You want a horse that'll be a real friend to you, don't you?"

"Yes." Kennie's voice was unsteady.

"Well, you'll never make a friend of that filly. She's all cut and scarred up already with tearing through barbed wire after that bitch of a mother of hers. No fence'll hold 'em——"

"I know," said Kennie, still more faintly.

"Change your mind?" asked Howard briskly.

"No."

Rob was grim and put out. He couldn't go back on his word. The boy had to have a reasonable amount of help in breaking and taming the filly, and he could envision precious hours, whole days, wasted in the struggle.

Nell McLaughlin despaired. Once again Ken seemed to have taken the wrong turn and was back where he had begun; stoical, silent, defensive.

But there was a difference that only Ken could know. The way he felt about his colt. The way his heart sang. The pride and joy that filled him so full that sometimes he hung his head so they wouldn't see it shining out of his eyes.

He had known from the very first that he would choose that particular yearling because he was in love with her.

The year before, he had been out working with Gus, the big Swedish ranch hand, on the irrigation ditch, when they had noticed Rocket standing in a gully on the hillside, quiet for once, and eying them cautiously.

"Ay bet she got a colt," said Gus, and they walked carefully up the draw. Rocket gave a wild snort, thrust her feet out, shook her head wickedly, then fled away. And as they reached the spot they saw standing there the wavering, pinkish colt, barely able to keep its feet. It gave a little squeak and started after its mother on crooked, wobbling legs.

"Yee whiz! Luk at de little *flicka!*" said Gus.

"What does *flicka* mean, Gus?"

"Swedish for little gurl, Ken."

Ken announced at supper, "You said she'd never been named. I've named her. Her name is Flicka."

The first thing to do was to get her in. She was running with a band of yearlings on the saddleback, cut with ravines and gullies, on section twenty.

They all went out after her, Ken, as owner, on old Rob Roy, the wisest horse on the ranch.

Ken was entranced to watch Flicka when the wild band of youngsters discovered that they were being pursued and took off across the mountain. Footing made no difference to her. She floated across the ravines, always two lengths ahead of the others. Her pink mane and tail whipped in the wind. Her long delicate legs had only to aim, it seemed, at a particular spot, for her to reach it and sail on. She seemed to Ken a fairy horse.

He sat motionless, just watching and holding Rob Roy in, when his father thundered past on Sultan and shouted, "Well, what's the matter? Why didn't you turn 'em?"

Kennie woke up and galloped after.

Rob Roy brought in the whole band. The corral gates were closed, and an hour was spent shunting the ponies in and out and through the chutes, until Flicka was left alone in the small round corral in which the baby colts were branded. Gus drove the others away, out the gate, and up the saddleback.

But Flicka did not intend to be left. She hurled herself against the poles which walled the corral. She tried to jump them. They were seven feet high. She caught her front feet over the top rung, clung, scrambled, while Kennie held his breath for fear the slender legs would be caught between the bars and snapped.

Her hold broke; she fell over backward, rolled, screamed, tore around the corral. Kennie had a sick feeling in the pit of his stomach, and his father looked disgusted.

One of the bars broke. She hurled herself again. Another went. She saw the opening and, as neatly as a dog crawls through a fence, inserted her head and forefeet, scrambled through, and fled away, bleeding in a dozen places.

As Gus was coming back, just about to close the gate to the upper range, the sorrel whipped through it, sailed across the road and ditch with her inimitable floating leap, and went up the side of the saddleback like a jack rabbit.

From way up the mountain Gus heard excited whinnies, as she joined the band he had just driven up, and the last he saw of them they were strung out along the crest running like deer.

"Yee whiz!" said Gus, and stood motionless and staring until the ponies had disappeared over the ridge. Then he closed the gate, remounted Rob Roy, and rode back to the corral.

Rob McLaughlin gave Kennie one more chance to change his mind. "Last chance, son. Better pick a horse that you have some hope of riding one day. I'd have got rid of this whole line of stock if they weren't so damned fast that I've had the fool idea that someday there might turn out one gentle one in the lot—and I'd have a race horse. But there's never been one so far, and it's not going to be Flicka."

"It's not going to be Flicka," chanted Howard.

"Perhaps she *might* be gentled," said Kennie; and Nell, watching, saw that although his lips quivered, there was fanatical determination in his eye.

"Ken," said Rob, "it's up to you. If you say you want her we'll get her. But she wouldn't be the first of that line to die rather than give in. They're beautiful and they're fast, but let me tell you this, young man, they're *loco!*"

Kennie flinched under his father's direct glance.

"If I go after her again I'll not give up whatever comes; understand what I mean by that?"

"Yes."

"What do you say?"

"I want her."

They brought her in again. They had better luck this time. She jumped over the Dutch half door of the stable and crashed inside. The men slammed the upper half of the door shut, and she was caught.

The rest of the band was driven away, and Kennie stood outside of the stable, listening to the wild hoofs beating, the screams, the crashes. His Flicka inside there! He was drenched with perspiration.

"We'll leave her to think it over," said Rob when dinnertime came. "Afterward we'll go up and feed and water her."

But when they went up afterward there was no Flicka in the barn. One of the windows, higher than the mangers, was broken.

The window opened onto a pasture an eighth of a mile square, fenced in barbed wire six feet high. Near the stable stood a wagonload of hay. When they went around the back of the stable to see where Flicka had hidden herself they found her between the stable and the hay wagon, eating.

At their approach she leaped away, then headed east across the pasture.

"If she's like her mother," said Rob, "she'll go right through the wire."

"Ay bet she'll go over," said Gus. "She yumps like a deer."

"No horse can jump that," said McLaughlin.

Kennie said nothing because he could not speak. It was, perhaps, the most terrible moment of his life. He watched Flicka racing toward the eastern wire.

A few yards from it she swerved, turned, and raced diagonally south.

"It turned her! It turned her!" cried Kennie, almost sobbing. It was the first sign of hope for Flicka. "Oh, Dad! She has got sense. She has! She has!"

Flicka turned again as she met the southern boundary of the pasture, again at the northern; she avoided the barn. Without abating anything of her whirlwind speed, following a precise, accurate calculation and turning each time on a dime, she investigated every possibility. Then, seeing that there was no hope, she raced south toward the range where she had spent her life, gathered herself, and shot into the air.

Each of the three men watching had the impulse to cover his eyes, and Kennie gave a sort of a howl of despair.

Twenty yards of fence came down with her as she hurled herself through. Caught on the upper strands, she turned a complete somersault, landing on her back, her four legs dragging the wires down on top of her, and tangling herself in them beyond hope of escape.

"Damn the wire!" cursed McLaughlin. "If I could afford decent fences . . ."

Kennie followed the men miserably as they walked to the filly. They stood in a circle watching, while she kicked and fought and thrashed until the wire was tightly wound and knotted about her, cutting, piercing, and tearing great three-cornered pieces of flesh and hide. At last she was unconscious, streams of blood running on her golden coat, and pools of crimson widening and spreading on the grass beneath her.

With the wire cutter which Gus always carried in the hip pocket of his overalls he cut all the wire away, and they drew her into the pasture, repaired the fence, placed hay, a box of oats, and a tub of water near her, and called it a day.

"I don't think she'll pull out of it," said McLaughlin.

Next morning Kennie was up at five, doing his lessons. At six he went out to Flicka.

She had not moved. Food and water were untouched. She was no longer bleeding, but the wounds were swollen and caked over.

Kennie got a bucket of fresh water and poured it over her mouth. Then he leaped away, for Flicka came to life, scrambled up, got her balance, and stood swaying.

Kennie went a few feet away and sat down to watch her. When he went in to breakfast she had drunk deeply of the water and was mouthing the oats.

There began then a sort of recovery. She ate, drank, limped about the pasture, stood for hours with hanging head and weakly splayed-out legs, under the clump of cottonwood trees. The swollen wounds scabbed and began to heal.

Kennie lived in the pasture too. He followed her around; he talked to her. He, too, lay snoozing or sat under the cottonwoods; and often, coaxing her with hand outstretched, he walked very quietly toward her. But she would not let him come near her.

Often she stood with her head at the south fence, looking off to the mountain. It made the tears come to Kennie's eyes to see the way she longed to get away.

Still Rob said she wouldn't pull out of it. There was no use putting a halter on her. She had no strength.

One morning, as Ken came out of the house, Gus met him and said, "De filly's down."

Kennie ran to the pasture, Howard close behind him. The right hind leg which had been badly swollen at the knee joint had opened in a festering wound, and Flicka lay flat and motionless, with staring eyes.

"Don't you wish now you'd chosen Doughboy?" asked Howard.

"Go away!" shouted Ken.

Howard stood watching while Kennie sat down on the ground and took Flicka's head on his lap. Though she was conscious and moved a little she did not struggle nor seem frightened. Tears rolled down Kennie's checks as he talked to her and petted her. After a few moments Howard walked away.

"Mother, what do you do for an infection when it's a horse?" asked Kennie.

"Just what you'd do if it was a person. Wet dressings. I'll help you, Ken. We mustn't let those wounds close or scab over until they're clean. I'll make a poultice for that hind leg and help you put it on. Now that she'll let us get close to her, we can help her a lot."

"The thing to do is see that she eats," said Rob. "Keep up her strength."

But he himself would not go near her. "She won't pull out of it," he said. "I don't want to see her or think about her."

Kennie and his mother nursed the filly. The big poultice was bandaged on the hind leg. It drew out much poisoned matter, and Flicka felt better and was able to stand again.

She watched for Kennie now and followed him like a dog, hopping on three legs, holding up the right hind leg with its huge knob of a bandage in comical fashion.

"Dad, Flicka's my friend now; she likes me," said Ken.

His father looked at him. "I'm glad of that, son. It's a fine thing to have a horse for a friend."

Kennie found a nicer place for her. In the lower pasture the brook ran over cool stones. There was a grassy bank, the size of a corral, almost on a level with the water. Here she could lie softly, eat grass, drink fresh running water. From the grass, a twenty-foot hill sloped up, crested with overhanging trees. She was enclosed, as it were, in a green, open-air nursery.

Kennie carried her oats morning and evening. She would watch for him to come, eyes and ears pointed to the hill. And one evening Ken, still some distance off, came to a stop and a wide grin spread over his face. He had heard her nicker. She had caught sight of him coming and was calling to him!

He placed the box of oats under her nose, and she ate while he stood beside her, his hand smoothing the satin-soft skin under her mane. It had a nap as deep as plush. He played with her long, cream-colored tresses, arranged her forelock neatly between her eyes. She was a bit dish-faced, like an Arab, with eyes set far apart. He lightly groomed and brushed her while she stood turning her head to him whichever way he went.

He spoiled her. Soon she would not step to the stream to drink but he must hold a bucket for her. And she would drink, then lift her dripping muzzle, rest it on the shoulder of his blue chambray shirt, her golden eyes dreaming off into the distance, then daintily dip her mouth and drink again.

When she turned her head to the south and pricked her ears and stood tense and listening, Ken knew she heard the other colts galloping on the upland.

"You'll go back there someday, Flicka," he whispered. "You'll be three, and I'll be eleven. You'll be so strong you won't know I'm on your back, and we'll fly like the wind. We'll stand on the very top where we can look over the whole world and smell the snow from the Neversummer Range. Maybe we'll see antelope. . . ."

This was the happiest month of Kennie's life.

With the morning Flicka always had new strength and would hop three-legged up the hill to stand broadside to the early sun, as horses love to do.

The moment Ken woke he'd go to the window and see her there, and when he was dressed and at his table studying he sat so that he could raise his head and see Flicka.

After breakfast she would be waiting at the gate for him and the box of oats, and for Nell McLaughlin with fresh bandages and buckets of disinfectant. All three would go together to the brook, Flicka hopping along ahead of them as if she were leading the way.

But Rob McLaughlin would not look at her.

One day all the wounds were swollen again. Presently they opened, one by one, and Kennie and his mother made more poultices.

Still the little filly climbed the hill in the early morning and ran about on three legs. Then she began to go down in flesh and almost overnight wasted away to nothing. Every rib showed; the glossy hide was dull and brittle and was pulled over the skeleton as if she were a dead horse.

Gus said, "It's de fever. It burns up her flesh. If you could stop de fever she might get vell."

McLaughlin was standing in his window one morning and saw the little skeleton hopping about three-legged in the sunshine, and he said, "That's the end. I won't have a thing like that on my place."

Kennie had to understand that Flicka had not been getting well all this time; she had been slowly dying.

"She still eats her oats," he said mechanically.

They were all sorry for Ken. Nell McLaughlin stopped disinfecting and dressing the wounds. "It's no use, Ken," she said gently, "you know Flicka's going to die, don't you?"

"Yes, Mother."

Ken stopped eating. Howard said, "Ken doesn't eat anything any more. Don't he have to eat his dinner, Mother?"

But Nell answered, "Leave him alone."

Because the shooting of wounded animals is all in the day's work on the western plains, and sickening to everyone, Rob's voice, when he gave the order to have Flicka shot, was as flat as if he had been telling Gus to kill a chicken for dinner.

"Here's the Marlin, Gus. Pick out a time when Ken's not around and put the filly out of her misery."

Gus took the rifle. "*Ja,* boss. . . ."

Ever since Ken had known that Flicka was to be shot he had kept his eye on the rack which held the firearms. His father allowed no firearms in the bunkhouse. The gun rack was in the dining room of the ranch house, and going through it to the kitchen three times a day for meals, Ken's eye scanned the weapons to make sure that they were all there.

That night they were not all there. The Marlin rifle was missing.

When Kennie saw that he stopped walking. He felt dizzy. He kept staring at the gun rack, telling himself that it surely was there—he counted again and again—he couldn't see clearly. . . .

Then he felt an arm across his shoulders and heard his father's voice.

"I know, son. Some things are awful hard to take. We just have to take 'em. I have to, too."

Kennie got hold of his father's hand and held on. It helped steady him.

Finally he looked up. Rob looked down and smiled at him and gave him a little shake and squeeze. Ken managed a smile too.

"All right now?"

"All right, Dad."

They walked in to supper together.

Ken even ate a little. But Nell looked thoughtfully at the ashen color of his face and at the little pulse that was beating in the side of his neck.

After supper he carried Flicka her oats but he had to coax her, and she would only eat a little. She stood with her head hanging but when he stroked it and talked to her she pressed her face into his chest and was content. He could feel the burning heat of her body. It didn't seem possible that anything so thin could be alive.

Presently Kennie saw Gus come into the pasture carrying the Marlin. When he saw Ken he changed his direction and sauntered along as if he was out to shoot some cottontails.

Ken ran to him. "When are you going to do it, Gus?"

"Ay was goin' down soon now, before it got dark. . . ."

"Gus, don't do it tonight. Wait till morning. Just one more night, Gus."

"Vell, in de morning den, but it got to be done, Ken. Yer fader gives de order."

"I know. I won't say anything more."

An hour after the family had gone to bed Ken got up and put on his clothes. It was a warm moonlit night. He ran down to the brook, calling softly. "Flicka! Flicka!"

But Flicka did not answer with a little nicker; and she was not in the nursery nor hopping about the pasture. Ken hunted for an hour.

At last he found her down the creek, lying in the water. Her head had been on the bank, but as she lay there the current of the stream had sucked and pulled at her, and she had had no strength to resist; and little by little her head had slipped down until when Ken got there only the muzzle was resting on the bank, and the body and legs were swinging in the stream.

Kennie slid into the water, sitting on the bank, and he hauled at her head. But she was heavy, and the current dragged like a weight; and he began to sob because he had no strength to draw her out.

Then he found a leverage for his heels against some rocks in the bed of the stream and he braced himself against these and pulled with all his might; and her head came up onto his knees, and he held it cradled in his arms.

He was glad that she had died of her own accord, in the

cool water, under the moon, instead of being shot by Gus. Then, putting his face close to hers, and looking searchingly into her eyes, he saw that she was alive and looking back at him.

And then he burst out crying and hugged her and said, "Oh, my little Flicka, my little Flicka."

The long night passed.

The moon slid slowly across the heavens.

The water rippled over Kennie's legs and over Flicka's body. And gradually the heat and fever went out of her. And the cool running water washed and washed her wounds.

When Gus went down in the morning with the rifle they hadn't moved. There they were, Kennie sitting in water over his thighs and hips, with Flicka's head in his arms.

Gus seized Flicka by the head and hauled her out on the grassy bank and then, seeing that Kennie couldn't move, cold and stiff and half-paralyzed as he was, lifted him in his arms and carried him to the house.

"Gus," said Ken through chattering teeth, "don't shoot her, Gus."

"It ain't fur me to say, Ken. You know dat."

"But the fever's left her, Gus."

"Ay wait a little, Ken. . . ."

Rob McLaughlin drove to Laramie to get the doctor, for Ken was in violent chills that would not stop. His mother had him in bed wrapped in hot blankets when they got back.

He looked at his father imploringly as the doctor shook down the thermometer.

"She might get well now, Dad. The fever's left her. It went out of her when the moon went down."

"All right, son. Don't worry. Gus'll feed her, morning and night, as long as she's——"

"As long as I can't do it," finished Kennie happily.

The doctor put the thermometer in his mouth and told him to keep it shut.

All day Gus went about his work, thinking of Flicka. He had not been back to look at her. He had been given no more orders. If she was alive the order to shoot her was still in effect. But Kennie was ill, McLaughlin making his second trip to town taking the doctor home, and would not be back till long after dark.

After their supper in the bunkhouse Gus and Tim walked down to the brook. They did not speak as they approached the filly, lying stretched out flat on the grassy bank, but their eyes were straining at her to see if she was dead or alive.

She raised her head as they reached her.

"By the powers!" exclaimed Tim. "There she is!"

She dropped her head, raised it again, and moved her legs and became tense as if struggling to rise. But to do so she must use her right hind leg to brace herself against the earth. That was the damaged leg, and at the first bit of pressure with it she gave up and fell back.

"We'll swing her onto the other side," said Tim. "Then she can help herself."

"Ja. . . ."

Standing behind her, they leaned over, grabbed hold of her left legs, front and back, and gently hauled her over. Flicka was as lax and willing as a puppy. But the moment she found hersef lying on her right side, she began to scramble, braced herself with her good left leg, and tried to rise.

"Yee whiz!" said Gus. "She got plenty strength yet."

"Hi!" cheered Tim. "She's up!"

But Flicka wavered, slid down again, and lay flat. This time she gave notice that she would not try again by heaving a deep sigh and closing her eyes.

Gus took his pipe out of his mouth and thought it over. Orders or no orders, he would try to save the filly. Ken had gone too far to be let down.

"Ay'm goin' to rig a blanket sling fur her, Tim, and get her on her feet, and keep her up."

There was bright moonlight to work by. They brought down the posthole digger and set two aspen poles deep into the ground either side of the filly, then, with ropes attached to the blanket, hoisted her by a pulley.

Not at all disconcerted, she rested comfortably in the blanket under her belly, touched her feet on the ground, and reached for the bucket of water Gus held for her.

Kennie was sick a long time. He nearly died. But Flicka picked up. Every day Gus passed the word to Nell, who carried it to Ken. "She's cleaning up her oats." "She's out of the sling." "She bears a little weight on the bad leg."

Tim declared it was a real miracle. They argued about it, eating their supper.

"Na," said Gus. "It was de cold water, washin' de fever outa her. And more dan dat—it was Ken—you tink it don't count? All night dot boy sits dere and says, 'Hold on, Flicka, Ay'm here wid you. Ay'm standin' by, two of us togedder'. . . ."

Tim stared at Gus without answering, while he thought it over. In the silence a coyote yapped far off on the plains, and the wind made a rushing sound high up in the jack pines on the hill.

Gus filled his pipe.

"Sure," said Tim finally. "Sure. That's it."

Then came the day when Rob McLaughlin stood smiling at the foot of Kennie's bed and said, "Listen! Hear your friend?"

Ken listened and heard Flicka's high, eager whinny.

"She don't spend much time by the brook any more. She's up at the gate of the corral half the time, nickering for you."

"For me!"

Rob wrapped a blanket around the boy and carried him out to the corral gate.

Kennie gazed at Flicka. There was a look of marveling in his eyes. He felt as if he had been living in a world where everything was dreadful and hurting but awfully real; and *this* couldn't be real; this was all soft and happy, nothing to struggle over or worry about or fight for any more. Even his father was proud of him! He could feel it in the way Rob's big arms held him. It was all like a dream and far away. He couldn't, yet, get close to anything.

But Flicka—Flicka—alive, well, pressing up to him, recognizing him, nickering . . .

Kennie put out a hand—weak and white—and laid it on her face. His thin little fingers straightened her forelock the way he used to do, while Rob looked at the two with a strange expression about his mouth and a glow in his eyes that was not often there.

"She's still poor, Dad, but she's on four legs now."

"She's picking up."

Ken turned his face up, suddenly remembering. "Dad! She did get gentled, didn't she?"

"Gentle—as a kitten. . . ."

They put a cot down by the brook for Ken, and boy and filly got well together.

Although MARY O'HARA's famous story is about ranch horses and the West, she was born in Brooklyn, the daughter of an Episcopal minister, and traces her ancestry back to William Penn and Jonathan Edwards. She attended schools in New York and New England, then went to Europe to study languages and music, and has published a number of her musical compositions.

It was after she returned to the United States and went to California that Miss O'Hara began writing in earnest. At this period she was writing film scripts, and worked on such noted motion pictures as "Prisoner of Zenda" and "Peg O' My Heart." After her marriage, she and her husband settled on a ranch in Wyoming, where they still live. Here Miss O'Hara developed her love and knowledge of horses, out of which grew the idea for "My Friend Flicka." Originally published as a short story, it first appeared in *Story* magazine and was included in the O. Henry Memorial Award volume. Then Miss O'Hara made it into a novel, and finally it became a popular motion picture, paralleling in this way Eric Knight's famous classic among dog stories, "Lassie Come Home." Miss O'Hara's "My Friend Flicka" is familiar to millions of American moviegoers and readers, and has become one of the best loved horse stories of our time.

Two against nature's fury

Beast of God

BY CECILIA DABROWSKA

THE deep blue surge of the windswept Tasman Sea drove in against the west coast of the North Island and laid down a white froth of foam like frost against the black ironstone sand of the shore.

And into the sand the little chestnut mare's black hooves thudded, pressing in their graceful prints in impermanent perfection, the sea foam clinging in coronets of lace to her hoof-tops. Spirited, she played with the bit, eager to lengthen her stride from canter to gallop and reach the thundering apex of her speed—setting herself against the sea's own white horses rearing and retreating ever before her.

Paul McPherson, tempted, slackened the reins and leaned a little in the saddle. "Go, Salaam, go!" he said, uttering the words as in a chant, and the dancing black hooves struck the sand like a drum beat, scattering it in showers, speed-spurned into the hot air. The light chestnut mane spread in the wind like a fan, lifting and whipping along the mare's curving crest as she galloped with whippet-like urgency, lengthening her body against the sandy flats—keeping just beyond the farthest reach of the foam-edged tide sighing restlessly toward her, and away from the cliffs soaring up on the other side.

One mile—two, and the faint sweat-marks showed along her neck. Eagerly she went forward, not balking at imaginary things but galloping with trustworthy concentration in full and lively participation in the ride. The swift stride carried her on, fleetly in passage like a winged thing, but the pressure of the reins brought her obediently to a canter, not chafing against the restriction. And her final halt came at the foot of the great sandstone cliffs that towered up from the shore. Far above, the stunted mountain flax lifted pointed leaves on the airy swell of the wind.

Paul McPherson looked up at the cliffs, seeking the time-worn trail that followed the cliff-face, sloping down along it, broad as a road. Station cattle long ago had been driven down it to the beach and taken in great droves along the wind-blown shore from one holding to another. He ran his gaze over the heights again, studying the cattle trail, calculating the shortening of time it represented, as the mare picked her way through a boulder-strewn stretch with delicate, unhesitating steps. He found the beginning of the path at the foot of the headlands and urged the mare over towards it, skirting a small rock-fall, thinking that if at any place the path became impassable there was room to turn around and descend again.

Salaam, the chestnut mare, stepped onto the rough pathway unhesitatingly, sensing that it had often borne others of her kind before her. She took the beginning of the ascent easily. Habitually docile, she went forward calmly, her head lowered level with her withers against the effort, her eyes glancing ahead and sideways to the swing of each step. She neither flinched at nor paid nervous attention to the increasing drop on her off side as the shore fell away below.

Three parts of the way up and in plain sight of the cliff-top, from out of the empty air itself the mare caught the prescient awareness of earth's betrayal.

Salaam it was who sensed what was coming. Laboring up the path she halted, snatching at the bit, pausing in the hot quiet —not the hesitation of an animal seeking a respite from labor, but the pause of a wild thing testing its senses, seeking the whereabouts of menace.

Like telepathy McPherson caught the alarm from the horse as though it touched him in tangible currents along the reins and through the leather of the saddle. He tightened the reins, not fully comprehending, and urged the mare forward with his legs, and for the first time ever she answered him with a balking refusal— only moving sideways, pressing against the cliff-face, halting there, head upflung.

All four feet planted squarely, Salaam stood motionless, and McPherson, looking ahead up the trail, saw it move before his disbelieving eyes, watched it crumble from the spray-beaten edges, breaking up as wet sand breaks out from outspread fingers. The voice of the quaking earth reached them on a rumbling pitch of terror, and the man, trapped on the chestnut mare in the midst of it, turned his head fearfully and looked behind him, down to where the summer waves hissed and lifted as though invisible bitter winds sought to tear them from the ocean bed. He watched the sea far below straining against the rock-face, gushing up beyond the spring tide line, hurtling at the cliff itself, tormented by the fearful surge below its own surging.

Feet braced, the mare stood, one side pressed in against the rock, the path disintegrating almost beneath her hooves. Another tremor, and she went down onto her knees in slow reluctance, sliding to them against the cliff-face, terror in the large-showing whites of her eyes.

There was the rumble of an avalanche somewhere beyond,

and a smothering crash as earth and sandstone blocks tore down from the cliff-top and surged over the path, obliterating it ahead.

The mare's nose rested against the fall. She drew a long sobbing breath, and McPherson could feel her sides move as she breathed hard like a creature whose last strength is almost spent. The seconds went past in a blur of fear, and then the man heard the faint splash of the falling sandstone rocks striking the sea far below.

Crouched over the mare's neck McPherson watched the damp sweat-marks grow over her withers until her whole neck and forequarters glistened wringing wet, and small trickles of sweat ran down dripping onto the pathway where she knelt. And still she did not move. McPherson let the reins lie as they were, slackly upon her neck. There in the now still heart of peril the man sat the kneeling mare rigidly, and neither of them moved a muscle.

Long seconds flickered away, clothing them in timelessness as does the immobility of the graven statues men erect of their living dead. The fear seeping into McPherson entrenched itself inside him, acknowledging the treachery of the unstable earth.

Then, with an almost imperceptible movement, the mare began to lift her off fore knee. For a sickening second her hoof swung over space, then she began slowly scraping away the earth and rock-pieces in front of her nose, making a place for her hoof. Small falls of earth and rock rolled away ahead of her, dropping down to the sea. Gently as a kitten's paw the hoof rested in the hollow. Again, almost imperceptibly at first she rested, weight on the hoof, testing the place until she knew in absolute certainty that it would bear her weight securely. Only then did she attempt to stand. Slowly the muscles of her foreleg straightened, tautening like a steel bar, and she began to lift her body up off the near knee against the cliff. Along her shoulder the muscles ridged like cables—her whole body quivered with endeavor. She lifted her other foreleg loosely—all her weight thrown onto the other three bracing legs. Then, with infinite tortuous care in that narrow space, she laid the near hoof in behind the other and slowly eased the proportionate share of the weight onto it.

Quietly she stood, the breath whistling in through wide-flared nostrils until, with the temporary easing of strain, the trembling of her whole body ceased.

McPherson's left leg was jammed against the cliff-face, protected at the knee by the jutting knee-pad of the saddle from the vise-like thrust of the mare's body against the rock-face. Crouched over her withers, his hands clenched on the saddle pommel, he had not altered his position as the mare rose to her feet, fully knowing that any touch on the reins would destroy her precarious balance and send them both somersaulting down to death below.

The mare inched forward, and McPherson dared not look down. Momentarily sick with vertigo, he stared ahead at some point between the gentle mare's ears, and somewhere inside of himself he reached out to the fringe of eternity humbly, like a beggar at the gates, desiring the bequest of life and the ceasing of peril. Looking in his mind at many things he saw that between the rawness of earth and all mankind come the beasts of God—the humble buffer between humanity and the primitive forces that molded creation.

The mare moved again—a small step like a hobbled creature, and never did she place a hoof without that gentle tentative pressure on the loose surface. Obeying inherent instinct, and the sure knowledge that this way lay her only chance of survival, she stole along the path; and so surely did she move that each hind hoof pressed into the imprint of the fore. The loose earth swirled over her fetlocks in the middle of the fall and from the outside it cascaded away in small runnels and slips. Halting, catlike, in her determination, assessing her passage, she braced, pawing again at the fall—shifting the slithering treachery of loose rock-pieces from beneath her hooves.

Then as she moved again her off hind hoof slipped, and she froze for one terrible moment, poised on the cliff-face, one hind leg dangling in space, braced in a desperate half-crouch, clinging with the other three hooves, fighting for balance.

McPherson thought she must fall, precipitated below as surely as if she were flung by a rebound from the cliff-face, but there could be no rebound, for there was no gap between the thrust of the rock and her side. Even as her hoof slipped and she went into the crouch the whole of her side slithered down against the cliff face. Holding herself to it, pressed against the rock, she slowly drew up the hind leg and, hunched like a crippled thing, placed it beneath her body, easing the weight upon it, mistrustfully at first, and then instinctively knowing that she could trust the small shelf beneath her.

Fractionally, McPherson turned his head, not allowing any portion of his body to move as he did so, and stared upward. Against the skyline the rough edge of the cliff-top was torn away in a great bite above them where the avalanche had broken loose. He stared, mesmerized by the fear of any more of the sandstone breaking away and falling, even of one single piece striking the mare.

And watching it McPherson realized it was the sense of betrayal that he could not bear. For the crust of earth which nourished him, even though he cherished it, had trembled into open cataclysm beneath him. The earth had joined some terrible subterranean force in malleable compliancy. The abrupt treachery which placed him in this predicament sent a ripple of shocked apprehension through him; for earth, the parent body, had yielded all things upon which he laid a hand even to the clothes he wore. He tasted the dry ash of fear, knowing she had reached out to take him back prematurely, perhaps for all time.

Fighting for every hold upon the path the mare moved forward, one slow pace after another until the fall was crossed. Each step was followed by the halt for rest—each move accompanied by the rasping slither of McPherson's leg against the cliff face. Then the original path lay before them, apparently undamaged. With unpredictable inconsequence the earthquake had seemingly left whole the equally vulnerable upper pathway.

Again, though the path ran broad as ever up the cliff and looked unchanged and untouched, the mare tested every step, until McPherson eased himself upright in the saddle and dared to look in hope to the cliff top where the path flowed over onto land that was smooth and undisturbed.

With infinite care Salaam laid one fore hoof upon the cliff top where the path petered out. The second black hoof swung into place behind it, her hind hooves followed onto solid earth, and like a thing released from secret chains she went forward without testing the earth beneath her.

Later McPherson swung himself slowly from the saddle, stiffly dismounting, woodenly feeling the firm ground beneath his feet with an air of disbelief. At his shoulder the mare stood, drawing great hard breaths through flaring nostrils. Automatically his hands went to the saddle, lifting the flap and loosening the girth buckles. He leaned against the saddle, feeling the exhausted heaving of the mare's sides. Her coat glistened wetly from the sweating inundation of terror and labor upon the cliff path. McPherson moved forward. The mare turned her head and rubbed her sweating poll against his arm. He slid his fingers in behind the bridle bands and rubbed gently. Salaam moved her head away and shook it, flapping the bridle loosely with a motion like a dog shaking water from its coat. They rested, lapped by the heavy warmth of the now quiescent earth, which held none of the menace of the cold sea, or the bitterness of empty air.

Then, recovering, with a colt-like gesture Salaam reached

out and lipped lightly at McPherson's arm, but not biting. Her small chestnut ears pricked, her alert eyes, watchful and benign, scanned the land rolling away inland. Long acres, broken here and there where the cabbage-palms interposed their lonely slenderness against the horizon, lay slumberous and heat-shrouded in the late afternoon. No mark upon them showed the bitter forces below, no rent or convulsive upthrust marred them.

The station cattle, whose heritage is that of the moment, though sensing the forces of cataclysm moving beneath them, had not yielded to panic. Looking at them as he rode among them, McPherson knew that. Tensed and fettered more surely by the abrupt deprivation of balance than by fear, they had stood, finding all movement rendered ineffectual, and when release came to them they had taken it slowly and cautiously, absorbing it into the tenor of that moment's way. But the beasts of the earth are not unaffected by its quaking—he knew that too: for the mare will look to her foal, and the she-dog, perturbed, tongue the coats of her blind pups.

McPherson mounted and rode the chestnut mare out onto the flats. The wind-shivered grass heeled over towards them with thin arboreal tremor. The mare's black hooves lifted and fell to the pendulum stroke of her stride, bridging the gap between fear and the bittersweet peace of respite.

CECILIA DABROWSKA'S story "Beast of God" is set in her native New Zealand, where she has lived most of her life. As a girl she learned to know and love animals through caring for them on her family's farm. The New Zealand country itself, with its earthquakes, avalanches and other spectacular phenomena, impressed her with how destructive nature can be.

After several years of teaching, Mrs. Dabrowska settled on her own farm with her Polish-born husband and began to write. Her stories now appear regularly in various magazines in Great Britain and the United States.

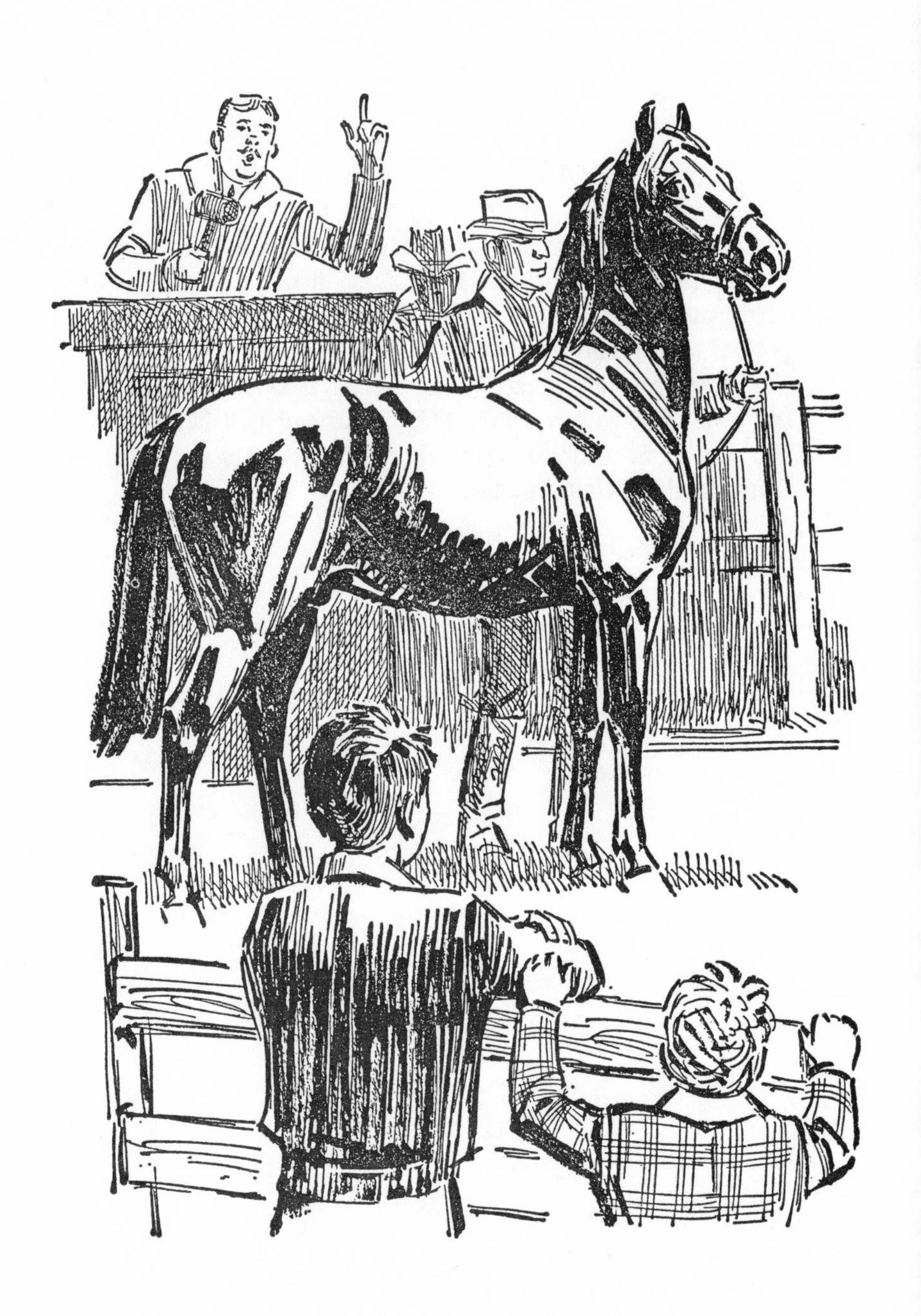

Looks aren't everything

Night Star

BY STEPHEN HOLT

ANDREW solemnly leaned an elbow on the top pole of the corral and watched the sale with sinking heart. Half a hundred ranchers ringed the auctioneer and a bewildered roan colt with a halter too big for him.

"At fifty once! At fifty twice! Fair warning!" the auctioneer, from his stand in the middle of the corral, droned. He was fat and bald and had a gold tooth that caught the early morning Alberta sunshine.

The roan draft colt pawed the loose corral dust and whinnied lonesomely.

"Going! Going!" intoned the auctioneer. Suddenly he hit the stand before him a sharp smack with his gavel and barked, "Sold to Hank Armstrong!"

A murmur of sympathy for the colt went around the group. Hank made outlaws of his colts.

Jamie, in the wagon box backed up to the corral, nudged Andrew beside him. Jamie was ten, and smart. He had blue eyes and sandy curls that disgusted him. "That's swell," he whispered. "Armstrong goes for rough colts."

Andrew nodded. "Yeah. He'll go for Night Star when he's put up this afternoon."

"Sure," Jamie chortled. "He'll buy Night Star, and that'll leave Playboy wide open for you to buy—that sorrel beauty!"

But Andrew couldn't get his mind off Night Star, the rough-looking little guy who'd lost his mom out in the hills when a rattler struck. He kept telling himself that he was glad Armstrong was going to buy Night Star.

"Playboy's the colt I really want," he whispered, dully. "He's smooth. Wonderful."

The sale droned on, with Armstrong buying most of the heavy colts.

After each purchase he'd go down, his big red face grinning, and yank the unlucky colt out of the corral.

"The big show-off!" Andrew muttered, his heart thudding. To save his life, he couldn't help looking out across the lot, over the corral top to where the little black guy, Night Star, stood tied to a fence. When he thought of Armstrong getting him—

Suddenly, he found himself crawling over the side of the wagon box. He was small for fifteen, with a dark serious face and a wide unsmiling mouth that seldom spoke. His deep-set brown eyes did most of the talking.

Jamie clambered after him. "I get it," he said, cannily. "You want to make sure that Armstrong will go for Night Star and leave Playboy for you."

Andrew jumped down from the wagon bed and turned to help Jamie. Hotly, he asked himself why he had to pay any attention to Night Star. He didn't own him, did he? And why did Night Star have to stand there with his head pointed right at Andrew?

Why didn't he act like Playboy? Playboy was sleek and pretty.

But Andrew's feet carried him around the outside of the

corral and over to a long row of mares with colts—Jim Schilling's dispersal stock. Jim had come from Kentucky with enough money to choke a cow. But he spent more time in Calgary than he did on his ranch at Skiff. So now he was broke and his stuff was going.

Andrew walked by Playboy, who didn't even turn his small beautiful head around.

"Don't pay any attention to him," Jamie warned. "If Hank'd see—"

But Andrew was looking at Night Star, tied to his post.

"That's the stuff," Jamie applauded. "Make a fuss over Night Star. You're as smart as Pop."

Andrew nodded. A wispy smile fell across his wide mouth. "Hi, ol' boy, ol' boy," he said huskily. "Lonesome?"

Night Star nuzzled Andrew's windbreaker. He nibbled a leather button. And his big wide head lay trustingly along Andrew's thin shoulder.

"You're sure smart," grinned Jamie. "It's only in the ring this afternoon you'll pay any attention to Playboy."

Andrew nodded. Fiercely, he told himself that it was his own money. Money he'd earned from Shorty, his fat steer who'd gone on to Chicago. And if he wanted to buy Playboy with it, instead of this, this— He started to walk over to watch the Hereford calves in the round corral back of the red barn.

But Night Star reared back against his halter. He jumped ahead and got his foot over his halter rope. He looked after Andrew and whinnied in a panic. It brought Andrew back to take his foot out of the rope and hold his big broad head between his trembling arms.

"Hey!" Jamie eyed him. "You're not going soft and buying this cayuse, are you, Andy?"

But before Andrew could deny it, a voice boomed, "I'll say he isn't. I'm buying him myself."

It was Armstrong. He put an arm under Night Star and lifted him clear off the ground; then dropped him, to pull his big left ear till Night Star fought him off.

Andrew got a sudden picture of himself leading Playboy the three miles home and wondering where Night Star might be. And what Armstrong would be doing to him. He said, against his better judgment and with Jamie's disgusted eyes on him, "Then you aren't interested in Playboy, there?"

"Him?" Armstrong's bullet head shook vehemently. "That sissy?"

Jamie stealthily kicked Andrew's shin. "You crazy?" he whispered.

But Armstrong was too busy to notice. "Nope, I'm buying this colt. I like him." He laughed and made another pass at Night Star's big right ear. "Well, I see the sale's stopped for eats. So long, jughead." He turned to Andrew. "You buy your sorrel sissy, Andy, but lay off jughead, here."

Armstrong sauntered off. Andrew stared after him. If it were possible to buy two colts . . . But his dad had been firm on that. "No, Andy, buy a colt—a good one. One's enough." Andrew knew that Night Star was no bargain, with his big head and rough build. Playboy was the horse.

After that, and because he'd finally made up his mind, he knew that the least he could do was to stay with Night Star till time to go in and buy Playboy. "Jamie," he said, "you go get my sandwiches and coffee. I'll stay here."

Jamie wandered off and presently came back with a big ham sandwich and a cup of milk. "Mrs. Schilling said you are too young for coffee. And you're to come back for apple pie."

But Andrew, much as he liked apple pie, didn't go back. The time for the sale of saddle mounts drew near. The auctioneer moved toward the corral and ice began to form around

Andrew's stiff heart. "Pretty soon," something whispered within him, "you'll own Playboy." He tried to grin. What a colt! What a horse! "And pretty soon, Armstrong will drag Night Star home to make an outlaw of him."

Andrew glimpsed his dad, tall and kindly, looking like a grown-up Jamie, red-faced and sandy-skinned. And his mom, little and dark, clinging to his arm.

"Dad," Andrew said, going across to him and his mom, standing talking to Mrs. Schilling. He pulled his dad off to one side. "Dad, will you take this money and buy that colt over there. That one—"

He didn't think he was looking at Night Star.

"Andrew—that jughead!" His dad was jarred. Although he wanted to remain impartial, he couldn't help now what he'd said.

That cinched it for Andrew. His dad, too, leery of Night Star. He wouldn't dare buy him now.

"No," Andrew said, "that sorrel. The one with the white stocking feet."

"Oh!" His dad half-reached for the money, then drew his hand back. "No, I was forgetting," he said. "No, Andy. It's good experience. Buy him in yourself."

Andrew gulped, and he knew argument was useless. When his dad said a thing, that settled it. He moved toward the corral and climbed up in the old wagon bed. Leaning over the top rail he had a swell view.

Jamie was already there, wide-eyed and canny. "Remember," he cautioned, "it's Playboy you want—"

And then the auctioneer shrilled: "And now, gentlemen, something a little special, even for Jim Schilling's line of stock."

A boy led Playboy in, mincing, dainty.

Andrew thought his heart was going to leap through his ribs. He feasted his eyes on Playboy's slim legs, his beautiful short-coupled back. He heard Jamie suck in his breath.

"What do I hear, gentlemen? Playboy, out of Sirocco, by Playgirl. Some of the best blood of Kentucky. Start your bids, gentlemen."

Armstrong, twenty feet from Andrew, turned and stared meaningly at him.

"F—F-orty dollars," Andy managed.

"Forty dollars, the young man says. Do I hear fifty—fifty—?"

The auctioneer did. He heard, "Sixty! Seventy! Eighty! Ninety!"

So did Andrew, with Jamie kicking his shins and breathing frantically, "Bid again! Bid! Bid!"

"Ninety-five!" Andy stuttered. High above it he could hear Night Star's whinny. Ice water ran down his spine.

"Ninety-five! Ninety-five! Ninety-five, once. Ninety-five, twice. Ninety-five, third and last call—fair warning! And—sold to the smart young man on the wagon—a McTavish, I believe." His gavel hit the stand a resounding smack.

A laugh ran around the crowd.

And Jamie chortled, "What a horse! Andy, you've bought Playboy. Got him for a song!"

Andrew knew he should have been glad. But he wondered if he'd ever smile again. He could see only Night Star. Little Night Star being led in as Playboy was led out, Playboy lashing out at him with a dainty hoof.

Then Night Star looked up at Andrew. He whinnied. He started over toward him, only to be yanked back by the boy attendant.

"And now," the auctioneer's voice said, patronizingly, "what am I bid for this one?" He looked at Night Star, then down at his card, as though there had been a mistake.

Andrew felt a rage. Slurring Night Star!

"Fifty dollars," Armstrong said.

"Fifty—fifty—fifty—" droned the auctioneer.

Andrew could tell that this sale would be shoved through. Night Star would be knocked down fast.

"Sixty! Sixty-five!"

"Seventy!" Always, Armstrong topped every bid.

Suddenly, the wagon box shook. A man stepped in by Andrew. A big man with flowing mustaches and white flowing hair. He carried a cane, and he had on a light gray suit with a red flower in his buttonhole.

"Now, Mr. McTavish—" he began, "Andrew McTavish—"

Andrew turned. His ears couldn't hear, at first, above the sound of the auctioneer selling Night Star to Armstrong.

"I'm Colonel Gleason—train held me up."

Andrew was beginning to get it.

"Wanted Playboy—take back to Kentucky. Give you a hundred and a quarter."

Andrew couldn't believe it. He grasped the side of the wagon box, staring.

"Well, make it a hundred and fifty. Right here."

"S-sold!" Andrew stuttered. His fingers closed on the money.

The auctioneer turned and checked his monotone, then droned on, "Night Star, at ninety-two fifty. Ninety-two fifty! Ninety-two fifty! Going—going—fair warning! And sold to—"

Andrew all but fell out of the wagon. "Ninety-five. Ninety-five for Night Star!" he called.

Jamie was sobbing, "Andy's sold Playboy. Sold the best horse that ever lived!"

"Hundred!" grunted Armstrong, red crawling up his bull-neck.

Andrew took hold of the wagon box. He didn't care. His heart sang. And Night Star was looking up at him and pawing the ground. He had a good heart girth. He'd make a cow horse.

What was beauty compared with love and companionship? "A hundred and ten!" Andrew said, firmly.

"Fifteen!" Armstrong glared.

"Twenty!" Andrew shot back.

"Twenty-five." Armstrong elbowed his way down to stand by Night Star, to take hold of the halter and jerk Night Star roughly around—as though he already owned him.

Andrew took a deep breath. "Fifty!" he said, burning inside.

For a moment, there was dead silence in the corral.

Andrew lived three lives. If Armstrong only knew how close he was! A hundred and fifty-one would have thrown Night Star to him. Andrew held his breath.

Then Armstrong shrugged, and stamped out of the corral, slamming the gate.

Night Star was his! Andrew climbed over the fence and down to take hold of Night Star's halter. "Hi, ol' boy," he whispered.

Night Star nuzzled deep inside Andrew's leather windbreaker.

Andrew's lips quivered. He leaned over and ploughed his wet eyes along Night Star's rough black mane, getting the sweet horse smell, the feel, of what he now owned.

"Now, let's get home," he said, raising his head and grinning. "We've got to start breakin' you—or me." He laughed shakily.

With his heart thudding against his thin ribs, he took Night Star's rope and led him out through the gate and toward the group of distant white buildings that was home. He guessed he had the right colt, all right, the way he felt inside. And the way the ground shook under Night Star's feet as they walked along.

There was nothing sissy about that walk!

STEPHEN HOLT might once have been in the same predicament as Andrew in "Night Star," for as a boy he seldom missed a horse auction. He lived in western Kansas and Nebraska, the setting of "Indian Fighter," until his family moved to a ranch in Alberta, Canada.

Even before he could read, Holt knew a great deal about horses. His father's T X ranch was one of the biggest and most prosperous in the Northwest, and he learned to rope and range and keep alert for signs of a stampede at the roundups.

Holt later left the ranch to be educated in Canada and California. Then he became a writer of books and stories. His favorite subject is still horses, however, and he usually draws on his boyhood experience for both plot and setting. Perhaps his best-loved book is *Phantom Roan,* about an aspiring young veterinarian who rescued a dying outlaw roan, only to see the horse later almost destroyed by the ruthless rodeo practices described in "Night Star."

The Summer of the Beautiful White Horse

BY WILLIAM SAROYAN

ONE day back there in the good old days when I was nine and the world was full of every imaginable kind of magnificence, and life was still a delightful and mysterious dream, my cousin Mourad, who was considered crazy by everybody who knew him except me, came to my house at four in the morning and woke me by tapping on the window of my room.

Aram, he said.

I jumped out of bed and looked out the window.

I couldn't believe what I saw.

It wasn't morning yet, but it was summer and with daybreak not many minutes around the corner of the world it was light enough for me to know I wasn't dreaming.

My cousin Mourad was sitting on a beautiful white horse.

I stuck my head out of the window and rubbed my eyes.

Yes, he said in Armenian. It's a horse. You're not dreaming. Make it quick if you want to ride.

I knew my cousin Mourad enjoyed being alive more than anybody else who had ever fallen into the world by mistake, but this was more than even I could believe.

In the first place, my earliest memories had been memories of horses and my first longings had been longings to ride.

This was the wonderful part.

In the second place, we were poor.

This was the part that wouldn't permit me to believe what I saw.

We were poor. We had no money. Our whole tribe was poverty-stricken. Every branch of the Garoghlanian family was living in the most amazing and comical poverty in the world. Nobody could understand where we ever got money enough to keep us with food in our bellies, not even the old men of the family. Most important of all, though, we were famous for our honesty. We had been famous for our honesty for something like eleven centuries, even when we had been the wealthiest family in what we liked to think was the world. We were proud first, honest next, and after that we believed in right and wrong. None of us would take advantage of anybody in the world, let alone steal.

Consequently, even though I could *see* the horse, so magnificent; even though I could *smell* it, so lovely; even though I could *hear* it breathing, so exciting; I couldn't *believe* the horse had anything to do with my cousin Mourad or with me or with any of the other members of our family, asleep or awake, because I *knew* my cousin Mourad couldn't have *bought* the horse, and if he couldn't have bought it he must have *stolen* it, and I refused to believe he had stolen it.

No member of the Garoghlanian family could be a thief.

I stared first at my cousin and then at the horse. There was a pious stillness and humor in each of them which on the one hand delighted me and on the other frightened me.

Mourad, I said, where did you steal this horse?

Leap out of the window, he said, if you want to ride.

It was true, then. He *had* stolen the horse. There was no question about it. He had come to invite me to ride or not, as I chose.

Well, it seemed to me stealing a horse for a ride was not the same thing as stealing something else, such as money. For all I knew, maybe it wasn't stealing at all. If you were crazy about horses the way my cousin Mourad and I were, it wasn't stealing. It wouldn't become stealing until we offered to sell the horse, which of course I knew we would never do.

Let me put on some clothes, I said.

All right, he said, but hurry.

I leaped into my clothes.

I jumped down to the yard from the window and leaped up onto the horse behind my cousin Mourad.

That year we lived at the edge of town, on Walnut Avenue. Behind our house was the country: vineyards, orchards, irrigation ditches, and country roads. In less than three minutes we were on Olive Avenue, and then the horse began to trot. The air was new and lovely to breathe. The feel of the horse running was wonderful. My cousin Mourad who was considered one of the craziest members of our family began to sing. I mean, he began to roar.

Every family has a crazy streak in it somewhere, and my cousin Mourad was considered the natural descendant of the crazy streak in our tribe. Before him was our uncle Khosrove, an enormous man with a powerful head of black hair and the largest mustache in the San Joaquin Valley, a man so furious in temper, so irritable, so impatient that he stopped anyone from talking by roaring, *It is no harm; pay no attention to it.*

That was all, no matter what anybody happened to be talking about. Once it was his own son Arak running eight blocks to the barber shop where his father was having his mustache trimmed to tell him their house was on fire. This man Khosrove sat up in the chair and roared, It is no harm; pay no attention to it. The barber said, But the boy says your house is on fire. So Khosrove roared, Enough, it is no harm, I say.

My cousin Mourad was considered the natural descendant of this man, although Mourad's father was Zorab, who was practical and nothing else. That's how it was in our tribe. A man could be the father of his son's flesh, but that did not mean that he was also the father of his spirit. The distribution of the various kinds of spirit of our tribe had been from the beginning capricious and vagrant.

We rode and my cousin Mourad sang. For all anybody knew we were still in the old country where, at least according to some of our neighbors, we belonged. We let the horse run as long as it felt like running.

At last my cousin Mourad said, Get down. I want to ride alone.

Will you let me ride alone? I said.

That is up to the horse, my cousin said. Get down.

The *horse* will let me ride, I said.

We shall see, he said. Don't forget that I have a way with a horse.

Well, I said, any way you have with a horse, I have also.

For the sake of your safety, he said, let us hope so. Get down.

All right, I said, but remember you've got to let me try to ride alone.

I got down and my cousin Mourad kicked his heels into the horse and shouted *Vazire,* run. The horse stood on its hind legs, snorted, and burst into a fury of speed that was the loveliest thing I had ever seen. My cousin Mourad raced the horse across a field of dry grass to an irrigation ditch, crossed the ditch on the horse, and five minutes later returned, dripping wet.

The sun was coming up.

Now it's my turn to ride, I said.

My cousin Mourad got off the horse.

Ride, he said.

I leaped to the back of the horse and for a moment knew the awfulest fear imaginable. The horse did not move.

Kick into his muscles, my cousin Mourad said. What are you waiting for? We've got to take him back before everybody in the world is up and about.

I kicked into the muscles of the horse. Once again it reared and snorted. Then it began to run. I didn't know what to do. Instead of running across the field to the irrigation ditch the horse ran down the road to the vineyard of Dikran Halabian where it began to leap over vines. The horse leaped over seven vines before I fell. Then it continued running.

My cousin Mourad came running down the road.

I'm not worried about you, he shouted. We've got to get that horse. You go this way and I'll go this way. If you come upon him, be kindly. I'll be near.

I continued down the road and my cousin Mourad went across the field toward the irrigation ditch.

It took him half an hour to find the horse and bring him back.

All right, he said, jump on. The whole world is awake now.

What will we do? I said.

Well, he said, we'll either take him back or hide him until tomorrow morning.

He didn't sound worried and I knew he'd hide him and not take him back. Not for a while, at any rate.

Where will we hide him? I said.

I know a place, he said.

How long ago did you steal this horse? I said.

It suddenly dawned on me that he had been taking these early morning rides for some time and had come for me this morning only because he knew how much I longed to ride.

Who said anything about stealing a horse? he said.

Anyhow, I said, how long ago did you begin riding every morning?

Not until this morning, he said.

Are you telling the truth? I said.

Of course not, he said, but if we are found out, that's what you're to say. I don't want both of us to be liars. All you know is that we started riding this morning.

All right, I said.

He walked the horse quietly to the barn of a deserted vineyard which at one time had been the pride of a farmer named Fetvajian. There were some oats and dry alfalfa in the barn.

We began walking home.

It wasn't easy, he said, to get the horse to behave so nicely. At first it wanted to run wild, but, as I've told you, I have a way with a horse. I can get it to want to do anything *I* want it to do. Horses understand me.

How do you do it? I said.

I have an understanding with a horse, he said.

Yes, but what sort of an understanding? I said.

A simple and honest one, he said.

Well, I said, I wish I knew how to reach an understanding like that with a horse.

You're still a small boy, he said. When you get to be thirteen you'll know how to do it.

I went home and ate a hearty breakfast.

That afternoon my uncle Khosrove came to our house for coffee and cigarettes. He sat in the parlor, sipping and smoking and remembering the old country. Then another visitor arrived, a farmer named John Byro, an Assyrian who, out of loneliness, had learned to speak Armenian. My mother brought the lonely visitor coffee and tobacco and he rolled a cigarette and sipped and smoked, and then at last, sighing sadly, he said, My white horse which was stolen last month is still gone. I cannot understand it.

My uncle Khosrove became very irritated and shouted, It's no harm. What is the loss of a horse? Haven't we all lost the homeland? What is this crying over a horse?

That may be all right for you, a city dweller, to say, John Byro said, but what of my surrey? What good is a surrey without a horse?

Pay no attention to it, my uncle Khosrove roared.

I walked ten miles to get here, John Byro said.

You have legs, my uncle Khosrove shouted.

My left leg pains me, the farmer said.

Pay no attention to it, my uncle Khosrove roared.

That horse cost me sixty dollars, the farmer said.

I spit on money, my uncle Khosrove said.

He got up and stalked out of the house, slamming the screen door.

My mother explained.

He has a gentle heart, she said. It is simply that he is homesick and such a large man.

The farmer went away and I ran over to my cousin Mourad's house.

He was sitting under a peach tree, trying to repair the hurt wing of a young robin which could not fly. He was talking to the bird.

What is it? he said.

The farmer, John Byro, I said. He visited our house. He wants his horse. You've had it a month. I want you to promise not to take it back until I learn to ride.

It will take you *a year* to learn to ride, my cousin Mourad said.

We could keep the horse a year, I said.

My cousin Mourad leaped to his feet.

What? he roared. Are you inviting a member of the Garoghlanian family to steal? The horse must go back to its true owner.

When? I said.

In six months at the latest, he said.

He threw the bird into the air. The bird tried hard, almost fell twice, but at last flew away, high and straight.

Early every morning for two weeks my cousin Mourad and I took the horse out of the barn of the deserted vineyard where we were hiding it and rode it, and every morning the horse, when it was my turn to ride alone, leaped over grapevines and small trees and threw me and ran away. Nevertheless, I hoped in time to learn to ride the way my cousin Mourad rode.

One morning on the way to Fetvajian's deserted vineyard we ran into the farmer John Byro who was on his way to town.

Let me do the talking, my cousin Mourad said. I have a way with farmers.

Good morning, John Byro, my cousin Mourad said to the farmer.

The farmer studied the horse eagerly.

Good morning, sons of my friends, he said. What is the name of your horse?

My Heart, my cousin Mourad said in Armenian.

A lovely name, John Byro said, for a lovely horse. I could swear it is the horse that was stolen from me many weeks ago. May I look into its mouth?

Of course, Mourad said.

The farmer looked into the mouth of the horse.

Tooth for tooth, he said. I would swear it *is* my horse if I didn't know your parents. The fame of your family for honesty is well known to me. Yet the horse is the twin of my horse. A suspicious man would believe his eyes instead of his heart. Good day, my young friends.

Good day, John Byro, my cousin Mourad said.

Early the following morning we took the horse to John Byro's vineyard and put it in the barn. The dogs followed us around without making a sound.

The dogs, I whispered to my cousin Mourad. I thought they would bark.

They would at somebody else, he said. I have a way with dogs.

My cousin Mourad put his arms around the horse, pressed his nose into the horse's nose, patted it, and then we went away.

That afternoon John Byro came to our house in his surrey

and showed my mother the horse that had been stolen and returned.

I do not know what to think, he said. The horse is stronger than ever. Better-tempered, too. I thank God.

My uncle Khosrove, who was in the parlor, became irritated and shouted, Quiet, man, quiet. Your horse has been returned. Pay no attention to it.

When "The Summer of the Beautiful White Horse" first appeared in *Esquire* in the late thirties, WILLIAM SAROYAN had already achieved distinction for his prize-winning story "The Daring Young Man on the Flying Trapeze" and for other stories.

"The Summer of the Beautiful White Horse" is based on an episode from his youth in California. Born to Ormenak and Takooki Saroyan in 1908, he grew up in close association with his Armenian relatives, whose warm, colorful personalities are described in this and other Saroyan stories and novels.

Saroyan decided to be an author early in life, and was selling newspapers at age eight in order to buy a typewriter. He read "every book in the Fresno Public Library" but didn't care for formal schooling, and quit at fifteen to read law and learn shorthand and typing in his uncle's office. For the next eleven years he wrote and submitted his writing to various magazines while working at a dozen different jobs.

Then he was included in O'Brien's *Best Short Stories of 1934*, and began to appear regularly in leading magazines.

Since then he has written several novels, stories and plays. For *The Time of Your Life* he was awarded the Drama Critics' Circle Award and, in 1940, the Pulitzer Prize in drama—which he refused!

A four-legged detective

Two-bits of Traffic C

BY IRVING CRUMP

BRONX Parkway reached away like a long wet ribbon through the night with a vista of jewel-like street lamps. At the intersection of 210th Street the white traffic post stood out, adding alternately green and red reflections along the wet pavement. There was not much traffic. Occasionally the glaring eyes of a car loomed up at the far-off turn, came down the wet pavement. Some of the cars skidded a little when they stopped at the traffic light. Others came to a stop with the tires squeejeeing the wet pavements with a rubbery squeak. But they all stopped for the light; that is all but one.

Two-bits, the fine, big, clean-limbed, chestnut police horse, the mount of Patrolman James Jennings, almost anticipated the fact that the driver of the car coming north intended to try and run the light. Some strange sixth sense, highly developed in horses of his breeding and training, and often called horse sense, warned him that the man driving this car was not the best kind of citizen. For one thing he was running with his bright lights on and that was not allowed within the city limits. Bright lights always annoyed Two-bits. He had heard Patrolman Jimmy say a lot of things about men who drove with brilliant headlights shining, and he had stood by and seen Jimmy give some of them one of those little slips of paper from the notebook he carried.

This fellow was going to get a bawling out, if not one of those slips. Two-bits knew it the minute he caught sight of the car coming up the drive. He and Jimmy had been standing in the shadow of some parkway shrubbery. Two-bits heard Jimmy grumble something and felt him fumble under his wet slicker for his whistle as his knees signaled to move forward. Two-bits stepped out carefully on the wet and slippery pavement, planting his rubber-calked shoes solidly to guard against slipping. And as he moved forward, he expected to hear Jimmy's whistle chirp shrilly.

Patrolman Jimmy did not blow his whistle, however, for the green light on the traffic post clicked to a change and red eyes gleamed in the darkness warning the oncoming motorist to stop. But as Two-bits advanced and the car came on with undiminished speed, the horse saw that the driver did not intend to stop for the light. In fact, Two-bits' quick ear heard the engine accelerate a little as the driver made a desperate effort to run the intersection on the red light.

The whistle chirped out a succession of quick blasts. And as it shrilled, Two-bits, with the fearlessness of a trained police horse, stepped forward into the glare of the oncoming headlights.

The driver of the big closed car saw the policeman and his horse and heard his warning whistle at the same time, and instinctively he stepped down on his brakes; stepped down hard, in fact. There was a shrill screech of bands clamping home followed by a hiss of tires sliding in the wet, then suddenly another shrill, rubbery squeak, and things happened.

The big car began to skid. The heavy rear end whipped around, straightened a little, twisted the other way, and the car slid sideways, straight for Two-bits and Patrolman Jennings. Two-bits tried to leap sideways out of the path, but his rubber-calked shoes skidded on the wet pavement as the car struck him

There was a crash of glass, a shout of anger from Patrolman Jennings as he struggled to throw himself clear of the saddle; then a general mix-up in which the slicker-clad policeman went sailing through the air to come down heavily on the wet pavement, while Two-bits fell to his knees. The big car had knocked his feet out from under him as it skidded past.

Patrolman Jennings landed on his shoulder with such force that his head snapped downward against the pavement with a terrific whack. But he was a fighter and he did not remain unconscious long. Indeed, a few seconds after he landed on the pavement he struggled to his knees and tried valiantly to get to his feet. But his head whirled and the landscape swam before his blurred vision. His hands and feet became entangled in his rubber coat, too, causing him to fall again, and as he rolled over on the pavement he heard the thunderous roar of the car's motor as the driver opened it up once more and went speeding on down the parkway out of sight.

"One of those blasted hit-and-run drivers," muttered Patrolman Jennings as he staggered weakly to his feet and turned toward his horse. Two-bits was on his feet, too, trembling in every limb and staring, ears cocked in the direction of the vanishing car.

The horse had not been down for long. Fortunately, the skidding car had not hit him solidly. He was falling when the tail end whipped around and sideswiped his left shoulder. He had felt the burning sensation of some broken glass hitting him and opening up a cut on his withers, but he had not been stunned as Jimmy was and he was back on his feet while Jennings was still rolling around on the wet pavement.

But his heart was pounding and his breath was coming in gasps, for his horse intelligence told him that he and his master had had a close call. With a snort he moved toward the policeman and nuzzled him affectionately.

"Reckless fools. They got away, too, and I didn't get a look at their license plates. Lights were too bright. They blinded me. Didn't even see what kind of a car it was. It looked like a Cadillac, but I couldn't be sure. Two-bits, I wish you had sense enough to get their number. We might stand a chance of finding that car again if you had."

But Two-bits, with his horse instinct, had marked that car more accurately than Jimmy could have marked it if he had seen the license plates. What did a set of numbers amount to, anyway? They could be changed too easily. Two-bits had other and better methods. His keen sense of hearing had indelibly registered the sound of the motor; marked it as a fearsome sound different from the sound of any other car, as the noises of motors differ from each other. His keen eyes, too, had registered the form, size and color of the car as it fled off into the night and he would never forget it. Two-bits, like all horses, never forgot anything that caused him an injury.

And that car had injured him. It had not broken any bones, fortunately, but it had bruised and skinned his side, and glass had opened a wound in his shoulder. Patrolman Jennings found the wound as he passed his hands gently over the horse's mud-smeared and quivering flanks.

"They did hurt you, didn't they, old fellow? Looks like we would have to have a few days off, you and I, to get over being banged up this way. I got jiggered up a little myself." He led Two-bits to the side of the road. Then he went back to where a lot of broken glass gleamed in the lamplight.

"Busted a window, and a headlight, too, and—what's this?" Jennings bent over a wet object in the road and picked it up. It was a bolt of silk wrapped in wet paper that showed a brand mark.

"Silk. Standard Mills, too. Jingo! No wonder those birds didn't want to stop! A bunch of silk thieves—part of Lefty

Colter's gang that has been robbing the Markison silk warehouses, I'll bet a hat. That's the second time I've had a brush with that gang and they've got away clean again. That car was full of silk, and this piece fell out when the window busted, that's what happened. I owe those birds something and I sure wish I could have nailed them that time."

With the bolt of silk in his hand Patrolman Jennings stood in the road staring in the direction the departed car had taken. But as he stood there, once more the lights began to swim in his blurred vision. He turned toward Two-bits and tried to reach him. But even as he took a forward step, his legs doubled under him and he crumpled in the road, only partly aware of the fact that Two-bits had come to his side and now stood over him protectingly as he nuzzled him affectionately with his cold wet muzzle. Only dimly did he realize, ages later it seemed, that a brother officer found him and took charge of his horse while an ambulance carried him to the hospital.

Jimmy Jennings and Two-bits had come into the New York police department at about the same time. Two-bits had come into the department after a course of rigorous training at the stock farm where police horses are reared and trained for service. Jimmy Jennings had become a member of the department by way of the civil service examinations and two months in the school for policemen.

Jennings was a westerner from Idaho, stranded in New York when a rodeo company in which he was doing some exhibition riding met financial disaster. Jimmy, just past twenty-one, had only a silver-mounted prize saddle and a few dollars to his name. The saddle brought him eighty dollars, capital on which to live while he started job hunting. The only job in the whole city that interested him was with the mounted squad of the police department. He found that there was soon to be an examination for new policemen. He made application, took the examination, and because of his high school education, had little difficulty in passing. Also, because of his excellent physical condition and the fact that he was such a superior horseman, there was no doubt in the minds of the officials where he would best fit into the department. He was immediately assigned to the mounted section of the traffic division, and Two-bits was his working companion.

"By Jingo, you're a horse," said Jimmy enthusiastically when he saw Two-bits for the first time in the department's stables. "You're a horse with a heap of intelligence. I reckon you and I are going to be good pals."

As for Two-bits, when Jimmy Jennings, in his blue uniform, came into his stall and ran a soothing hand over his flanks and scratched him under his jaw, where all horses like to be scratched, he took one sniff, then rubbed his nose affectionately against Jimmy's shoulder, as if to say:

"By Jingo, you're a man. You're the kind who knows horses and loves them. I'm going to be proud to work for you and we sure are going to be good buddies."

And they were. For a year now they had been working together on the parkway, where all young horses and young cops of the mounted department are stationed first. Together they had experienced the hardships and unpleasant weather that go with the life of a policeman. They had had some thrills and made some arrests together and once they had heard bullets whistle their deadly chorus close to them. That had been their first close shave with the Colter gang of silk thieves. They had got a broadcast to watch for a certain stolen car with bogus license plates, and one afternoon the very car they were watching for turned into the parkway at Harrison Street right under their noses.

Patrolman Jimmy spotted the vehicle and blew his whistle for it to stop. But it did not stop. Instead it swung around the corner and into the parkway at full tilt. Patrolman Jimmy and

Two-bits tried to get in front of the machine. But they did not move fast enough. As it sped past them, Jimmy yanked his Police Special and fired a shot over the top of the car to warn the driver. But the short, dark-faced, ratty-eyed man did not stop. Instead he stepped on the gas, and at the same time three men in the car opened up at Jimmy and Two-bits with automatics, through the car window. Those bullets hummed close, but Two-bits was not afraid of gunfire. He had been pretty well schooled in that sort of work at the stock farm where he was trained. Nor did the bullets disturb Jimmy. The only thing that annoyed him was the fact that, after blazing six shots at the car and perforating the back of it thoroughly, it got away from him.

He had managed to cripple it up pretty well, however. One of his slugs went through the gas tank, and the machine was later found on the outskirts of New Rochelle, out of gas. It had been abandoned and left at the curb, and it was found to be loaded with silk, stolen from the Markison silk warehouses.

And here, evidently, was a second car used by the same gang that had got away from Jimmy, for there was no doubt in his mind and in the minds of his superiors that some of the members of the Colter gang had been in the automobile that had skidded into him and Two-bits.

They were a happy pair when they were together again and back on patrol duty. Some shifts had been made. Younger policemen had come into the mounted department and were placed on patrol up on the parkway, and Jimmy, with Two-bits, was transferred to Traffic C, down in the vicinity of Thirty-fourth Street and Fifth Avenue. Jimmy protested at first. He explained to Captain Mulcare that he wanted to continue on the parkway patrol and catch some of those Colter thieves.

But Captain Mulcare told him that some of their best detectives had been put on the Colter silk job, and that he was a traffic cop and not a sleuth. Anyway he was going down in the busy silk district where the Colter gang operated, so he might run up against them again.

They had miles of city streets to patrol, moving from one traffic post to another, relieving officers on duty for brief intervals during the day, and at night, when they were on the late shift, traveling block after block east and west of Fifth Avenue watching for trouble on the side streets, or keeping the late traffic moving on the main thoroughfares.

Patrolman Jimmy, in a measure, forgot about the accident and the car that had caused it, with his new duties. But Two-bits did not, and had he been able to communicate more plainly with Patrolman Jimmy he would have told him some things that would have startled him and made him marvel at his own stupidity. For instance, he would have told him that once during the six o'clock rush of traffic up Fifth Avenue that car passed so close to them that he, if he had not been afraid of it, could have touched it with his nose. Patrolman Jimmy, directing traffic, felt Two-bits shy and heard him snort. He saw his ear cock as he stared up Fifth Avenue, but Jimmy ignorantly blamed the animal's restlessness on the fact that they were just taking in a big flag that hung out of the windows of one of the hotels, and he laughed at Two-bits.

But that was not the last time the car passed them. On two other occasions it was part of the steady stream of traffic that flowed up Fifth Avenue while Two-bits and Jimmy were on patrol, and once it actually stalled within thirty feet of them, in a traffic jam. Two-bits did a lot of backing and filling then and considerable snorting and pawing trying to tell Jimmy that the car was there, and that the man at the driver's wheel, the one with the pasty yellow complexion and the mean eyes, was the fellow who always drove it. But one car in a jam of traffic did not mean anything to Jimmy, and anyway he was too busy trying to help two brother officers unsnarl a tangle at Thirty-ninth Street before the lights changed and made things worse.

Two-bits could not understand why, when he told him so plainly on more than one occasion that the car that had injured them both was within his grasp, Jimmy did not stop it and give the driver one of those white slips. Yet Jimmy Jennings did many things that were beyond Two-bits' understanding, so the horse let it go at that and continued to keep a watchful eye and equally attentive ear on the alert for the car that had run them down.

It was an evening when they were on the shift from twelve o'clock in the afternoon to twelve o'clock at night. Two-bits directed traffic for Jimmy for twenty minutes while Jimmy gossiped with Pat McCarthy. Then he and Jimmy started toward Herald Square, where they looked things over. They crossed Sixth Avenue and moved east along the now quiet and deserted block of Thirty-fifth Street. There was a car parked well up the block in front of one of the several dingy, old and apparently unoccupied brownstone houses toward Fifth Avenue. It was out of the glow of the street lamp and Two-bits could not make it out very well, though he had a premonition that he knew the vehicle, and he cocked his ears at it and sniffed hard as he moved forward.

Jimmy saw those cocked ears and remarked about them.

"Only some old night-hawker of a taxicab, Two-bits. What you so suspicious about? Driver's probably gone to get a bite to eat. It's funny, though, why he should leave it in the middle of the block that—sa-a-ay you, what's the matter, Two-bits? You're jumpy.

"By George. Been in a smash some time ago. Left side was hit. Lamp busted. It's a Cadillac, too, and . . ." Jimmy rode closer and bent out of the saddle. "Front door handle has been knocked off. That's a new one on there now, and . . . sa-a-ay, it couldn't be this is the car that hit us? And you sort of recognize it, don't you, Two-bits? I wonder now . . ."

Jimmy glanced up and down the deserted street, then back at the house again. But he did not look back quickly enough to see a face vanish from one of the darkened windows of the second floor, although Two-bits saw it and snorted anxiously. It was the pasty face of the man who always drove the car.

"I should investigate that place, I reckon. But if I try it alone, whoever is in there will get away from me," cogitated Jimmy. "It's too easy for them to slip out the back way while I'm getting in the front, or pile out the front way while I'm muscling my way in through the rear. I'd better get help. Come on, Two-bits."

Jimmy swung the horse around. There was a police signal light and call box at the end of the block on the Fifth Avenue corner.

But even as his fingers shoved in the little brass stub that set the green light flashing, Two-bits snorted and threw up his head as he cocked his ears forward. At the same time Jimmy heard the rumble of a motor starting to life down the block.

"They saw me snooping and they're trying to make a getaway. Come on, Two-bits. We've got to stop 'em and look 'em over."

The motor was under way already. In low gear it was drawing away from the curb. Jimmy realized that if they were going to overtake the machine they would have to catch it before it shifted into high. Fast as Two-bits was, the animal could never hope to overtake the car once it really got going. Two-bits put every ounce of strength and speed into his dash down the block.

Faster and faster traveled Two-bits, cutting down the lead of the car. But faster and faster traveled the car, too. When Two-bits was twenty feet behind the machine it was rolling along in second speed, almost as fast as Two-bits was galloping. Ugly faces were peering out of the window. Two-bits thought he saw the gleam of a revolver. So did Jimmy. He yanked his own then, and leaning low along Two-bits' neck, he spoke to him.

"Faster, feller! Faster! We've got to get that outfit this time. We'll look like a pair of palookas if we let 'em get away from us again."

Two-bits seemed to realize that they would be disgraced if they let that car lose them and with a valiant effort he redoubled his speed. In three or four terrific jumps he was almost beside the car as it sped toward Sixth Avenue. But the driver was stepping down harder on the gas as he strove to accelerate the engine and shift into high. The motor coughed and sputtered for a moment, and bucked a little with the way the gasoline was flooding the carburetor. Then suddenly came a wrenching, grating sound and the clash of gears as the driver threw the machine into high and shot it forward.

Jimmy Jennings, in the saddle and within a few feet of the machine, knew that there was but a split second left to him and Two-bits to apprehend the fugitives. There was only one thing for Jimmy Jennings to do, and he did it.

Leaning forward in his saddle, he hooked the fingers of his left hand under the upper edge of the open window beside the driver; at the same time he allowed the momentum of the car to drag him clear of his saddle. It was a simple trick. He had done it many a time bulldogging steers or changing horses at a fast canter out West. But a lot depended upon it this time. From the saddle he must swing down onto the running board of the car and hold fast, in spite of the high speed the car was traveling. If he missed that running board and failed to swing aboard that racing car, he might fall and be dragged under the wheels.

But Patrolman Jimmy did not miss the running board. As he shot clear of the saddle, he pulled himself toward the car and timed his feet to drop nicely. They landed perfectly on the running board with a heavy thump, and the next instant Jimmy was standing beside the driver, fiercely clinging fast with one hand and shoving the hard barrel of his service revolver into the man's back with the other.

"Stop that car and do it quick, if you don't want to be stopped yourself," snapped Jimmy crisply.

But the man stopped for another reason than the revolver prodding him between the ribs. At that instant, the car had reached the corner of Sixth Avenue, and without warning a trolley car rumbled to the crossing and stopped, blocking the way. The driver of the car saw that a fatal crash was imminent unless he applied the brakes forcefully, and he stepped down on them hard. And while Patrolman Jimmy was grimly trying to keep from being flung from the running board, a policeman leaped from the trolley car while another one sped across Sixth Avenue, and a third, none other than Sergeant Peacock, Jimmy's immediate superior, came running up from Thirty-fourth Street, all summoned by the flashing police light and the shrill of Jimmy's whistle.

"What's all this? What's the trouble, Jennings?" demanded the sergeant as Jimmy dropped from the running board, still keeping the driver covered with his revolver. Then, as he peered into the car window, he exclaimed, "Why, by Jove, you've arrested Lefty Colter and four of his gang! Good work!"

"I don't know who my prisoners are, but this is the car that ran me and Two-bits down on Bronx Parkway a couple of months ago. And if one of those birds is Lefty Colter, I've found the gang's hangout all right. It's in a brownstone house up the block there," exclaimed Patrolman Jimmy.

"It's the hangout of the Colter gang, I'm sure. We've got the silk robbers, fellows, and got them cold. Jennings, this is a mighty fine piece of work and you'll get a lot of credit for it, let me tell you. There have been a dozen department detectives on the trail of these fellows."

"Well," said Patrolman Jimmy with a smile, "my little ol' horse, Two-bits, he deserves most of the credit. If it hadn't been for him, I never would have identified that Cadillac car nor stumbled onto this place either. Look at him. Sergeant, he's a horse and I don't mean maybe. He gets an extra quart of oats for this when we get back to the stables tonight if I have to buy 'em myself."

IRVING CRUMP met the spirited hero of "Two-bits of Traffic C" while gathering material for two books about New York City's Police Department. "Two-bits was a fine, intelligent example of the horses used by the mounted men of the force," the author recalls.

Before he came to New York City as a newspaper reporter, Crump had grown up in a small town at the foot of the Catskill Mountains, where he used to spend his spare time exploring the woods and fields near his home. The love he felt for the outdoors, combined with his writing talent, led to the editorship of the Boy Scouts' magazine *Boys' Life*. While working there, Crump met Ernest Thompson Seton, whose stories about the outdoors had influenced his own. Later, on a visit to a ranch in Montana, he "became very well acquainted with horses, because it was impossible to get anywhere without one!"

The author of nearly forty books for boys, Crump has also written many radio scripts, among them, "Jack Armstrong, the All American Boy."

A bad scholar, a good patriot

The Royal Greens

BY RUSSELL GORDON CARTER

ON a cool, misty autumn morning in the year 1777, as David Wethervale led the small black mare from the stable, his father said to him, "After today I reckon you'll have to go to school afoot."

David's hand tightened on the bridle, and he swallowed hard. He said, "Then—you have at last found a buyer for her?"

"Aye," Seth Wethervale replied. "A man from over Danbury way is coming tomorrow. I'm sorry, lad, for your sake."

As David rode slowly westward toward the schoolhouse at the Corners, some three miles distant, he was miserable. No one knew the full depths of his feelings for the little mare. "Hobgoblin" she was named, because of her swift, ambling gait and her curious facial markings—a spattering of little white flecks that gave her a strangely humorous look.

Halfway to school, as they were crossing the old wooden bridge over the swift waters of Dog Creek, one of the rotten planks gave way under Hobgoblin's weight. She stumbled and pitched her rider sidewise into the stream.

David scrambled out, breathless and shaken, his hose and breeches dripping. Hobgoblin gazed at him wonderingly, then began to nuzzle at his shoulder.

David threw an arm impulsively over her drooping neck. " 'Twasn't your fault," he said. " 'Twas that rotten plank. Lucky you didn't break a leg!"

School was in session when David tethered the mare in a pine grove across the road. As he entered the small square building, Mr. Verrill, the schoolmaster, frowned and tightened his thin lips.

"What made you late?" he demanded. "Did you dawdle?"

"No, sir, I pitched off my horse," David replied. "She went through a plank in the bridge, and I landed in the water."

Several of the smaller girls tittered.

Mr. Verrill glowered at them, and the sound subsided at once. "Take your seat," he said to the boy.

After David had sat down between Mary Jacobus and Joseph Trumbull, the schoolmaster reopened the brown-covered speller on his desk and proceeded to call upon the pupils at the front of the room. But David's mind was not on the lesson. He was thinking of Hobgoblin, and what would become of her.

"David! Stand up and spell 'independent'!"

Joseph Trumbull's elbow against his ribs roused David to the realization that the schoolmaster had called on him. He got slowly to his feet. What was the word Mr. Verrill had asked him to spell? He heard Mary Jacobus whisper something.

"Indignant," he began. "I-n-"

"The word was 'independent'!" Mr. Verrill broke in sharply.

David's thoughts cleared. "Oh, yes, sir. Independent. I-n-d-e-p-e-n-d-a-n-t."

"Wrong!" cried the master. "Who can spell it correctly?"

The schoolroom buzzed with eager voices.

"Now try it again, David."

The boy wrinkled his forehead. Even amid the buzz of eager voices, his thoughts had again strayed to the mare. He began, "I-n-d-i-g-"

Mr. Verrill sprang from the chair, his face flushed. Seizing his birchwood ruler, he motioned with it to a corner. "Stand over yonder with your face to the wall!" he ordered. "Maybe 'twill help you gather your wits."

Half an hour dragged past. With his head against the wall, David was listening to Mary Jacobus trying to spell "beatific," when she suddenly uttered a startled exclamation and then began to laugh.

Glancing sidewise, David saw a surprising sight. Through the open window close to Mary protruded Hobgoblin's white-flecked head, her ears twitching, her jaws gently chewing a wisp of grass that hung from her lips. Others began to laugh, but a sharp crack of the ruler on the desk brought sudden silence.

"David!"

"Yes, sir?"

"Why did you not tie up your horse?"

"I—I did, sir."

"It does not look so!"

"She must have freed herself, sir."

"Well, go and tie her up again! You and your horse are a vexation!"

David hurried outside. He thought he had tied the bridle rein securely to a young pine, but here it was hanging free. Gathering up the rein, he led the horse away from the schoolhouse. Not back to the pine grove, but up the hill to where a solitary apple tree stood above grass that was still long and green.

"There now," he said, as he secured the rein to a limb. "You can graze here all you please."

He lingered, caressing Hobgoblin's smooth neck and letting her nibble playfully at his shoulder. To the east he could see the clustered houses of the village and, to the north of it, the round powder house built of field stones. Close by stood Amos Thatcher's big barn, which now held all the supplies for the militia.

His gaze lowered to the road, winding among patches of woodland, dropping to Dog Creek, then gradually twisting upward toward the Corners.

Suddenly David stiffened and caught his breath. There on the road, a quarter of a mile from the Corners, a band of men was marching. Men with muskets, clad in dusty green uniforms! He stared with mouth agape, almost unable to believe his eyes. Men in green uniforms marching toward the town!

His throat went abruptly dry, as the explanation leaped to his mind. Tories! A detachment of the Royal Greens—Johnson's Tories! They must have come up the old logging road that joined the main road some two hundred yards below the Corners. Now they were doubtless on their way to destroy the militia supplies, while the menfolks were at work in the fields!

David jerked Hobgoblin's bridle free from around the limb. A moment later, his leg was across the gray blanket that served as saddle and he was on his way down the slope.

Reaching the main road, David drew rein and held Hobgoblin to a slow walk. He knew exactly what he would do.

Just beyond Dog Creek, a second logging road joined the main road from the north. He would follow the raiding party at a safe distance, until he was across the bridge. Then he would strike northward up the logging road till he came to open country, and then push eastward as fast as possible. He was sure he could reach the town in time to give the alarm.

David was riding now through an old beech wood, the mare's hoofs making hardly a sound on the soft earth at the right of the road. Ahead of him, he could hear Dog Creek tumbling over its stony bed as it raced southward to join a branch of the Housatonic. The sound grew louder as he approached the base of the valley. Overhead, a pair of crows cawed raucously.

Just ahead of him, the road turned to the right before it dropped steeply to the creek. David drew rein and listened, but heard nothing except the roaring of the creek and the cawing of the crows. The raiders were probably across the bridge.

David urged the horse around the turn—and then jerked her to a sudden halt, his heart almost in his throat. Less than fifty yards in front, on the near side of the bridge, marched the raiders! Several greencoats in the rear spied him and called to those ahead.

For an instant, David sat rigid, viewing the collapse of his careful plan. He could never reach the north logging road now. And if he turned back, the town would be completely surprised.

The thought was intolerable. Acting on swift impulse, David clapped both heels to the mare's flanks, and away she went straight down the incline.

The suddenness of his charge took the Tories unawares. He saw green-clad figures hurriedly drawing apart in front of him. The wind sang in his ears. The woods rang with the clatter of hoofs and the shouts of men as Hobgoblin thundered downward —her haunches straining, her mane flying, sparks leaping outward from beneath her pounding feet.

Something slashed at David as he bent low over the mare's neck. A musket butt glanced off his shoulder. Another swished through the air and struck the mare's haunch, causing her to leap sidewise. A branch raked David's face as he swung her back to the middle of the road.

Only one man was between David and the bridge! He saw the fellow raise his musket. But before he could fire, Hobgoblin struck him with her shoulder, sending him spinning.

The bridge now was only a score of yards distant, and seemed to David to be rushing at him at breakneck speed. In a terrified instant, he pictured what would happen if one of Hobgoblin's feet should go through the hole in the bridge.

Then he steeled himself. He had taught Hobgoblin to jump. She must jump now—for her life! Almost at the edge of the bridge, he tightened his legs under the mare and let his weight fall backward. "Now, girl, now!"

Hobgoblin responded beautifully, landing almost in the center of the bridge. Then she thundered up the slope beyond. Two or three musket shots rang out as the mare reached the first turn, and David heard the bullets snap overhead. A moment later, horse and rider were around the turn—safe!

But there was no time to waste. David dug his heels against

the mare's flanks, urged her to her utmost. When they reached the first house on the outskirts of town, she was wet and glistening.

A woman appeared in the doorway, wide-eyed.

"Tories!" David shouted, slowing down. "A big band of them on the road!"

Through the heart of the town he clattered, shouting the warning on all sides: "Tories! Two score of the Royal Greens!" Then he made off across the fields, toward where he saw men working.

"Tories!" he shouted. "They're on their way up the west road!"

Somewhere in the town a bugle blared, the uncertain notes quivering across the countryside. On a rise of ground, David brought the mare to a halt. He had done his best.

From all directions, from the woods to the north and the fields to the east and south and west, men in shirt sleeves were running toward the town—sun-browned, resolute men with scythes or axes in their hands. He saw the first arrivals enter Amos Thatcher's barn, saw them emerge with muskets and powder horns. Others joined them, and as they formed ranks, David caught sight of his father. Then the column moved off down the road.

It was not until well past noon that the militiamen began to return. David saw them come straggling up the hill. In one group, to his profound relief, he spied his father.

Seth Wethervale came forward at a quick walk. His face was powder-stained.

David ran to meet him. "The Tories—" he began.

"They're well away from here by now—them as is left," his father replied grimly. Then he clutched his son's shoulder.

"Lad, I be proud o' ye!" he said. "What ye done an' all—"

David smiled and shook his head. " 'Twas Hobgoblin," he protested.

Seth Wethervale looked at him, then nodded. "I reckon ye're right. The mare shares the credit." Then he added in a tone meant to be matter-of-fact, "And I reckon, after what's happened, 'twould be a mite unfair to part the two o' ye."

David felt the warm blood come flooding into his face. "You—you mean you'll not sell her after all?"

"Aye, lad, that is what I mean. You've earned her keep."

David stared with eyes bright and lips parted, too moved to speak.

With a boisterous shout, he suddenly whirled and ran to where Hobgoblin was patiently waiting. A moment later his arm was across her neck and her soft lips were against his shoulder, as he told her the joyous news.

Although RUSSELL GORDON CARTER was a city boy brought up in Brooklyn, N. Y., he learned to care for and ride horses during summer vacations on the farm of a relative. But it was in Europe with the American Expeditionary Force during World War I that Carter discovered how important the relationship between a man and his horse can be in time of danger. With his horse Prince he took part in many successful European campaigns, and traveled hundreds of miles, finally crossing the Rhine to Rengsdorf, Germany. For his "gallantry in action" Carter was awarded a Silver Star. Later he paid tribute to the horses and mules of the A.E.F. who performed "such tasks as no others could possibly have accomplished." The citation is inscribed on the memorial statue at the entrance of the War Building in Washington, D. C.

A one-time editor of *Youth's Companion,* Carter has also written historical fiction for young readers. "The Royal Greens" reveals his keen interest in both horses and history.

A clever renegade

Coaly-bay, the Outlaw Horse

BY ERNEST THOMPSON SETON

FIVE years ago in the Bitterroot mountains of Idaho, there was a beautiful little foal. His coat was bright bay; his legs, mane and tail were glossy black—coal black and bright bay—so they named him Coaly-bay.

"Coaly-bay" sounds like "Koli-bey," which is an Arab title of nobility, and those who saw the handsome colt and did not know how he came by the name, thought he must be of Arab blood. No doubt he was, in a faraway sense; just as all our best horses have Arab blood, and once in a while it seems to come out strong and show in every part of the creature, in his frame, his power, and his wild, free roving spirit.

Coaly-bay loved to race like the wind; he gloried in his speed, his tireless legs; and when, careering with the herd of colts he met a fence or ditch, it was as natural to Coaly-bay to overleap it as it was for the others to sheer off.

So he grew up strong of limb, restless of spirit, and rebellious at any thought of restraint. Even the kindly curb of the hay yard or the stable was unwelcome, and he soon showed that he would rather stand out all night in a driving storm than be locked in a comfortable stall where he had no vestige of the liberty he loved so well.

He became very clever at dodging the horse wrangler whose

job it was to bring the horse herd to the corral. The very sight of that man set Coaly-bay going. He became what is known as a "quit-the-bunch"—that is, a horse of such independent mind that he will go his own way the moment he does not like the way of the herd.

So each month the colt became more set on living free, and more cunning in the means he took to win his way. Far down in his soul, too, there must have been a streak of cruelty, for he stuck at nothing and spared no one that seemed to stand between him and his one desire.

When he was three years of age, just in the perfection of his young strength and beauty, his real trouble began, for now his owner undertook to break him to ride. He was as tricky and vicious as he was handsome, and the first day's experience was a terrible battle between the horse trainer and the beautiful colt.

But the man was skillful. He knew how to apply his power, and all the wild plunging, bucking, rearing and rolling of the wild one had no desired result. With all his strength, the horse was hopelessly helpless in the hands of the skillful horseman, and Coaly-bay was at length so far mastered that a good rider could use him. But each time the saddle went on, he made a new fight. After a few months of this the colt seemed to realize that it was useless to resist—it simply won for him lashings and spurrings—so he pretended to reform. For a week he was ridden each day and not once did he buck, but on the last day he came home lame.

His owner turned him out to pasture. Three days later he seemed all right; he was caught and saddled. He did not buck, but within five minutes he went lame as before. Again he was turned out to pasture, and after a week, saddled, only to go lame.

His owner did not know what to think, whether the horse really had a lame leg or was only shamming, but he took the first chance to get rid of him, and though Coaly-bay was easily worth fifty dollars, he sold him for twenty-five. The new owner felt he had a bargain, but after being ridden half a mile Coaly-bay went lame. The rider got off to examine the foot, whereupon Coaly-bay broke away and galloped back to his old pasture. Here he was caught, and the new owner, being neither gentle nor sweet, applied spur without mercy, so that the next twenty miles was covered in less than two hours and no sign of lameness appeared.

Now they were at the ranch of this new owner. Coaly-bay was led from the door of the house to the pasture, limping all the way, and then turned out. He limped over to the other horses.

On one side of the pasture was the garden of a neighbor. This man was very proud of his fine vegetables and had put a six-foot fence around the place. Yet the very night after Coaly-bay arrived, certain of the horses got into the garden somehow and did a great deal of damage. But they leaped out before daylight, and no one saw them.

The gardener was furious, but the ranchman stoutly maintained that it must have been some other horses, since his were behind a six-foot fence.

Next night it happened again. The ranchman went out very early and saw all his horses in the pasture, with Coaly-bay behind them. His lameness seemed worse now instead of better. In a few days, however, the horse was seen walking all right, so the ranchman's son caught him and tried to ride him. But this seemed too good a chance to lose; all his old wickedness returned to the horse; the boy was bucked off at once and hurt. The ranchman himself now leaped into the saddle. Coaly-bay bucked for ten minutes but finding he could not throw the man, he tried to crush his leg against a post, but the rider guarded himself well. Coaly-bay reared and threw himself backward; the rider slipped off, the horse fell, jarring heavily, and before he could rise the man was in the saddle again. The horse now ran away, plunging and bucking. He stopped short, but the rider did not go over his head, so Coaly-bay turned, seized the man's foot in his teeth, and but for heavy blows on the nose would have torn him dreadfully. It was quite clear now that Coaly-bay was an outlaw, an incurably vicious horse.

The saddle was jerked off, and he was driven, limping, into the pasture.

The raids on the garden continued, and the two men began to quarrel over it. To prove that his horses were not guilty, the ranchman asked the gardener to sit up with him and watch. That night as the moon was brightly shining they saw, not all the horses, but Coaly-bay, walk straight up to the garden fence—no sign of a limp now—easily leap over it, and proceed to gobble the finest things he could find. After they had made sure of his identity, the men ran forward. Coaly-bay cleared the fence like a deer, lightly raced over the pasture to mix with the horse herd, and when the men came near he had—oh, such an awful limp.

"That settles it," said the rancher. "He's a fraud but he's a beauty, and good stuff, too."

"Yes, but it settles who took my garden truck."

"Wal, I suppose so," was the answer; "but luk a-here, neighbor, you ain't lost more'n ten dollars in truck. That horse is easily worth—a hundred. Give me twenty-five dollars, take the horse, an' call it square."

"Not much I will," said the gardener. "I'm out twenty-five dollars' worth of truck; the horse ain't worth a cent more. I take him and call it even."

And so the thing was settled. The ranchman said nothing about Coaly-bay being vicious as well as cunning. The gardener found it out the very first time he tried to ride him; the horse was as bad as he was beautiful.

Next day a sign appeared on the gardener's gate:

FOR SALE
First-class horse, sound
and gentle. $10.00

Now at this time a band of hunters came riding by. There were three mountaineers, two men from the city and the writer of this story. The city men were going to hunt bear. They had guns and everything needed for bear-hunting, except bait. It is usual to buy some worthless horse or cow, drive it into the mountains where the bears are, and kill it there. So, seeing the sign up, the hunters called to the gardener: "Haven't you got a cheaper horse?"

The gardener replied: "Look at him there, ain't he a beauty? You won't find a cheaper horse if you travel a thousand miles."

"We are looking for an old bear-bait and five dollars is our limit," replied the hunter.

Horses were cheap and plentiful in that country; buyers were scarce. The gardener feared that Coaly-bay would escape. "Wal, if that's the best you can do, he's yourn."

The hunter handed him five dollars, then said:

"Now, stranger, bargain's settled. Will you tell me why you sell this fine horse for five dollars?"

"Mighty simple. He can't be rode. He's dead lame when he's going your way and sound as a dollar going his own; no fence in the country can hold him; he's a dangerous outlaw. He's wickeder nor old Nick."

"Well, he's an almighty handsome bear-bait," and the hunters rode on.

Coaly-bay was driven with the pack horses, and limped dreadfully on the trail. Once or twice he tried to go back, but he was easily turned by the men behind him. His limp grew worse, and toward night it was painful to see him.

The leading guide remarked: "That thar limp ain't no fake. He's got some deep-seated trouble."

Day after day the hunters rode farther into the mountains, driving the horses along and hobbling them at night. Coaly-bay went with the rest, limping along, tossing his head and his long splendid mane at every step. One of the hunters tried to ride him and nearly lost his life, for the horse seemed possessed of a demon as soon as the man was on his back.

The road grew harder as it rose. A very bad bog had to be crossed one day. Several horses were mired in it, and as the men rushed to the rescue, Coaly-bay saw his chance of escape. He wheeled in a moment and turned himself from a limping, low-headed, sorry, bad-eyed creature into a high-spirited horse. Head and tail aloft now, shaking their black streamers in the wind he gave a joyous neigh, and without a trace of lameness, dashed for his home one hundred miles away, threading each narrow trail with perfect certainty though he had seen them but once before. In a few minutes he had streamed away from their sight.

The men were furious, but one of them, saying not a word, leaped on his horse—to do what? Follow that free-ranging racer? Sheer folly. Oh, no—he knew a better plan. He knew the country. Two miles around by the trail, half a mile by the rough cutoff that he took, was Panther Gap. The runaway must pass through that, and Coaly-bay raced down the trail to find the guide below awaiting him. Tossing his head with anger, he wheeled on up the trail again and within a few yards recovered his monotonous limp and his evil expression. He was driven into camp and there he vented his rage by kicking in the ribs of a harmless little pack horse.

This was bear country, and the hunters resolved to end his dangerous pranks and make him useful for once. They dared not catch him, it was not really safe to go near him, but two of the guides drove him to a distant glade where bears abounded. A thrill of pity came over me as I saw that beautiful untamable creature going away with his imitation limp.

"Ain't you coming along?" called the guide.

"No, I don't want to see him die," was the answer. Then, as the tossing head was disappearing, I called, "I wish you would bring me that mane and tail when you come back!"

Fifteen minutes later I heard a distant rifle crack, and in my mind's eye I saw that proud head and those superb limbs, robbed of their sustaining indomitable spirit, falling flat and limp—to suffer the unsightly end of fleshly things. Poor Coaly-bay; he would not bear the yoke. Rebellious to the end, he had fought against the fate of all his kind. It seemed to me the spirit of an eagle or a wolf it was that dwelt behind those full bright eyes, that ordered all his wayward life.

I tried to put the tragic finish out of mind, and had not long to battle with the thought—not even one short hour, for the men came back.

Down the long trail to the west they had driven him; there was no chance for him to turn aside. He must go on, and the men behind felt safe in that.

Farther away from his old home on the Bitterroot River he had gone each time he journeyed. And now he had passed the high divide and was keeping the narrow trail that leads to the valley of bears and on to Salmon River, and still away to the open wild Columbian Plains, limping sadly as though he knew. His glossy hide flashed back the golden sunlight, still richer than it fell, and the men behind followed like hangmen in the death train of a nobleman condemned—down the narrow trail till it opened into a little beaver meadow, with rank rich grass, a lovely mountain stream, and winding bear paths up and down the waterside.

"Guess this'll do," said the older man. "Well, here goes for a sure death or a clean miss," said the other confidently, and waiting till the limper was out in the middle of the meadow, he gave a short, sharp whistle. Instantly Coaly-bay was alert. He swung and faced his tormentors, his noble head erect, his nostrils flaring, a picture of horse beauty—yes, of horse perfection.

The rifle was leveled, the very brain its mark, just on the crossline of the eyes and ears that meant sudden, painless death.

The rifle cracked. The great horse wheeled and dashed

away. It was sudden death or miss—and the marksman had *missed.*

Away went the wild horse at his famous best, not for his eastern home but down the unknown western trail, away and away; the pine woods hid him from view, and left behind was the rifleman vainly trying to force the empty cartridge from his gun.

Down that trail with an inborn certainty he went, and on through the pines, then leaped a great bog and splashed an hour later through the limpid Clearwater and on, responsive to some unknown guide that subtly called him from the farther west. And so he went till the dwindling pines gave place to scrubby cedars and these in turn were mixed with sage, and onward still, till the faraway flat plains of Salmon River were about him, and ever on, tireless as it seemed, he went, and crossed the canyon of the mighty Snake, and up again to the high wild plains where the wire fence still is not, and on beyond the Buffalo Hump, till moving specks on the far horizon caught his eager eyes, and coming on and near, they moved and rushed aside to wheel and face about. He lifted up his voice and called to them, the long shrill neigh of his kindred when they bugled to each other on the far Chaldean plain, and back their answer came. This way and that they wheeled and sped and caracoled, and Coaly-bay drew nearer, called and gave the countersigns his kindred know, till this they were assured—he was their kind, he was of the wild free blood that man had never tamed. And when the night came down on the purpling plain his place was in the herd as one who after many a long hard journey in the dark had found his home.

There you may see him yet, for still his strength endures, and his beauty is not less. The riders tell me they have seen him many times by Cedra. He is swift and strong among the swift ones, but it is that flowing mane and tail that mark him chiefly from afar.

There on the wild free plains of sage he lives: the storm

wind smites his glossy coat at night and the winter snows are driven hard on him at times; the wolves are there to harry all the weak ones of the herd, and in the spring the mighty grizzly, too, may come to claim his toll. There are no luscious pastures made by man, no grain foods; nothing but the wild hard hay, the wind and the open plains. But here at last he found the thing he craved—the one worth all the rest. Long may he roam—this is my wish, and this—that I may see him once again in all the glory of his speed with his black mane on the wind, the spur-galls gone from his flanks, and in his eye the blazing light that grew in his far-off forebears' eyes as they spurned Arabian plains to leave behind the racing wild beast and the fleet gazelle—yes, too, the driving sandstorm that overwhelmed the rest, but strove in vain on the dusty wake of the desert's highest born.

ERNEST THOMPSON SETON was five when his family moved from England to the backwoods of Ontario, Canada, where he developed his lifelong passion for the outdoors. His father sent him to study at the Royal Academy of Art in London, but Seton wanted to be a naturalist, and when tuberculosis interrupted his studies he went camping and hunting to regain his health.

In 1898 Seton published eight of his realistic animal stories under the title *Wild Animals I Have Known.* An immediate success, it was followed by more than forty books, which he wrote and illustrated. This great naturalist felt a sense of mission about Americans growing up with a love for their outdoor world, and was instrumental in establishing the Boy Scouts of America. In 1930 he moved to New Mexico where he founded a great animal preserve, the Seton Institute, at Santa Fe. His story "Coaly-bay" from *Wild Animal Ways* shows his admiration for the freedom-loving spirit of wild animals, a theme that runs through many of his stories.

A herd of castaways

Before Misty

BY MARGUERITE HENRY

1. LIVE CARGO!

A WILD, ringing neigh shrilled up from the hold of the Spanish galleon. It was not the cry of an animal in hunger. It was a terrifying bugle. An alarm call.

The captain of the *Santo Cristo* strode the poop deck. "Cursed be that stallion!" he muttered under his breath as he stamped forward and back, forward and back.

Suddenly he stopped short. The wind! It was dying with the sun. It was spilling out of the sails, causing them to quiver and shake. He could feel his flesh creep with the sails. Without wind he could not get to Panama. And if he did not get there and get there soon, he was headed for trouble. The Moor ponies to be delivered to the viceroy of Peru could not be kept alive much longer. Their hay had grown musty. The water casks were almost empty. And now this sudden calm, this heavy warning of a storm.

He plucked nervously at his rusty black beard as if that would help him think. "We lie in the latitude of white squalls," he said, a look of vexation on his face. "When the wind does strike, it will strike with fury." His steps quickened as he made up his mind. "We must shorten sail."

Cupping his hands to his mouth he bellowed orders: "Furl the topgallant sail! Furl the coursers and the main-topsail! Shorten the fore-topsail!"

The ship burst into action. From forward and aft all hands came running. They fell to work furiously, carrying out orders.

The captain's eyes were fixed on his men, but his thoughts raced ahead to the rich land where he was bound. In his mind's eye he could see the mule train coming to meet him when he reached land. He could see it snaking its way along the Gold Road from Panama to the seaport of Puerto Bello. He could almost feel the smooth, hard gold in the packs on the donkeys' backs.

His eyes narrowed greedily. "Gold!" he mumbled. "Think of trading twenty ponies for their weight in gold!" He clasped his hands behind him and resumed his pacing and muttering. "The viceroy of Peru sets great store by the ponies, and well he may. Without the ponies to work the mines, there will be no more gold." He clenched his fists. "We must keep the ponies alive!"

His thoughts were brought up sharply. That shrill horse call! Again it filled the air about him with a wild ring. His beady eyes darted to the lookout man in the crow's-nest, then to the men on deck. He saw fear spread among the crew.

Meanwhile, in the dark hold of the ship a small bay stallion was pawing the floor of his stall. His iron shoes with their sharp rims and turned-down heels threw a shower of sparks, and he felt strong charges of electricity. His nostrils flared. The moisture in the air! The charges of electricity! These were storm warnings —things he knew. Some inner urge told him he must get his mares to high land before the storm broke. He tried to escape, charging against the chest board of his stall again and again. He threw his head back and bugled.

From stalls beside him and from stalls opposite him, nineteen heads with small pointed ears peered out. Nineteen pairs of brown eyes whitened. Nineteen young mares caught his anxiety. They, too, tried to escape, rearing and plunging, rearing and plunging.

But presently the animals were no longer hurling themselves. They were *being* hurled. The ship was pitching and tossing to the rising swell of the sea, flinging the ponies forward against their chest boards, backward against the ship's sides.

A cold wind spiraled down the hatch. It whistled and screamed above the rough voice of the captain. It gave way only to the deep *flump-flump* of the thunder.

The sea became a wildcat now, and the galleon her prey. She stalked the ship and drove her off her course. She slapped at her, rolling her victim from side to side. She knocked the spars out of her and used them to ram holes in her sides. She clawed the rudder from its sternpost and threw it into the sea. She cracked the ship's ribs as if they were brittle bones. Then she hissed and spat through the seams.

The pressure of the sea swept everything before it. Huge baskets filled with gravel for ballast plummeted down the passageway between the ponies, breaking up stalls as they went by.

Suddenly the galleon shuddered. From bow to stern came an endless rasping sound. The ship had struck a shoal. And with a ripping and crashing of timber the hull cracked open. In that split second the captain, his men, and his live cargo were washed into the boiling foam.

The wildcat sea yawned. She swallowed the men. Only the captain and fifteen ponies managed to come up again. The captain bobbed alongside the stallion and made a wild grasp for his tail, but a great wave swept him out of reach.

The stallion neighed encouragement to his mares, who were struggling to keep afloat, fighting the wreckage and the sea. For long minutes they thrashed about helplessly, and just when their strength was nearly spent, the storm died as suddenly as it had risen. The wind calmed.

The sea was no longer a wildcat. She became a kitten, fawning and lapping about the ponies' legs. Now their hooves touched land. They were able to stand! They were scrambling up the beach, up on Assateague Beach, that long, sandy island which shelters the tidewater country of Virginia and Maryland. They were far from the mines of Peru.

2. THE ISLAND OF THE WILD THINGS

The ponies were exhausted and their coats were heavy with water, but they were free, free, *free!* They raised their heads and snuffed the wind. The smell was unlike that of the lowland moors of Spain, but it was good. They sucked in the sharp, sweet pungence of pine woods, and somewhere mixed in with the piney smell came the enticing scent of salt grass.

Their stomachs were pinched with hunger, but the ponies did not seek the grass at once. They shook the water from their coats. Then they rolled back and forth in the sand, enjoying the solid feel of the land.

At last the stallion's hunger stirred him to action. He rounded up his mares, and with only a watery moon to light the way he drove them through the needle-carpeted woods. The mares stopped to eat the leaves of some myrtle bushes, but the stallion jostled them into line. Then he took the lead. So direct was his progress it seemed almost as if he had trodden here before. Through bramble and thicket, through brackish pools of water, he led the way.

The moon was high overhead when the little band came out on grassy marshland. They stopped a moment to listen to the wide blades of grass whisper and squeak in the wind, to sniff the tickling smell of salt grass.

This was it! This was the exciting smell that had urged them on. With wild snorts of happiness they buried their noses in the long grass. They bit and tore great mouthfuls—frantically, as if they were afraid it might not last. Oh, the salty goodness of it! Not bitter at all, but juicy-sweet with rain. It was different from any grass they knew. It billowed and shimmered like the sea. They could not get enough of it. That delicious salty taste! Never had they known anything like it. Never. And sometimes they came upon tender patches of lespedeza, a kind of clover that grew among the grasses.

The ponies forgot the forty days and forty nights in the dark hold of the Spanish galleon. They forgot the musty hay. They forgot the smell of bilge water, of oil and fishy odors from the cooking galley.

When they could eat no more, they pawed shallow wells with their hooves for drinking water. Then they rolled in the wiry grass, letting out great whinnies of happiness. They seemed unable to believe that the island was all their own. Not a human being anywhere. Only grass. And sea. And sky. And the wind.

At last they slept.

The seasons came and went, and the ponies adopted the New World as their own. They learned how to take care of themselves. When summer came and with it the greenhead flies by day and the mosquitoes by night, they plunged into the sea, up to their necks in the cool surf. The sea was their friend. Once it had set them free; now it protected them from their fiercest enemies.

Winter came and the grass yellowed and dried, but the ponies discovered that close to the roots it was still green and good to eat.

Even when a solid film of ice sealed the land, they did not

go hungry. They broke through the ice with their hooves or went off to the woods to eat the myrtle leaves that stayed green all winter.

Snow was a new experience, too. They blew at it, making little snow flurries of their own. They tasted it. It melted on their tongues. Snow was good to drink!

If the Spaniards could have seen their ponies now, they would have been startled at their changed appearance. No longer were their coats sleek. They were as thick and shaggy as the coat of any sheep dog. This was a good thing. On bitter days, when they stood close-huddled for comfort, each pony could enjoy the added warmth of his neighbor's coat as well as his own.

There were no wolves or wildcats on the island, but there was deep, miry mud to trap creatures and suck them down. After a few desperate struggles the ponies learned how to fall to their knees, then sidle and wriggle along like crabs until they were well out of it.

With each season the ponies grew wiser. And with each season they became tougher and more hardy. Horse colts and fillies were born to them. As the horse colts grew big they rounded up mares of their own, and started new herds that ranged wild—wild as the wind and the sea that had brought them there long ago.

Years went by. And more years. Changes came to Assateague. The red men came. The white men came. The white men built a lighthouse to warn ships of dangerous reefs. They built a handful of houses and a white church But soon the houses stood empty. The people moved their homes and their church to nearby Chincoteague Island, for Assateague belonged to the wild things—to the wild birds that nestled on it, and the wild ponies whose ancestors had lived on it since the days of the Spanish galleon.

The first horse that MARGUERITE HENRY knew well was the family mare Bonnie, who was sold because she was bad-tempered and inclined to bite. In spite of this unpleasant early encounter, Mrs. Henry got a horse of her own as soon as she and her husband had bought some land in Illinois. She has kept one or more, along with numerous other animals, ever since.

One of the nation's best known writers of horse stories, Mrs. Henry began writing soon after graduation from Milwaukee State Teachers College. She had been encouraged by her father, who also wrote, and by her sister Gertrude, still her most trusted critic.

Her *Misty of Chincoteague,* from which the selection "Before Misty" was taken, won the Newbery Award, was made into a motion picture, and has become one of the best-loved books of our time. In gathering material for *Misty* Mrs. Henry lived for awhile on Chincoteague Island off the Virginia coast. She also visited the neighboring island of Assateague. There she saw for herself the famous herd of wild horses, whose history she so eloquently describes in "Before Misty."

End of a dream

The Gift

BY JOHN STEINBECK

AT daybreak Billy Buck emerged from the bunk-house and stood for a moment on the porch looking up at the sky. He was a broad, bandy-legged little man with a walrus mustache, with square hands, puffed and muscled on the palms. His eyes were a contemplative, watery gray, and the hair which protruded from under his Stetson hat was spiky and weathered. Billy was still stuffing his shirt into his blue jeans as he stood on the porch. He unbuckled his belt and tightened it again. The belt showed, by the worn shiny places opposite each hole, the gradual increase of Billy's middle over a period of years. When he had seen to the weather, Billy cleared each nostril by holding its mate closed with his forefinger and blowing fiercely. Then he walked down to the barn, rubbing his hands together. He curried and brushed two saddle horses in the stalls, talking quietly to them all the time; and he had hardly finished when the iron triangle started ringing at the ranch house. Billy stuck the brush and currycomb together and laid them on the rail, and went up to breakfast. His action had been so deliberate and yet so wasteless of time that he came to the house while Mrs. Tiflin was still ringing the triangle. She nodded her gray head to him and withdrew into the kitchen. Billy Buck sat down on the steps, because he was a cow hand, and it wouldn't be fitting that he should go first into the dining room. He heard Mr. Tiflin in the house, stamping his feet into his boots.

The high jangling note of the triangle put the boy Jody in motion. He was only a little boy, ten years old, with hair like dusty yellow grass and with shy, polite gray eyes, and with a mouth that worked when he thought. The triangle picked him up out of sleep. It didn't occur to him to disobey the harsh note. He never had: no one he knew ever had. He brushed the tangled hair out of his eyes and skinned his nightgown off. In a moment he was dressed—blue chambray shirt and overalls. It was late in the summer, so of course there were no shoes to bother with. In the kitchen he waited until his mother got from in front of the sink and went back to the stove. Then he washed himself and brushed back his wet hair with his fingers. His mother turned sharply on him as he left the sink. Jody looked shyly away.

"I've got to cut your hair before long," his mother said. "Breakfast's on the table. Go on in, so Billy can come."

Jody sat at the long table which was covered with white oilcloth washed through to the fabric in some places. The fried eggs lay in rows on their platter. Jody took three eggs on his plate and followed with three thick slices of crisp bacon. He carefully scraped a spot of blood from one of the egg yolks.

Billy Buck clumped in. "That won't hurt you," Billy explained. "That's only a sign the rooster leaves."

Jody's tall stern father came in then. Jody knew from the noise on the floor that he was wearing boots, but he looked under the table anyway, to make sure. His father turned off the oil lamp over the table, for plenty of morning light now came through the windows.

Jody did not ask where his father and Billy Buck were riding that day, but he wished he might go along. His father was a disciplinarian. Jody obeyed him in everything without questions of any kind. Now, Carl Tiflin sat down and reached for the egg platter.

"Got the cows ready to go, Billy?" he asked.

"In the lower corral," Billy said. "I could just as well take them in alone."

"Sure you could. But a man needs company. Besides, your throat gets pretty dry." Carl Tiflin was jovial this morning.

Jody's mother put her head in the door. "What time do you think to be back, Carl?"

"I can't tell. I've got to see some men in Salinas. Might be gone till dark."

The eggs and coffee and big biscuits disappeared rapidly. Jody followed the two men out of the house. He watched them mount their horses and drive six old milk cows out of the corral and start over the hill toward Salinas. They were going to sell the old cows to the butcher.

When they had disappeared over the crown of the ridge Jody walked up the hill in back of the house. The dogs trotted around the house corner, hunching their shoulders and grinning horribly with pleasure. Jody patted their heads—Doubletree Mutt with the big thick tail and yellow eyes, and Smasher, the shepherd, who had killed a coyote and lost an ear in doing it. Smasher's one good ear stood up higher than a collie's ear should. Billy Buck said that always happened. After the frenzied greeting the dogs lowered their noses to the ground in a businesslike way and went ahead, looking back now and then to make sure that the boy was coming. They walked up through the chicken yard and saw the quail eating with the chickens. Smasher chased the chickens a little to keep in practice in case there should ever be sheep to herd. Jody continued on through the large vegetable patch where the green corn was higher than his head. The cow-pumpkins were green and small yet. He went on to the sagebrush line where the cold spring ran out of its pipe and fell into a round wooden tub. He leaned over and drank close to the green mossy wood where the water tasted best. Then he turned and looked back on the ranch, on the low, whitewashed house girded with red geraniums, and on the long bunkhouse by the cypress tree where Billy Buck lived alone. Jody could see the great black kettle under the cypress tree. That was where the pigs were scalded. The sun was coming over the ridge now, glaring on the whitewash of the houses and barns, making the wet grass blaze softly. Behind him, in the tall sagebrush, the birds were scampering on the ground, making a great noise among the dry leaves; the squirrels piped shrilly on the side hills. Jody looked along at the farm buildings. He felt an uncertainty in the air, a feeling of change and of loss and of the gain of new and unfamiliar things. Over the hillside two big black buzzards sailed low to the ground, and their shadows slipped smoothly and quickly ahead of them. Some animal had died in the vicinity. Jody knew it. It might be a cow or it might be the remains of a rabbit. The buzzards overlooked nothing. Jody hated them as all decent things hate them, but they could not be hurt because they made away with carrion.

After a while the boy sauntered down hill again. The dogs had long ago given him up and gone into the brush to do things in their own way. Back through the vegetable garden he went, and he paused for a moment to smash a green muskmelon with his heel, but he was not happy about it. It was a bad thing to do, he knew perfectly well. He kicked dirt over the ruined melon to conceal it.

Back at the house his mother bent over his rough hands, inspecting his fingers and nails. It did little good to start him clean to school, for too many things could happen on the way. She sighed over the black cracks on his fingers, and then gave him his books and his lunch and started him on the mile walk to school. She noticed that his mouth was working a good deal this morning.

Jody started his journey. He filled his pockets with little pieces of white quartz that lay in the road, and every so often he took a shot at a bird or at some rabbit that had stayed sunning itself in the road too long. At the crossroads over the bridge he met two friends and the three of them walked to school together, making ridiculous strides and being rather silly. School had just opened two weeks before. There was still a spirit of revolt among the pupils.

It was four o'clock in the afternoon when Jody topped the hill and looked down on the ranch again. He looked for the saddle horses, but the corral was empty. His father was not back yet. He went slowly, then, toward the afternoon chores. At the ranch house, he found his mother sitting on the porch, mending socks.

"There's two doughnuts in the kitchen for you," she said. Jody slid to the kitchen and returned with half of one of the doughnuts already eaten and his mouth full. His mother asked him what he had learned in school that day, but she didn't listen to his doughnut-muffled answer. She interrupted, "Jody, tonight see you fill the woodbox clear full. Last night you crossed the sticks and it wasn't only about half full. Lay the sticks flat tonight. And Jody, some of the hens are hiding eggs, or else the dogs are eating them. Look about in the grass and see if you can find any nests."

Jody, still eating, went out and did his chores. He saw the quail come down to eat with the chickens when he threw out the grain. For some reason his father was proud to have them come.

He never allowed any shooting near the house for fear the quail might go away.

When the woodbox was full, Jody took his twenty-two rifle up to the cold spring at the brush line. He drank again and then aimed the gun at all manner of things, at rocks, at birds on the wing, at the big black pig-kettle under the cypress tree; he didn't shoot, for he had no cartridges and wouldn't have until he was twelve. If his father had seen him aim the rifle in the direction of the house he would have put the cartridges off another year. Jody remembered this and did not point the rifle down the hill again. Two years was enough to wait for cartridges. Nearly all of his father's presents were given with reservations which hampered their value somewhat. It was good discipline.

The supper waited until dark for his father to return. When at last he came in with Billy Buck, Jody could smell the delicious brandy on their breaths. Inwardly he rejoiced, for his father sometimes talked to him when he smelled of brandy, sometimes even told things he had done in the wild days when he was a boy.

After supper, Jody sat by the fireplace and his shy polite eyes sought the room corners, and he waited for his father to tell what it was he contained, for Jody knew he had news of some sort. But he was disappointed. His father pointed a stern finger at him.

"You'd better go to bed, Jody. I'm going to need you in the morning."

That wasn't so bad. Jody liked to do the things he had to do as long as they weren't routine things. He looked at the floor and his mouth worked out a question before he spoke it. "What are we going to do in the morning, kill a pig?" he asked softly.

"Never you mind. You better get to bed."

When the door closed behind him, Jody heard his father and Billy Buck chuckling and he knew it was a joke of some kind. And later, when he lay in bed, trying to make words out of the murmurs in the other room, he heard his father protest, "But, Ruth, I didn't give much for him."

Jody heard the hoot owls hunting mice down by the barn, and he heard a fruit tree limb tap-tapping against the house. A cow was lowing when he went to sleep.

When the triangle sounded in the morning, Jody dressed more quickly even than usual. In the kitchen, while he washed his face and combed back his hair, his mother addressed him irritably. "Don't you go out until you get a good breakfast in you."

He went into the dining room and sat at the long white table. He took a steaming hotcake from the platter, arranged two fried eggs on it, covered them with another hotcake and squashed the whole thing with his fork.

His father and Billy Buck came in. Jody knew from the sound on the floor that both of them were wearing flat-heeled shoes, but he peered under the table to make sure. His father turned off the oil lamp, for the day had arrived, and he looked stern and disciplinary; but Billy Buck didn't look at Jody at all. He avoided the shy questioning eyes of the boy and soaked a whole piece of toast in his coffee.

Carl Tiflin said crossly, "You come with us after breakfast!"

Jody had trouble with his food then, for he felt a kind of doom in the air. After Billy had tilted his saucer and drained the coffee which had slopped into it, and had wiped his hands on his jeans, the two men stood up from the table and went out into the morning light together, and Jody respectfully followed a little behind them. He tried to keep his mind from running ahead, tried to keep it absolutely motionless.

His mother called, "Carl! Don't you let it keep him from school."

They marched past the cypress, where a singletree hung

from a limb to butcher the pigs on, and past the black iron kettle, so it was not a pig-killing. The sun shone over the hill and threw long, dark shadows of the trees and buildings. They crossed a stubble field to short-cut to the barn. Jody's father unhooked the door and they went in. They had been walking toward the sun on the way down. The barn was black as night in contrast, and warm from the hay and from the beasts. Jody's father moved over toward the one box stall. "Come here!" he ordered. Jody could begin to see things now. He looked into the box stall and then stepped back quickly.

A red pony colt was looking at him out of the stall. Its tense ears were forward and a light of disobedience was in its eyes. Its coat was rough and thick as an Airedale's fur and its mane was long and tangled. Jody's throat collapsed in on itself and cut his breath short.

"He needs a good currying," his father said, "and if I ever hear of you not feeding him or leaving his stall dirty, I'll sell him off in a minute."

Jody couldn't bear to look at the pony's eyes any more. He gazed down at his hands for a moment, and he asked very shyly, "Mine?" No one answered him. He put his hand out toward the pony. Its gray nose came close, sniffing loudly, and then the lips drew back and the strong teeth closed on Jody's fingers. The pony shook its head up and down and seemed to laugh with amusement. Jody regarded his bruised fingers. "Well," he said with pride—"Well, I guess he can bite all right." The two men laughed, somewhat in relief. Carl Tiflin went out of the barn and walked up a side hill to be by himself, for he was embarrassed, but Billy Buck stayed. It was easier to talk to Billy Buck. Jody asked again—"Mine?"

Billy became professional in tone. "Sure! That is, if you look out for him and break him right. I'll show you how. He's just a colt. You can't ride him for some time."

Jody put out his bruised hand again, and this time the red

pony let his nose be rubbed. "I ought to have a carrot," Jody said. "Where'd we get him, Billy?"

"Bought him at a sheriff's auction," Billy explained. "A show went broke in Salinas and had debts. The sheriff was selling off their stuff."

The pony stretched out his nose and shook the forelock from his wild eyes. Jody stroked the nose a little. He said softly, "There isn't a—saddle?"

Billy Buck laughed. "I'd forgot. Come along."

In the harness room he lifted down a little saddle of red morocco leather. "It's just a show saddle," Billy Buck said disparagingly. "It isn't practical for the brush, but it was cheap at the sale."

Jody couldn't trust himself to look at the saddle either, and he couldn't speak at all. He brushed the shining red leather with his fingertips, and after a long time he said, "It'll look pretty on him though." He thought of the grandest and prettiest things he knew. "If he hasn't a name already, I think I'll call him Gabilan Mountains," he said.

Billy Buck knew how he felt. "It's a pretty long name. Why don't you just call him Gabilan? That means hawk. That would be a fine name for him." Billy felt glad. "If you will collect tail hair, I might be able to make a hair rope for you sometime. You could use it for a hackamore."

Jody wanted to go back to the box stall. "Could I lead him to school, do you think—to show the kids?"

But Billy shook his head. "He's not even halter broke yet. We had a time getting him here. Had to almost drag him. You better be starting for school though."

"I'll bring the kids to see him here this afternoon," Jody said.

Six boys came over the hill half an hour early that afternoon, running hard, their heads down, their forearms working, their breath whistling. They swept by the house and cut across the stubble field to the barn. And then they stood self-consciously before the pony, and then they looked at Jody with eyes in which there was a new admiration and a new respect. Before today Jody had been a boy dressed in overalls and a blue shirt, quieter than most, even suspected of being a little cowardly. And now he was different. Out of a thousand centuries they drew the ancient admiration of the footman for the horseman. They knew instinctively that a man on a horse is spiritually as well as physically bigger than a man on foot. They knew that Jody had been miraculously lifted out of equality with them and had been placed over them. Gabilan put his head out of the stall and sniffed them.

"Why'n't you ride him?" the boys cried. "Why'n't you braid his tail with ribbons like in the fair?" "When you going to ride him?"

Jody's courage was up. He too felt the superiority of the horseman. "He's not old enough. Nobody can ride him for a long time. I'm going to train him on the long halter. Billy Buck is going to show me how."

"Well, can't we even lead him around a little?"

"He isn't even halter broke," Jody said. He wanted to be completely alone when he took the pony out the first time. "Come and see the saddle."

They were speechless at the red morocco saddle, completely shocked out of comment. "It isn't much use in the brush," Jody explained. "It'll look pretty on him though. Maybe I'll ride bareback when I go into the brush."

"How you going to rope a cow without a saddle horn?"

"Maybe I'll get another saddle for everyday. My father might want me to help him with the stock." He let them feel the red saddle and showed them the brass chain throatlatch on the bridle and the big brass buttons at each temple where the headstall and brow band crossed. The whole thing was too wonderful.

They had to go away after a little while, and each boy, in his mind, searched among his possessions for a bribe worthy of offering in return for a ride on the red pony when the time should come.

Jody was glad when they had gone. He took brush and currycomb from the wall, took down the barrier of the box stall and stepped cautiously in. The pony's eyes glittered, and he edged around into kicking position. But Jody touched him on the shoulder and rubbed his high arched neck as he had always seen Billy Buck do, and he crooned "so-o-o boy" in a deep voice. The pony gradually relaxed his tenseness. Jody curried and brushed until a pile of dead hair lay in the stall and until the pony's coat had taken on a deep red shine. Each time he finished he thought it might have been done better. He braided the mane into a dozen little pigtails, and he braided the forelock, and then he undid them and brushed the hair out straight again.

Jody did not hear his mother enter the barn. She was angry when she came, but when she looked in at the pony and at Jody working over him, she felt a curious pride rise up in her. "Have you forgot the woodbox?" she asked gently. "It's not far off from dark and there's not a stick of wood in the house, and the chickens aren't fed."

Jody quickly put up his tools. "I forgot, ma'am."

"Well, after this do your chores first. Then you won't forget. I expect you'll forget lots of things now if I don't keep an eye on you."

"Can I have carrots from the garden for him, ma'am?"

She had to think about that. "Oh—I guess so, if you only take the big tough ones."

"Carrots keep the coat good," he said, and again she felt the curious rush of pride.

Jody never waited for the triangle to get him out of bed after the coming of the pony. It became his habit to creep out of bed even before his mother was awake, to slip into his clothes and to go quietly down to the barn to see Gabilan. In the gray quiet mornings when the land and the brush and the houses and the trees were silver-gray and black like a photograph negative, he stole toward the barn, past the sleeping stones and the sleeping cypress tree. The turkeys, roosting in the tree out of coyotes' reach, clicked drowsily. The fields glowed with a gray frostlike light, and in the dew the tracks of rabbits and of field mice stood out sharply. The good dogs came stiffly out of their little houses, hackles up and deep growls in their throats. Then they caught Jody's scent, and their stiff tails rose up and waved a greeting—Doubletree Mutt with the big thick tail, and Smasher, the incipient shepherd—then went lazily back to their warm beds.

It was a strange time and a mysterious journey to Jody—an extension of a dream. When he first had the pony he liked to torture himself during the trip by thinking Gabilan would not be in his stall, and worse, would never have been there. And he had other delicious little self-induced pains. He thought how the rats had gnawed ragged holes in the red saddle, and how the mice had nibbled Gabilan's tail until it was stringy and thin. He usually ran the last little way to the barn. He unlatched the rusty hasp of the barn door and stepped in, and no matter how quietly he opened the door, Gabilan was always looking at him over the barrier of the box stall and Gabilan whinnied softly and stamped his front foot, and his eyes had big sparks of red fire in them like oakwood embers.

Sometimes, if the work horses were to be used that day, Jody found Billy Buck in the barn harnessing and currying. Billy stood with him and looked long at Gabilan and he told Jody a great many things about horses. He explained that they were terribly afraid for their feet, so that one must make a practice of lifting the legs and patting the hooves and ankles to remove their terror. He told Jody how horses love conversation. He must talk to the pony all the time and tell him the reasons for everything. Billy wasn't sure a horse could understand everything that was said to him, but it was impossible to say how much was understood. A horse never kicked up a fuss if someone he liked explained things to him. Billy could give examples, too. He had known, for instance, a horse nearly dead beat with fatigue to perk up when told it was only a little farther to his destination. And he had known a horse paralyzed with fright to come out of it when his rider told him what it was that was frightening him. While he talked in the mornings, Billy Buck cut twenty or thirty straws into neat three-inch lengths and stuck them into his hatband. Then, during the whole day, if he wanted to pick his teeth or merely to chew on something, he had only to reach up for one of them.

Jody listened carefully, for he knew and the whole country knew that Billy Buck was a fine hand with horses. Billy's own horse was a stringy cayuse with a hammer head, but he nearly always won the first prizes at the stock trials. Billy could rope a steer, take a double half-hitch about the horn with his riata, and dismount; and his horse would play the steer as an angler plays a fish, keeping a tight rope until the steer was down or beaten.

Every morning, after Jody had curried and brushed the pony, he let down the barrier of the stall, and Gabilan thrust past him and raced down the barn and into the corral. Around and around he galloped, and sometimes he jumped forward and landed on stiff legs. He stood quivering, stiff ears forward, eyes rolling so that the whites showed, pretending to be frightened. At last he walked snorting to the water trough and buried his nose in the water up to the nostrils. Jody was proud then, for he knew that was the way to judge a horse. Poor horses only touched their lips to the water, but a fine spirited beast put his whole nose and mouth under, and only left room to breathe.

Then Jody stood and watched the pony, and he saw things

he had never noticed about any other horse; the sleek, sliding flank muscles and the cords of the buttocks, which flexed like a closing fist, and the shine the sun put on the red coat. Having seen horses all his life, Jody had never looked at them very closely before. But now he noticed the moving ears which gave expression and even inflection of expression to the face. The pony talked with his ears. You could tell exactly how he felt about everything by the way his ears pointed. Sometimes they were stiff and upright and sometimes lax and sagging. They went back when he was angry or fearful, and forward when he was anxious and curious and pleased; and their exact position indicated which emotion he had.

Billy Buck kept his word. In the early fall the training began. First there was the halter-breaking, and that was the hardest because it was the first thing. Jody held a carrot and coaxed and promised and pulled on the rope. The pony set his feet like a burro when he felt the strain. But before long he learned. Jody walked all over the ranch leading him. Gradually he took to dropping the rope until the pony followed him unled wherever he went.

And then came the training on the long halter. That was slower work. Jody stood in the middle of a circle, holding the long halter. He clucked with his tongue and the pony started to walk in a big circle, held in by the long rope. He clucked again to make the pony trot, and again to make him gallop. Around and around Gabilan went, thundering and enjoying it immensely. Then Jody called "whoa," and the pony stopped. It was not long until Gabilan was perfect at it. But in many ways he was a bad pony. He bit Jody in the pants and stomped on Jody's feet. Now and then his ears went back and he aimed a tremendous kick at the boy. Every time he did one of these bad things, Gabilan settled back and seemed to laugh to himself.

Billy Buck worked at the hair rope in the evenings before

the fireplace. Jody collected tail hair in a bag, and he sat and watched Billy slowly constructing the rope, twisting a few hairs to make a string and rolling two strings together for a cord, and then braiding a number of cords to make the rope. Billy rolled the finished rope on the floor under his foot to make it round and hard.

The long halter work rapidly approached perfection. Jody's father, watching the pony stop and start and trot and gallop, was a little bothered by it.

"He's getting to be almost a trick pony," he complained. "I don't like trick horses. It takes all the—dignity out of a horse to make him do tricks. Why, a trick horse is kind of like an actor—no dignity, no character of his own." And his father said, "I guess you better be getting him used to the saddle pretty soon."

Jody rushed for the harness room. For some time he had been riding the saddle on a sawhorse. He changed the stirrup length over and over, and could never get it just right. Sometimes, mounted on the sawhorse in the harness room, with collars and hames and tugs hung all about him, Jody rode out beyond the room. He carried his rifle across the pommel. He saw the fields go flying by, and he heard the beat of the galloping hoofs.

It was a ticklish job, saddling the pony the first time. Gabilan hunched and reared and threw the saddle off before the cinch could be tightened. It had to be replaced again and again until at last the pony let it stay. And the cinching was difficult, too. Day by day Jody tightened the girth a little more until at last the pony didn't mind the saddle at all.

Then there was the bridle. Billy explained how to use a stick of licorice for a bit until Gabilan was used to having something in his mouth. Billy explained, "Of course we could force-break him to everything, but he wouldn't be as good a horse if we did. He'd always be a little bit afraid, and he wouldn't mind because he wanted to."

The first time the pony wore the bridle he whipped his head about and worked his tongue against the bit until the blood oozed from the corners of his mouth. He tried to rub the headstall off on the manger. His ears pivoted about and his eyes turned red with fear and with general rambunctiousness. Jody rejoiced, for he knew that only a mean-souled horse does not resent training.

And Jody trembled when he thought of the time when he would first sit in the saddle. The pony would probably throw him off. There was no disgrace in that. The disgrace would come if he did not get right up and mount again. Sometimes he dreamed that he lay in the dirt and cried and couldn't make himself mount again. The shame of the dream lasted until the middle of the day.

Gabilan was growing fast. Already he had lost the long-leggedness of the colt; his mane was getting longer and blacker. Under the constant currying and brushing his coat lay as smooth and gleaming as orange-red lacquer. Jody oiled the hoofs and kept them carefully trimmed so they would not crack.

The hair rope was nearly finished. Jody's father gave him an old pair of spurs and bent in the side bars and cut down the strap and took up the chainlets until they fitted. And then one day Carl Tiflin said, "The pony's growing faster than I thought. I guess you can ride him by Thanksgiving. Think you can stick on?"

"I don't know," Jody said shyly. Thanksgiving was only three weeks off. He hoped it wouldn't rain, for rain would spot the red saddle.

Gabilan knew and liked Jody by now. He nickered when Jody came across the stubble field, and in the pasture he came running when his master whistled for him. There was always a carrot for him, every time.

Billy Buck gave him riding instructions over and over. "Now when you get up there, just grab tight with your knees and keep your hands away from the saddle, and if you get throwed, don't let that stop you. No matter how good a man is, there's always some horse can pitch him. You just climb up again before he gets to feeling smart about it. Pretty soon he won't throw you no more, and pretty soon he can't throw you no more. That's the way to do it."

"I hope it don't rain before," Jody said.

"Why not? Don't want to get throwed in the mud?"

That was partly it, and also he was afraid that in the flurry of bucking Gabilan might slip and fall on him and break his leg or his hip. He had seen that happen to men before, had seen how they writhed on the ground like squashed bugs, and he was afraid of it.

He practiced on the sawhorse how he would hold the reins in his left hand and a hat in his right hand. If he kept his hands thus busy, he couldn't grab the horn if he felt himself going off. He didn't like to think of what would happen if he did grab the horn. Perhaps his father and Billy Buck would never speak to him again, they would be so ashamed. The news would get about and his mother would be ashamed too. And in the schoolyard—it was too awful to contemplate.

He began putting his weight in a stirrup when Gabilan was saddled, but he didn't throw his leg over the pony's back. That was forbidden until Thanksgiving.

Every afternoon he put the red saddle on the pony and cinched it tight. The pony was learning already to fill his stomach out unnaturally large while the cinching was going on, and then to let it down when the straps were fixed. Sometimes Jody led him up to the brush line and let him drink from the round green tub, and sometimes he led him up through the stubble field to the hilltop from which it was possible to see the white town of Salinas and the geometric fields of the great valley, and the oak trees clipped by the sheep. Now and then they broke through the brush and came to little cleared circles so hedged in that the world was gone and only the sky and the circle of brush were left from the old life. Gabilan liked these trips and showed it by keeping his head very high and by quivering his nostrils with interest. When the two came back from an expedition they smelled of the sweet sage they had forced through.

Time dragged on toward Thanksgiving, but winter came fast. The clouds swept down and hung all day over the land and brushed the hilltops, and the winds blew shrilly at night. All day the dry oak leaves drifted down from the trees until they covered the ground, and yet the trees were unchanged.

Jody had wished it might not rain before Thanksgiving, but it did. The brown earth turned dark and the trees glistened. The cut ends of the stubble turned black with mildew; the haystacks grayed from exposure to the damp, and on the roofs the moss, which had been all summer as gray as lizards, turned a brilliant yellow-green. During the week of rain, Jody kept the pony in the box stall out of the dampness, except for a little time after school when he took him out for exercise and to drink at the water trough in the upper corral. Not once did Gabilan get wet.

The wet weather continued until little new grass appeared. Jody walked to school dressed in a slicker and short rubber boots. At length one morning the sun came out brightly. Jody, at his work in the box stall, said to Billy Buck, "Maybe I'll leave Gabilan in the corral when I go to school today."

"Be good for him to be out in the sun," Billy assured him. "No animal likes to be cooped up too long. Your father and me are going back on the hill to clean the leaves out of the spring." Billy nodded and picked his teeth with one of his little straws.

"If the rain comes, though—" Jody suggested.

"Not likely to rain today. She's rained herself out." Billy pulled up his sleeves and snapped his arm bands. "If it comes on to rain—why a little rain don't hurt a horse."

"Well, if it does come on to rain, you put him in, will you, Billy? I'm scared he might get cold so I couldn't ride him when the time comes."

"Oh sure! I'll watch out for him if we get back in time. But it won't rain today."

And so Jody, when he went to school left Gabilan standing out in the corral.

Billy Buck wasn't wrong about many things. He couldn't be. But he was wrong about the weather that day, for a little after noon the clouds pushed over the hills and the rain began to pour down. Jody heard it start on the schoolhouse roof. He considered holding up one finger for permission to go to the outhouse, and once outside, running for home to put the pony in. Punishment would be prompt both at school and at home. He gave it up and took ease from Billy's assurance that rain couldn't hurt a horse. When school was finally out, he hurried home through the dark rain. The banks at the sides of the road spouted little jets of muddy water. The rain slanted and swirled under a cold and gusty wind. Jody dog-trotted home, slopping through the gravelly mud of the road.

From the top of the ridge he could see Gabilan standing miserably in the corral. The red coat was almost black, and streaked with water. He stood head down with his rump to the rain and wind. Jody arrived running and threw open the barn door and led the wet pony in by his forelock. Then he found a gunny sack and rubbed the soaked hair and rubbed the legs and ankles. Gabilan stood patiently, but he trembled in gusts like the wind.

When he had dried the pony as well as he could, Jody went up to the house and brought hot water down to the barn and soaked the grain in it. Gabilan was not very hungry. He nibbled at the hot mash but he was not very much interested in it, and he still shivered now and then. A little steam rose from his damp back.

It was almost dark when Billy Buck and Carl Tiflin came home. "When the rain started we put up at Ben Herche's place, and the rain never let up all afternoon," Carl Tiflin explained. Jody looked reproachfully at Billy Buck and Billy felt guilty.

"You said it wouldn't rain," Jody accused him.

Billy looked away. "It's hard to tell, this time of year," he said, but his excuse was lame. He had no right to be fallible, and he knew it.

"The pony got wet, got soaked through."

"Did you dry him off?"

"I rubbed him with a sack and I gave him hot grain."

Billy nodded in agreement.

"Do you think he'll take cold, Billy?"

"A little rain never hurt anything," Billy assured him.

Jody's father joined the conversation then and lectured the boy a little. "A horse," he said, "isn't any lap-dog kind of thing." Carl Tiflin hated weakness and sickness, and he held a violent contempt for helplessness.

Jody's mother put a platter of steaks on the table, and boiled potatoes and boiled squash, which clouded the room with their steam. They sat down to eat. Carl Tiflin still grumbled about weakness put into animals and men by too much coddling.

Billy Buck felt bad about his mistake. "Did you blanket him?" he asked.

"No. I couldn't find any blanket. I laid some sacks over his back."

"We'll go down and cover him up after we eat, then." Billy felt better about it then. When Jody's father had gone in to the fire and his mother was washing dishes, Billy found and lighted a lantern. He and Jody walked through the mud to the barn. The barn was dark and warm and sweet. The horses still munched their evening hay. "You hold the lantern!" Billy ordered. And he felt the pony's legs and tested the heat of the flanks. He put his cheek against the pony's gray muzzle and then he rolled up the eyelids to look at the eyeballs and he lifted the lips to see the gums, and he put his fingers inside the ears. "He don't seem so chipper," Billy said. "I'll give him a rubdown."

Then Billy found a sack and rubbed the pony's legs violently and he rubbed the chest and the withers. Gabilan was strangely spiritless. He submitted patiently to the rubbing. At last Billy brought an old cotton comforter from the saddle room and threw it over the pony's back and tied it at neck and chest with string.

"Now he'll be all right in the morning," Billy said.

Jody's mother looked up when he got back to the house. "You're late up from bed," she said. She held his chin in her hard hand and brushed the tangled hair out of his eyes and she said, "Don't worry about the pony. He'll be all right. Billy's as good as any horse doctor in the country."

Jody hadn't known she could see his worry. He pulled gently away from her and knelt down in front of the fireplace until it burned his stomach. He scorched himself through and then went in to bed, but it was a hard thing to go to sleep. He awakened after what seemed a long time. The room was dark but there was a grayness in the window like that which precedes the dawn. He got up and found his overalls and searched for the legs, and then the clock in the other room struck two. He laid his clothes down and got back into bed. It was broad daylight when he awakened again. For the first time he had slept through the ringing of the triangle. He leaped up, flung on his clothes and went out of the door still buttoning his shirt. His mother looked after him for a moment and then went quietly back to her work. Her eyes were brooding and kind. Now and then her mouth smiled a little, but without changing her eyes at all.

Jody ran on toward the barn. Halfway there he heard the sound he dreaded, the hollow rasping cough of a horse. He broke into a sprint then. In the barn he found Billy Buck with the pony. Billy was rubbing its legs with his strong thick hands. He looked up and smiled gaily. "He just took a little cold," Billy said. "We'll have him out of it in a couple of days."

Jody looked at the pony's face. The eyes were half closed and the lids thick and dry. In the eye corners a crust of hard mucus stuck. Gabilan's ears hung loosely sideways and his head was low. Jody put out his hand, but the pony did not move close to it. He coughed again and his whole body constricted with the effort. A little stream of thin fluid ran from his nostrils.

Jody looked back at Billy Buck. "He's awful sick, Billy."

"Just a little cold, like I said," Billy insisted. "You go get some breakfast and then go back to school. I'll take care of him."

"But you might have to do something else. You might leave him."

"No, I won't. I won't leave him at all. Tomorrow's Saturday. Then you can stay with him all day." Billy had failed again, and he felt badly about it. He had to cure the pony now.

Jody walked up to the house and took his place listlessly at the table. The eggs and bacon were cold and greasy, but he didn't notice it. He ate his usual amount. He didn't even ask to stay home from school. His mother pushed his hair back when she took his plate. "Billy'll take care of the pony," she assured him.

He moped through the whole day at school. He couldn't answer any questions nor read any words. He couldn't even tell anyone the pony was sick, for that might make him sicker. And when school was finally out he started home in dread. He walked slowly and let the other boys leave him. He wished he might continue walking and never arrive at the ranch.

Billy was in the barn, as he had promised, and the pony was worse. His eyes were almost closed now, and his breath whistled shrilly past an obstruction in his nose. A film covered that part of the eyes that was visible at all. It was doubtful whether the pony could see any more. Now and then he snorted, to clear his nose, and by the action seemed to plug it tighter. Jody looked dispiritedly at the pony's coat. The hair lay rough and unkempt and seemed to have lost all its old luster. Billy stood quietly beside the stall. Jody hated to ask, but he had to know."

"Billy, is he—is he going to get well?"

Billy put his fingers between the bars under the pony's jaw and felt about. "Feel here," he said and he guided Jody's fingers to a large lump under the jaw. "When that gets bigger, I'll open it up and then he'll get better."

Jody looked quickly away, for he had heard about that lump. "What is it the matter with him?"

Billy didn't want to answer, but he had to. He couldn't be wrong three times. "Strangles," he said shortly, "but don't you worry about that. I'll pull him out of it. I've seen them get well when they were worse than Gabilan is. I'm going to steam him now. You can help."

"Yes," Jody said miserably. He followed Billy into the grain room and watched him make the steaming bag ready. It was a long canvas nose bag with straps to go over a horse's ears. Billy filled it one-third full of bran and then he added a couple of handfuls of dried hops. On top of the dry substance he poured a little carbolic acid and a little turpentine. "I'll be mixing it all up while you run to the house for a kettle of boiling water," Billy said.

When Jody came back with the steaming kettle, Billy buckled the straps over Gabilan's head and fitted the bag tightly around his nose. Then through a little hole in the side of the bag he poured the boiling water on the mixture. The pony started away as a cloud of strong steam rose up, but then the soothing fumes crept through his nose and into his lungs, and the sharp steam began to clear out the nasal passages. He breathed loudly. His legs trembled in an ague, and his eyes closed against the biting cloud. Billy poured in more water and kept the steam rising for fifteen minutes. At last he set down the kettle and took the bag from Gabilan's nose. The pony looked better. He breathed freely, and his eyes were open wider than they had been.

"See how good it makes him feel," Billy said. "Now we'll wrap him up in the blanket again. Maybe he'll be nearly well by morning."

"I'll stay with him tonight," Jody suggested.

"No. Don't you do it. I'll bring my blankets down here and put them in the hay. You can stay tomorrow and steam him if he needs it."

The evening was falling when they went to the house for their supper. Jody didn't even realize that someone else had fed the chickens and filled the woodbox. He walked up past the house to the dark brush line and took a drink of water from the tub. The spring water was so cold that it stung his mouth and drove a shiver through him. The sky above the hills was still light. He saw a hawk flying so high that it caught the sun on its breast and shone like a spark. Two blackbirds were driving him down the sky, glittering as they attacked their enemy. In the west, the clouds were moving in to rain again.

Jody's father didn't speak at all while the family ate supper, but after Billy Buck had taken his blankets and gone to sleep in the barn, Carl Tiflin built a high fire in the fireplace and told stories. He told about the wild man who ran naked through the country and had a tail and ears like a horse, and he told about the rabbit-cats of Moro Cojo that hopped into the trees for birds. He revived the famous Maxwell brothers who found a vein of gold and hid the traces of it so carefully that they could never find it again.

Jody sat with his chin in his hands; his mouth worked nervously, and his father gradually became aware that he wasn't listening very carefully. "Isn't that funny?" he asked.

Jody laughed politely and said, "Yes, sir." His father was angry and hurt, then. He didn't tell any more stories. After a while, Jody took a lantern and went down to the barn. Billy Buck was asleep in the hay, and except that his breath rasped a little in his lungs, the pony seemed to be much better. Jody stayed a little while, running his fingers over the red rough coat, and then he took up the lantern and went back to the house. When he was in bed, his mother came into the room.

"Have you enough covers on? It's getting winter."

"Yes, ma'am."

"Well, get some rest tonight." She hesitated to go out, stood uncertainly. "The pony will be all right," she said.

Jody was tired. He went to sleep quickly and didn't awaken until dawn. The triangle sounded, and Billy Buck came up from the barn before Jody could get out of the house.

"How is he?" Jody demanded.

Billy always wolfed his breakfast. "Pretty good. I'm going to open that lump this morning. Then he'll be better maybe."

After breakfast, Billy got out his best knife, one with a

needle point. He whetted the shining blade a long time on a little carborundum stone. He tried the point and the blade again and again on his calloused thumb-ball, and at last he tried it on his upper lip.

On the way to the barn, Jody noticed how the young grass was up and how the stubble was melting day by day into the new green crop of volunteer. It was a cold sunny morning.

As soon as he saw the pony, Jody knew he was worse. His eyes were closed and sealed shut with dried mucus. His head hung so low that his nose almost touched the straw of his bed. There was a little groan in each breath, a deep-seated, patient groan.

Billy lifted the weak head and made a quick slash with the knife. Jody saw the yellow pus run out. He held up the head while Billy swabbed out the wound with weak carbolic acid salve.

"Now he'll feel better," Billy assured him. "That yellow poison is what makes him sick."

Jody looked unbelieving at Billy Buck. "He's awful sick."

Billy thought a long time what to say. He nearly tossed off a careless assurance, but he saved himself in time. "Yes, he's pretty sick," he said at last. "I've seen worse ones get well. If he doesn't get pneumonia, we'll pull him through. You stay with him. If he gets worse, you can come and get me."

For a long time after Billy went away, Jody stood beside the pony, stroking him behind the ears. The pony didn't flip his head the way he had done when he was well. The groaning in his breathing was becoming more hollow.

Doubletree Mutt looked into the barn, his big tail waving provocatively, and Jody was so incensed at his health that he found a hard black clod on the floor and deliberately threw it. Doubletree Mutt went yelping away to nurse a bruised paw.

In the middle of the morning, Billy Buck came back and made another steam bag. Jody watched to see whether the pony improved this time as he had before. His breathing eased a little, but he did not raise his head.

The Saturday dragged on. Late in the afternoon Jody went to the house and brought his bedding down and made up a place to sleep in the hay. He didn't ask permission. He knew from the way his mother looked at him that she would let him do almost anything. That night he left a lantern burning on a wire over the box stall. Billy had told him to rub the pony's legs every little while.

At nine o'clock the wind sprang up and howled around the barn. And in spite of his worry, Jody grew sleepy. He got into his blankets and went to sleep, but the breathy groans of the pony sounded in his dreams. And in his sleep he heard a crashing noise which went on and on until it awakened him. The wind was rushing through the barn. He sprang up and looked down the lane of stalls. The barn door had blown open, and the pony was gone.

He caught the lantern and ran outside into the gale, and he saw Gabilan weakly shambling away into the darkness, head down, legs working slowly and mechanically. When Jody ran up and caught him by the forelock, he allowed himself to be led back and put into his stall. His groans were louder, and a fierce whistling came from his nose. Jody didn't sleep any more then. The hissing of the pony's breath grew louder and sharper.

He was glad when Billy Buck came in at dawn. Billy looked for a time at the pony as though he had never seen him before. He felt the ears and flanks. "Jody," he said. "I've got to do something you won't want to see. You run up to the house for a while."

Jody grabbed him fiercely by the forearm. "You're not going to shoot him?"

Billy patted his hand. "No. I'm going to open a little hole in his windpipe so he can breathe. His nose is filled up. When he gets well, we'll put a little brass button in the hole for him to breathe through."

Jody couldn't have gone away if he had wanted to. It was awful to see the red hide cut, but infinitely more terrible to know it was being cut and not to see it. "I'll stay right here," he said bitterly. "You sure you got to?"

"Yes. I'm sure. If you stay, you can hold his head. If it doesn't make you sick, that is.

The fine knife came out again and was whetted again just as carefully as it had been the first time. Jody held the pony's head up and the throat taut, while Billy felt up and down for the right place. Jody sobbed once as the bright knife point disappeared into the throat. The pony plunged weakly away and then stood still, trembling violently. The blood ran thickly out and up the knife and across Billy's hand and into his shirtsleeve. The sure square hand sawed out a round hole in the flesh, and the breath came bursting out of the hole, throwing a fine spray of blood. With the rush of oxygen, the pony took a sudden strength. He lashed out with his hind feet and tried to rear, but Jody held his head down while Billy mopped the new wound with carbolic salve. It was a good job. The blood stopped flowing and the air puffed out the hole and sucked it in regularly with a little bubbling noise.

The rain brought in by the night wind began to fall on the barn roof. Then the triangle rang for breakfast. "You go up and eat while I wait," Billy said. "We've got to keep this hole from plugging up."

Jody walked slowly out of the barn. He was too dispirited to tell Billy how the barn door had blown open and let the pony out. He emerged into the wet gray morning and sloshed up to the house, taking a perverse pleasure in splashing through all the puddles. His mother fed him and put dry clothes on. She didn't question him. She seemed to know he couldn't answer questions. But when he was ready to go back to the barn she brought him a pan of steaming meal. "Give him this," she said.

But Jody did not take the pan. He said, "He won't eat anything," and ran out of the house. At the barn, Billy showed him how to fix a ball of cotton on a stick, with which to swab out the breathing hole when it became clogged with mucus.

Jody's father walked into the barn and stood with them in front of the stall. At length he turned to the boy, "Hadn't you better come with me? I'm going to drive over the hill." Jody shook his head. "You better come on, out of this," his father insisted.

Billy turned on him angrily. "Let him alone. It's his pony, isn't it?"

Carl Tiflin walked away without saying another word. His feelings were badly hurt.

All morning Jody kept the wound open and the air passing in and out freely. At noon the pony lay wearily down on his side and stretched his nose out.

Billy came back. "If you're going to stay with him tonight, you better take a little nap," he said. Jody went absently out of the barn. The sky had cleared to a hard thin blue. Everywhere the birds were busy with worms that had come to the damp surface of the ground.

Jody walked to the brush line and sat on the edge of the mossy tub. He looked down at the house and at the old bunkhouse and at the dark cypress tree. The place was familiar, but curiously changed. It wasn't itself any more, but a frame for things that were happening. A cold wind blew out of the east now, signifying that the rain was over for a little while. At his feet Jody could see the little arms of new weeds spreading out over the ground. In the mud about the spring were thousands of quail tracks.

Doubletree Mutt came sideways and embarrassed up through

the vegetable patch, and Jody, remembering how he had thrown the clod, put his arm about the dog's neck and kissed him on his wide black nose. Doubletree Mutt sat still, as though he knew some solemn thing was happening. His big tail slapped the ground gravely. Jody pulled a swollen tick out of Mutt's neck and popped it dead between his thumbnails. It was a nasty thing. He washed his hands in the cold spring water.

Except for the steady swish of the wind, the farm was very quiet. Jody knew his mother wouldn't mind if he didn't go in to eat his lunch. After a little while he went slowly back to the barn. Mutt crept into his own little house and whined softly to himself for a long time.

Billy Buck stood up from the box and surrendered the cotton swab. The pony still lay on his side and the wound in his throat bellowsed in and out. When Jody saw how dry and dead the hair looked, he knew at last that there was no hope for the pony. He had seen the dead hair before on dogs and on cows, and it was a sure sign. He sat heavily on the box and let down the barrier of the box stall. For a long time he kept his eyes on the moving wound, and at last he dozed, and the afternoon passed quickly. Just before dark his mother brought in a deep dish of stew and left it for him and went away. Jody ate a little of it, and when it was dark he set the lantern on the floor by the pony's head so he could watch the wound and keep it open. And he dozed again until the night chill awakened him. The wind was blowing fiercely, bringing the north cold with it. Jody brought a blanket from his bed in the hay and wrapped himself in it. Gabilan's breathing was quiet at last; the hole in his throat moved gently. The owls flew through the hayloft, shrieking and looking for mice. Jody put his hands down on his head and slept. In his sleep he was aware that the wind had increased. He heard it slamming about the barn.

It was daylight when he awakened. The barn door had

swung open. The pony was gone. He sprang up and ran out into the morning light.

The pony's tracks were plain enough, dragging through the frostlike dew on the young grass, tired tracks with little lines between them where the hoofs had dragged. They headed for the brush line halfway up the ridge. Jody broke into a run and followed them. The sun shone on the sharp white quartz that stuck through the ground here and there. As he followed the plain trail, a shadow cut across in front of him. He looked up and saw a high circle of black buzzards, and the slowly revolving circle dropped lower and lower. The solemn birds soon disappeared over the ridge. Jody ran faster then, forced on by panic and rage. The trail entered the brush at last and followed a winding route among the tall sage bushes.

At the top of the ridge Jody was winded. He paused, puffing noisily. The blood pounded in his ears. Then he saw what he was looking for. Below, in one of the little clearings in the brush, lay the red pony. In the distance, Jody could see the legs moving slowly and convulsively. And in a circle around him stood the buzzards, waiting for the moment of death they know so well.

Jody leaped forward and plunged down the hill. The wet ground muffled his steps and the brush hid him. When he arrived, it was all over. The first buzzard sat on the pony's head and its beak had just risen dripping with dark eye fluid. Jody plunged into the circle like a cat. The black brotherhood arose in a cloud, but the big one on the pony's head was too late. As it hopped along to take off, Jody caught its wing tip and pulled it down. It was nearly as big as he was. The free wing crashed into his face with the force of a club, but he hung on. The claws fastened on his leg and the wing elbows battered his head on either side. Jody groped blindly with his free hand. His fingers found the neck of the struggling bird. The red eyes looked into his face, calm and fearless and fierce; the naked head turned from side to side. Then the beak opened and vomited a stream of putrefied fluid. Jody brought up his knee and fell on the great bird. He held the neck to the ground with one hand while his other found a piece of sharp white quartz. The first blow broke the beak sideways and black blood spurted from the twisted, leathery mouth corners. He struck again and missed. The red fearless eyes still looked at him, impersonal and unafraid and detached. He struck again and again, until the buzzard lay dead, until its head was a red pulp. He was still beating the dead bird when Billy Buck pulled him off and held him tightly to calm his shaking.

Carl Tiflin wiped the blood from the boy's face with a red bandana. Jody was limp and quiet now. His father moved the buzzard with his toe. "Jody," he explained, "the buzzard didn't kill the pony. Don't you know that?"

"I know it," Jody said wearily.

It was Billy Buck who was angry. He had lifted Jody in his arms and had turned to carry him home. But he turned back on Carl Tiflin. " 'Course he knows it!" Billy said furiously. "Can't you see how he'd feel about it?"

Like many of JOHN STEINBECK'S novels and stories, *The Red Pony* ("The Gift") is about people and a locale that the author knew intimately from his own experience. As a child of German-Irish parentage growing up in Salinas, California, in the early twentieth century, he may well have been a sensitive, impressionable boy like Jody, and one of the many jobs he held after leaving Stanford University was that of ranch hand. He was also fruit picker, hod carrier, bricklayer, newspaperman. For two winters he lived alone in the High Sierras, and he shipped on a freighter to New York. He was writing all the time, and finally in 1929 he published his first book, *Cup of Gold,* about Henry Morgan the pirate.

But Steinbeck gained wide recognition only when he turned to his own experiences and the surroundings he knew well. He set them down in such books as *Tortilla Flat, Of Mice and Men, The Red Pony,* and *The Grapes of Wrath.* Written in 1939, this last is considered the most important novel of the Depression, and it brought Steinbeck both success and literary fame. He was awarded the Pulitzer Prize for it in 1940.

During World War II he was a correspondent for the *New York Herald Tribune* in Africa and on the Italian front. His more recent writing, such as *Travels with Charley,* combines travel, journalism and commentary on questions of the day. In 1962 Steinbeck received the world's highest literary honor—The Nobel Prize for Literature.

Picking a perilous path

The Seeing Eye

BY WILL JAMES

IT'S worse than tough for anybody to be blind, but I don't think it's as tough for an indoor born and raised person, as it is for one whose life is with the all out-of-doors the most of his life from childhood on. The outdoor man misses his freedom to roam over the hills and the sight of 'em ever changing. A canary would die outside his cage, but a free-born eagle would dwindle away inside of one.

Dane Gruger was very much of an out-of-door man. He was born on a little ranch along a creek bottom, in the heart of the cow country, growed up with it to be a good cowboy; then, like with his dad, went on in the cow business. A railroad went through the lower part of the ranch, but stations and little towns was over twenty miles away either way.

He had a nice little spread when I went to work for him, was married and had two boys who done some of the riding. I'd been riding for Dane for quite a few days before I knew he was blind; not totally blind but, as his boys told me, he couldn't see any further than his outstretched hand, and that was blurred. He couldn't read, not even big print, with any kind of glasses, so he never wore any.

That's what fooled me, and he could look you "right square in the eye" while talking to you. What was more he'd go straight down to the corral, catch his horse, saddle him and ride away like any man with full sight. The thing I first noticed and wondered at was that he never rode with us, and after the boys told me, I could understand. It was that he'd be of no use out on the range and away from the ranch.

Dane had been blind a few years when I come there and he'd of course got to know every foot of the ten miles which the ranch covered on the creek bottom before that happened. The ranch itself was one to two miles wide in some places and taking in some brakes. The whole of that was fenced and cross-fenced into pastures and hay lands, and Dane knew to within an inch when he came to every fence, gate or creek crossing. He knew how many head of cattle or horses might be in each pasture, how all was faring, when some broke out or some broke in, and where. He could find bogged cattle, cow with young calf needing help, and know everything that went well or wrong with what stock would be held on the ranch.

He of course seldom could do much toward helping whatever stock needed it or fixing the holes he found in the fences, but when he'd get back to the ranch house he could easy tell the boys when there was anything wrong and the exact spot where, in which field or pasture, how far from which side of the creek or what fence, and what all the trouble might be. It would then be up to the boys to set things to rights, and after Dane's description of the spot it was easy found.

During the time I was with that little outfit I got to know Dane pretty well, well enough to see that I don't think he could of lived if he hadn't been able to do what he was doing. He was so full of life and gumption and so appreciating of all around him that he could feel, hear and breathe in. I'd sometimes see him hold his horse to a standstill while he only listened to birds or the faraway bellering of cattle, even to the yapping of prairie dogs, which most cowboys would rather not hear the sound of.

To take him away from all of that, the open air, the feel of his saddle and horse under him, and set him on a chair to do nothing but sit and babble and think, would of brought a quick end to him.

With the riding he done he felt satisfied he was doing something worth doing instead of just plain riding. He wouldn't of cared for that, and fact was, he well took the place of an average rider.

But he had mighty good help in the work he was doing, and that was the two horses he used, for they was both as well trained to his wants and care as the dogs that's used nowadays to lead the blind and which are called "The Seeing Eye."

Dane had the advantage over the man with the dog, for he didn't have to walk and use a cane at every step. He rode, and he had more confidence in his horses' every step than he had in his own, even if he could of seen well. As horses do, they naturally sensed every foot of the earth under 'em without ever looking down at it, during sunlight, darkness or under drifted snow.

Riding into clumps of willows or thickets which the creek bottoms had much of, either of the two horses was careful to pick out a wide enough trail through so their rider wouldn't get scratched or brushed off. If they come to a place where the brush was too thick and Dane was wanting to go through that certain thicket, the ponies, regardless of his wants, would turn back for a ways and look for a better opening. Dane never argued with 'em at such times. He would just sort of head 'em where he wanted to go and they'd do the rest to pick out the best way there.

Them horses was still young when I got to that outfit, seven and eight years of age, and would be fit for at least twenty years more with the little riding and good care they was getting. Dane's boys had broke 'em especially for their dad's use that way and they'd done a fine job of it.

One of the horses, a gray of about a thousand pounds, was called Little Eagle. That little horse never missed a thing in sight or sound. With his training, the rustling of the brush close by would make him investigate and learn the cause before leaving that spot. Dane would know by his actions whether it was a newborn calf that had been hid or some cow in distress. It was the same at the boggy places along the creek or alkali swamps. If Little Eagle rode right on around and without stopping, Dane knew that all was well. If he stopped at any certain spot, bowed his neck and snorted low, then Dane knew that some horse or cow was in trouble. Keeping his hand on Little Eagle's neck he'd have him go on, and by the bend of that horse's neck as he went, like pointing, Dane could tell the exact location of where that animal was that was in trouble, or whatever it was that was wrong.

Sometimes, Little Eagle would line out on a trot of his own accord, and as though there was something needed looking into right away. At times he'd even break into a lope, and then Dane wouldn't know what to expect, whether it was stock breaking through a fence, milling around an animal that was down, oı what. But most always it would be when a bunch of stock, horses or cattle, would be stringing out in single file, maybe going to water or some other part of the pasture.

At such times Little Eagle would get just close enough to the stock so Dane could count 'em by the sounds of the hoofs going by, a near-impossible thing to do for a man that can see, but Dane got so he could do it and get a mighty close count on what stock was in each pasture that way. Close enough so he could tell if any had got out or others got in.

With the horses in the pastures, there was bells on the leaders of every bunch and some on one of every little bunch that sort of held together and separate from others. Dane knew by the sound of every bell which bunch it was and about how many there would be to each. The boys kept him posted on that, every time they'd run a bunch in for some reason or other. Not many horses was ever kept under fence, but there was quite a few of the purebred cattle for the upbreeding of the outside herds.

At this work of keeping tab on stock, Little Eagle was a

cowboy by himself. With his natural intellect so developed as to what was wanted of him, he could near tell of what stock was wanted or not and where they belonged. The proof of that was when he turned a bunch of cattle out of a hayfield one time, and other times, and drove 'em to the gate of the field where they'd broke out of, circled around 'em when the gate was reached and went to it for Dane to open. He then drove the cattle through; none got away, not from Little Eagle, and Dane would always prepare to ride at such times, for if any did try to break away Little Eagle would be right on their tail to bring 'em back, and for a blind man, not knowing when his horse is going to break into a sudden run, stop or turn, that's kind of hard riding, on a good cow horse.

About all Dane would have to go by most of the time was the feel of the top muscles on Little Eagle's neck, and he got to know by them about the same as like language to him. With one hand most always on them muscles, he felt what the horse seen. Tenseness, wonder, danger, fear, relaxation and about all that a human feels at the sight of different things. Places, dangerous or smooth, trouble or peace.

Them top muscles told him more, and more plainly than if another rider had been riding constantly alongside of him and telling him right along of what he seen. That was another reason why Dane liked to ride alone. He felt more at ease, no confusion, and wasn't putting anybody out of their way by talking and describing when they maybe wouldn't feel like it.

And them two horses of Dane's, they not only took him wherever he wanted to go but never overlooked any work that needed to be done. They took it onto themselves to look for work which, being they always felt so good, was like play to them. Dane knew it when such times come and he then would let 'em go as they chose.

Neither of the horses would of course go out by themselves

without a rider and do that work. They wouldn't of been interested in doing that without Dane's company. What's more they couldn't have opened the gates that had to be gone through and besides they wasn't wanted to do that. They was to be the company of Dane and with him in whatever he wanted to do.

Dane's other horse was a trim bay about the same size as Little Eagle, and even though just as good, he had different ways about him. He was called Ferret, and a ferret he was for digging up and finding out things, like a cow with new-born calf or mare with colt, and he was even better than Little Eagle for finding holes in fences or where some was down.

All that came under the special training the boys had given him and Little Eagle, and if it wasn't for automobiles these days, such as them would be mighty valuable companions in the city, even more useful in the streets than the dog is; for the horse would soon know where his rider would want to go after being ridden such places a few times.

Unlike most horses it wasn't these two's nature to keep wanting to turn back to the ranch (home) when Dane would ride 'em away, and they wouldn't turn back until they knew the ride was over and it was time to. Sometimes Dane wouldn't show up for the noon meal, and that was all right with the ponies too, for he'd often get off of 'em and let 'em graze with reins dragging. There was no danger of either of them ever leaving Dane, for they seemed as attached to him as any dog could be to his master.

It was the same way with Dane for them, and he had more confidence in their trueness and senses than most humans have in one another.

A mighty good test and surprising outcome of that came one day as a powerful big cloudburst hit above the ranch a ways and left Dane acrost the creek from home. The creek had turned into churning wild waters the size of a big river in a few minutes, half a mile wide in some places and licking up close to the higher land where the ranch buildings and corrals was.

It kept on a-raining hard after the cloudburst had fell and it didn't act like it was going to let up for some time, and the wide river wouldn't be down to creek size or safe to cross, at least not for a day or so.

The noise of the rushing water was a-plenty to let Dane know of the cloudburst. It had come with a sudden roar and without a drop of warning, and Dane's horse, he was riding Little Eagle that day, plainly let him know the danger of the wide stretch of swirling fast waters. It wasn't the danger of the water only, but uprooted trees and all kinds of heavy timber speeding along would make the crossing more than dangerous, not only dangerous but it would about mean certain death.

Little Eagle would of tackled the swollen waters or anything Dane would of wanted him to, but Dane knew a whole lot better than to make that wise horse go where he didn't want to, any time.

Dane could tell by the noise, and riding to the edge of the water and the location where he was, how wide the body of wild waters was. He knew that the stock could keep out of reach of it on either side without being jammed against the fences, but he got worried about the ranch, wondering if the waters had got up to the buildings. He worried too about his family worrying about him, and maybe trying to find and get to him.

That worrying got him to figuring on ways of getting back. He sure couldn't stay where he was until the waters went down, not if he could help it. It wouldn't be comfortable being out so long in the heavy rain either, even if he did have his slicker on, and it wouldn't do to try to go to the neighbor's ranch which was some fifteen miles away. He doubted if he could find it anyway, for it was acrost a bunch of rolling hills, nothing to go by, and Little Eagle wouldn't know that *there* would be where Dane would be wanting him to go. Besides there was the thought of his family worrying so about him and maybe risking their lives in trying to find him.

He'd just have to get home somehow, and it was at the thought of his neighbor's ranch, and picturing the distance and country to it in his mind, that he thought of the railroad, for he would of had to cross it to get there. And then, thinking of the railroad, the thought came of the trestle crossing along it and over the creek. Maybe he could make that. That would be sort of a dangerous crossing too, but the more he thought of it the more he figured it worth taking the chances of trying. That was the only way of his getting on the other side of the high waters and back to the ranch.

The railroad and trestle was only about half a mile from where he now was, and that made it all the more tempting to try. So after thinking it over in every way, including the fact that he'd be taking chances with losing his horse also, he finally decided to take the chance, at the risk of both himself and his horse—that is, if his horse seen it might be safe enough. He felt it had to be done and it could be done, and there went to show his faith and confidence in that Little Eagle horse of his.

And that confidence sure wasn't misplaced, for a cooler-headed, brainier horse never was.

There was two fences to cross to get to the railroad and trestle, and it wasn't at all necessary to go through gates to get there, for the swollen waters with jamming timbers had laid the fence down for quite a ways on both sides of the wide river, some of the wire strands to break and snap and coil all directions.

A strand of barbed wire, even if flat to the ground, is a mighty dangerous thing to ride over, for a horse might pick it up with a hoof, and as most horses will scare, draw their hind legs up under 'em and act up. The result might be a wicked sawing wire cut at the joint by the hock, cutting veins and tendons and often crippling a horse for life. In such cases the rider is also very apt to get tangled up in the wire, for that wicked stuff seems to have the ways of the tentacles of a devilfish at such times.

Loose wire laying around on the ground is the cowboys'

worst fear, especially so with Dane, for, as he couldn't see, it was many times more threatening as he rode most every day from one fenced-in field to the other. But the confidence he had in his two coolheaded ponies relieved him of most all his fear of the dangerous barbed wire, and either one of 'em would stop and snort a little at the sight of a broken strand coiled to the ground. Dane knew what that meant and it always brought a chill to his spine. He'd get down off his saddle, feel around carefully in front of his horse, and usually the threatening coil would be found to within a foot or so of his horse's nose. The coil would then be pulled and fastened to the fence, to stay until a ranch hand, with team and buckboard, would make the rounds of all fences every few months and done a general fixing of 'em.

It's too bad barbed wire *has* to be used for fences. It has butchered and killed many good horses, and some riders. But barbed wire is about the only kind of fence that will hold cattle most of the time, and when there has to be many long miles of it, even with the smaller ranches, that's about the only kind of fence that can be afforded or used. Cattle (even the wildest) seldom get a scratch by it, even in breaking through a four-strand fence of it or going over it while it's loose and coiled on the ground, for they don't get rattled when in wire as a horse does, and they hold their hind legs straight back when going through, while the horse draws 'em under him instead and goes to tearing around.

Both Little Eagle and Ferret had been well trained against scaring and fighting wire if they ever got into it, also trained not to get into it, and stop whenever coming to some that was loose on the ground. That training had been done with a rope and a piece of smooth wire at one end, and being they was naturally coolheaded they soon learned all the tricks of the wire and how to behave when they come near any of that coiled on the ground.

There was many such coils as the flood waters rampaged along the creek bottom, and as Dane headed Little Eagle toward the railroad and trestle he then let him pick his own way through and around the two fence entanglements on the way there, along the edge of the rushing water.

Little Eagle done considerable winding around and careful stepping as he come to the fences that had been snapped and washed to scattering, dangerous strands over the field. Dane gave him his time, let him go as he choose, and finally the roar of the waters against the high banks by the trestle came to his ears. It sounded as though it was near up to the trestle, which he knew was plenty high, and that gave him a good idea of what a cloudburst it had been.

He then got mighty dubious about trying to cross the trestle, for it was a long one, there was no railing of any kind on the sides, and part of it might be under water or even washed away. There was some of the flood water in the ditch alongside the railroad grade and it wasn't so many feet up it to the track level.

Riding between the rails a short ways he come to where the trestle begun and there he stopped Little Eagle. The swirling waters made a mighty roar right there, and how he wished he could of been able to see then, more than any time since his blindness had overtook him.

Getting off Little Eagle there, he felt his way along to the first ties to the trestle and the space between each, which was about five inches and just right for Little Eagle's small hoofs to slip in between, Dane thought. One such a slip would mean a broken leg, and the horse would have to be shot right there, to lay between the rails. The rider would be mighty likely to go over the side of the trestle, too.

Dane hardly had any fear for himself, but he did have for Little Eagle. Not that he feared he would put a foot between the ties, for that little horse was too wise, coolheaded and careful to do anything like that, Dane knew. What worried him most was if the trestle was still up and above water all the way acrost. There would be no turning back, for in turning is when Little Eagle would be mighty liable to slip a hoof between the ties. The rain had let up but the wind was blowing hard and the tarred ties was slippery as soaped glass.

It all struck Dane as fool recklessness to try to cross on that long and narrow trestle at such a time, but he felt he should try, and to settle his dubiousness he now left it to Little Eagle and his good sense as to whether to tackle it or not.

If he went he would *ride* him across, not try to crawl, feel his way and lead him, for in leading the horse he wouldn't be apt to pay as much attention to his footing and to nosing every dangerous step he made. Besides, Dane kind of felt that if Little Eagle should go over the side he'd go with him.

So, getting into the saddle again, he let Little Eagle stand for a spell, at the same time letting him know that he wanted to cross the trestle, for him to size it up and see if it could be done. It was up to him, and the little gray well understood.

It might sound unbelievable, but a good sensible horse and rider have a sort of feel-language which is mighty plain between 'em, and when comes a particular dangerous spot the two can discuss the possibilities of getting over or acrost it as well as two humans can, and even better, for the horse has the instinct which the human lacks. He can tell danger where the human can't, and the same with the safety.

It was that way with Little Eagle and Dane, only even more so, because as Little Eagle, like Ferret, had been trained to realize Dane's affliction, cater and sort of take care of him, they was always watchful. Then with Dane's affection and care for them, talking to 'em and treating 'em like the true pardners they was, there was an understanding and trust between man and horse that's seldom seen between man and man.

Sitting in his saddle with his hand on Little Eagle's neck the two "discussed" the dangerous situation ahead in such a way that the loud roar of the water foaming by and under the trestle didn't interfere any with the decision that was to come.

There was a tenseness in the top muscles of Little Eagle's

neck as he looked over the scary, narrow, steel-ribboned trail ahead, nervous at the so-careful investigation, that all sure didn't look well. But Dane'd now left it all to Little Eagle's judgment, and just as he had about expected he'd be against trying, Little Eagle, still all tense and quivering some, planted one foot on the first tie, and crouching a bit, all nerves and muscles steady, started on the way of the dangerous crossing.

Every step by step from the first seemed like a long minute to Dane. The brave little horse, his nose close to the ties, at the same time looking ahead, was mighty careful how he placed each front foot, and sure that the hind one would come up to the exact same place afterward, right where that front one had been. He didn't just plank his hoof and go on, but felt for a sure footing on the wet and slippery tarred ties before putting any weight on it and making another step. Something like a mountain climber, feeling and making sure of his every hold while going on with his climbing.

The start wasn't the worst of the crossing. That begin to come as they went further along and nearer to the center. There, with the strong wind blowing broadside of 'em, the swift waters churning, sounding like to the level of the slippery ties, would seem about scary enough to chill the marrow in any being. But there was more piled onto that, for as they neared the center it begin to tremble and sway as if by earth tremors. This was by the high rushing waters swirling around the tall and now submerged supporting timbers.

Little Eagle's step wasn't so sure then, and as careful as he was, there come a few times when he slipped, and a time or two when a hoof went down between the ties, leaving him to stand on three shaking legs until he got his hoof up and on footing again.

With most any other horse it would of been the end of him and his rider right then. As it was, Little Eagle went on, like a tightrope walker, with every muscle at work. And Dane, riding mighty light on him, his heart up his throat at every slip or loss of footing, done his best not to get him off balance but help him that way when he thought he could.

If the shaking, trembling and swaying of the trestle had been steady it would of been less scary and some easier, but along with the strong vibrations of the trestle there'd sometimes come a big uprooted tree to smash into it at a forty-mile speed. There'd be a quiver all along the trestle at the impact. It would sway and bend dangerously, to slip back again as the tree would be washed under and on.

Such goings-on would jar Little Eagle's footing to where he'd again slip a hoof between the ties, and Dane would pray, sometimes cuss a little. But the way Little Eagle handled his feet and every part of himself, sometimes on the tip of his toes, the sides of his hoofs and even to his knees, he somehow managed to keep right side up.

Good thing, Dane thought, that the horse wasn't shod, for shoes without sharp calks would have been much worse on than none, on the slippery ties. As it was, and being his shoes had been pulled off only a couple of days before to ease his feet some between shoeings, his hoofs was sharp at the edges and toe, and that gave him more chance.

The scary and most dangerous part of the trestle was reached, the center, and it was a good thing maybe that Dane couldn't see while Little Eagle sort of juggled himself over that part, for the trestle had been under repair and some of the old ties had been taken away in a few places, to later be replaced by new ones; but where each tie had been taken away, that left an opening of near two feet wide. Mighty scary for Little Eagle too, but he eased over them gaps without Dane knowing.

Dane felt as though it was long weary miles and took about that much time to finally get past the center and most dangerous part of the five-hundred-yard trestle, for them five hundred yards put more wear on him during that time than five hundred miles would of.

And he was far from near safe going as yet, for he'd just passed center and the trestle was still doing some tall trembling and dangerous weaving, when, as bad and spooky as things already was, there come the sound of still worse fear and danger, and Dane's heart stood still. It was a train whistle he'd heard above the roar of the waters. It sounded like the train was coming his way, facing him, and there'd sure be no chance for him to turn and make it back, for he'd crossed over half of the trestle, the worst part, and going back would take a long time.

All the dangers and fears piling together now, instead of exciting Dane, seemed to cool and steady him, like having to face the worst and make the best of it. He rode right on toward the coming train.

He knew from memory that the railroad run a straight line to the trestle, that there was no railroad crossing nor other reason for the engineer to blow his whistle, unless it was for him, himself. Then it came to him that the engineer must of seen him on the trestle and would sure stop his train, if he could.

Standing up in his stirrups he raised his big black hat high as he could and waved it from side to side as a signal for the engineer to stop his train. Surely they could see that black hat of his and realize the predicament he was in. That getting off the trestle would mean almost certain death.

But the train sounded like it was coming right on, and at that Dane wondered if maybe it was coming too fast to be able to stop. He got a little panicky then, and for a second he was about to turn Little Eagle off the trestle and swim for it. It would of been a long and risky swim, maybe carried for miles down country before they could of reached either bank, and it would of taken more than luck to've succeeded. But if they'd got bowled over by some tree trunk and went down the churning waters that would be better, Dane thought, than to have Little Eagle smashed to smithereens by the locomotive. He had no thought for himself.

About the only thing that made him take a bigger chance

and ride on some more was that he knew that the whole train and its crew would be doomed before it got halfways on the trestle, and what if it was a passenger train?

At that thought he had no more fear of Little Eagle keeping his footing on the trestle. His fear now went for the many lives there might be on the train, and he sort of went wild and to waving his big black hat all the more in trying to warn of the danger.

But he didn't put on no such action as to unbalance the little gray in any way. He still felt and helped with his every careful step, and then there got to be a prayer with each one, like with the beads of the rosary.

He rubbed his moist eyes and also prayed he could see, now of all times and if only just for this once, and then the train whistle blew again, so close this time that it sounded like it was on the trestle, like coming on, and being mighty near to him.—Dane had done his best, and now was his last and only chance to save Little Eagle and himself, by sliding off the trestle. He wiped his eyes like as though to see better, and went to reining Little Eagle off the side of the trestle. But to his surprise, Little Eagle wouldn't respond to the rein. It was the first time excepting amongst the thick brush or bad creek crossings that horse had ever went against his wishes that way. But this was now very different, and puzzled, he tried him again and again, with no effect, and then, all at once, *he could see.*

Myself and one of Dane's boys had been riding, looking for Dane soon after the cloudburst hit, and seeing the stopped passenger train with the many people gathered by the engine, we high-loped toward it, there to get the surprise of seeing Dane on Little Eagle on the trestle and carefully making each and every dangerous step toward us and solid ground.

We seen we sure couldn't be of no use to the little gray nor Dane, only maybe a hindrance, and being there was only a little ways more we held our horses and watched. Looking on the length of the trestle we noticed that only the rails and ties showed above the high water; there was quite a bend in it from the swift and powerful pressure, and the rails and ties was leaning, like threatening to break loose at any time.

How the little horse and Dane ever made it, with the strong wind, slippery ties and all a-weaving, was beyond us. So was it with the passengers who stood with gaping mouths and tense watching. What if they'd known that the rider had been blind while he made the dangerous crossing?

And as the engineer went on to tell the spellbound passengers how that man and horse on the trestle had saved all their lives, they was more than thankful, for as the heavy cloudburst had come so sudden and hit in one spot, there'd been no report of it, and as the engineer said, he might of drove onto the trestle a ways before knowing. Then it would of been too late.

But Little Eagle was the one who played the biggest part in stopping what would have been a terrible happening. He was the one who decided to make the dangerous crossing, the one who had to use his head and hoofs with all his skill and power, also the one who at the last of the stretch would not heed Dane's pull of the reins to slide off the trestle. His first time not to do as he was wanted to. He'd disobeyed and had saved another life. He'd been "The Seeing Eye."

The fuss over with as Dane finally rode up on solid ground and near the engine, we then was the ones due for a big surprise. For Dane *spotted* us out from the crowd, and smiling, rode straight for us and looked us both square in the eye.

The shock and years he lived crossing that trestle, then the puzzling over Little Eagle not wanting to turn at the touch of the rein had done the trick, had brought his sight back.

After that day, Little Eagle and Ferret was sort of neglected, neglected knee-deep in clover, amongst good shade and where clear spring water run. The seeing eyes was partly closed in contentment.

WILL JAMES was born in Montana, and always contended that the first sounds he ever heard were the jangling of his father's spurs, the nickering of horses and the "bellering" of cattle. His mother died when he was only a year old, and his father was killed in a cattle-herding accident three years later. A kindly Canadian trapper took care of James until he was thirteen. But when the trapper died, the boy was on his own. He rode for some of the biggest cow and horse outfits in the West, and became known for his ability to capture wild horses. As he grew older, he began to draw and then to write about horses.

"The Seeing Eye," like all of Will James' stories, is true and unglamorized. He never went to school, and his stories were criticized when they were first published because he wrote in the rough, everyday idiom of the cowboy. Today, however, his genius is generally recognized. In 1927 he received the Newbery Award for *Smoky,* now considered to be an American classic. Will James died when he was fifty, but his name continues to live through his vivid, realistic tales of the West.

Trapped

BY SAM SAVITT

THE wind was edged with ice. It was blowing from the northwest and struck Vicki Jordan full blast when she stepped down from the school bus in front of her house. She hunched forward hugging her books against her chest as she scrambled up the slippery drive. Rocky, her Irish setter, met her halfway, then bounded ahead through the banked snow. He was waiting at the door when she got there and scooted inside when she opened it. She roughed up his grinning face, kicked loose her boots in the hallway, and without taking off her parka made a beeline for the kitchen and the cookie jar on the second shelf above the counter.

Her quick eye immediately caught the note on the kitchen table, and while she munched her cookie she read: "Dear Vicki, Pat is turned out. Bring him in when you feed the animals. Wayne is at basketball practice and I'll be home at six. Love, Mom."

It was four-fifteen and would start getting dark in about twenty minutes—so she had better get going.

The thermometer outside the window read eighteen degrees above zero, but as she trudged down to the barn it felt more like eighteen below. It was starting to snow again. The gray sky had deepened and a thin film of blowing white was beginning to fog over the dark woods that bordered the pasture.

By comparison, the inside of the barn seemed warm. The stall door was open. Poor Pat, Vicki thought, out on a day like this. But he has to stretch the kinks out of his muscles even if it's too cold for anyone to ride him.

She plugged in the water heater, then cleaned out the stall and fluffed up the soft dry shavings with a rake. She would bring Pat in as soon as she got his dinner mixed. He would love a hot mash tonight—bran and oats and molasses and hot water made the most delicious-smelling concoction. She tasted it occasionally, as a mother samples a dish before giving it to her baby.

Just thinking about Pat made her green eyes grow misty. He looked exactly like Fury of the movies—sleek and black, with one white star on his forehead. He was her Dad's horse, but Vicki had wished he belonged to her from the first day he came to Random Farm. He was sick then with a horrible cough, but Dan Jordan patiently nursed him along with special feed and Vicki's untiring help. She used to walk him slowly along the dirt road that ran for miles from their barnyard through the countryside.

Dr. Regan, the veterinarian, was a frequent visitor, and after long months Pat began to get well. Vicki used to think he had more ribs than any horse she had ever seen, but as he recovered they faded and his taut hide was replaced by a coat that shone like black satin. His neck filled out and arched into alert ears and a fine Thoroughbred head. When his breathing eased, his step came alive, and Vicki knew then that he was the most wonderful horse she had ever known.

Now she dumped the mash into his feed bucket. She stepped

outside and around the corner of the barn, cupped her mittened hand around her mouth and shouted, "Hey, Black Horse, come and get it!"

It was snowing harder and blowing harder. The driving wind stifled her words, drowning them out. The drifts were thigh-deep here but she could still make out Pat's tracks and used them as a pathway as she trudged toward the pasture fence.

Pat was nowhere to be seen. She called again and again. Maybe there was an answering whinny, but she couldn't be sure.

As yet she felt no real alarm, only an odd tightening in her throat and quivering in her stomach. "Pat, hey Pat—Pat!" A cold chill settled between her shoulder blades and began creeping slowly up the back of her neck. She ducked under the barway, then floundered along the rail fence to the upper pasture where she hoped he would be. He *had* to be there. He was there—standing like a statue facing the wind. Her first reaction was relief. But why wasn't his back to the wind and why was he so still with an icy blast slashing against his chest? His head was low, watching her weaving approach. The black mane was lashing about in quick erratic bursts as sharp gusts of wind tore at it. As she came closer she could see the frost collected around his muzzle and the dark eyes blinking against the sharp sting of snow.

"Pat, for gosh sakes why don't you come—"

Then she *saw* the answer. Pat was trapped—in wire, barbed wire! Wire that had lain unnoticed, buried deep in snow these many winter months. Now it reached up like an octopus and held the horse in its twisted coils and quivering strands. Suddenly all the terrifying stories of horses caught in wire descended upon her like an avalanche—stories of horses who became ensnarled this way and fought for their freedom until they died from loss of blood and exhaustion. Only last month one of the McLean's prize hunters had gotten tangled up in barbed wire so badly he had to be destroyed. And the Watkins' mare, Loli, just across the way, had been seriously cut up in the same manner six months ago and wasn't sound yet. It was strange how some horses would panic and practically commit suicide.

All this flashed through Vicki's mind in the space of a heartbeat. She turned and stumbled down the back trail. She no longer felt the cold or the buffeting wind. The wire cutters, she thought, I've got to get the wire cutters. She found them where her dad had always hung them, next to the hay chute.

Darkness was beginning to creep in, blending with the storm.

"Oh, Pat, don't move. Wait for me. Don't panic! Wait for me." He was where she had left him, still standing, but trembling all over. He must have been enmeshed here for hours. The cold was beginning to get to him—and the fear.

Pat was a Thoroughbred—bred to race, and more highstrung than most of the other breeds. Every instinct within him cried, bolt—fight—run—run! But some vague, outer good sense held him in place, like a dyke shuddering before the onslaught of a flood.

Vicki's parka hood had blown back and now her short dark hair was whipping wildly against Pat's belly as she crouched.

The situation looked worse than she had expected. The old garden used to be here. Last fall Vicki's father had converted it to pasture. He had spent days digging up old fence and rusted wire which had been in the ground for more than twenty years. Vicki and Wayne had helped, and when they finished, figured they'd gotten all of it. How they had overlooked this section she would never know. But Pat, pawing through the snow, had disturbed the remains. Now he stood ensnared with two heavy strands of tangled wire running between his front and hind legs, parallel to his body and only six inches below it. His feet were immobilized deep in a cobweb of barbed coils. His knees were shaking and beginning to buckle.

Vicki clamped the cutters down on the upper wire and

pressed the handles with all her might. Snap—ping! The strand parted and recoiled sharply in opposite directions. Pat started but held fast as the loose ends slapped against his legs. Be careful now, she told herself, steady—no quick moves—he is close to the breaking point; almost anything might trigger him off.

The wire cutters were fastened on the second wire. Vicki's face twisted into a grimace of pain and frustration as the grips dug into the palms of her hands. The grips wouldn't close—the wire was too thick. She shifted to another spot and tried again. Her breath came in short explosive grunts. She threw the cutters down in the snow and seized the wire in her hands. Back and forth, back and forth. "Break! please break!" she said aloud. Her teeth cut into her lower lip. The rusty wire turned red under the desperate efforts of her bleeding hands, but she never felt the hurt. The strand finally gave way with a jerk that threw her down to her hands and knees. She was gasping for air. It was bitterly cold, but the hair above her eyes was matted to her glistening brow. Her fingers were numb as she dug down through the snow, frantically searching for the wire around Pat's front feet. She could feel it now; it was wrapped and twisted around his hoofs. She reached for the wire cutters again. On her belly now, the snow almost blinding her, she struggled with the wire. Cut . . . cut . . . cut, and Pat was free—but only in front! She lurched to her feet, dizzy with exhaustion. She held on to his halter for support, her face against his neck.

"Steady, Pat," she gasped. "We're almost through, just a little longer."

She pressed gently against his shoulder, pushing sideways. He stepped clear reluctantly, fearfully, still not sure. As he turned, his back legs, still trapped, stayed where they were, but crossed slightly as he pivoted away from them.

"Hold it, you're not clear yet!"

The black horse seemed to understand what she was saying —to know that this girl was trying to help him.

On her knees again, she found the wire behind. There seemed to be no sensation left in her hands. They worked automatically like things apart, on a mission of their own. All that mattered in the whole world was to get Pat through this. His complete faith and trust gave her a strength she hadn't thought she possessed.

She cut the last strand and dragged it aside. At Pat's head she led him slowly forward, one step at a time, until he was in the clear. She reeled back away from him as he reared, then plunged ahead in the exuberance of his freedom. All his pent-up nerves and control exploded in a series of bucks and kicks as he headed toward the barn. Vicki staggered along behind, but once inside she quickly cross-tied and carefully examined him from the tip of his nose to the end of his tail. There wasn't a mark on him!

It was a miracle. She could hardly believe her eyes. Nobody would believe anything like this could happen—but it did. The palms of her hands, torn and crusted with blood, and the ripped sleeves of her parka were witnesses. But Pat, wonderful Pat, was alive and unhurt!

Vicki's father had come home late. He had been detained at his law office, then had had to walk a couple of miles through heavy snow when his car couldn't make it. As soon as he heard what had happened he hurried up to Vicki's room.

He sat at the edge of her bed, the glow from the hall light silhouetting the line of his dark hair and high cheekbones.

"Mom just told me about you and Pat." He tenderly patted her bandaged hands. "You're wonderful, honey. I'm proud of you." He leaned forward and kissed her cheek.

"I've never heard of anything like it. That black horse couldn't have impressed me more if he'd won a blue ribbon at Madison Square Garden. Standing out there like that—waiting for you to cut him free." He shook his head, scratching the back of his neck. "Beats me! The most remarkable thing was the confidence he had in you. Somehow he knew you would help him if he waited. And you didn't let him down!"

Dan Jordan rose to his feet and let his fingers gently ruffle her hair. "Come spring we'll have to do something about that pony you've been saving for. A girl like you should have a pony of her own."

SAM SAVITT'S first contacts with horses in his native town of Wilkes-Barre, Pennsylvania, were feeding the milkman's nag, reading Will James' stories and seeing cowboy movies on Saturday afternoons. But however limited these experiences, he developed a passion for horses that has never left him.

One of America's leading horse artists, Savitt first learned to ride during a hitchhiking trip through the Southwest, where he worked on ranches, went to rodeos, and stored up the impressions he later portrayed so vividly in his illustrations. He is an expert horseman, particularly interested in training hunters and jumpers. His star pupil War Bride was selected for the United States Equestrian Team, and Savitt is the team's official artist. When he's not drawing or writing, he loves to ride a horse that looks very much like Pat in "Trapped." The episode of the wire also happens to be true.

Among the many books which Savitt has written and illustrated is *Midnight,* the story of a rodeo horse who never was "rode." Savitt first heard about him when he was in the West. He talked with many cowboys who had tried and failed, and wrote and illustrated the story of this spirited horse who has become a legend.

Two ladies with racing blood

First Day Finish

BY JESSAMYN WEST

"THEE'S home, Lady," Jess told his mare.

They had made the trip in jig time. The sun was still up, catalpa shadows long across the grass, and mud daubers still busy about the horse trough, gathering a few last loads before nightfall, when Lady turned in the home driveway.

Jess loosened the reins, so that on their first homecoming together they could round the curve to the barn with a little flourish of arrival. It was a short-lived flourish, quickly subsiding when Jess caught sight of the Reverend Marcus Augustus Godley's Black Prince tied to the hitching rack.

"Look who's here," Jess told his mare and they came in slow and seemly as befitted travelers with forty weary miles behind them.

The Reverend Godley himself, shading his eyes from the low sun, stepped to the barn door when his Black Prince nickered.

Jess lit stiffly down and was standing at Lady's head when the Reverend Marcus Augustus reached them.

"Good evening, Marcus," said Jess. "Thee run short of something over at thy place?"

"Welcome home," said Reverend Godley, never flinching. "I was hunting, with Enoch's help, a bolt to fit my seeder," he told Jess, but he never took his eyes off Lady.

He was a big man, fat but not pursy, with a full red face preaching had kept supple and limber. A variety of feelings, mostly painful, flickered across it now as he gazed at Jess's mare.

He opened and shut his mouth a couple of times, but all he managed to say was, "Where'd you come across that animal, Friend Birdwell?"

"Kentucky," Jess said shortly.

"I'm a Kentuckian myself." The Reverend Godley marveled that the state that had fathered him could have produced such horseflesh.

"You trade Red Rover for this?" he asked.

Jess rubbed his hand along Lady's neck. "The mare's name is Lady," he said.

"Lady!" the preacher gulped, then threw back his big head and disturbed the evening air with laughter.

"Friend," Jess said, watching the big bulk heave, "thy risibilities are mighty near the surface this evening."

The Reverend Godley wiped the tears from his face and ventured another look. "It's just the cleavage," he said. "The rift between the name and looks."

"That's a matter of opinion," Jess told him, "but Lady is the name."

The preacher stepped off a pace or two as if to try the advantage of a new perspective on the mare's appearance, clapped a handful of Sen-sen into his mouth, and chewed reflectively.

"I figure it this way," he told Jess. "You bought that animal Red Rover. Flashy as sin and twice as unreliable. First little brush you have with me and my cob, Red Rover curdles on you—goes sourer than a crock of cream in a June storm. What's the natural thing to do?"

The Reverend Godley gave his talk a pulpit pause and rested his big thumbs in his curving watch chain.

"The natural thing to do? Why, just what you done. Give

speed the go-by. Say farewell to looks. Get yourself a beast sound in wind and limb and at home behind a plow. Friend," he commended Jess, "you done the right thing, though I'm free to admit I never laid eyes before on a beast of such dimensions.

"Have some Sen-sen?" he asked amiably. "Does wonders for the breath." Jess shook his head.

"Well," he continued, "I want you to know—Sunday mornings on the way to church, when I pass you, there's nothing personal in it. That morning when I went round you and Red Rover, I somehow got the idea you's taking it personal. Speed's an eternal verity, friend, an eternal verity. Nothing personal. The stars shine. The grass withereth. The race is to the swift. A fast horse passes a slow one. An eternal verity, Friend Birdwell. You're no preacher, but your wife is. She understands these things. Nothing personal. Like gravitation, like life, like death. A law of God. Nothing personal.

"The good woman will be hallooing for me," he said, gazing up the pike toward his own farm a quarter of a mile away. He took another look at Jess's new mare.

"Name's Lady," he said, as if reminding himself. "Much obliged for the bolt, Friend Birdwell. Me and my cob'll see you Sunday."

Enoch stepped out from the barn door as the Reverend Godley turned down the driveway.

"Figure I heard my sermon for the week," he said.

"He's got an endurin' flock," Jess told his hired man.

"Cob?" Enoch asked. "What's he mean always calling that animal of his a cob? He ignorant?"

"Not ignorant—smooth," Jess said. "Cob's just his way of saying Black Prince's no ordinary beast without coming straight out with so undraped a word as stallion."

The two men turned with one accord from Godley's cob to

Jess's Lady. Enoch's green eyes flickered knowingly; his long freckled hand touched Lady's muscled shoulder lightly, ran down the powerful legs, explored the deep chest.

"There's more here, Mr. Birdwell, than meets the eye?"

Jess nodded.

"As far as looks goes," Enoch said, "the Reverend called the turn."

"As far as looks goes," Jess agreed.

"She part Morgan?"

"Half," Jess said proudly.

Enoch swallowed. "How'd you swing it?"

"Providence," Jess said. "Pure Providence. Widow woman wanted a pretty horse and one that could be passed."

"Red Rover," Enoch agreed, and added softly, "The Reverend was took in."

"He's a smart man," said Jess. "We'd best not bank on it. But by sugar, Enoch, I tell thee I was getting tired of taking Eliza down the pike to Meeting every First Day like a tail to Godley's comet. Have him start late, go round me, then slow down so's we'd eat dust. Riled me so I was arriving at Meeting in no fit state to worship."

"You give her a tryout—coming home?" Enoch asked guardedly.

"I did, Enoch," Jess said solemnly. "This horse, this Morgan mare named Lady, got the heart of a lion and the wings of a bird. Nothing without pinfeathers is going to pass her."

"It's like Mr. Emerson says," said Enoch earnestly.

Jess nodded. "Compensation," he agreed. "A clear case of it and her pure due considering the looks she's got."

"You figure on this Sunday?" Enoch asked.

"Well," Jess said, "I plan to figure on nothing. Thee heard the Reverend Marcus Augustus. A fast horse goes round a slow one. Eternal law. If Black Prince tries to pass us First Day—and don't—it's just a law, just something eternal. And mighty pretty, Enoch, like the stars."

"A pity," Enoch said reflecting. "The Reverend's young 'uns all so piddling and yours such busters. It'll tell on your mare."

"A pity," Jess acquiesced, "but there it is. Eliza'd never agree to leave the children home from Meeting."

Enoch ruminated, his fingers busy with Lady's harness. "What'll your wife say to this mare? Been a considerable amount of trading lately."

"Say?" said Jess. "Thee heard her. 'Exchange Red Rover for a horse not racy-looking.' This mare racy-looking?"

"You have to look twice to see it," Enoch admitted.

"Eliza don't look twice at a horse. I'll just lead Lady up now for Eliza to see. She don't hold with coming down to the barn while men's about."

Jess took Lady from the shafts and led her between rows of currant bushes up to the house. Dusk was come now, lamps were lit. Inside, Eliza and the children were waiting for their greeting until the men had had their talk.

"Lady," Jess said fondly, "I want thee to see thy mistress."

The rest of the week went by, mild and very fair, one of those spells in autumn when time seems to stand still. Clear days with a wind which would die down by afternoon. The faraway Sandusky ridges seemed to have moved up to the orchard's edge. The purple ironweed, the farewell summer, the goldenrod, stood untrembling beneath an unclouded sky. Onto the corn standing shocked in the fields, gold light softer than arrows, but as pointed, fell. A single crow at dusk would drop in a slow arc against the distant wood to show that not all had died. Indian summer can be a time of great content.

First Day turned up pretty. Just before the start for Meeting,

Jess discovered that there was a hub cap missing off the surrey.

"Lost?" asked Eliza.

"I wouldn't say lost," Jess told her. "Missing."

Odd thing, a pity to be sure, but there it was. Nothing for it but for him and Eliza to ride to Meeting in the cut-down buggy and leave the children behind. Great pity, but there it was.

Eliza stood in the yard in her First Day silk. "Jess," she said in a balky voice, "this isn't my idea of what's seemly. A preacher going to Meeting in a cut-down rig like this. Looks more like heading for the trotting races at the county fair than preaching."

Jess said, "Thee surprises me, Eliza. Thee was used to put duty before appearance. Friend Fox was content to tramp the roads to reach his people. Thee asks for thy surrey, fresh blacking on the dashboard and a new whip in the socket."

He turned away sadly. "The Lord's people are everywhere grown more worldly," he said, looking dismally at the ground.

It didn't set good with Jess, pushing Eliza against her will that way—and he wasn't too sure it was going to work. But the name Fox got her. When she was a girl she'd set out to bring the Word to people, the way Fox had done, and he'd have gone, she knew, to Meeting in a barrow, if need be.

So that's the way they started out, and in spite of the rig, Eliza was lighthearted and holy-feeling. When they pulled out on the pike, she was pleased to note the mare's gait was better than her looks. Lady picked up her feet like she knew what to do with them.

"Thee's got a good-pulling mare, Jess," she said kindly.

"She'll get us there, I don't misdoubt," Jess said.

They'd rounded the first curve below the clump of maples that gave Maple Grove Nursery its name when the Reverend Godley bore down upon them. Neither bothered to look back, both knew the heavy, steady beat of Black Prince's hoofs.

Eliza settled herself in the cut-down rig, her Bible held comfortably in her lap. "It taxes the imagination," she said, "how a man church-bound can have his mind so set on besting another. Don't thee think so, Jess?"

"It don't tax mine," Jess said, thinking honesty might be the only virtue he'd get credit for that day.

Eliza was surprised not to see Black Prince pulling abreast them. It was here on the long stretch of level road that Black Prince usually showed them his heels.

"Thee'd best pull over, Jess," she said.

"I got no call to pull out in the ditch," Jess said. "The law allows me half the road."

The mare hadn't made any fuss about it—no head-shaking, no fancy footwork—but she'd settled down in her harness, she was traveling. It was plain to Eliza they were eating up the road.

"Don't thee think we'd better pull up, Jess?" Eliza said it easy, so as not to stir up the contrary streak that wasn't buried very deep in her husband.

"By sugar," Jess said, "I don't see why."

As soon as Eliza heard that "by sugar" spoken as bold-faced as if it were a weekday, she knew it was too late for soft words. "By sugar," Jess said again, "I don't see why. The Reverend Godley's got half the road and I ain't urging my mare."

It depended on what you called urging. He hadn't taken to lambasting Lady with his hat yet, the way he had Red Rover, but he was sitting on the edge of his seat—and sitting mighty light, it was plain to see—driving the mare with an easy rein and talking to her like a weanling.

"Thee's a fine mare. Thee's a tryer. Thee's a credit to thy dam. Never have to think twice about thy looks again."

Maybe, strictly speaking, that was just encouraging, not urging, but Eliza wasn't in a hairsplitting mood.

She looked back at the Reverend Marcus Augustus, and no two ways about it: he *was* urging Black Prince. The Reverend Godley's cob wasn't a length behind them, and the Reverend himself was half standing, slapping the reins across Black Prince's rump and exhorting him like a sinner newly come to the mourner's bench.

This was a pass to which Eliza hadn't thought to come twice in a lifetime—twice in a lifetime to be heading for Meeting like a county fair racer in a checkered shirt.

"Nothing lacking now," she thought bitterly, "but for bets to be laid on us."

That wasn't lacking, either, if Eliza had only known it. They'd come in view of the Bethel Church now, and more than one of Godley's flock had got so carried away by the race as to try for odds on their own preacher. It didn't seem loyal not to back up their Kentucky brother with hard cash. Two to one the odds were—with no takers.

The Bethel Church sat atop a long, low rise, not much to the eye—but it told on a light mare pulling against a heavy stallion, and it was here Black Prince began to close in; before the rise was half covered, the stallion's nose was pressing toward the buggy's back wheel.

Jess had given up encouraging. He was urging, now. Eliza lifted the hat off his head. Come what might, there wasn't going to be any more hat-whacking if she could help it—Jess was beyond knowing whether his head was bare or covered. He was pulling with his mare now, sweating with her, sucking the air into scalding lungs with her. Lady had slowed on the rise—she'd have been dead if she hadn't—but she was still a-going, still trying hard. Only the Quaker blood in Jess's veins kept him from shouting with pride at his mare's performance.

The Reverend Godley didn't have Quaker blood in his veins. What he had was Kentucky horse-racing blood, and when Black Prince got his nose opposite Lady's rump, Godley's racing blood got the best of him. He began to talk to his cob in a voice that got its volume from camp-meeting practice—and its vocabulary, too, as a matter of fact—but he was using it in a fashion his camp-meeting congregation had never heard.

They were almost opposite the Bethel Church now; Black Prince had nosed up an inch or two more on Lady, and the Reverend Godley was still strongly exhorting—getting mighty personal, for a man of his convictions.

But Lady was a stayer and so was Jess. And Eliza too, for that matter. Jess spared her a glance out of the corner of his eye to see how she was faring. She was faring mighty well—sitting bolt upright, her Bible tightly clasped, and clucking to the mare. Jess couldn't credit what he heard. But there was no doubt about it—Eliza was counseling Lady. "Thee keep a-going, Lady," she called. Eliza hadn't camp-meeting experience, but she had a good clear pulpit voice, and Lady heard her.

She kept a-going. She did better. She unloosed a spurt of speed Jess hadn't known was in her. Lady was used to being held back, not yelled at in a brush. Yelling got her dander up. She stretched out her long neck, lengthened her powerful stride, and pulled away from Black Prince just as they reached the Bethel Church grounds.

Jess thought the race was won and over, that from here on the pace to Meeting could be more suitable to First Day travel. But the Reverend Godley had no mind to stop at so critical a juncture. He'd wrestled with sinners too long to give up at the first setback. He figured the mare was weakening. He figured that with a strong stayer like his Black Prince he'd settle the matter easy in the half mile that lay between Bethel Church and the Quaker Meetinghouse at Rush Branch. He kept a-coming.

But one thing he didn't figure—that was that the slope from Bethel to Rush Branch was against him. Lady had a downhill grade now. It was all she needed. She didn't pull away from Black Prince in any whirlwind style, but stride by stride she pulled away.

It was a great pity Jess's joy in that brush had to be marred.

He'd eaten humble pie some time now, and he was pleasured through and through to be doing the dishing up himself. And he was pleasured for the mare's sake.

But neither winning nor his mare's pleasure was first with Jess. Eliza was. There she sat, white and suffering, holding her Bible like it was the Rock of Ages from which she'd come mighty near to clean slipping off. Jess knew Eliza had a forgiving heart when it came to others—but whether she could forgive herself for getting heated over a horse race the way she'd done, he couldn't say.

And the worst for Eliza was yet to come. Jess saw that clear enough. When Lady and Black Prince had pounded past Godley's church, a number of the Bethel brethren who had arrived early and were still in their rigs set out behind the Reverend Marcus Augustus to be in at the finish. And they were going to be. Their brother was losing, but they were for him still, close behind and encouraging him in a wholehearted way. The whole caboodle was going to sweep behind Jess and Eliza into the Quaker churchyard. They wouldn't linger, but Jess feared they'd turn around there before heading back. And that's the way it was.

Lady was three lengths ahead of Black Prince when they reached the Rush Branch Meetinghouse. Jess eased her for the turn, made it on two wheels, and drew in close to the church. The Bethelites swooped in behind him and on out—plainly beat but not subdued. The Reverend Marcus Augustus was the only man among them without a word to say. He was as silent as a tombstone and considerably grimmer. Even his fancy vest looked to have faded.

The Quakers waiting in the yard for Meeting to begin were quiet, too. Jess couldn't tell from their faces what they were feeling, but there was no use thinking that they considered what they'd just witnessed an edifying sight. Not for a weekday even, that mess of rigs hitting it down the pike with all that hullabaloo

—let alone to First Day and their preacher up front, leading it.

Jess asked a boy to look after Lady. He was so taken up with Eliza he no more than laid a fond hand on Lady's hot flank in passing. He helped Eliza light down, and set his hat on his head when she handed it to him. Eliza looked mighty peaked and withdrawn, like a woman communing with her Lord.

She bowed to her congregation and they bowed back and she led them out of the sunshine into the Meetinghouse with no word being spoken on either side. She walked to the preacher's bench, laid her Bible quietly down, and untied her bonnet strings.

Jess sat rigid in his seat among the men. Jess was a birthright Quaker—and his father and grandfathers before him—and he'd known Quakers to be read out of Meeting for less.

Eliza laid her little plump hands on her Bible and bowed her head in silent prayer. Jess didn't know how long it lasted—sometimes it seemed stretching out into eternity, but Quakers were used to silent worship, and he was the only one who seemed restive. About the time the ice around Jess's heart was hardening past his enduring, Eliza's sweet, cool, carrying voice said, "If the spirit leads any of thee to speak, will thee speak now?"

Then Eliza lowered her head again—but Jess peered around the Meetinghouse. He thought he saw a contented look on most of the faces—nothing that went so far as to warm into a smile, but a look that said they were satisfied the way the Lord had handled things. And the spirit didn't move any member of the congregation to speak that day except for the prayers of two elderly Friends in closing.

The ride home was mighty quiet. They drove past Bethel Church, where the sermon had been short—for all the hitching racks were empty. Lady carried them along proud and untired. Enoch and the children met them down the pike a ways from home and Jess nodded the good news to Enoch—but he couldn't glory in it the way he'd like, because of Eliza.

Eliza was kind, but silent. Very silent. She spoke when spoken to, did her whole duty by the children and Jess, but in all the ways that made Eliza most herself, she was absent and withdrawn.

Toward evening Jess felt a little dauncy—a pain beneath the ribs, heart or stomach, he couldn't say which. He thought he'd brew himself a cup of sassafras tea, take it to bed and drink it there, and maybe find a little ease.

It was past nightfall when Jess entered his and Eliza's chamber, but there was a full moon and by its light he saw Eliza sitting at the east window in her white nightdress, plaiting her black hair.

"Jess," asked Eliza, noting the cup he carried, "has thee been taken ill?"

"No," Jess said, "no," his pain easing off of itself when he heard by the tones of Eliza's voice that she was restored to him—forgiving and gentle, letting bygones be bygones.

"Eliza," he asked, "wouldn't thee like a nice hot cup of sassafras tea?"

"Why, yes, Jess," Eliza said. "That'd be real refreshing."

Jess carried Eliza her cup of tea, walking down a path of roses the moon had lit up in the ingrain carpet.

He stood, while she drank it, with his hand on her chair, gazing out of the window: the whole upcurve and embowered sweep of the earth soaked in moonlight—hill and wood lot, orchard and silent river. And beneath that sheen his own rooftree, and all beneath *it,* peaceful and at rest. Lady in her stall, Enoch reading Emerson, the children long abed.

" 'Sweet day,' " he said, " 'so cool, so calm, so bright, the bridal of the earth and sky.' "

And though he felt so pensive and reposeful, still the bridge of his big nose wrinkled up, his ribs shook with laughter.

Eliza felt the movement of his laughing in her chair. "What is it, Jess?" she asked.

Jess stopped laughing, but said nothing. He figured Eliza had gone about as far in one day as a woman could in enlarging her appreciation of horseflesh; still, he couldn't help smiling when he thought of the sermon that might have been preached in the Bethel Church upon eternal verities.

JESSAMYN WEST understands the Quakers and knows a great deal about them for the simple reason that she was born into the religion. She attended Whittier College, a Quaker institution, and she often listened to her parents' stories about her Indiana forebears. Miss West had rarely thought of being a writer until an attack of tuberculosis forced her to stay in bed for almost two years. During her illness, she began to write a series of sketches about a family of Quakers living in Southern Indiana during the Civil War. The wife was a Quaker minister; the husband's devotion was to horse racing. These short stories eventually became her first book, *The Friendly Persuasion,* from which "First Day Finish" was taken. Later, when the novel was made into a film, Miss West wrote *To See the Dream,* an account of her experiences as a Hollywood script consultant.

She has written other popular books, such as *The Witch Diggers* and *Cress Delehanty,* but *The Friendly Persuasion* is her most heartwarming book, born as it was out of the affection for family ties.

The Black Horse

BY JIM KJELGAARD

THE July sun was hot, and the mountain was high. Jed Hale brushed the perspiration from his forehead as he mounted over the top. The coil of rope about his middle started to chafe. Jed unwrapped it and threw it on the ground while he sat down to rest.

He chewed thoughtfully on a straw and gazed down on the range of low hills that stretched as far as he could see. The big, saucerlike hoofmarks of the horse led down, but there was no particular hurry. The horse was not traveling fast. A man on foot, if he had two good legs, could see him as many times a day as he chose. But the horse could not be caught. Jed had known that when he started.

After an hour Jed rose to his feet, and at the limping hobble that was his fastest pace, started down the hill on the trail of the horse. If he could bring him back—something that fifteen men, each mounted on a good saddle horse, had not been able to do—he would get five hundred dollars. Raglan would pay that much for the black horse.

Jed had seen the black horse scatter Raglan's men. After two days of constant chasing they had finally run him into the stout log corral that they had built. The corral had been strong enough to hold any ordinary animal, but the black horse had crashed through it as though it had been matchwood when they tried to put a rope on him. The man on the wiry saddle pony, who had roped the horse as he ran, had barely escaped with his life. The pony had been dragged along for fifty yards, and would have been killed if the saddle girth had not broken. The black horse had rid himself of the rope somehow. It had not been on him when Jed caught up with him.

Jed's crippled leg gave him trouble going downhill. He was glad when he passed the summits of the low hills and descended into the valley where it was level. From a stream in the valley, Jed drank and ate his fill of the ripe raspberries that hung over the stream. He had had no money to buy supplies to bring along. But he needn't starve. More than once he had lived off the country.

A mile down the valley he came upon the black horse. It stood with its head in the shade of a tree, swishing the flies away with its tail. Noiselessly, Jed sank behind a patch of brush, and for four hours lost himself in staring.

It was the biggest and most magnificent horse Jed had ever seen. He knew horses. Product of a wastrel mother and father, victim of paralysis in his childhood, he had spent all his life doing chores for Raglan and other stockmen in the hills. He had never earned more than ten dollars a month, but he had dreams and ambitions. If he could get only ten acres of land for himself, he would somehow or other procure a mare and make a living raising horses. That, for Jed, would be all he wanted of happiness.

The hill men had said that nobody could capture this horse; nothing could tame it. Every man in the hills had tried. The black horse wasn't fast. Three riders besides Raglan's men had had their ropes on him, two had had their ropes broken, and the third had cut his rather than risk having his saddle horse dragged to death. Jed looked at the manila rope that he had again looped about his waist and shook his head. It was the best and strongest rope to be had, but it would not hold the black horse. Still—Raglan offered five hundred dollars.

Dusk fell. The black horse moved lazily out of the shade of the tree and began cropping at the rich grass that grew along the creek. For another half hour Jed watched him. When Jed was near the horse, he was not Jed Hale, crippled chore boy and roustabout. In some mysterious way he borrowed from the horse's boundless vitality. When the horse grazed too close to him and there was danger of his being discovered, Jed slipped out of his hiding place and moved half a mile up the valley. There, under the side of a mossy log, he made his bed for the night.

With sunup he rolled from under the log. He had slept well enough and he was not tired, but even the summer nights were chilly in the hills. As briskly as he could, he set off down the valley to where he had last seen the horse.

The black horse was browsing peacefully in the center of a patch of wild grass that grew along the creek. For all the world he might have been one of Raglan's Percherons grazing in his home pasture. But the black horse was bigger than any Percheron that Raglan owned. There was another difference too, a subtle one, not to be noticed by the casual eye. When grazing, the black horse raised his head at least once every minute to look about him. It was the mark of the wild thing that must be aware of danger; no tame horse did that.

For a quarter of an hour Jed studied him from the shelter of some aspen trees. Then, as slowly as he could, he walked into the little field where the horse grazed. As soon as he left the shelter of the trees the horse stopped grazing and looked at him steadily. Jed's pulse pounded; the vein in his temple throbbed. Men with years more experience than he had said the horse was bad—a natural killer.

Recklessly Jed walked on. He came to within fifty feet of the horse. It made a nervous little start and trotted a few steps. Jed paused to make soothing noises with his mouth. The rope he had been carrying he threw to the ground. Two yards farther on the horse stopped and swung his head to look at the crippled man. Jed advanced another twenty feet.

The black horse swung about. There was no fear in him, but neither was there any viciousness. His ears tipped forward, not back, and his eyes betrayed only a lively curiosity.

In low tones that scarcely carried across the few feet that separated them, Jed talked to the horse. Still talking, he walked forward. The black horse tossed his head in puzzled wonderment and made nervous little motions with his feet. Fifteen feet separated them, then ten feet. The horse shone like a mountain of muscle and strength. With a sudden, blasting snort he wheeled and thundered down the valley. Jed sank to the ground; perspiration covered his face. He had done what no other man in the hills had ever done, been unarmed in striking distance of the horse. But the horse was not a killer. If he were, Jed knew that he would not be alive now.

Jed took a fish line and hook from his pocket and picked some worms from the bottom of an overturned stone. He cut a willow pole with his sheath knife and caught three trout from the stream. He built a fire and broiled the fish over the flames. He was on a fool's mission. He should be back among the stockmen earning the money that would provide him with food during the winter to come. Deliberately he ate the trout. Getting to his feet, he put out the fire and struck off in the direction taken by the horse.

For another six days he followed the black horse about the low hills. Jed rested when the horse rested and went on when the horse moved again. For the six days the horse stayed within a mile radius of the small meadow where Jed had tried to approach him.

Then on the seventh day, moved by some unaccountable impulse within his massive head, the horse struck across the low hills and did not stop at any of his customary grazing grounds. Patiently, Jed gathered up his coil of rope and followed.

The horse had been foaled in Raglan's back pasture and somehow he had been overlooked when Raglan took his stock in for the winter. They were, Jed guessed, traveling in a great circle and within a month or six weeks they would come back to Raglan's pasture again. It was only at rare intervals that the horse appeared at the pasture. His visits were always unwelcome. Numberless times he had lured mares into the hills with him, and only with difficulty had they been recaptured.

All day he traveled without stopping. It marked the first day that Jed did not see the horse. He was a little fearful when he made his bed that night under a ledge of rocks a dozen miles from where they had started. For two hours he lay peering into the dark, unable to sleep. He did not own the horse and could not catch him, and by spending his time following him he was only making it certain that he would have to live all the next winter on boiled corn meal when he was lucky enough to get it.

Nevertheless, he had to chase the black horse. If he could not come up to him again and somehow contrive a way to capture him, then nothing else mattered either. Finally Jed slept.

He was up the next morning with the first streak of dawn and he did not bother with a cooked meal. Some low-hanging juneberries served him for breakfast. He ate a few and picked a great handful to eat as he walked. Only when he was again on the trail of the horse did he feel at ease.

At twilight he found the horse again. He was quietly grazing in the bottom of a low and rocky ravine. Jed lay on top of the ravine and watched him. He had never been in this country before and he did not like it. The valleys were not gently sloping as in the low hills he had just left. It was a place of rocks, of steep ravines, and oddly enough, of swamps. The creeks were low and muddy; it was a good country to stay out of.

With night Jed moved a quarter-mile back from the lip of the ravine and built a fire. He supped on berries, but rabbit sign was plentiful. With his knife he cut a yard from the end of his rope and unbraided it. Within a hundred yards of his fire he set a dozen snares, and curled on the ground beside the fire to sleep.

He awoke in the middle of the night. The air was cool. A high wind soared across the rocky ledge upon which he slept. Thunder rolled in the sky. The night was made fearfully light by flashes of lightning. Jed picked up a fat pine knot that dripped sticky pitch and stirred the embers of his fire. He lighted the knot at the embers and with it blazing in his hands he made the rounds of his snares. There were rabbits in two of them. Gathering them up along with the unsprung snares, Jed made his way along the rocky ledge by the light of the pine torch.

Halfway around it he came to the place he sought. Close to the wall of the cliff a huge flat rock lay across two small boulders. The natural cave thus formed was full of leaves blown in by the wind. Laying the pair of rabbits on top of the rock, Jed crawled in among the leaves and in a few seconds he was fast asleep.

The second time he awoke in a wet world. Torrential rain had fallen while he slept. The sluggish stream that he could see from his retreat flowed out of its banks. Every leaf on every tree dripped water. A light rain still fell. Jed shrugged and turned to the back of the cave. He built a fire in the dry leaves and fed it with wood that he split with his knife so it would burn. When both the rabbits were cooked and eaten, he wound the rope about him and set out once more to look for the black horse.

The horse was not in the same ravine where Jed had seen him last night. Jed glanced at the steep wall of the ravine and at the swamp at its mouth. The horse could neither climb one nor cross the other. Jed walked along the edge of the ravine; descending into it when he did not have to would be hard work and unnecessary. At the head of the ravine, where it ran onto the summit of the hill, he found the horse's tracks. He followed them.

For five miles the horse had walked across the level top of the hill. Finally, between a cleft in its rocky side, he went down into another of the steep little ravines. There was a trail five feet wide where he had half walked, half slid down.

The rain had stopped, but a wind still blew. Jed stood at the top of the path where the horse had gone down and watched it critically. The walls of the ravine were forty feet high and steep. At the bottom it was scarcely twenty feet across.

Jed worked his way along the rim of the ravine toward its mouth. He would descend into it ahead of the horse and chase him up the ravine to safe travel on top.

Where the ravine led into the main valley was another of the dismal swamps, a big one this time, fully a mile across, and it ran as far up and down the main valley as Jed was able to see. The black horse stood at the edge of the swamp, pawing the soft ground anxiously with a front hoof. Jed watched as he galloped a few yards up the grassless floor of the ravine, then turned to test the swamp again.

For the first time since he had been following him, Jed saw that the black horse was worried. He peered anxiously about. Somewhere in the ravine was an enemy that he could not see. There were rattlesnakes and copperheads to be found in great numbers in just such places, but the black horse was snake-wise; he could avoid these. Occasionally, a wandering cougar was known to cross the hills and to take a colt or calf from the stockmen's herds. That must be it. A big cougar might possibly be able to fasten itself on the horse's back and to kill it with fangs and raking claws.

Ten feet below him a little ledge jutted out from the side of the ravine. Jed doubled his rope around a tree and slid down.

For several seconds after he gained the ledge, he lay gasping for breath.

At a blasting neigh of terror from the horse he crawled to the side of the ledge and looked over. Below him the black horse stood with his head thrown erect, his nostrils flaring and his eyes reflecting the terror they felt. Jed yanked the rope down to him and looped it over a rock. The horse was in danger, he had to get to him. A cougar would run from a man, even such a man as himself.

For fifteen painful feet he struggled down the face of the ravine. His crippled leg sent spasms of pain shooting over his entire body. Grimly he held on. Five feet more he descended. Then his crippled leg proved unequal to the task his mind had given it. He lost his hold on the rope and landed in a heap at the bottom of the ravine.

He sat up to look about. Ten feet in front of him the black horse stood rigid, staring up the ravine.

Jed shook his head to clear it and took his knife from its sheath. There was no time now for anything save finding and coping with whatever nameless terror beset the horse. He rose to his feet by sheer will power putting strength into his legs. When he walked up the ravine, he passed so close to the black horse that he might have reached out and touched him if he had wanted to. The horse merely sidestepped a few paces and followed him with questioning eyes.

The cougar would now either attack or slink away. Walking slowly, searching every ledge with his eyes and missing nothing, Jed advanced. He could not see anything. But there was a sinister thing here that could be neither seen nor heard, only sensed. The air was growing more gushy; pebbles rattled into the ravine. Jed glanced anxiously back over his shoulder. If somehow he had missed the enemy and it had got behind him to attack the horse—. But the black horse still stood; from all appearances he had not moved a muscle.

Suddenly the silence broke. The black horse screamed, a long and chilling blast of fear. There came the pound of his hooves as he fled back down the ravine. Jed heard him splashing into the swamp. Simultaneously there came a deep-throated rumble from up the ravine, as a huge boulder loosed its hold on the canyon's lip to thunder down the side. It gathered others as it rolled. There was a staccato rattling as shale mingled with the avalanche.

Jed sheathed his knife. Within a minute everything was over. A pall of shale dust hung in the air, but that was wafted away by its own weight. The avalanche, then, was the enemy. Animal instinct had told the horse that the slide was coming. The ravine was blocked to a third of its depth by a wall of shale and rock. A man could get over the block, a horse never could. With a shrug, Jed turned back to the swamp and to the horse.

The horse was a raving-mad thing. Ten feet from the rocky floor of the ravine he struggled in the grip of swamp mud that was already up to his belly. His breath came in agonized gasps as he strove with all his mighty strength to free himself of the slimy hand of the swamp. Slowly, inexorably, he sank. As Jed watched, he flung himself four inches out of the mud, and fell back again to sink deeper than before.

Jed walked into the swamp. It sucked at his bare feet, and sighed because it could not grip them. If he stayed out of holes and stepped on grass tussocks wherever he could, he would not sink.

The horse was fast in the grip of the mud when Jed reached its side. It could not move but still tossed its head wildly. A sublime elation gripped Jed when he first laid a hand on the horse's back. He had, he felt, at last known a full moment in his life.

"Easy, old boy," he crooned. "Take it easy."

The horse swung its head about and knocked him sprawling in the mud. Coolly Jed picked himself up to walk back to the mired animal. Kneeling by the horse's shoulder, he ran his hand slowly up its neck.

"Don't be worried, horse," he pleaded. "Don't fight so, old fellow. I'll get you out."

Wildly the black horse struggled. Slowly, carefully, making no move that might alarm, Jed scratched his neck and talked to him. Finally the black horse stopped his insane thrashing and held his head still. Calmly Jed walked to the front of him. Instantly the black horse closed his jaws on Jed's arm. Jed gritted his teeth as the horse squeezed, but his free hand played soothingly around the animal's ears.

The horse unclenched his jaws. He pressed his muzzle against Jed's mud-caked body and smelled him over. Jed grinned happily. The black horse and he were acquainted. Now he could go to work.

The frenzied flight of the black horse had carried him a dozen feet from the floor of the ravine and left him facing into the swamp. Still keeping up his murmuring undertone, Jed studied the situation. He had no lifts or hoists and no way of getting any. It was useless for him to try to pit his own strength against the sucking mud. Likewise there was no way whatever to make the horse obey his commands, and first he would have to get him facing toward the ravine.

With his knife Jed set to work by the horse's side. When the carpet of grass on top of the mud had been cut away he could dig faster with his hands, but as soon as he scooped out a handful of mud another handful seeped in to take its place. Jed took off his shirt and returned to the ravine, where he filled the shirt with loose shale from the rock slide. As soon as he scooped away a handful of mud he packed the remaining wall with shale. That held. The horse moved against the wall as soon as Jed made enough room for him to move, and Jed was much encouraged. Then darkness stopped the work. After eight hours of steady labor he had turned the horse around at least six inches.

In the last faint light of day Jed returned to the ravine and got the coil of rope. The night would be a bad time. He did not think the horse could sink any deeper, but if he became panicky again he might easily render useless all the work done. With his knife Jed hacked off a dozen slender saplings, and carried them back along with the coil of rope. The black horse turned his head to watch when Jed started back to where he was; almost it seemed that he was glad of company. Jed threw the saplings down beside the horse; they were to be his bed. The rope he passed about the horse's neck and made a hackamore that fitted over his jaw. With his head resting on the horse's back, he lay down on the saplings. The end of the rope was in his hand. If the horse should start to sink he would hold his head up as long as he could.

All night long Jed talked to the mired horse, calling him endearing names, soothing him with quiet voice whenever he became restless. A full two hours he spent caressing the horse's head with his shale-torn hands. An hour before dawn he went again to the bottom of the ravine. Daylight was just breaking when he scrambled over the rock slide. He picked a great armful of the wild grass that grew in patches on the other side of the slide and carried it to the horse. Half of it he threw down in front of him, but when the animal had eaten that he took the rest from Jed's hand.

Doggedly Jed set to work with his knife and hands. It was devastatingly slow work. Take out as much mud as he could, and pack the sides with shale. Before the sun set the black horse was again facing the ravine. Furiously he plunged to reach firm ground. Jed quieted him. The time to make the test had not yet come.

Jed slept again beside the horse. When morning came he once more scaled the slide to get him grass, then he resumed his digging. He worked from a different angle this time. It was scarcely ten feet to stony footing. A yard in front of the horse he set to work clearing the mud away. When he got down to the level of the horse's feet he filled the hole with rocks and shale, and packed the sides with shale alone. As the day wore on he gradually worked up to the horse's breast. Two hours before sunset all was ready.

In front of the black horse was a ramp of shale and rocks, a foot high, a yard long, and four feet wide. Jed took the rope, one end of which still formed the hackamore, and ran it into the ravine. He returned to the horse. With his knife and hands he scraped the mud away from one of his mired front legs. As soon as the pressure eased, the horse brought his freed leg to rest on the ramp and he raised his entire body two inches from the mud.

Jed ran back to the ravine. Taking the rope in both hands he pulled gently but steadily. The horse fought the rope a minute before he yielded to it. With a prodigious effort he placed his other forefoot on the ramp, and arching his back, he sent all the elastic strength of his muscles into his mired rear quarters. Jed heaved madly on the rope. The horse cleared the ramp with both front legs; for the first time his belly was clear of the mud. Jed gritted his teeth and pulled, the horse's hind hoofs slid on the ramp. He leaped and threw himself a yard through the mud. His front feet found a wisp of hard footing; he pawed wildly. A second later the black horse scrambled to the stony floor of the ravine.

Jed fell back, and for a few seconds yielded to the fatigue that was upon him. He had slept little and eaten nothing for three days. Dimly he was aware of an immense black beast standing over him, pushing him with its muzzle and nibbling him with its lips.

The horse's mane fell about him. Jed grasped it and pulled himself erect. He could not rest yet. The black horse followed close behind him. He nickered anxiously when Jed climbed over the slide, and pranced playfully when he came back, his arms laden with wild grass.

Half the grass Jed left on top of the slide, the rest he carried into the ravine with him. He took away the hackamore as the horse ate, and fashioned a breast strap in the end of the rope. With utter freedom he dodged under the horse's neck and arranged the crude harness. Then he climbed to the top of the slide for the rest of the grass.

Jed shook his head worriedly as he surveyed the slide; a good team might not move some of the boulders in it. But perhaps the black horse . . . He banished fear from his mind as he hitched the free end of the rope about one of the boulders and with the grass in his arms went to the horse's head.

He patted the horse as it pulled at the hay in his arms. Slowly he backed away. The horse followed, and the rope stretched taut. The black horse stopped and swung his head as he edged nervously sideways. Jed gasped. If the horse fought the harness now he could never get it on him again and he could never get him out of the ravine. Jed stepped close to the horse.

"This way, horse," he murmured. "Look this way. Come this way."

He stepped back again, the grass held out invitingly. The black horse trembled and took a step forward. Pebbles flew from beneath his hooves as he gave all his enormous strength to the task in hand. The tight rope almost hummed. The boulder moved an inch, six inches.

Then, in a steady creeping that did not stop at all, it came away from the slide.

A week later a great black horse appeared in the upper pasture where Tom Raglan was counting his colts. The horse stopped while the tiny, emaciated figure of a man slid from his back. Incredulously Raglan approached them. The horse stood fearlessly behind the wasted man.

"You got him, Jed," Raglan said.

Raglan was no waster of words, but words were not needed. He was unable to tear his eyes away from the horse's massive legs, his splendid head, his flawless body, all the qualities that had here combined to form the perfect living thing.

"I got him, Tom," Jed Hale said, "and I brought him back like I said I would."

Raglan coughed hesitantly. Above all else he was a horseman. There was no need for Jed to tell him of the chase, or how the horse had been captured. Jed's sunken eyes, his skeleton body, his tattered clothes, the fingers from which the nails had been torn, told that story for all who could read. There was a world of difference between himself, the successful stockman, and Jed, the crippled stable hand. But they were brothers by a common bond —the love of a good horse. Raglan coughed again. Jed had indeed brought the horse back, but by all the rules known, the black horse could belong to only one man, the man who had brought him back.

"Jed," Raglan said slowly, "I never went back on my word yet, and I'll stick by the bargain I made. But that horse is no good to me." Jed stood without speaking.

"He'd kill anybody except you, that tried to monkey 'round him," Raglan continued. "I can't risk that. But I'll go a long way to get his blood in my stock. Now there's a house and barn in my north pasture. I'll give both of 'em to you along with fifty acres of ground, if you'll take that horse up there and let me turn my best mares in with him. I can pay you thirty dollars a month, and you can keep every seventh colt. Do you think you'd just as soon do that as to have the five hundred?"

Jed Hale gasped, and put a hand against the black horse's withers to steady himself. The black horse laid his muzzle against

Jed's shoulder. Jed encircled it with an arm. The black horse, the horse that could do anything, was his now. It was a little too much to stand all at once. Suddenly Jed remembered that he was now a hard-boiled stock owner.

"Why, yes," he said finally. "If that's the way you'd rather have it, Tom. Yes, I guess I'd just as soon."

JIM KJELGAARD grew up on a 150-acre farm in the Black Forest region of Pennsylvania. Much of the land was wooded, so that besides taking care of the farm's dairy cattle, horses, and other animals, he and his brothers hunted and trapped right on their own property. Kjelgaard once spent an entire hunting season living in the woods, fishing, hunting and running trap lines. During that time, he gained an understanding of the hardships men face when living in the outdoors, and later wrote about some of them in "The Black Horse."

After high school, Kjelgaard worked at almost any kind of job that would keep him out in the open. He has been a teamster, a surveyor's assistant and a laborer. Of the more than forty books that he has written about dogs, horses, sports and the outdoors, *Big Red,* the story of an Irish setter, is perhaps his most famous.

A strange vengeance

Metzengerstein

BY EDGAR ALLAN POE

A grand master of horror and suspense, Poe was fascinated by the various theories, scientific and pseudo-scientific, of his day. In "Metzengerstein" he uses the idea of reincarnation or the transmigration of souls to create a "horse" story both supernatural and terrifying.

THE Hungarian families of Berlifitzing and Metzengerstein had been at variance for centuries. Never before were two such illustrious houses so mutually embittered by hostility so deadly. The origin of this enmity seems to lie in the words of an ancient prophecy: "A lofty name shall have a fearful fall when, as the rider over his horse, the mortality of Metzengerstein shall triumph over the immortality of Berlifitzing."

To be sure, the words themselves had little or no meaning. But more trivial causes have given rise to consequences equally eventful. Besides the estates, which were contiguous, had long exercised a rival influence in the affairs of a busy government. Moreover, near neighbors are seldom friends, and the inhabitants of the castle Berlifitzing might look from their lofty buttresses into the very windows of the palace Metzengerstein. Nor had the more-than-feudal magnificence of the palace, thus closely viewed, tended to allay the irritable feelings of the less ancient and less wealthy Berlifitzing. What wonder then that the words, however silly, of that prediction should have succeeded in keeping at variance two families, already predisposed to quarrel by every instigation of hereditary jealousy? The prophecy seemed to imply, if it implied anything, a final triumph on the part of the already more powerful house; and was of course remembered with the more bitter animosity by the weaker and less influential.

Wilhelm, Count Berlifitzing, although loftily descended, was at the time of this narrative an infirm and doting old man, remarkable for his inordinate personal antipathy to the family of his rival, and a love of horses and hunting so passionate that neither bodily infirmity and great age nor mental incapacity prevented his daily participation in the dangers of the chase.

Frederick, Baron Metzengerstein, on the other hand, was not yet of age. His father, the Minister G——, died young, and his mother, the Lady Mary, soon followed. Frederick was at that time in his eighteenth year. In a city, eighteen years is no great age, but in a wilderness, in so magnificent a wilderness as that old principality, the pendulum vibrates with deeper meaning.

From some peculiar circumstances attending the administration of his father, the young Baron Metzengerstein, after his father's decease, entered immediately upon his vast possessions.

Such estates were seldom held by a nobleman of Hungary. The baron's castles were without number, the chief, in point of splendor and extent, being the Palace Metzengerstein. The boundary line of his dominions was never clearly defined, but his principal park embraced an area of fifty miles.

On the succession of a proprietor so young and with a character so well known, to a fortune so unparalleled, there was little speculation regarding his probable course of conduct. And indeed, for the space of three days, the behavior of the heir well surpassed the expectations of his most enthusiastic admirers. Shameful debaucheries, flagrant treacheries, unheard-of atrocities, gave his trembling vassals quickly to understand that no servile submission on their part, no punctilios of conscience on his own, were henceforward any security against the remorseless fangs of this petty Caligula. On the night of the fourth day, fire broke out in the stables of the Castle Berlifitzing. The unanimous opinion of the neighborhood added this crime to the already hideous list of the baron's enormities.

But during the tumult occasioned by the flames, the young baron himself sat apparently buried in meditation, in a vast and desolate upper apartment of the family palace of Metzengerstein. The rich although faded tapestry hangings which swung gloomily upon the walls represented the shadowy and majestic forms of a thousand illustrious ancestors. Here, rich ermined priests were familiarly seated with the autocrat and the sovereign; there, the tall, dark figures of the Princes Metzengerstein on their muscular war coursers that plunged over the carcasses of fallen foes, startled the steadiest nerves. Here, again, the voluptuous and swanlike forms of the dames of days gone by floated away in the mazes of an unreal dance to the strains of imaginary melody.

But as the baron listened, or appeared to listen, to the gradually increasing uproar in the stables of Berlifitzing—or perhaps pondered some even more decided act of audacity—his eyes turned unwittingly to the figure of an enormous and unnaturally colored horse, represented in the tapestry as belonging to a Saracen ancestor of the rival Berlifitzing family. The horse itself, in the foreground of the design, stood motionless and statue-like—while farther back, its discomfited rider perished by the dagger of a Metzengerstein.

On Frederick's lip arose a fiendish expression as he became aware of the direction in which his glance had unconsciously turned. Yet he did not look away. And he could not account for the overwhelming anxiety which seemed to fall like a pall upon his senses. It was difficult, in his dreamy state, to be certain he was awake. The longer he gazed, the more absorbed he became—the more impossible did it appear that he could ever tear his eyes from that tapestry. But the tumult without became suddenly more violent, and he forcibly turned his attention to the glare of ruddy light from the flaming stables upon the windows of the apartment.

The action, however, was but momentary; his gaze returned mechanically to the wall. To his extreme horror and astonishment, the head of the gigantic steed had in the meantime altered its position. The neck of the animal, before arched as if in compassion over the prostrate body of its lord, was now extended at full length, in the direction of the baron. The eyes, before invisible, now wore an energetic and human expression, while they gleamed with a fiery and unusual red; and the distended lips of the apparently enraged horse left in full view his sepulchral and disgusting teeth.

Stupefied with terror, the young nobleman tottered to the door. As he threw it open, a flash of red light streaming far into the chamber flung his shadow with a clear outline against the quivering tapestry; and he shuddered to perceive that shadow—

as he staggered awhile upon the threshold—assuming the exact position and the precise contour of his ancestor, the relentless and triumphant murderer of the Saracen Berlifitzing.

To lighten the depression of his spirits Baron Metzengerstein hurried into the open air. He encountered three equerries at the principal gate of the palace. With much difficulty, and at the imminent peril of their lives, they were restraining the wild plunges of a gigantic and fiery-colored horse.

"Whose horse? Where did you get him?" demanded the youth in a querulous and husky tone. He was instantly aware that the mysterious steed in the tapestried chamber was the very counterpart of the furious animal before his eyes.

"He is your own property, sire," replied one of the equerries, "at least he is claimed by no other owner. We caught him flying, all smoking and foaming with rage, from the burning stables of the castle Berlifitzing. Supposing him to have belonged to the old count's stud of foreign horses, we led him back as an estray. But the grooms there disclaim any knowledge of the creature, which is strange, since he bears evident marks of having made a narrow escape from the flames."

"The letters W. V. B. are also branded very distinctly on his forehead," interrupted a second equerry. "I supposed them of course to be the initials of William Von Berlifitzing—but all at the castle are positive they have never seen him before."

"Extremely singular!" said the young baron with a musing air, apparently unconscious of the meaning of his words. "He is, as you say, a remarkable horse, a prodigious horse, although as you very justly observe, of a suspicious and untractable character. Let him be mine, however," he added, after a pause. "Perhaps a rider like Frederick of Metzengerstein may tame even the devil from the stable of Berlifitzing."

"You are mistaken, my lord. The horse, as I think we mentioned, is *not* from the stables of the count. If such had been the case, we know our duty better than to bring him into the presence of a noble of your family."

"True!" observed the baron dryly. At that instant a page of the bedchamber came from the palace with an ashen color and a precipitate step. He whispered into his master's ear a strange account—of the sudden disappearance of a small portion of the tapestry in a certain apartment, entering into particulars of a minute and circumstantial character. But from the low tone of voice in which these details were communicated, nothing escaped to gratify the excited curiosity of the equerries.

During the conference, the young Frederick seemed agitated by various emotions. He soon, however, recovered his composure, and an expression of determined malignancy settled on his countenance as he gave peremptory orders that the apartment in question should be immediately locked up, and the key placed in his own possession.

"Have you heard of the unhappy death of the old hunter Berlifitzing?" said one of his vassals to the baron as, after the departure of the page, the huge steed which that nobleman had adopted as his own plunged and curveted with redoubled fury down the long avenue which extended from the palace to the stables of Metzengerstein.

"No!" said the baron, turning abruptly toward the speaker. "Dead, say you?"

"It is indeed true, my lord; and to a noble of your name it is, I imagine, no unwelcome intelligence."

A rapid smile shot over the countenance of the listener. "How died he?"

"In his rash exertions to rescue a favorite portion of the hunting stud he has himself perished miserably in the flames."

"I-n-d-e-e-d!" ejaculated the baron, as if slowly and deliberately impressed with the truth of some exciting idea.

"Indeed!" repeated the vassal.

"Shocking!" said the youth calmly, and turned quietly into the palace.

From this date a marked alteration took place in the outward demeanor of the dissolute young Baron Frederick von Metzengerstein. Indeed, his behavior disappointed every expectation and little accorded with the views of many a maneuvering mamma. His habits and manner were if anything even less congenial than formerly, with those of the neighboring aristocracy. He was never seen beyond the limits of his own domain, and in his wide and socially limitless world, was utterly companionless—unless indeed that unnatural, impetuous and fiery-colored horse which he henceforward continually rode had any mysterious right to the title of his friend.

Numerous invitations on the part of the neighborhood for a long time, however, periodically came in. "Will the baron honor our festivals with his presence?" "Will the baron join us in a hunting of the boar?"—"Metzengerstein does not hunt," "Metzengerstein will not attend," were the haughty and laconic answers.

These repeated insults were not to be endured by an imperious nobility. Such invitations became less cordial, less frequent; in time they ceased altogether. The widow of the unfortunate Count Berlifitzing was even heard to express a hope that the baron might be at home when he did not wish to be at home, since he disdained the company of his equals; and ride when he did not wish to ride, since he preferred the society of a horse. This, to be sure, was a very silly explosion of hereditary pique, and merely proved how singularly unmeaning our sayings are apt to become when we desire to be unusually energetic.

The charitable, nevertheless, attributed the alteration in the conduct of the young nobleman to the natural sorrow of a son for the untimely loss of his parents—forgetting, however, his atrocious and reckless behavior during the short period immediately succeeding that bereavement. Some, indeed, suggested a too-haughty idea of self-consequence and dignity. Others again (among whom may be mentioned the family physician) did not hesitate in speaking of morbid melancholy and hereditary ill-health; while dark hints of a more equivocal nature were current among the multitude.

Indeed, the baron's perverse attachment to his lately acquired charger—an attachment which seemed to attain new strength from every fresh example of the animal's ferocious and demonlike propensities—at length became, in the eyes of all reasonable men, a hideous and unnatural fervor. In the glare of noon, at the dead hour of night, in sickness or in health, in calm or in tempest, the young Metzengerstein seemed to be riveted to the saddle of that colossal horse, whose intractability so well accorded with the baron's own spirit.

There were circumstances, moreover, which, coupled with late events, gave an unearthly and portentous character to the mania of the rider and to the capabilites of the steed. The space passed over in a single leap had been accurately measured and was found to exceed, by an astounding difference, the wildest expectations of the most imaginative. The baron, besides, had no particular name for the animal, although all the others in his stables bore distinctive names. This horse's stable, too, was at a distance from the rest, and with regard to grooming and other necessary offices, none but the owner in person had ventured to officiate, or even to enter the enclosure of that horse's particular stall.

Furthermore, of the three grooms who had caught the steed as he fled from the conflagration at Berlifitzing, and had succeeded in arresting his course by means of a chain-bridle and noose, not one could with any certainty affirm that he had actually placed his hand upon the beast during that dangerous struggle or at any period thereafter. Instances of peculiar intelligence in the demeanor of a noble and high-spirited horse do not usually excite unreasonable attention, but certain circumstances intruded themselves upon the most skeptical. It is also said there were times when the animal caused the gaping crowd who stood around to recoil in horror from the deep and impressive meaning of his terrible stamp—times when the young Metzengerstein turned pale and shrunk away from the rapid and searching expression of his human-looking eye.

Among all the retinue of the baron, however, none doubted the ardor of that extraordinary affection which existed on the part of the young nobleman for the fiery qualities of his horse; at least, none but an insignificant and misshapen little page, whose deformities were in everybody's way and whose opinions were of the least possible importance. He (if his ideas are worth mentioning at all) had the effrontery to assert that his master never vaulted into the saddle without an unaccountable and almost imperceptible shudder; and that, upon his return from every long-continued and habitual ride, an expression of triumphant malignity distorted every muscle in his countenance.

One tempestuous night, Metzengerstein, awaking from a heavy slumber, descended like a maniac from his chamber, and mounting in hot haste, bounded away into the mazes of the forest. An occurrence so common attracted no particular attention, but his return was awaited with intense anxiety on the part of his domestics, when, after some hours' absence, the stupendous and magnificent battlements of the palace Metzengerstein were discovered crackling and rocking to their very foundation in a dense and livid mass of ungovernable fire.

As the flames when first seen had already made such terrible progress that all efforts to save any portion of the building were evidently futile, the astonished neighborhood stood idly around in silent if not pathetic wonder. But a new and fearful object soon riveted the attention of the multitude, and proved how much more intense is the excitement wrought in the feelings of a crowd by the contemplation of human agony than that brought about by the most appalling spectacles of inanimate matter.

Up the long avenue of aged oaks which led from the forest to the main entrance of the palace Metzengerstein a steed, bearing an unbonneted and disordered rider, was seen leaping with an impetuosity which outstripped the very demon of the tempest.

The career of the horseman was indisputably, on his own part, uncontrollable. The agony of his countenance, the convulsive struggle of his frame gave evidence of superhuman exertion; but no sound save a solitary shriek escaped from his lacerated lips, which were bitten through and through in the intensity of terror. One instant, and the clattering of hoofs resounded sharply and shrilly above the roaring of the flames and the shrieking of the winds—another and, clearing at a single plunge the gateway and the moat, the steed bounded far up the tottering staircases of the palace, and with its rider disappeared amid the whirlwind of chaotic fire.

The fury of the tempest immediately died away, and a dead calm sullenly succeeded. A white flame still enveloped the building like a shroud, and, streaming far away into the quiet atmosphere, shot forth a glare of preternatural light; while a cloud of smoke settled heavily over the battlements in the distinct colossal figure of—*a horse.*

Although EDGAR ALLAN POE was one of our earliest American writers, his horror tales are even more popular today than when he first wrote them. "The Tell-Tale Heart," "The Pit and the Pendulum," "The Cask of Amontillado," and "The Fall of the House of Usher" are familiar to everyone, but the lesser known "Metzengerstein" is an equally thrilling tale of horror and revenge.

Poe was a truly dedicated writer. A thin, tense, almost emaciated figure, he worked feverishly all his short life, never able to overcome the illness and poverty that dogged him. Some physicians believe that a brain lesion from youth on caused his moodiness, his morbid imagination and the violent effects that even slight amounts of alcohol had on him. Yet he wrote with brilliance and clarity, and is now internationally recognized as a fine poet and critic as well as short story writer.

Poe was born in Boston in 1809. His actor parents died when he was three and he was raised by a wealthy merchant in Baltimore named Allan. After several years at school in England, Poe attended the University of Virginia. He then enlisted in the Army to support himself, and was finally sent to West Point. This did not work out, either, and Poe was in dire need when his story "Ms. Found in a Bottle" led to his becoming editor of the Richmond *Messenger*. After frequent quarrels with authors, Poe went on to become a magazine editor in Philadelphia. He had meanwhile married his cousin Virginia, and they lived with his aunt, who was the stabilizing influence in Poe's life. By 1844 the three were settled in New York. Poe Cottage, where Virginia later died, is still standing in the Bronx. All this time Poe was publishing books of poems and stories, writing and lecturing. On one of his lecture trips to Baltimore he was stricken and taken unconscious to the hospital. He died at forty, on the threshold of literary fame.

Easy Does It!

BY ROBERT L. MCGRATH

ROD McLEAN slowly picked himself up out of the dirt of the corral, the laughter of the Diamond Bar hands echoing in his burning ears. At the far side of the enclosure, the young bay horse—Rod's horse—stood still now, trembling with the excitement of what had just happened. "Too soon," Rod said to himself. "I tried to ride him too soon."

"Try 'im again!" urged Hub Watkins, the foreman, from his place on the fence. "Don't let 'im think he can get away with it."

"No," Rod said. "He's not ready."

"Better let somebody else ride 'im that can," the foreman said with a sneer. "He'll never be any good this way."

Rod stopped in the middle of the corral and turned to face the others. "You know what Uncle Caddo promised me, Hub," he said quietly. "I break Lucky my own way. He's not getting any more riding today."

"Told you he was chicken," Rod heard the foreman say, and it hurt—more than being thrown from Lucky had hurt. But Rod chose to ignore it.

He took a long time to unsaddle the bay horse, talking quietly and soothingly all the while, and rubbing the horse down carefully after taking the saddle off. It gave him time to think about all this—time to wonder if maybe he was trying to do something that just wouldn't work.

It all started about a year before. Everything was fine then, or so it seemed. Rod was in high school in a large eastern city —plenty of friends, plenty of activities, everything smooth. And then, just like snapping your finger, everything changed. An auto accident. Mom killed outright. Dad lingering for a week, and then he too passing on. And Rod left with almost nothing except a will that said he was to be placed under the guardianship of his uncle, Caddo McLean, whom Rod had seen only once in his sixteen years. Uncle Caddo was a sort of dream to Rod, who had heard of the Diamond Bar ranch in the West but had never seen it. Not until a year ago, that is.

It wasn't exactly the way he'd pictured it. In his mind, he'd seen beautiful white buildings, well-kept wooden fences, green pastures stretching endlessly across the plains. And when he saw the squat, faded buildings, the drooping barbed-wire fences, the sun-scorched prairies, he couldn't help being disappointed.

Of course, there was good reason for the Diamond Bar to look that way. In his day, Caddo McLean had been one of the best of ranchmen, but years ago he'd taken a bad fall. He'd been a semi-invalid ever since—handling the affairs of the ranch from his wheel chair, but having to depend on others to do the work. And so the proud Diamond Bar had lost some of the luster it once wore.

Rod McLean thought about all of this now, rubbing down Lucky and getting him gentled again after the incident in the corral. It had been a hard year for Rod—a year filled with harder work than he'd ever dreamed possible. But it had its rewards, too. Lucky, for instance. He'd earned ownership of the colt, same as the other hands earned their wages. And long before Lucky was actually his, he'd begun gentling the horse the way he thought an animal ought to be handled.

"Why can't a horse be trained by being kind and gentle to

him?" Rod had asked his Uncle Caddo. "Looks like you'd get lots better results."

Uncle Caddo was gentle and kind himself, always a square shooter. "Guess it's one of the traditions of the West," he said mildly. "Bronc bustin' is something that's been done ever since the first time a man ever straddled a cayuse." He pulled at his pipe thoughtfully. "Reckon you could try it, though," he said. "You pick the colt you want out of that string in the south pasture, and you break him any way you want. You can work out his price."

And that was how it had been. Now, Lucky was his—all his—and it was time he was being broken to ride, the same as the other colts his age. But they were broken by the time-honored bronc-busting routine of being ridden and reridden until they accepted the load.

The worst of the past year had been Hub Watkins. Hub was a good range boss—no doubt of that. But he didn't have much sympathy for the city boy who'd been thrown on the ranch. To Hub, a man not born to the range just didn't fit.

But even though Hub gave him all the unpleasant jobs that nobody else wanted, Rod knew he was learning more every day about how a ranch is run.

One Sunday he was driving Uncle Caddo out across the range in the pickup truck to check the stock. They suddenly came up to the ten palomino mares—the most valuable animals on the ranch.

"Aren't they beauties?" Rod exclaimed. "Just look at those cream-colored manes and tails!"

"Makes life worth livin' to see critters like that," Uncle Caddo said. "Be some more before long, too."

"You mean you're taking some more in for pasture?" Rod asked. The mares, like much of the other stock on the Diamond Bar, belonged to other people, who paid Caddo McLean to look after them.

The old man smiled, a twinkle in his eye. "Wait and see," he suggested.

"Oh—you mean more colts," Rod said. "Boy, isn't Golden Lady a honey?" He pointed to a mare walking toward them.

"Sure is," Uncle Caddo agreed. "Ten thousand bucks worth of horse there, son. Might' near worth her weight in gold."

The rich tan of her body, the slender sturdy legs, the quiet friendliness in her eyes made Golden Lady something out of a picture book as she approached.

"See," Rod said, as she nuzzled his arm. "She likes the way I treat her."

Caddo McLean nodded. "She trusts you," he said. "That's mighty important, sometimes."

On a Saturday afternoon about a month after Lucky had first thrown Rod, he stayed at the ranch instead of tagging along to town with the hands. Putting saddle and bridle on Lucky, he headed for an open pasture some distance from the ranch house, where he could work with the horse by himself. Lucky accepted saddle and bridle without protest and followed Rod without hesitation. In the middle of the open field, Rod gently tested the horse by putting his weight on the stirrup, talking soothingly all the time. Lucky looked around, but seemed not to mind.

Keeping a tight rein, Rod slowly eased his leg over the saddle, keeping his weight on the left stirrup. Lucky looked around again, but with Rod's reassuring hands along his withers, he gave no sign that he intended to buck, bolt, or pitch. In fact, he just stood stock-still, waiting.

"Good boy!" Rod said. "We made it!"

Gently he nudged the horse to a walk, keeping the reins tight lest Lucky suddenly decide to put his head between his legs and lose the weight on his back. But the horse never faltered. Rod urged him into a lope, reined him to both left and right, and let him stretch into a run along the well-worn path back toward the house. And when he pulled back on the reins, Lucky slowed to a walk as though he'd been ridden for years.

Not noticing the darkened clouds scudding across the sky, Rod rubbed his horse down and then rushed into the house to see his uncle. He was unable to conceal his excitement, and old Caddo McLean sensed something unusual at once.

"What is it, boy?" he said. "What's happened?"

"I did it!" Rod fairly shouted. "It worked—just like I thought it would!"

"Now hold on a minute," the old rancher said. "What worked—what did you do that's so all-fired remarkable?"

Panting for breath, Rod explained in quick bursts. "Lucky—I rode him," he said. "Didn't buck! Gentle as a lamb! See, it worked!"

Caddo McLean leaned back and smiled, his mane of white hair giving him an unusual appearance of dignity. "And not the first time," the old man said. "You'll never go wrong by handling any animal with kindness."

Rod started to say more, but the door was flung open and Hub Watkins, his face clouded with anger, burst into the room. "You leave the big gate open?" His words were directed at Rod.

"Why—I—I don't know," Rod faltered. "I had Lucky down in the south pasture. But I—"

"I thought so," the foreman interrupted. "Now we've got a mess on our hands!"

"Just a minute." It was the stern voice of Caddo McLean. "What kind of a mess?"

"Golden Lady," Hub said. "She's due to foal any time, and I had her in the barn lot." He looked meaningfully at Rod. "Now she's gone—and there's a winger of a storm brewin'!"

Rod's heart sank. The pride and joy of the whole ranch—Golden Lady—missing, because he'd left the gate open. And worst of all, she didn't belong to Uncle Caddo. That made her an even bigger responsibility—she and her unborn colt!

"No tellin' where she'll head," Hub went on. His words were punctuated by the distant rumble of thunder rolling across the sky. "Reckon I got a job on my hands now, tryin' to find her an' get her back before the rain hits."

"All right." Caddo McLean was sober, his brow wrinkled in a frown. "Better take Rod with you."

"Ain't no horse in but mine," the foreman said.

"I'll ride Lucky," Rod said quietly. "He's in."

"That good-for-nothin' bronc!" Hub Watkins snorted. "I need help—not a millstone tied on my neck."

"Take the boy along," Caddo McLean said. "Better check those draws by the creek. She might head there."

Without a word, Hub Watkins turned and stalked through the door, with Rod at his heels. The less said the better, Rod thought to himself. I made the mess—now maybe I can help get us out of it.

Stopping only long enough to get his oilskin slicker from his room, Rod went to the barn where he'd left Lucky, and carefully re-saddled the bay horse. Hub, he noticed, was not wasting any time, nor was he waiting for Rod to get ready. He was astride his horse, already cutting across the rolling land east of the ranch house, by the time Rod had Lucky ready to go.

He swung carefully to the bay's back again, uncertain what to expect, but Lucky stool still and waited. Rod spent a moment rubbing the horse's withers, then clucked him to a start and followed after Hub Watkins.

He had barely started across the rolling prairie on Hub's trail when the first giant drops of rain began to pelt down on him, and he knew that if the rain lasted any time at all, Golden Lady could very well be in grave danger. Water running off the slopes of the gullies in the far-flung ranch could create flash floods that would sweep animals or anything else along with them.

Rod nudged Lucky into a gallop, anxious to overtake the Diamond Bar foreman. The rain came faster, with more lightning and thunder, and as he rode, Rod slipped into the slicker. Lucky galloped smoothly along, as though he'd been ridden all his life.

When Rod came abreast of Hub, the foreman said nothing for a time, merely throwing Rod a grim glance through the spattering rain. They rode side by side for a time, and then Hub suddenly veered off to the left.

"Come on," he shouted through the rain. "She probably came off down this way."

Hub was wise in the ways of the range and its animals, Rod knew, and he followed without question. They rode for what seemed an age when Lucky suddenly whinnied and threw his head up and down. Hub pulled his mount to a stop.

"Think we're close to the crick," he announced. "You see anything?"

Rod tried to force himself to see through the heavy rain, but it was no use. Despite frequent flashes of lightning, there was too much water falling for him to see ten feet in front of his nose. Then, through the gloom, came an answering nicker, faint but unmistakable; Lucky shook his head and neighed again.

Hub looked at Rod. "Looks like she's over there somewhere," he said. "Come on!"

But they had gone only a few yards when both horses shied back away from the torrent of water that rushed across their path. "Crick bed," Hub stated. "She's on the other side—got to get her back or we'll lose her sure!"

Rod nodded, uncertain what to say or do.

"Here!" Hub handed Rod the loop of the spare lariat hanging on the back of his saddle. "Hook this on your saddle horn, so I can find my way back."

"Okay." Rod fastened the loop securely and watched while Hub urged his horse toward the churning waters of the creek. But the horse, fearful of the uncertainty of the flooding torrent, backed away. Hub brought his lariat down the horse's rump, he kicked and scolded, but the horse would not step into the current. At last, Hub reined back beside Rod.

"No use," he said. "No horse in his right mind will tackle that stuff. Reckon we better head back up to the bridge."

The only bridge across the creek, Rod knew, was several miles from here—miles that might mean the difference between saving Golden Lady or losing her.

"Let me try it," Rod said quietly. "Maybe Lucky will go across."

The foreman looked skeptical, and for a moment, Rod thought he'd be denied the chance to attempt the crossing. Then, "Won't hurt to try," Hub drawled, and Rod unfastened the lariat from his saddle horn, exchanging the loop for the other end of the rope.

"Come on, Lucky boy," he said, and reined the horse toward the raging waters of the creek bed. How deep it might be, Rod did not know. Normally, the creek was only a trickle. Now, fed by the slashing rain, it was deep, wide, and treacherous.

The horse went willingly to the edge of the water, and there he stopped. "Come on, Lucky," Rod urged. "Come on, boy, we can make it!" Gently, he nudged the bay's ribs with his boots, rubbing the horse's withers with his hands and talking quietly all the time. "Easy, boy, easy does it."

Gingerly, the horse put his left foot into the water, found solid footing, and moved forward. It was slow going, and in only a moment, Rod could feel the water swirling around the horse's legs. Still Lucky moved on, guided by Rod's confident voice. The water deepened, washed over Rod's boots, and filled them with the chill of the flood.

Then, when a blinding flash of lightning crashed nearby, Rod saw a splotch of tan ahead of him, and he knew they'd found Golden Lady. Lucky whinnied again, but moved steadily forward through the water. Then, abruptly, he scrambled up the side of a small island where Golden Lady stood. Beyond lay more of the raging flood waters. There would be no choice but to take the palomino mare back across the way they had come.

And then Rod saw something else. A small, whitish figure nestled at Golden Lady's front feet, and Rod's heart thrilled with surprise. For there were not one, but two animals to return across the churning waters. Golden Lady had foaled, and this tiny object she was licking was her colt. Rod swung to the ground.

Carefully, talking softly, Rod rubbed the palomino mare, gently soothing her and getting her used to him here in the driving rain. He took the lariat hanging from the pommel of the saddle and, shaking out a loop, carefully placed it over the mare's head. Then, using all the care he could there in the wet of the storm, he scooped his arms under the spindly-legged colt and lifted it up.

The colt, for all its small size, was heavy, and Rod wondered for a moment just how he'd get the tiny new life back across the water. But there would be only one way. Somehow, he'd have to get the colt up on the saddle in front of him. He'd have to trust Lucky to carry both him and the foal back across the creek.

He felt a nudge in his ribs, and he spoke softly and reassuringly to the palomino mare watching his every movement. "Easy, Lady," he said. "Everything's okay. Easy now. Whoa, Lucky—whoa, boy."

Thinking about lifting the colt and getting it on the saddle were two different things, Rod found now. It took an almost superhuman effort for him to get the spindly legs up and across the saddle, and Rod was fearful that Lucky might shy away from this new burden. The horse stood his ground, however, and with the colt safely straddled over the saddle, Rod himself swung up, putting his feet in the straps holding the stirrups.

He was thankful then for the lariat that stretched back across the driving rain and the churning creek to where Hub Watkins waited. Carefully, he nudged the bay horse back the way they'd come. There was little need, he found, for the lariat around Golden Lady's neck. The mare would follow her colt, no matter where it went.

Afterward, Rod saw the ride back through the creek as a bad dream. Halfway across, in the deepest part, Lucky slipped and went down. But with the colt to protect, Rod stayed astride the horse, even though the plunging water threatened to tear him and the colt in his arms away from each other and from Lucky. Then the horse found footing again, and moments later Rod saw Hub Watkins loom up out of the murk ahead of him.

"Good work!" Hub said. "Here, let me take the little guy."

"He's all right," Rod said. Now that the worst was over, he wanted to keep Golden Lady's foal himself—to give Lucky all the credit due for the rescue.

They stood there a moment, while Golden Lady nuzzled her colt and satisfied herself that her firstborn was all right. Then Hub reined away from the creek, and the trek back began.

The rain lasted all the way back, and more than once Hub Watkins led them up on ridges to avoid the chance of more flash floods down the gullies. But the wet didn't bother Rod now. Lucky had proved himself to be everything Rod had expected—everything and more.

After bedding down the mare and the colt and rubbing them dry, during which time Hub Watkins said not a word, Rod and the foreman saw to their own horses and then, still without speaking, headed for the ranch house.

The rain had let up some now, and Rod could see the weather-beaten buildings around him with a new sense of pride. This was his life, this was where he belonged—on the Diamond Bar—whether Hub Watkins liked it or not.

They reached the house and went directly to the big room Caddo McLean used as an office. Then, for the first time since Rod brought back the colt and the palomino mare across the creek, the foreman spoke.

"Reckon you can send that wire, Caddo," he said quietly. "Lady's got a mighty nice stud colt—and both in fine shape, thanks to my partner here."

My partner! The words echoed in Rod's ears.

"Trouble?" Caddo McLean asked.

"Oh, just a mite," Hub Watkins said. "Nothin' serious." He turned to Rod McLean. "Any time you and that horse of yours —Lucky, or whatever you call him—want to ride with me, you hop to it," he said. "Takes a lot more than bein' lucky to do what you did!"

He turned and walked out, and Rod's happy smile followed him. "Reckon I better go change my duds," he drawled, and his voice sounded strangely like Hub Watkins'. "Got a mite wet."

"Reckon so." Caddo McLean grinned. "Reckon you'll be one of the regular hands from now on."

When ROBERT McGRATH saw a cowboy friend breaking a string of horses the "easy way," the idea intrigued him. The result of his interest was "Easy Does It!" McGrath, who grew up on a farm in southeastern Colorado, has had a great deal of experience with horses. Since his family's farm didn't have a tractor, he was able to learn a lot of "horse sense" by working with a sturdy draft team in the alfalfa hay and wheat fields. He spent most of the time from age eight to age sixteen astride an "opinionated and rather tired old buckskin" which he loved because the horse was his own.

Though he's now a city dweller in Downey, California, and doesn't have much chance to ride, his inborn affection for horses is expressed in all his writings.

Killer or champion?

The Winning of Dark Boy

BY JOSEPHINE NOYES FELTS

"I DON'T believe it. I just don't believe it!" whispered Ginger Grey to herself as she watched Dark Boy, the beautiful black steeplechaser, going round and round on the longe, the training rope to which he was tethered in the O'Malleys' yard. She was stroking him with her eyes, loving every curve, every flowing muscle of his slender, shining body.

But the voice of Tim O'Malley, Dark Boy's owner, still echoed in her ears. "You're a brave little horsewoman, Ginger, but Dark Boy would kill you. I'm getting rid of him next week. He's thrown three experienced men and run away twice since I've had him. You are not to get on him!"

Ginger wiped a rebellious tear from her cheek, looking quickly around to make sure that neither ten-year-old Tommy nor the two younger children had seen her. She was alone at the O'Malley farm, several miles away from home, looking after the O'Malley children for the day while their father and mother were in town. Why couldn't she have had the exercising and training of this glorious horse! Her heart ached doubly, for she longed to ride him next week in the horse show at Pembroke.

Ginger glanced now at the two little girls playing in the yard. They needed their noses wiped. She took care of this, patted them gently, and went back to where Dark Boy was loafing at the end of the longe. He didn't seem to mind the light saddle she had put on him. The reins of the bridle trailed the ground. She must go soon and take it off. He'd had a good workout today, she thought with satisfaction. Exercise was what he needed. And now with nobody riding him . . .

She shivered suddenly and noticed how much colder it had turned. A great bank of black clouds had mounted up over the woods behind the meadow. She studied the clouds anxiously. Bad storms sometimes rose quickly out of that corner of the sky. The air seemed abnormally still, and there was a weird copper light spreading from the west.

If it was going to storm she'd better get the children in the house, put Dark Boy in the barn, and find Tommy. Here came Tommy now, dirty, tousled, one leg of his jeans torn and flapping as he walked.

"Barbed wire," he explained cheerfully, pointing to his pants. "Zigafoos has fenced his fields with it!"

A sharp gust of wind rounded the house. Tommy flapped in it like a scarecrow. A shutter on the house banged sharply; the barn door creaked shrilly as it slammed. Dark Boy reared and thudded to the ground.

"Look!" yelled Tommy suddenly. "What a close funny cloud!"

A thin spiral of smoke was rising from behind O'Malleys'

barn. Ginger's heart froze within her. Fire! She raced around the barn. Then she saw with horror that the lower part of that side was burning. The wind must have blown a spark from a smoldering trash pile. Already the blaze was too much for anything she and Tommy could do. She'd have to get help at once!

As she tore back toward the house, pictures flashed through her mind. The big red fire truck was in the village six miles down the road. There were no phones. Any cars in the scattered neighborhood would be down in the valley with the men who used them to get to work at the porcelain factory. She'd have to get to the village and give the fire alarm herself immediately. Perhaps on Dark Boy . . .

She dashed over to him and caught his bridle. He tossed his head and sidled away from her, prancing with excitement. As she talked quietly to him, with swift fingers she loosened the longe, letting it fall to the ground. She felt sure that she could guide him if only she could get on him and stay on him when he bolted. She thrust her hand deep in her pocket and brought out two of the sugar lumps she had been saving for him.

"Sugar for a good boy," she panted and reached up to his muzzle. Dark Boy lipped the sugar swiftly, his ears forward.

With a flying leap Ginger was up, had swung her right leg over him and slipped her right foot in the stirrup. She sat lightly forward as jockeys do. Would he resent her? Throw her off? Or could she stick?

Indignant, Dark Boy danced a wide circle of astonishment. The wind was whistling furiously now around the house, bending the trees. Ginger held the reins firmly and drew Dark Boy to a prancing halt. Then, suddenly, he reared. She clung with her lithe brown knees and held him tight. Precious minutes were flying. She thought of the bright tongues of flame licking up the side of the barn.

"Tommy! Take care of the children!" she shouted over

her shoulder as Dark Boy angrily seized the bit between his teeth and whirled away. "I'll get help!"

Ginger's light figure in a red blob of sweater flashed down the road through the twisting trees. Fast as Dark Boy's bright hooves beat a swift rhythm on the hard clay road, Ginger's thoughts raced ahead. She glanced at her watch. By the road it was six miles to the town. At Dark Boy's throbbing gallop they might make it in fifteen minutes. By the time the fire department got back it might well be much too late.

There was a crash like thunder off in the woods to her left as the first dead tree blew down. Dark Boy shied violently, almost throwing her headlong, but she bent lower over his neck and clung. Suddenly her heart stiffened with dread. What had she done! She'd been wrong to leave the children. Suppose Tommy took them into the house, and the house caught fire from the barn! She hadn't thought of the wind and the house. She'd only thought of saving the barn!

Desperately she pulled at Dark Boy's mouth. But he was going at a full runaway gallop, the bit between his teeth. Stop now? Go back? No!

There was one way that she might save precious seconds: take him across the fields, the short cut, the way the children went to school. That way it was only two miles! There were fences between the fields, but Dark Boy was a steeplechaser and trained to jump. She'd have to take a chance on jumping him now. They thundered toward the cutoff.

Peering ahead for fallen trees as the branches groaned and creaked above her, she guided him into the little lane that ran straight into a field where the main road turned sharply. Now he was responding to her touch, his great muscles flowing under his glossy coat like smoothly running water. She held him straight toward the stile at the far end of the field. Here was the place to take their first jump. Would he shy before it and make them lose the moments they were saving? Or would he take it smoothly?

She leaned anxiously forward and patted Dark Boy's silky neck. "Straight into it, beautiful! Come on, Boy!"

Dark Boy laid back an ear as he listened. A few yards ahead of the stile she tightened the reins, lifted his head, and rose lightly in the stirrups. Dark Boy stretched out his neck, left the ground almost like a bird, she thought. His bright hooves cleared the stile.

"Wonderful, beautiful Boy!" Ginger cried as they thudded on.

Now to the second fence! Over it they went, smooth as silk. Her heart lifted.

Down below them in the valley the little town of Honeybrook flashed in and out of sight behind the tortured trees. She thought briefly of the steep bank from the lower field onto the road below. What would Dark Boy do there? Would he go to pieces and roll as horses did sometimes to get down steep banks? Or could she trust him, count on his good sense, hold him firmly while he put his feet together and slid with her safely to within reach of the fire alarm?

They were headed now across a rounded field. Dark Boy lengthened his glistening neck, stretched his legs in a high gallop. Just then, irrelevantly, Tommy flashed into Ginger's mind, his torn jeans flapping in the wind. "Barbed wire! Oh, Dark Boy!"

Here was a danger she had not considered, a danger that stretched straight across their path, one she could not avoid! The lower end of Zigafoos' field, the one they were crossing now at such headlong speed, was fenced with it. Dark Boy couldn't possibly see it! This time she would be helpless to lift him to the jump. He'd tear into it, and at this pace he would be killed. She would never give her warning. Her heart beating wildly, she pulled the reins up to her chest.

"This way, Boy!" turning his head.

He curved smoothly. There weren't two of them now; horse and rider were one. They made the wide circle of the field. First at a gallop, then dropping to a canter and a walk. She stopped him just in time. He was quivering, shaking his head, only a few feet from the nearly invisible, vicious wire. As she slid to her feet the wind threw her against him.

"Here, Boy, come on," she urged breathlessly. Dark Boy, still trembling, followed her. She skinned out of her sweater and whipped its brilliant red over the barbed wire, flagging it for him. "There it is, Boy, now we can see it!"

Dark Boy was breathing heavily. Without protest this time, he let her mount. She dug her heels into his flanks and put him back into a gallop for the jump. Amid a thunder of hooves she took him straight for the crimson marker. Dark Boy lifted his feet almost daintily, stretched out his head, and they were clear!

He galloped now across the sloping field. "Good Boy, good Boy!" she choked, patting his foaming withers as he stretched out on the last lap of their race against fire and time.

The wind was still sharp in her face, but the terrifying black clouds had veered to the south, traveling swiftly down the Delaware valley. She could see distinctly the spire of the old church rising above the near grove of trees. How far beneath them it still seemed! That last fifty feet of the trail they would have to slide.

"Come on!" she urged, holding the reins firmly, digging her heels into his flanks to get one last burst of speed from his powerful frame. They flew along the ledge. Ahead in the clearing she could see the long bank that dropped to the road leading into the town. Just under top runaway speed but breathing hard, Dark Boy showed that the race was telling on him. With gradual pressure she began to pull him in.

"Slow, Boy, slow," she soothed. "You're doing fine! Don't overshoot the mark. Here we are, old fellow. Slide!"

His ears forward, his head dipped, looking down, quivering in every inch of his spent flanks, Dark Boy responded to the pressure of her knees and hands. Putting his four feet together, he half slid, half staggered down the bank and came to a quivering stop on the empty village street not ten feet from the great iron ring that gave the fire alarm. He was dripping and covered with foam.

As Ginger's hand rose and fell with the big iron clapper, the clang of the fire alarm echoed, and people ran to their doors. The alarm boomed through the little covered bridge up to Smith's machine shop. The men working there heard it, and dropping their tools, came running, not bothering to take off their aprons. It rang out across Mrs. Harnish's garden. Mr. Harnish and the oldest Harnish boy heard it and vaulted lightly over the fence, then ran, pulling on their coats.

While the big red engine roared out of the Holms' garage and backed up toward the canal bridge to get under way, Ginger called out the location of the fire. She fastened Dark Boy securely to a fence and climbed into the fire truck. They roared away up the hill.

Ginger looked at her watch again. In just eight minutes she and Dark Boy had made their race through the storm. It seemed eight hours! A few more minutes would tell whether or not they had won.

"Please, God," Ginger whispered, "take care of Tommy and the girls!"

They slowed briefly at Erwin's corner to pick up two more volunteers, then sent the big red truck throbbing up Turtle Hill. Tears trickled down between Ginger's fingers. Ned Holm threw an arm gently around her shoulders.

"Good girl!" he said smiling at her reassuringly. "We go the hill up! We get there in time!"

Ginger shook the tears from her eyes and thanked him with

a smile. But at the wheel Rudi set his lips in a grim line as he gave the truck all the power it had and sent it rocking over the rough road. The siren screamed fatefully across the valley. A barn can burn in little time and catch a house, too, if the wind is right, and this wind was right!

"How'd you come?" he growled.

"Across the fields—on Dark Boy."

"Dark Boy!" Rudi's eyes narrowed and he held them fixed on the road as he steered.

Ned Holm gasped. "You mean that steeplechaser nobody can stay on?"

"I stayed on!"

They rounded the turn at the top of the hill. Now they could see the great black cloud of smoke whirling angrily over the O'Malleys' trees. As they came to a throbbing stop in the O'Malleys' yard and the men set up the pump at the well, a corner of the house burst into flames. Five minutes more and . . . !

Tommy ran panic-stricken toward them. The barn was blazing fiercely now and in a little while all that would be left of it would be the beautiful Pennsylvania Dutch stonework. A stream of water played over the house. Sparks were falling thick and fast but the stream was soaking the shingles.

Ginger caught Tommy in her arms. "Where are the kids?" she shouted.

"In—in the house. I carried them up and then put the fence at the stairs. They don't like it much!"

Ned Holm ran with Ginger up the steep, narrow stairs and helped her carry out the squirming, indignant children.

That night when the fire was out and the big O'Malleys were home, the little O'Malleys safely in bed, Ginger at home told her mother all about the day. She was a little relieved that nobody scolded her about riding Dark Boy. Her mother just cried a little and hugged her.

Next morning they saw Tim O'Malley riding Dark Boy up the Greys' lane. Ginger raced out to meet him. Tim swung down and led the black horse up to Ginger.

"Here's your horse," he said simply. "You've won him!"

Ginger stared at him speechless.

Tim went on. "I want you to ride Dark Boy next week in the Pembroke show. And I expect you to win!"

"We'll try, sir," said Ginger.

JOSEPHINE NOYES FELTS is familiar with the beautiful Delaware valley which is the locale of "The Winning of Dark Boy." As the story demonstrates, she knows the dangers of a fire such as the one that destroyed the fine old Pennsylvania Dutch barn in the story, and she shows her sympathetic realization of a teen-aged babysitter's problems as well as her love and understanding of both children and horses. Ginger Grey's anxiety and heroic effort are as real as the "iron ring" alarm that could once be seen at village crossroads, as real as the community spirit that still exists in a country town in time of crisis.

"The Winning of Dark Boy" was originally published in *Calling All Girls* magazine in 1945.

Faith in a "worthless" colt

The Horse of the Sword

MANUEL BUAKEN

BOY, get rid of that horse," said one of the wise old men from Abra, where the racing horses thrive on the good Bermuda grass of the Luzon uplands. "That's a bandit's horse. See that sign of evil on him? Something tragic will happen to you if you keep him."

But another one of the old horse traders who had gathered at that auction declared, "That's a good omen. The sword he bears on his shoulder means leadership and power. He's a true mount for a chieftain. He's a free man's fighting horse."

As for me, I knew this gray colt was a wonder horse the moment I saw him. These other people were blind. They only saw that this gray shaggy horse bore the marks of many whips, that his ribs almost stuck through his mangy hide, that his great eyes rolled in defiance and fear as the auctioneer approached him. They couldn't see the meaning of that sword he bore—a marking not in the color, which was a uniform gray, but in the way that the hair had arranged itself permanently; it was parted to form an outline of a sword that was broad on his neck and tapered to a fine point on his shoulder.

Father, too, was blind against this horse. He argued with me and scolded: "Maning, when I promised you a pony as a reward for good work in high school English, I thought you'd use good judgment in choosing. It is true this horse has good blood, for he came from the Santiago stables—they have raised many fine racers, but this colt has always been worthless. He is bad-tempered, would never allow himself to be bathed and curried, and no one has ever been able to ride him. Now, that black over there is well trained—"

"Father, you promised I could choose for myself," I insisted. "I choose this horse. None of them can tame him, but I can. He's wild because his mouth is very tender—see how it has bled. That's his terrible secret."

My father always kept his promises, so he paid the few pesos they asked for this outlaw colt and made arrangements to have the animal driven, herded, up to our summer home in the hills.

"I used to play, but now I have work to do," I told father. "I'll show you and everybody else what a mistake you made about my horse."

Father agreed with me solemnly and smiled over my head at mother, but she wasn't agreeing at all. "Don't you go near that bad horse your father foolishly let you buy. You know he has kicked so many people."

It hurt me to disobey mother, and I consoled myself with the thought she'd change her mind when I had tamed my Horse of the Sword.

But could I win where all others, smart grown men, had failed? I could, if I was right. So early in the morning I slipped off to the meadow. The Horse of the Sword was cropping the grass industriously, but defiantly, alert for any whips. He snorted a warning at me, and backed away skittishly as I approached. "What a body you have," I said, talking to accustom him to my voice and to assure him of my peaceful intentions. "Wide between the shoulders—that's for strength and endurance. Long legs for speed, and a proud arched neck—that's some Arabian aristocracy you have in you, Sword Horse."

I kept walking slowly toward him and talking softly until he stopped backing away. He neighed defiance at me and his eyes rolled angrily, those big eyes that were so human in their dare and their appeal. He didn't move now as I inched closer, but I could see his muscles twitch. Very softly and gently I put my hand on his shoulder. He jumped away. I spoke softly and again put my hand on the sword of his shoulder. This time he stood. I kept my hand on his shaggy shoulder. Then slowly I slipped it up to his head, then down again to his shoulder, down his legs to his fetlocks. It was a major victory.

That very day I began grooming him, currying his coat, getting out the collection of insects that had burrowed into his skin. He sometimes jumped away but he never kicked at me. And next day I was able to lead my gray horse across the meadow to the spring, with my hand on his mane as his only guide—this "untamable outlaw" responded to my light touch. It was the simple truth: his mouth was too tender for a jerking bridle bit. The pain just drove him wild; that's all that had made him an outlaw. Gentle handling, no loud shouts, no jerks on his tender mouth, good food and a cleaned skin—these spelled health and contentment. Kindness had conquered. In a few days the gaunt hollows filled out with firm flesh to give the gray horse beauty. Reckless spirit he always had.

Every morning I slipped off to the meadow—mother was anxious to have the house quiet so father could write his pamphlet on the language and Christianization of the Tinggians, so I had a free hand. It didn't take more than a month to change my find from a raging outlaw to a miracle of glossy horseflesh. But was his taming complete? Could I ride him? Was he an outlaw at heart?

In the cool of a late afternoon, I mounted to his back. If he threw me I should be alone in my defeat and my fall would be cushioned by the grass. He trembled a little as I leaped to his back. But he stood quiet. He turned his head, his big eyes questioning me. Then, obedient to my *"Kiph"*—"Go"—he trotted slowly away.

I knew a thrill then, the thrill of mastery and of fleet motion on the back of this steed whose stride was so smooth, so much like flying. He ran about the meadow eagerly, and I turned him into the mountain lane. "I know how a butterfly feels as he skims along," I crowed delightedly. Down the lane where the trees made dappled shade around our high-roofed bungalow we flew along. Mother stood beside her cherished flame tree, watching sister Dominga as she pounded the rice.

The Horse of the Sword pranced into the yard. Mother gasped in amazement. "Mother, I disobeyed you," I blurted out quickly. "I'm sorry, but I had to show you, and you were wrong, everybody was wrong about this horse."

Mother tried to be severe with me, but soon her smile warmed me and she said, "Yes, I was wrong, Maning. What have you named your new horse?"

"A new name for a new horse, that's a good idea. Mother, you must name him."

Mother's imagination was always lively. It gave her the name at once. "Glory, that's his name. *Moro Glorioso.* Gray Glory." So Moro Glory it was.

Too soon, vacation was over and I had to go back to school. But Moro Glory went with me. "You take better care of that horse than you do of yourself," father complained. "If you don't stop neglecting your lessons, I'll have the horse taken up to the mountain pasture again."

"Oh, no, Father, you can't do that," I exclaimed. "Moro Glory must be here for his lessons too. Every day I teach him and give him practice so the next spring, at the *feria,* he is going to show his heels to all those fine horses they boast about so much."

Father knew what I meant. Those boasts had been mosquito bites in his mind too, for our *barrio* of Santa Lucia was known to be horse-crazy.

For instance, it was almost a scandal the way the priest, Father Anastacio, petted his horse Tango. Tango ate food that was better than the priest's, they said. He was a beauty, nobody denied that, but the good Father's boasts were a little hard to take, especially for the presidente.

The presidente had said in public, "My Bandirado Boyo is a horse whose bloodlines are known all the way back to an Arabian stallion imported by the conquistadores—these others are mere plow animals."

But the horse that really set the tongues wagging in Santa Lucia and in Candon was Allahsan, a gleaming sorrel who belonged to Bishop Aglipay and was said to share the bishop's magic power. There were magic wings on his hooves, it was said, that let him carry the bishop from Manila to Candon in one flying night.

Another boaster was the municipal treasurer—the *tesero,* who had recently acquired a silver-white horse, Purao, the horse with the speed and power of the foam-capped waves.

The chief of police hung his head in shame now. His Castano had once been the pride of Santa Lucia, had beaten Katarman—the black satin horse from the nearby barrio of Katarman who had so often humbled Santa Lucia's pride. Much as the horses of Santa Lucia set their owners to boasting against one another, all united against Katarman. Katarman, so the tale went, was so enraged if another horse challenged him that he ran until the muscles of his broad withers parted and blood spattered from him upon his rider, but he never faltered till his race was won.

These were the boasts and boasters I had set out to dust with defeat.

Winter was soon gone, the rice harvested, the sugar cane milled, and high school graduation was approaching. At last came the feria day, and people gathered, the ladies in sheer flowing gowns of many colors, the men in loose flowing shirts over cool white trousers. Excitement was a wild thing in the wind at the feria, for news of the challenge of the wonder horse Moro Glory had spread. I could hear many people shouting *"Caballo a Bintuangin*—The Horse of the Sword." These people were glad to see the once-despised outlaw colt turn by magic into the barrio's pride. They were cheering for my horse, but the riders of the other horses weren't cheering. I was a boy, riding an untried yet much feared horse. They didn't want me there, so they raised the entrance fee. But father had fighting blood also, and he borrowed the money for the extra fee.

As we paraded past the laughing, shouting crowds in the plaza, the peddlers who shouted *"Sinuman*—delicious *cascarones,"* stopped selling these coconut sweets and began to shout the praises of their favorite. I heard them calling: "Allahsan for me. Allahsan has magic hooves." The people of Katarman's village were very loud. They cried out, "Katarman will win. Katarman has the muscles of the carabao. Katarman has the speed of the deer."

The race was to be a long-distance trial of speed and endurance, run on the Provincial Road for a race track. A mile down to the river, then back to the judge's stand in the plaza.

Moro Glory looked them over, all the big-name horses. I think he measured his speed against them and knew they didn't have enough. I looked them over too. I was so excited, yet I knew I must be on guard as the man who walks where the big snakes hide. These riders were experienced; so were their horses. Moro Glory had my teaching only. I had run him this same course many times. Moro Glory must not spend his strength on the first mile; he must save his speed for a sprint. In the high school, I had made the track team. An American coach had taught me, and I held this teaching in my head now.

The starter gave his signal and the race began. Allahsan led out at a furious pace; the other horses set themselves to overtake him. It hurt my pride to eat the dust of all the others—all the way out the first mile. I knew it must be done. "Oomh, easy," I commanded, and Moro Glory obeyed me as always. We were last, but Moro Glory ran that mile feather-light on his feet.

At the river's bank all the horses turned quickly to begin the fateful last mile. The flagman said, "Too late, boy," but I knew Moro Glory.

I loosened the grip I held and he spurted ahead in flying leaps. In a few space-eating strides he overtook the tiring Allahsan. The pace-setter was breathing in great gasps. "Where are your magic wings?" I jeered as we passed.

"Kiph," I urged Moro Glory. I had no whip. I spoke to my horse and knew he would do his best. I saw the other riders lashing their mounts. Only Moro Glory ran as he willed.

Oh, it was a thrill, the way Moro Glory sped along, flew along, his hooves hardly seeming to touch the ground. The wind whipped at my face and I yelled just for pleasure. Moro Glory thought I was commanding more speed and he gave it. He flattened himself closer to the ground as his long legs reached forward for more and more. Up, and up. Past the strong horses from Abra, past the bright Tango. Bandirado Boyo was next in line. "How the presidente's daughter will cry to see her Bandirado Boyo come trailing home, his banner tail in the dust," I said to myself as Moro Glory surged past him. The tesero's Purao yielded his place without a struggle.

Now there was only Katarman, the black thunder horse ahead, but several lengths ahead. Could Moro Glory make up this handicap in this short distance? Already we were at the big mango tree—this was the final quarter.

"Here it is, Moro Glory. This is the big test." I shouted. "Show Katarman how your sword conquers him."

Oh, yes, Moro Glory could do it. And he did. He ran shoulder to shoulder with Katarman.

I saw that Katarman's rider was swinging his whip wide. I saw it come near to Moro Glory's head. I shouted to the man and the wind brought his answering curse at me. I must decide now—decide between Moro Glory's danger and the winning of the race. That whip might blind him. I knew no winning was worth that. I pulled against him, giving up the race.

Moro Glory had always obeyed me. He always responded to my lightest touch. But this time my sharp pull at his bridle brought no response. He had the bit between his teeth. Whip or no whip, he would not break his stride. And so he pulled ahead of Katarman.

"Moro Glory—the Horse of the Sword," the crowd cheered as the gray horse swept past the judges, a winner by two lengths.

I leaped from his back and caught his head. Blood streamed down the side, but his eyes were unharmed. The sword on his shoulder was touched with a few drops of his own blood.

Men also leaped at Katarman, dragged his rider off and punished him before the judges could interfere. The winner's wreath and bright ribbon went to Moro Glory, and we paraded in great glory. I was so proud. The Horse of the Sword had run free, without a whip, without spurs. He had proved his leadership and power. He had proved himself "a true mount for a chieftain, a free man's fighting horse," as the old wise man had said.

Golden days followed for Moro Glorioso. Again and again we raced—in Vigan, in Abra, and always Moro Glory won.

Then came the day when my father said, "The time has come for you, my son, to prove your sword, as Moro Glory proved his. You must learn to be a leader," father said.

And so I sailed away to America, to let the world know my will. As Moro Glory had proved himself, so must I.

MANUEL BUAKEN'S moving story about a boy and a great racer is undoubtedly based on an incident from his early youth in the Philippines, and vividly portrays the people and life of his village as well as his feeling for horses. Buaken was born on those islands and educated in American Universities. He joined the First Filipino Infantry of the United States Army in 1943, the year his story first appeared in *Asia Magazine*. It has since been included in *A World of Great Stories,* edited by Haydn and Cournos, as well as in the present volume.

The Adventures of Black Beauty

BY ANNA SEWELL

The following selections are from the famous book, Black Beauty, *written in an age when horses were almost the only means of transport. Important historically as an eloquent plea for a wiser, more humane treatment of horses, it is, above all, a powerful and moving account of a spirited horse who faced life's ups and downs with stoic courage.*

1. A RUNAWAY HORSE

EARLY in the spring, Lord W— and part of his family went up to London. Ginger and I and some other horses were left at home for use, and the head groom was left in charge.

The Lady Harriet, who remained at the Hall, was a great invalid and never went out in the carriage, and the Lady Anne preferred riding on horseback with her brother or cousins. She was a perfect horsewoman, and as gay and gentle as she was beautiful. She chose me for her horse and named me Black Auster. I enjoyed these rides very much in the clear cold air, sometimes with Ginger, sometimes with Lizzie. This Lizzie was a bright bay mare, almost thoroughbred, and a great favorite with the gentlemen, on account of her fine action and lively spirit. But Ginger, who knew more of her than I did, told me she was rather nervous.

There was a gentleman of the name of Blantyre staying at the Hall; he always rode Lizzie, and praised her so much that one day Lady Anne ordered the sidesaddle to be put on her, and the other saddle on me. When we came to the door, the gentleman seemed very uneasy.

"How is this?" he said. "Are you tired of your good Black Auster?"

"Oh! no, not at all," she replied, "but I am amiable enough to let you ride him for once, and I will try your charming Lizzie. You must confess that in size and appearance she is far more like a lady's horse than my own favorite."

"Do let me advise you not to mount her," he said. "She is a charming creature, but she is too nervous for a lady. I assure you she is not perfectly safe; let me beg you to have the saddles changed."

"My dear cousin," said Lady Anne laughing, "pray do not trouble your good careful head about me. I have been a horsewoman ever since I was a baby, and I have followed the hounds a great many times, though I know you do not approve of ladies hunting. But still that is the fact, and I intend to try this Lizzie that you gentlemen are all so fond of; so please help me to mount like the good friend you are."

There was no more to be said; he assisted her carefully onto the saddle, looked to the bit and curb, gave the reins gently into her hand, and then mounted me. Just as we were moving off a footman came out with a slip of paper and message from the Lady Harriet. "Would they ask this question for her at Dr. Ashley's and bring the answer?"

The village was about a mile off, and the doctor's house was the last one in it. We went along gaily enough till we came to his gate. There was a short drive up to the house between tall evergreens. Blantyre alighted at the gate and was going to open it for Lady Anne, but she said, "I will wait for you here; you can hang Auster's rein on the gate."

He looked at her doubtfully. "I will not be five minutes," he said.

"Oh, do not hurry yourself. Lizzie and I shall not run away from you."

He hung my rein on one of the iron spikes and was soon hidden among the trees. Lizzie was standing quietly by the side of the road a few paces off with her back to me. My young mistress was sitting easily with a loose rein, humming a little song. I listened to my rider's footsteps until they reached the house, and heard him knock at the door. There was a meadow on the opposite side of the road, the gate of which stood open. Just then some cart horses and several young colts came trotting out in a very disorderly manner, while a boy behind was cracking a great whip. The colts were wild and frolicsome, and one of them bolted across the road and blundered up against Lizzie's hind legs; and whether it was the stupid colt or the loud cracking of the whip or both together, I cannot say, but she gave a violent kick and dashed off into a headlong gallop. It was so sudden that Lady Anne was nearly unseated, but she soon recovered herself. I gave a loud, shrill neigh for help; again and again I neighed, pawing the ground impatiently and tossing my head to get the rein loose. I had not long to wait. Blantyre came running to the gate; he looked anxiously about and just caught sight of the flying figure, now far away on the road. In an instant he sprang to the saddle. I needed no whip or spur, for I was as eager as my rider; he saw it, and giving me a free rein and leaning a little forward, we dashed after them.

For about a mile and a half the road ran straight and then bent to the right, after which it divided into two roads. Long before we came to the bend they were out of sight. Which way had they turned? A woman was standing at her garden gate, shading her eyes with her hand and looking eagerly up the road. Scarcely drawing the rein Blantyre shouted, "Which way?" "To the right," cried the woman, pointing with her hand, and away we went up the right-hand road; then for a moment we caught sight of them; another bend and they were hidden again. Several times we caught glimpses and then lost them. We scarcely seemed to gain ground upon them at all. An old road mender was standing near a heap of stones, his shovel lying on the ground and his hand raised. As we came near he made a sign to speak. Blantyre drew rein a little. "To the common, to the common, sir; she has turned off there." I knew this common very well; it was for the most part very uneven ground, covered with heather and dark green furze bushes, with here and there a scrubby old thorn tree; there were also open spaces of fine short grass, with anthills and mole turns everywhere. It was the worst place I ever knew for a headlong gallop.

We had hardly turned on the common when we caught sight again of the green habit flying on before us. My lady's hat was gone, and her long brown hair was streaming behind her. Her head and body were thrown back as if she were pulling with all her remaining strength, and as if that strength were nearly exhausted. It was clear that the roughness of the ground had very much lessened Lizzie's speed, and there seemed a chance that we might overtake her.

While we were on the highroad Blantyre had given me my head, but now, with a light hand and a practiced eye he guided me over the ground in such a masterly manner that my pace was scarcely slackened, and we were decidedly gaining on them.

About halfway across the heath there had been a wide dyke recently cut, and the earth from the cutting was cast up roughly on the other side. Surely this would stop them! but no; with scarcely a pause Lizzie took the leap, stumbled among the rough clods and fell. Blantyre groaned, "Now, Auster, do your best!" He gave me a steady rein. I gathered myself well together and with one determined leap cleared both dyke and bank.

Motionless among the heather, with her face to the earth, lay my poor young mistress. Blantyre kneeled down and called her name. There was no sound. Gently he turned her face upward. It was ghastly white, and the eyes were closed. "Annie, dear Annie, do speak!" but there was no answer. He unbuttoned her habit, loosened her collar, felt her hands and wrists, then started up and looked wildly around him for help.

At no great distance, two men had been cutting turf; upon seeing Lizzie running wild without a rider they had left their work to catch her.

Blantyre's halloo soon brought them to the spot. The foremost man looked troubled and asked what he could do.

"Can you ride?"

"Well, sir, I bean't much of a horseman, but I'd risk my neck for the Lady Anne; she was uncommon good to my wife in the winter."

"Then mount this horse, my friend—your neck will be quite safe—and ride to the doctor's and ask him to come instantly—then on to the Hall. Tell them all that you know, and bid them send me the carriage with Lady Anne's maid and help. I shall stay here."

"All right, sir, I'll do my best, and I pray God the dear young lady may open her eyes soon." Then, seeing the other man, he called out, "Here, Joe, run for some water and tell my missus to come as quick as she can to the Lady Anne."

He then somehow scrambled into the saddle, and with a "Gee-up" and a clap on my sides with both his legs he started on his journey, making a little circuit to avoid the dyke. He had no whip, which seemed to trouble him, but my pace soon cured that difficulty, and he found the best thing he could do was to stick to the saddle and hold me in, which he did manfully. I shook him as little as I could help, but once or twice on the rough ground he called out, "Steady! Whoa! Steady!" On the highroad we were all right, and at the doctor's and the Hall he did his errand like a good man and true. They asked him in to take a drop of something. "No, no!" he said, "I'll be back to 'em again by a short cut through the fields and be there afore the carriage."

There was a great deal of hurry and excitement after the news became known. I was just turned into my box, the saddle and the bridle were taken off, and a cloth thrown over me.

Ginger was saddled and sent off in great haste for Lord George, and I soon heard the carriage roll out of the yard.

It seemed a long time before Ginger came back and before we were left alone; and then she told me all that she had seen.

"I can't tell much," she said. "We went at a gallop nearly all the way and got there just as the doctor rode up. There was a woman sitting on the ground with the lady's head in her lap. The doctor poured something into her mouth, but all that I heard was, 'She is not dead.' Then I was led off by a man to a little distance. After a while she was taken to the carriage, and we came home together. I heard my master say to a gentleman who stopped him to inquire, that he hoped no bones were broken but that she had not spoken yet."

Two days after the accident, Blantyre paid me a visit. He patted me and praised me very much; he told Lord George that he was sure the horse knew of Annie's danger as well as he did. "I could not have held him in if I would," said he. "She ought never to ride any other horse." I found by their conversation that my young mistress was now out of danger and would soon be able to ride again. This was good news to me, and I looked forward to a happy life.

Through the carelessness of a drunken groom Black Beauty has a bad fall, which ruins his knees and his appearance as a gentleman's horse. He is thereupon put up for sale.

2. A HORSE FAIR

No doubt a horse fair is a very amusing place to those who have nothing to lose; at any rate, there is plenty to see.

Long strings of young horses out of the country, fresh from the marshes; and droves of shaggy little Welsh ponies no higher than Merrylegs; and hundreds of cart horses of all sorts, some of them with their long tails braided up and tied with scarlet cord; and a good many like myself, handsome and high-bred, but fallen into the middle class through some accident or blemish, unsoundness of wind or some other complaint. There were some splendid animals quite in their prime and fit for anything; they were throwing out their legs and showing off their paces in high style as they were trotted out with a leading rein, the groom running by the side. But around in the background there were a number of poor things sadly broken down with hard work, with their knees knuckling over and their hind legs swinging out at every step; and there were some very dejected-looking old horses with the underlip hanging down and the ears lying back heavily, as if there was no more pleasure in life, and no more hope; there were some so thin you might see all their ribs, and some with old sores on their backs and hips. These were sad sights for a horse to look upon, who knows not but he may come to the same state.

There was a great deal of bargaining, of running up and beating down, and if a horse may speak his mind as far as he understands, I should say there were more lies told and more trickery at the horse fair than a clever man could give an account of. I was put with two or three other strong, useful-looking horses, and a good many people came to look at us. The gentlemen always turned from me when they saw my broken knees, though the man who had me swore it was only a slip in the stall.

The first thing was to pull my mouth open, then to look at my eyes, then feel all the way down my legs and give me a hard feel of the skin and flesh, and then try my paces.

It was wonderful what a difference there was in the way these things were done. Some did it in a rough, offhand way, as if one was only a piece of wood; while others would take their hands gently over one's body with a pat now and then, as much as to say, "By your leave." Of course I judged a good many of the buyers by their manners to myself.

There was one man about whom I thought, if he would buy me I should be happy. He was not a gentleman nor yet one of the loud, flashy sort that called themselves so. He was rather a small man but well made and quick in all his motions: I knew in a moment by the way he handled me that he was used to horses. He spoke gently and his gray eye had a kindly, cheery look in it. It may seem strange to say—but it is true all the same—that the clean, fresh smell there was about him made me take to him; no smell of old beer and tobacco, which I hated, but a fresh smell as if he had come out of a hayloft. He offered twenty-three pounds for me; but that was refused and he walked away. I looked after him but he was gone, and a very hard-looking, loud-voiced man came. I was dreadfully afraid he would have me, but he walked off. One or two more came who did not mean business.

Then the hard-faced man came back again and offered twenty-three pounds. A very close bargain was being driven, for my salesman began to think he should not get all he asked and must come down; but just then the gray-eyed man came back again. I could not help reaching out my head toward him. He stroked my face kindly.

"Well, old chap," he said, "I think we should suit each other. I'll give twenty-four for him."

"Say twenty-five and you shall have him."

"Twenty-four ten," said my friend, in a very decided tone, "and not another sixpence—yes or no?"

"Done," said the salesman, "and you may depend upon it there's a monstrous deal of quality in that horse, and if you want him for cab work, he's a bargain."

The money was paid on the spot and my new master took my halter, and led me out of the fair to an inn, where he had a saddle and bridle ready. He gave me a good feed of oats and stood by while I ate it, talking to himself and talking to me. Half an hour afterward we were on our way to London through pleasant lanes and country roads, until we came into the great London thoroughfare, on which we traveled steadily till in the twilight we reached the great city.

Black Beauty is very happy for some time with Jerry, the kind London cab driver who bought him at the fair. Then Jerry's health fails. He retires to become coachman at a country estate and Black Beauty again is sold.

3. JAKES AND THE LADY

I was sold to a corn dealer and baker whom Jerry knew, and with him he thought I should have good food and fair work. In the first he was quite right, and if my master had always been on the premises I do not think I should have been overloaded, but there was a foreman who was always hurrying and driving everyone, and frequently when I had quite a full load he would order something else to be taken on. My carter, whose name was Jakes, often said it was more than I ought to take, but the other always overruled him. " 'Twas no use going twice when once would do and he chose to get business forward."

Jakes, like the other carters, always had the bearing rein up, which prevented me from drawing easily, and by the time I had been there three or four months I found the work telling very much on my strength.

One day I was loaded more than usual, and part of the road was a steep uphill. I used all my strength, but I could not get on and was obliged continually to stop. This vexed my driver and he laid his whip on badly. "Get on, you lazy fellow," he said, "or I'll make you."

Again I started the heavy load and struggled on a few yards; again the whip came down and again I struggled forward. The pain of that great cart whip was sharp, but my mind was hurt quite as much as my poor sides. To be punished and abused when I was doing my very best was so hard it took the heart out of me. A third time he was flogging me cruelly when a lady stepped quickly up to him and said in a sweet, earnest voice:

"Oh! pray do not whip your good horse any more. I am sure he is doing all he can; the road is very steep. I am sure he is doing his best."

"If doing his best won't get this load up he must do something more than his best; that's all I know, ma'am," said Jakes.

"But is it not a very heavy load?" she said.

"Yes, yes, too heavy," he said, "but that's not my fault. The foreman came just as we were starting and would have three hundredweight more put on to save him trouble, and I must get on with it as well as I can."

He was raising the whip again when the lady said:

"Pray, stop, I think I can help you if you will let me."

The man laughed.

"You see," she said, "you do not give him a fair chance; he cannot use all his power with his head held back as it is with that bearing rein. If you would take it off I am sure he would do better—*do* try it," she said persuasively. "I should be very glad if you would."

"Well, well," said Jakes, with a short laugh, "anything to please a lady of course. How far do you wish it down, ma'am?"

"Quite down, give him his head altogether."

The rein was taken off and in a moment I put my head down to my very knees. What a comfort it was! Then I tossed it up and down several times to get the aching stiffness out of my neck.

"Poor fellow! that is what you wanted," said she, patting and stroking me with her gentle hand. "And now if you will speak kindly to him and lead him on I believe he will be able to do better."

Jakes took the rein. "Come on, Blackie." I put down my head and threw my whole weight against the collar. I spared no strength; I pulled the load steadily up the hill and then stopped to take breath.

The lady had walked along the footpath, and now came across into the road. She stroked and patted my neck, as I had not been patted for many a long day.

"You see he was quite willing when you gave him the chance. I am sure he is a fine-tempered creature and I dare say he has known better days. You won't put that rein on again, will you?" for he was just going to hitch it up on the old plan.

"Well, ma'am, I can't deny that having his head has helped him up the hill, and I'll remember it another time, and thank you, ma'am; but if he went without a bearing rein I should be the laughing stock of all the carters. It is the fashion, you see."

"Is it not better," she said, "to lead a good fashion than to follow a bad one? A great many gentlemen do not use bearing reins now. Our carriage horses have not worn them for fifteen years and work with much less fatigue than those who have them; besides," she added in a very serious voice, "we have no right to distress any of God's creatures without a very good reason; we call them dumb animals, and so they are for they cannot tell us how they feel, but they do not suffer less because they have no words. But I must not detain you now; I thank you for trying my plan with your good horse, and I am sure you will find it far better than the whip. Good day," and with another soft pat on my neck she stepped lightly across the path, and I saw her no more.

"That was a real lady, I'll be bound for it," said Jakes to himself. "She spoke just as polite as if I was a gentleman, and I'll try her plan, uphill, at any rate"; and I must do him the justice to say that he let my rein out several holes, and going uphill after that he always gave me my head; but the heavy loads went on. Good feed and fair rest will keep one's strength under full work, but no horse can stand against overloading, and I was getting so thoroughly pulled down from this cause that a younger horse was bought in my place. I may as well mention here what I suffered at this time from another cause. I had heard horses speak of it but had never myself had experience of the evil. This was a badly lighted stable. There was only one very small window at the end, and the consequence was that the stalls were almost dark.

Besides the depressing effect this had on my spirits it very much weakened my sight, and when I was suddenly brought out of the darkness into the glare of daylight it was very painful to my eyes. Several times I stumbled over the threshold and could scarcely see where I was going.

I believe, had I stayed there very long, I should have become purblind, and that would have been a great misfortune, for I have heard men say that a stone-blind horse was safer to drive than one which had imperfect sight, as it generally makes them very timid. However, I escaped without any permanent injury to my sight, and was sold to a large cab owner.

4. HARD TIMES

I shall never forget my new master; he had black eyes and a hooked nose, his mouth was as full of teeth as a bulldog's, and his voice was as harsh as the grinding of cart wheels over gravel stones. His name was Nicholas Skinner, and I believe he was the same man that poor Seedy Sam drove for.

I have heard men say that seeing is believing, but I should say that feeling is believing; for much as I had seen before, I never knew till now the utter misery of the life of a cab horse.

Skinner had a low set of cabs and a low set of drivers; he was hard on the men and the men were hard on the horses. In this place we had no Sunday rest, and it was in the heat of summer.

Sometimes on a Sunday morning a party of fast men would hire the cab for the day—four of them inside and another with the driver, and I had to take them ten or fifteen miles out into the country and back again. Never would any of them get down to walk up a hill let it be ever so steep, or the day ever so hot—unless, indeed, when the driver was afraid I should not manage it, and sometimes I was so fevered and worn that I could hardly touch my food. How I used to long for the nice bran mash with niter in it that Jerry used to give us on Saturday nights in hot weather that used to cool us down and make us so comfortable. Then we had two nights and a whole day for unbroken rest, and on Monday morning we were as fresh as young horses again. But here, there was no rest and my driver was just as hard as his master. He had a cruel whip with something so sharp at the end that it sometimes drew blood, and he would even whip me under the belly and flip the lash out at my head. Indignities like these took the heart out of me terribly but still I did my best and never hung back; for as poor Ginger had said, it was no use; men are the strongest.

My life was now so utterly wretched that I wished I might, like Ginger, drop down dead at my work and be out of my misery, and one day my wish very nearly came to pass.

I went on the stand at eight in the morning and had done a good share of work when we had to take a fare to the railway. A long train was just expected in, so my driver pulled up at the back of some of the outside cabs to take the chance of a return fare. It was a very heavy train, and as all the cabs were soon engaged ours was called for. There was a party of four—a noisy, blustering man with a lady, a little boy and a young girl, and a great deal of luggage. The lady and the boy got into the cab, and while the man ordered about the luggage the young girl came and looked at me.

"Papa," she said, "I am sure this poor horse cannot take us and all our luggage so far, he is so very weak and worn out. Do look at him."

"Oh! he's all right, miss," said my driver, "he's strong enough."

The porter, who was pulling about some heavy boxes suggested to the gentleman, as there was so much luggage, whether he would not take a second cab.

"Can your horse do it or can't he?" said the blustering man.

"Oh! he can do it all right, sir. Send up the boxes, porter. He could take more than that," and he helped to haul up a box so heavy that I could feel the springs go down.

"Papa, papa, do take a second cab," said the young girl in a beseeching tone. "I am sure we are wrong; I am sure it is very cruel."

"Nonsense, Grace, get in at once and don't make all this fuss; a pretty thing it would be if a man of business had to examine every cab horse before he hired it—the man knows his own business of course. There, get in and hold your tongue!"

My gentle friend had to obey, and box after box was dragged up and lodged on the top of the cab or settled by the side of the driver. At last all was ready, and with his usual jerk at the rein and slash of the whip, my driver drove out of the station.

The load was very heavy, and I had had neither food nor rest since the morning; but I did my best, as I always had done, in spite of cruelty and injustice.

I got along fairly till we came to Ludgate Hill, but there the heavy load and my own exhaustion were too much. I was struggling to keep on, goaded by constant chucks of the rein and use of the whip, when, in a single moment—I cannot tell how—my feet slipped from under me and I fell heavily to the ground on my side. The suddenness and the force with which I fell seemed to beat all the breath out of my body. I lay perfectly still; indeed, I had no power to move, and I thought now I was going to die. I heard a sort of confusion round me, loud, angry voices and the getting down of the luggage, but it was all like a dream. I thought I heard that sweet, pitiful voice saying, "Oh! that poor horse! it is our fault." Someone came and loosened the throat strap of my bridle and undid the traces which kept the collar so tight upon me. Someone said, "He's dead, he'll never get up again." Then I could hear the policeman giving orders, but I did not even open my eyes. I could only draw a gasping breath now and then. Some cold water was thrown over my head and some cordial was poured into my mouth, and something was covered over me. I cannot tell how long I lay there, but I found my life coming back and a kind-voiced man was patting me and encouraging me to rise. After some more cordial had been given me, and after one or two attempts, I staggered to my feet and was gently led to some stables which were close by. Here I was put into a well-littered stall, and some warm gruel was brought to me which I drank thankfully.

In the evening I was sufficiently recovered to be led back to Skinner's stables, where I think they did the best for me they could. In the morning Skinner came with a farrier to look at me. He examined me very closely and said:

"This is a case of overwork more than disease. If you could give him a run-off for six months he would be able to work again; but now there is not an ounce of strength in him."

"Then he must just go to the dogs," said Skinner. "I have no meadows to nurse sick horses in—he might get well or he might not. That sort of thing don't suit my business; my plan is to work 'em as long as they'll go, and then sell 'em for what they'll fetch, at the knacker's or elsewhere."

"If he was broken-winded," said the farrier, "you had better have him killed out of hand, but he is not. There is a sale of horses coming off in about ten days. If you rest him and feed him up he may pick up, and you may get more than his skin is worth, at any rate."

Upon this advice Skinner, rather unwillingly I think, gave orders that I should be well fed and cared for, and the stable man, happily for me, carried out the orders with a much better will than his master had in giving them. Ten days of perfect rest, plenty of good oats, hay, bran mashes, with boiled linseed mixed in them, did more to get up my condition than anything else could have done; those linseed mashes were delicious, and I began to think, after all, it might be better to live than go to the dogs. When the twelfth day after the accident came, I was taken to the sale a few miles out of London. I felt that any change from my present place must be an improvement, so I held up my head and hoped for the best.

5. FARMER THOROUGHGOOD AND HIS GRANDSON WILLIE

At this sale, of course I found myself in company with the old, broken-down horses—some lame, some broken-winded, some old, and some that I am sure it would have been merciful to shoot.

The buyers and sellers, too, many of them, looked not much better off than the poor beasts they were bargaining about. There were poor old men trying to get a horse or a pony for a few pounds that might drag about some little wood or coal cart. There were poor men trying to sell a worn-out beast for two or three pounds rather than have the greater loss of killing him. Some of them looked as if poverty and hard times had hardened them all over; but there were others that I would have willingly used the last of my strength in serving; poor and shabby but kind and human, with voices that I could trust. There was one tottering old man that took a great fancy to me and I to him, but I was not strong enough. It was an anxious time! Then I noticed a man coming from the better part of the fair who looked like a gentleman farmer, with a young boy by his side. The man had a broad back and round shoulders, a kind, ruddy face, and he wore a broad-brimmed hat. When he came up to me and my companions he stood still, and gave a pitying look around at us. I saw his eye rest on me; I had still a good mane and tail, which did something for my appearance. I pricked my ears and looked at him.

"There's a horse, Willie, that has known better days."

"Poor old fellow!" said the boy. "Do you think, grandpapa, he was ever a carriage horse?"

"Oh yes! my boy," said the farmer, coming closer, "he might have been anything when he was young; look at his nostrils and his ears, the shape of his neck and shoulders. There's a deal of breeding about that horse." He put out his hand and gave me a kind pat on the neck. I put out my nose in answer to his kindness; the boy stroked my face.

"Poor old fellow! see, grandpapa, how well he understands kindness. Could not you buy him and make him young again as you did with Ladybird?"

"My dear boy, I can't make all old horses young. Besides, Ladybird was not so very old as she was run down and badly used."

"Well, grandpapa, I don't believe that this one is old; look at his mane and tail. I wish you would look into his mouth, and then you could tell; though he is so very thin, his eyes are not sunk like some old horses'."

The old gentleman laughed. "Bless the boy! he is as horsey as his old grandfather."

"But do look at his mouth, grandpapa, and ask the price; I am sure he would grow young in our meadows."

The man who had brought me for sale now put in his word.

"The young gentleman's a real knowing one, sir. Now the fact is, this 'ere hoss is just pulled down with overwork in the cabs; he's not an old one, and I heerd as how the vetenary should say that a six months' runoff would set him right up, being as how his wind was not broken. I've had the tending of him these ten days past, and a gratefuller, pleasanter animal I never met with, and 'twould be worth a gentleman's while to give a five-pound note for him, and let him have a chance. I'll be bound he'd be worth twenty pounds next spring."

The old gentleman laughed and the little boy looked up eagerly.

"Oh! grandpapa, did you not say the colt sold for five pounds more than you expected? You would not be poorer if you did buy this one."

The farmer slowly felt my legs, which were much swelled and strained; then he looked at my mouth. "Thirteen or fourteen, I should say; just trot him out, will you?"

I arched my poor thin neck, raised my tail a little, and threw out my legs as well as I could, for they were very stiff.

"What is the lowest you will take for him?" said the farmer as I came back.

"Five pounds, sir; that was the lowest price my master set."

" 'Tis a speculation," said the old gentleman, shaking his head, but at the same time slowly drawing out his purse, "quite a speculation! Have you any more business here?" he said, counting the sovereigns into his hand.

"No, sir, I can take him for you to the inn, if you please."

"Do so. I am now going there."

They walked forward, and I was led behind. The boy could hardly control his delight, and the old gentleman seemed to enjoy his pleasure. I had a good feed at the inn and was then gently ridden home by a servant of my new master's and turned into a large meadow with a shed in one corner of it.

Mr. Thoroughgood, for that was the name of my benefactor, gave orders that I should have hay and oats every night and morning, and the run of the meadow during the day, and "you, Willie," said he, "must take the oversight of him. I give him in charge to you."

The boy was proud of his charge and undertook it in all seriousness. There was not a day when he did not pay me a visit, sometimes picking me out among the other horses and giving me a bit of carrot or something good, or sometimes standing by me while I ate my oats. He always came with kind words and caresses and of course I grew very fond of him. He called me Old Crony, as I used to come to him in the field and follow him about. Sometimes he brought his grandfather, who always looked closely at my legs.

"This is our point, Willie," he would say. "But he is improving so steadily that I think we shall see a change for the better in the spring."

The perfect rest, the good food, the soft turf and gentle exercise soon began to tell on my condition and my spirits. I had a good constitution from my mother and I was never strained when I was young, so that I had a better chance than many horses who have been worked before they came to their full strength.

During the winter my legs improved so much that I began to feel quite young again. The spring came round, and one day in

March Mr. Thoroughgood determined that he would try me in the phaeton. I was well pleased, and he and Willie drove me a few miles. My legs were not stiff now and I did the work with perfect ease.

"He's growing young, Willie. We must give him a little gentle work now, and by midsummer he will be as good as Ladybird. He has a beautiful mouth and good paces; they can't be better."

"Oh! grandpapa, how glad I am you bought him!"

"So am I, my boy, but he has to thank you more than me; we must now be looking out for a quiet, genteel place for him where he will be valued."

6. MY LAST HOME

One day during this summer the groom cleaned and dressed me with such extraordinary care that I thought some new change must be at hand; he trimmed my fetlocks and legs, passed the tarbrush over my hoofs, and even parted my forelock. I think the harness had an extra polish. Willie seemed half anxious, half merry, as he got into the chaise with his grandfather.

"If the ladies take to him," said the old gentleman, "they'll be suited and he'll be suited. We can but try."

At the distance of a mile or two from the village we came to a pretty, low house, with a lawn and shrubbery at the front and a drive up to the door. Willie rang the bell and asked if Miss Blomefield or Miss Ellen was at home. Yes, they were. So while Willie stayed with me, Mr. Thoroughgood went into the house. In about ten minutes he returned, followed by three ladies: one tall, pale lady, wrapped in a white shawl, leaned on a younger lady with dark eyes and a merry face; the other, a very stately looking person, was Miss Blomefield. They all came and looked at me and asked questions. The younger lady—that was Miss Ellen—took to me very much; she said she was sure she should like me, I had such a good face. The tall, pale lady said that she should always be nervous in riding behind a horse that had once been down, as I might come down again, and if I did she should never get over the fright.

"You see, ladies," said Mr. Thoroughgood, "many first-rate horses have had their knees broken through the carelessness of their drivers, without any fault of their own, and from what I see of this horse I should say that is his case; but of course I do not wish to influence you. If you incline, you can have him on trial, and then your coachman will see what he thinks of him."

"You have always been such a good adviser to us about our horses," said the stately lady, "that your recommendation would go a long way with me, and if my sister Lavinia sees no objection we will accept your offer of a trial with thanks."

It was then arranged that I should be sent for the next day.

In the morning a smart-looking young man came for me. At first he looked pleased; but when he saw my knees he said in a disappointed voice:

"I didn't think, sir, you would have recommended to my ladies a blemished horse like that."

"Handsome is as handsome does," said my master. "You are only taking him on trial, and I am sure you will do fairly by him, young man, and if he is not as safe as any horse you ever drove, send him back."

I was led home, placed in a comfortable stable, fed and left to myself. The next day, when my groom was cleaning my face, he said:

"That is just like the star that Black Beauty had; he is much the same height too. I wonder where he is now."

A little further on he came to the place in my neck where I was bled, and where a little knot was left in the skin. He almost started, and began to look me over carefully, talking to himself.

"White star in the forehead, one white foot on the off side, this little knot just in that place"—then looking at the middle of my back—"and as I am alive, there is that little patch of white hair that John used to call 'Beauty's threepenny bit.' It *must* be Black Beauty! Why, Beauty! Beauty! do you know me? little Joe Green that almost killed you?" And he began patting and patting me as if he was quite overjoyed.

I could not say that I remember him, for now he was a fine grown young fellow with black whiskers and a man's voice, but I was sure he knew me, and that he was Joe Green, and I was very glad. I put my nose up to him and tried to say that we were friends. I never saw a man so pleased.

"Give you a fair trial! I should think so indeed! I wonder who the rascal was that broke your knees, my old Beauty! You must have been badly served out somewhere; well, well, it won't be my fault if you haven't good times of it now. I wish John Manly was here to see you."

In the afternoon I was put into a low park chair and brought to the door. Miss Ellen was going to try me, and Green went with her. I soon found that she was a good driver, and she seemed pleased with my paces. I heard Joe telling her about me and that he was sure I was Squire Gordon's old Black Beauty.

When we returned, the other sisters came out to hear how I had behaved myself. She told them what she had just heard, and said:

"I shall certainly write to Mrs. Gordon and tell her that her favorite horse has come to us. How pleased she will be!"

After this I was driven every day for a week or so, and as I appeared to be quite safe, Miss Lavinia at last ventured out in the small close carriage. After this it was quite decided to keep me and call me by my old name of "Black Beauty."

I have now lived in this happy place a whole year. Joe is

the best and kindest of grooms. My work is easy and pleasant and I feel my strength and spirits all coming back again. Mr. Thoroughgood said to Joe the other day:

"In your place he will last till he is twenty years old—perhaps more."

Willie always speaks to me when he can, and treats me as his special friend. My ladies have promised that I shall never be sold, and so I have nothing to fear; and here my story ends. My troubles are all over and I am at home; and often before I am quite awake I fancy I am still in the orchard at Birtwick, standing with my old friends under the apple trees.

As a little girl ANNA SEWELL often saw the overworked cart horses of nineteenth century London beaten and abused. Because she had been taught to believe that animals have feelings and should be loved, she was horrified by this cruelty. One horse, even more mistreated than the rest, became the main object of the sensitive child's sympathy, and years later, the model for *Black Beauty*.

Though an accident when she was twelve left her an invalid, Miss Sewell never stopped trying to help people and animals in trouble. When her family moved to the country she was given a pony and cart of her own so that she could come and go as she pleased. The girl loved the pony, and without him she would rarely have been able to leave the house. During outings in her cart she talked to neighbors and listened to the talk of stable hands and grooms. Many of these conversations were eventually recorded in her novel.

Quite late in life Miss Sewell's mother began writing ballads, and from her mother, Miss Sewell herself learned how to write in a clear, direct style. She was past fifty before she began work on the one book of her life—*Black Beauty*. It was published a few months before her death in 1877 and had a tremendous world impact in the battle against man's cruelty toward animals. In spite of its Victorian style, *Black Beauty* still has a universal appeal and is loved by young readers everywhere.

Battle for an old warrior

Indian Fighter

BY STEPHEN HOLT

JOE rode Baldy out to the spring on the edge of the ravine. Sliding to the ground he led the old sorrel pony over to where the clear water burbled from the ground.

"Take a last drink, pal," he whispered.

Baldy dropped his head and began to drink. Joe stared at him and thought of the time the old codger in the buckskin shirt had come along riding him. Seeing Joe standing in the barn door, he had come in and said, "Want to buy a good Indian fighter for ten dollars, Bub?"

Suddenly a coyote yipped across the ravine, jolting Joe's thoughts. And another. And another—till it seemed the air was alive with the cries. An icy wind sprang up. A snowflake hit Joe's pug nose.

"Winter!" Joe whispered, his stomach going fuzzy, and his eyes following Baldy's down the ravine to where the chemist, Mr.

Graham from Omaha, prodded exploringly around in the shale. Joe's fingers twined in Baldy's mane. "And winter spells coyotes pulling you down, Baldy," he whispered. "Unless——" He broke off talking to pull a cockle burr from Baldy's mane. Joe's dad had gone broke. Graham had bought the farm. The family was clearing out for California—after his dad shot Baldy.

Baldy's head came slowly around to Joe. With old gray lips he began nibbling at a button on Joe's leather jacket.

Joe's heart turned to water. "There's no other way," he babbled. "Nobody bid you in at the sale. Mr. Graham doesn't want you. And we can't turn you loose to let the coyotes finish you in the snow."

Baldy's ears drooped. He gave a big sigh, easing his weight to his left hip, then raised his head to rest on Joe's thin shoulder.

Joe got a picture of his lonesomeness without Baldy. He began to spar with the old horse. Baldy used his head to dodge around. And the pain within Joe mounted steadily. He said, "Count three, Baldy!" using the sign they'd practiced—Joe pressing Baldy's thin old shoulder with his elbow. The kids down at the country school at the crossroads used to eat it up.

Joe felt his face go stiff with anguish at the thought of Baldy lying stiff and cold down in the coulee back of the barn where all animals were hauled after they had died.

It wasn't as though he hadn't tried to save Baldy. And his dad's farm. He had written to Graham Robinson and Wade, chemists at Omaha, and sent a sample of shale from the canyon, pleading, in a pencil-scrawled note, that it must be good for something.

But nothing seemed to come of it, beyond Mr. Graham's coming out at the last minute—the day of the sale—to buy the farm without saying more than two words. Then he had gone wandering down along the ravine.

"Now, pretend there are Indians," Joe commanded Baldy "Indians, Baldy. Indians!"

Dutifully, Baldy dropped to his bent old knees, then to his stomach, and finally stretched full length on the ground, his head hugging the grass. The old codger had shown Joe this.

Joe stared at the old horse stretched silently on the ground. And suddenly, something inside him stiffened. There must be a way to save Baldy. Some way. And he'd have to find it.

He clucked to Baldy to get up, then mounted him by shinnying up his side. He rode down by the barn where his dad, George Straka, stood chewing a straw and just staring around him.

His father had had a bad day. His best bay team, Rock and Babe, sold. His new plow. The two sets of brass-studded harness.

"Dad, I've just got to make a last try to save Baldy," Joe said, slipping to the ground.

George Straka looked at the sun setting in the west behind a black bank of snow clouds. "It's thirty miles to Grand Island, and your mom's anxious to get started," he said.

"If I had an hour, I could try three places," Joe pleaded. "Please, Dad, let me."

"Whose places?" George Straka's tired brown eyes probed Joe's.

"Blaha's—" Joe began.

"Got ten horses and six kids and no feed for either," George Straka said softly.

"Creswell's—"

"Plenty of money, but Thaddeus Creswell spends half his time bragging how he hasn't a horse on the place—that he's a power-machine farmer from the word 'go.' "

"I've got to try," Joe pleaded. "I just got to, Dad."

George Straka's answer was to go get a pair of shears. "I'll work on his mane," he said gently. "It'll make him look trimmer."

Joe's heart leaped. "And his hoofs?" Joe asked. "He'll step better then."

His father eyed Baldy's bent old knees, his long, broken hoofs, especially the right front foot with the wire scar from the time Baldy got caught in the barbed-wire fence.

"And his hoofs," he agreed. "You go get the hoof trimmers, Joe, while I get rid of this cockle-burred mane."

Joe got the hoof pincers and brought them to his dad. He got a bucket of water and washed Baldy's old winter coat.

In less than fifteen minutes, Baldy was a changed horse—to Joe. "Boost me on, Dad," he said.

George took Joe by the bent right leg and heaved him on to Baldy's shining back. "One hour," he said softly. "And good luck, Joey." He looked wistfully at the boy.

Joe gently nudged Baldy's thin ribs and rode toward the gate that led to Blaha's.

"Throw in the bridle, if you make a deal," his father called.

Joe nodded, and riding out the gate, turned down the road toward Blaha's.

By the time he rode the two miles to turn in at the Blaha gate, Baldy's winter hair was plastered smooth with sweat. He looked swell. Swell! Joey gently nudged his old ribs and rode up to the ramshackle house with a flourish. Hope for a quick sale made his heart thump under his worn cotton shirt.

But suddenly, from the unpainted house, poured six Blaha kids—two sets of twin boys, a hollow-eyed girl of ten, and Jimmy, the oldest.

"Hi!" Jimmy said, eyeing Baldy enviously. "Gonna sell Baldy to Pop?"

Joe's eyes swept around toward the lean-to barn, to take in the meager pile of wheat straw—all the feed Blaha would have to pull four horses and a milk cow through the Nebraska winter.

Joe shook his head and turned old Baldy to go, but Mr. Blaha came out of the barn and hailed him. Joe nudged Baldy, and with the Blahas trailing, rode down to him.

Mr. Blaha was a Pole. He had a flat face, a stub nose, and high cheek bones, but his brown eyes were warm and steady. "I hear you're going out to California," he said with a touch of envy. "Where you can pick oranges right off the trees."

Joe wished he hadn't said that. The sound of six Blaha kids sucking in their lips would be hard to shake.

"Lucky . . ." Jimmy muttered softly.

"I don't know," Joe said carefully. "I'd rather stick around —with Dad."

"I know—you hate to let go." Blaha's eyes swept the bleak, flat farm and came doggedly back to Joe.

But Joe caught sight of the sun, red and sinking on the western horizon. A panic seized him. Baldy's time was running out. He turned the horse's head and nudged him in the ribs.

"Well, so long," he said. "See you sometime."

Jimmy sprang to catch Baldy's bit. "Hey, wait a minute, Joe," he pleaded.

Joe pulled Baldy up, and six Blahas went into a huddle with their dad.

It wasn't hard for Joe, sitting there, to get the drift. Blaha was being crowded. His old voice trembled as he said for Joe to hear, "What can I do? I got no feed, no money!"

Joe nudged Baldy's ribs and got out of there quick.

Thaddeus Creswell was fixing a snowplow as Joe rode up to the big woven-wire gate that led to Creswell's glistening gray buildings—a huge barn, a two-story house, and a red machine shed that housed enough power machinery to start a business.

Creswell was a big man with an open red face, huge blue

eyes, and a hearty laugh. He'd made no secret of always liking Joe. He'd even listened to Joe talk about the shale beds.

He came down to the gate and opened it to let Joe through. "Well, Joe, did you come to say good-by?" he boomed. "Wish I had sense enough to quit and go to California!" His laugh made old Baldy's ears twitch.

Joe grinned, then sobered. "I, I came to sell you Baldy," he blurted. Suddenly, the dam burst within him and he poured out a babble of words. "Dad's got to kill him if I don't sell him in an hour," he said. "You've got a boy—buy Baldy for him. Look!"

He leaped from Baldy and pressed his elbow in his ribs. "Count five, Baldy!"

Baldy paused as if in deep thought, then pawed till Jimmy took his elbow from his ribs—five it was.

Creswell took off his Stetson. "Well, now," he said, "I'm a machine man. No horses!"

Joe's heart thumped. "Indians, Baldy, Indians!" he said sharply.

Once more, Baldy lowered his tottering frame to the Creswell yard.

Jimmy flopped beside him and looked over his old paunch to Creswell. "An old Indian fighter," he said hopefully.

Creswell whistled softly. "What do you know—a regular circus horse!"

"Then, you will buy him—five dollars! A dollar! Fifty cents—and the bridle thrown in!" Joe's insides were one big pain. He waited—and waited.

Then a noise behind him swung him around, and there sat the reason Creswell couldn't buy Baldy—Alan, his spoiled boy, with blond, curly hair and scornful gray eyes that looked Baldy over as though he already lay dead and cold.

"Buy that old plug, Pop?" he screeched. "If you do, I'll run away from home."

Joe shinnied up the side of Baldy and got out of that yard, fast.

There remained only Mr. Graham himself as the last hope. Joe rode into their own yard and down to the spring. He circled the house and went down to the hen house. No Mr. Graham.

The gully back of the barn, where all dead animals were hauled, taunted Joe. He couldn't keep it out of his eyes.

He rode over to the west fence and stared off at an evening thunderhead, as though a stack of hay might come out of it that would feed Baldy for the winter.

The gully beckoned. And still no Mr. Graham.

Joe dropped to lie along Baldy's neck, the reins lying loose. With a sigh, the old horse turned and walked toward the barn, around behind it, and down to the gully.

Joe's dad came up behind them with his thirty-thirty in the crook of his arm. He was blinking hard.

"No sale," Joe whispered.

George Straka nodded, then said gently, "You go on up to the house, Joey."

This was Baldy's finish. Joe knew it. His dad knew it. In a minute Joe'd go up the hill; when he got out of sight there'd be the sharp crack of his dad's thirty-thirty, and Baldy would drop in his tracks.

But suddenly Joe's eyes, staring off across the fields, caught the shape of a thunderhead in the western sky. It was big and black—the shape of an old Indian warrior's head. There was a war bonnet of fleecy lighter clouds down his back.

It gave Joe an idea.

He slipped off Baldy's back and took the rifle from his dad's hands. "You go on up the hill, Dad," he said. "I'll tend to this."

He stood and watched his dad's feet carry him over the hill. His dad knew he could shoot. Joe had killed plenty of coyotes with the thirty-thirty.

Suddenly, he came close to Baldy.

"Indians, Baldy! Indians!" he whispered.

Baldy lowered himself to the ground.

Joe flopped beside him and pulled the rifle across Baldy's neck. There would be five shots across the hill, then the sixth one into Baldy's brain. He'd lived an Indian fighter; he'd die one, too.

"One!"

A little puff of dust danced halfway up the hill.

"Two!"

The whine of a bullet ricocheting from a rock came back to Joe.

Baldy lay quiet—a genuine Indian fighter, all right.

"Three! Four! Five!" whined from the gun to find distant marks.

Baldy still lay, not moving a muscle. Even his eyes were closed.

Jim swung the barrel of the gun around with the muzzle pointing just back of Baldy's ear. His finger twined on the trigger—he hesitated, then closed his eyes.

"Hey!" A hand from behind knocked the gun barrel up. "What are you going to run in the milk cows with if you shoot Baldy?" Mr. Graham's voice demanded.

Joe looked around. "M-milk cows?" he stuttered. "We're moving."

Old Baldy hadn't twitched.

"Oh, no," Mr. Graham said. "You're staying—you and your dad—to run the farm. All I want is the shale beds. I've tested it and it'll make the finest unbreakable glass in the world."

Suddenly Baldy raised his head and looked Joe in the eye. "Fine thing—talking, with Indians all around," his old eyes seemed to say.

Joe couldn't help laughing, and Mr. Graham joined in.

Then Joe took Baldy's reins and clucked to him. "Come on, old timer," he said softly. "The Indians have pulled out—for good."

"Do you know what I'm going to do tomorrow, Mr. Graham?" he asked, as they started up the hill together.

"Nope."

Joe grinned. "I'm going to buy the Blahas the biggest sack of oranges they've ever seen."

"Swell!" Mr. Graham said.

"Swell is right," Joe agreed, happily. He gave Baldy a gentle slap along his neck and steered him into the barn.

A biographical note on STEPHEN HOLT is given on page 75, following the story, "Night Star."

Fanfare for a flawless artist

An Imperial Performance

BY FELIX SALTEN

The dancing white horses of Lipizza have been a tradition of the Spanish Riding Academy in Vienna for several centuries. Originally owned by the Austrian Emperors, these magnificently large and spirited stallions are trained to execute stately, intricate and truly amazing dancing steps and formations.

Their dramatic rescue in World War II by General Patton, their performances in the various cities in the

United States, and in Walt Disney's film The Miracle of the White Stallions, *have made them familiar to most Americans. This selection from Felix Salten's noted biography of the Lipizzan stallion Florian recreates an imperial performance in all its faultless detail and august splendor.*

AN eighteenth-century fanfare sounded through the wide hall as the Emperor stepped into the court box at the Riding School in Vienna. Above the box was the escutcheon held aloft by genii and martial emblems. Behind it had been placed the bugle sextet, musicians from the orchestra of the opera.

Purple velvet hangings covered the balcony and enlivened the hall with their luminous tints. Few people occupied the balcony; officers, ladies, chamberlains of the archdukes present, ladies-in-waiting and the wives of various court officials. In the court box five archdukes sat waiting.

Then the fanfare.

Franz Joseph entered. After their obeisances the princes remained silent. The archduchesses rose from their deep curtsies.

A brief "good morning" from the Emperor was accompanied by a circular movement of his hand. The moment he sat down, a door in the opposite wall was thrown wide, and four horsemen rode into the arena. In a straight line they swept toward the court box and stopped at an appropriate distance. Simultaneously they doffed their two-cornered hats and swung them until their arms were horizontal. Then they wheeled and to the strains of the *Gypsy Baron* began their quadrille.

The circle and capers cut by the four horses were precisely alike, and gave the effect of music in the flowing rhythm of their execution. The regularity of the horses' strides, and the horsemanship of the four riders aroused the spectators to a gay pitch, for it was sheer rapture evoked by the beautiful, blooded animals and their artistry. Everyone in the hall could ride, knew horse flesh, and enjoyed the spectacle with the relish of a connoisseur.

The quadrille was over, the horsemen had made their exit. The wooden door remained wide open.

Next, seven mounted stallions entered and filed in front of the court box. Seven bicornes were removed from seven heads, swung to a horizontal position, and replaced.

Florian stood in the center. To his right stood three older stallions, thoroughly trained, and to his left three equally tested ones. He resembled a fiery youth among men. In a row of white steeds he stood out as the only *pure* white one. His snowy skin, unmarred by a single speck, called up memories of cloudless sunny days, of nature's gracious gifts. His liquid dark eyes, from whose depths his very soul shone forth, sparkled with inner fire and energy and health. Ennsbauer sat in the saddle like a carved image. With his brown frock coat, his chiseled, reddish-brown features and his fixed mien, he seemed to have been poured in metal.

The Emperor had just remarked, "Ennsbauer uses no stirrups or spurs," when the sextet began to play.

The horses walked alongside the grayish-white wainscoting. Their tails were braided with gold, with gold also their waving manes. Pair by pair they were led through the steps of the high school; they approached from the far side toward the middle and went into their syncopated, cadenced stride.

The Emperor had no eyes for any but Florian. Him he watched, deeply engrossed. His connoisseur's eye tested the animal, tested the rider, and could find no flaw that might belie the unstinted praise he had heard showered on them. His right hand played with his mustache, slowly, not with the impatient flick that spelled disappointment over something.

Ennsbauer felt the Emperor's glance like a physical touch. He stiffened. He could hope for no advancement. Nor did he need to fear a fall. Now—in the saddle, under him, this unexcelled stallion whose breathing he could feel between his legs and whose readiness and willingness to obey he could sense like some organic outpouring—now doubt and pessimism vanished. The calm, collected, resolute animal gave him calmness, collectedness, resolution.

At last he rode for the applause of the Emperor, of Franz Joseph himself, and by imperial accolade for enduring fame. Now it was his turn. . . .

Away from the wall he guided Florian, into the center of the ring. An invisible sign, and Florian, as if waiting for it, fell into the Spanish step.

Gracefully and solemnly, he lifted his legs as though one with the rhythm of the music. He gave the impression of carrying his rider collectedly and slowly by his own free will and for his own enjoyment. Jealous of space, he placed one hoof directly in front of the other.

The old Archduke Rainer could not contain himself: "Never have I seen a horse *piaffe* like that!"

Ennsbauer wanted to lead Florian out of the Spanish step, to grant him a moment's respite before the next tour. But Florian insisted on prolonging it, and Ennsbauer submitted.

Florian strode as those horses strode who, centuries ago, triumphantly and conscious of the triumphant occasion, bore Cæsars and conquerors into vanquished cities or in homecoming processions. The rigid curved neck, such as ancient sculptors modeled, the heavy short body that seemed to rock on the springs of his legs, the interplay of muscle and joint, together constituted a stately performance, one that amazed the more as it gradually compelled the recognition of its rising out of the will to perfect performance. Every single movement of Florian's revealed nobility, grace, significance and distinction all in one; and in each one of his poses he was the ideal model for a sculptor, the composite of all the equestrian statues of history.

The music continued, and Florian, chin pressed against chest, deliberately bowed his head to the left, to the right.

"Do you remember," Elizabeth whispered to her husband, "what our boy once said about Florian? He sings—only one does not hear it."

Ennsbauer also was thinking of the words of little Leopold von Neustift as he led Florian from the Spanish step directly into the *volte*. The delight with which Florian took the change, the effortless ease with which he glided into the short, sharply cadenced gallop, encouraged Ennsbauer to try the most precise and exacting form of the *volte,* the *redoppe,* and to follow that with the *pirouette.*

As though he intended to stamp a circle into the tanbark of the floor, Florian pivoted with his hind legs fixed to the same place, giving the breathtaking impression of a horse in full gallop that could not bolt loose from the spot, nailed to the ground by a sorcerer or by inner compulsion.

And when, right afterward, with but a short gallop around, Florian rose into the *pesade,* his two forelegs high in the air and hind legs bent low, and accomplished this difficult feat of balance twice, three times, as if it were child's play, he needed no more spurring on. Ennsbauer simply had to let him be, as he began to *courbette,* stiffly erect. His forelegs did not beat the air, now, but hung limply side by side, folded at the knee. Thus he carried his rider, hopped forward five times without stretching his hind legs. In the eyes of the spectators, Florian's execution of the *courbette* did not impress by its bravura, or by the conquest of body heaviness through careful dressure and rehearsal, but rather as an exuberant means of getting rid of a superabundance of controlled gigantic energy.

Another short canter around the ring was shortened by Florian's own impatience when he voluntarily fell into the Spanish step. He enjoyed the music, rocked with its rhythm. These men and women and their rank were nothing to him. Still, the presence of onlookers fired him from the very outset. He wanted to please, he had a sharp longing for applause, for admiration; his ambition, goaded on by the music, threw him into a state of intoxication; youth and fettle raced through his veins like a stream overflowing on a steep grade. Nothing was difficult any longer. With his rider and with all these human beings around him, he celebrated a feast. He did not feel the ground under his feet, the light burden on his back. Gliding, dancing with the melody, he could have flown had the gay strains asked for it.

On Florian's back as he hopped on his hind legs once, twice, Ennsbauer sat stunned, amazed.

Following two successive *croupades,* a tremendous feat, Florian went into the Spanish step still again. Tense and at the same time visibly exuberant, proud and amused, his joyously shining eyes made light of his exertions. From the *ballotade* he thrust himself into the *capriole,* rose high in the air from the standing position, forelegs and hind legs horizontal. He soared above the ground, his head high in jubilation. Conquering!

Frenetic applause burst out all over the hall, like many fans opening and shutting, like the rustle of stiff paper being torn.

Surrounded by the six other stallions Florian stepped

before the court box, and while the riders swung their hats in unison, he bowed his proud head just once, conscious, it seemed, of the fact that the ovation was for him, and he was giving gracious thanks in return.

FELIX SALTEN lived in Vienna during the pre-World War I era, when that imperial Austrian city was the proudest capital of Europe. In *Florian, the Emperor's Stallion* he recreates those old splendid days through the character of Florian, one of the famous Lipizzan white horses whose début before Franz Joseph is eloquently recorded in "An Imperial Performance."

Although Salten had no formal schooling, he was a journalist at age seventeen, already launched on what was to be a long, distinguished career as a writer of articles, essays, novels and stories about animals.

Soon after Vienna was occupied by the Nazis in 1938, Salten left the city in which he had lived for seventy years, and settled in Switzerland. He died at Zurich in 1946.

Of all his writing, his animal stories alone were translated into English and are famous throughout the world. His understanding of animals and his sensitivity to their feelings toward people and nature are unequaled in such stories as *Florian, Perri,* and *Bambi.* This last has become an immortal children's classic, and Walt Disney's filming of the story has made *Bambi* standard fare for young readers.

A king runs free

Flame

BY WILLIS LINDQUIST

"TOMORROW I'll be fifteen," Mike told his father, "and there is only one thing I want: a chance to catch Flame."

For three years Flame, the wild mustang of Blackman's Rock, had been a legend in the cow country. This powerful stallion with fiery mane and tail was as unconquerable as the wild mountain winds he breathed. Many there were who had attempted his capture. All had failed.

Mr. Hutchinson scowled at his son. An attempt to capture Flame would cost a great deal of money; but being the wealthy owner of the Sanora spread, money was the least of his worries.

"Mike," he said with a sigh. "That's like chasing a shadow. I was hoping you'd grow up and give your attention to the ranch for a change. For two years you've talked of nothing but that horse. It's no good. You could no more own Flame than you could own the stars."

Mike tightened his lips. "Max Denton almost caught him."

"Denton is an expert with wild horses, one of the best in the country," his father reminded him.

"You promised," Mike said grimly, determined not to be talked out of it this time. "You said if I still wanted to have a go at Flame when I turned fifteen, you'd give me the chance."

"Well, it's nonsense," said his father. "But if you insist . . . I suppose you've got a plan."

Mike did have. For weeks he had been studying the habits of Flame and his band of wild horses. He knew the kind of a trap he'd need and exactly where it should be built.

With a dozen ranch hands to help him, he labored for three weeks on the building of a fence across Blackman's valley, a V-shaped fence which he cleverly disguised with juniper and brush. At the bottom of the V was a gate, and beyond it a corral formed by a circular six-feet-high fence of woven wire. When it was completed, even Trimble, the ranch foreman, had to admit it was the most beautiful job of camouflaged fencework he had ever seen.

"Son, you've given a heap of thought to this," he said with admiration. "But that hoss is a smart one. Reckon you can get him to go in?"

Mike nodded confidently. He hadn't been dreaming and planning these last two years for nothing.

"Flame and his band will come in at the head of the valley. Then we'll push them right in. They don't have wings, and there's no place else for them to go. I want twelve riders tomorrow at noon."

The next day was clear and bright, perfect in every way, and he posted the men at the head of the valley behind a jumble of boulders. With Trimble for company, he rode over Blackman's pass into the next valley and concealed himself in a clump of junipers.

"Might have to wait a couple of hours," he explained to Trimble. "Flame always takes his band down this way to water. When he passes that brush, you get out ahead of him and cut him off. I'll swing in behind so they can't turn back. They'll have to take the pass."

Mike studied the valley about him. For him it was an enchanted valley, for it was Flame's private kingdom, his home, which echoed with the sounds of his comings and goings.

Presently they heard a shrill neighing. Mike held his breath, listening to the distant rumble of flying hoofs. Then a magnificent sorrel with four white socks and streaming mane and tail the color of living flame swept into sight. With his head held high, he swung down the slope in an easy ground-eating trot, the sun flashing on his rippling muscles, his legs driving smoothly like pistons.

"Jumping jay birds!" gasped Trimble. "What a beauty!"

Mike's heart hammered. He had watched Flame often, and always it brought a hurting lump to his throat.

As the big stallion and his band plunged on, he tossed his head, looking over the countryside as if the whole world were his. Then suddenly he stopped, head high, staring at the juniper thicket with suspicion.

"Now!" whispered Mike.

They rode out in different directions. Flame reared with

a snort, wheeling back to his band, trying to lead them again the way they had come.

"No you don't," said Mike, swinging his horse down the slope at full gallop.

A moment later the band with Flame in the lead headed for the pass. Mike gave a shout of triumph. They were as good as caught. He and Trimble pressed them hard until they were through the pass. The rest was up to the boys in the valley.

Mike ran his horse along the ridge to have a clear view. He saw the boys give chase, saw the band rush down the valley and into the trap. It was as easy as that.

"We got him!" he shouted to Trimble.

The foreman came galloping up. "Look at Flame go!" he said. "He's wheeling round and round in that corral faster and faster. Wait a minute."

Suddenly Flame turned from his circle, cut straight across the center of the corral and leaped the fence with a tail-flirting bound. Then he was off, a flaming streak of speed.

Mike stared speechless until he was lost from sight.

"You'll never get him into a trap like that again," Trimble said. "That hoss learns fast."

"I'll get him yet," said Mike.

The next afternoon the men were posted at five-mile intervals through the whole chain of valleys. Trimble found the stallion on a ridge above the corral where he could keep watch on his band, and Trimble gave chase. Several times the big stallion circled back toward the corral, galloping easily. But Trimble hung on doggedly.

After half an hour of furious riding, another rider burst from cover and took up the chase with a fresh horse, and then another, and another, and another. So the afternoon went, and finally, after eight riders had used up their horses with reckless speed, the big stallion swept past the rocks where Mike was hidden.

The stallion was beginning to tire. Foam and sweat and dust streaked his body, and yet he moved in a flowing motion as if scarcely touching the ground. Out over the flat open country he raced, with Mike gaining at every stride.

Mike was chuckling in his throat. It had turned out perfectly. He, Mike Hutchinson, would be the first to drop a rope over the stallion's head. He made his loop, began swinging it.

But Flame was wise in the ways of men. He had heard the whistling of rope before. He stopped suddenly. Then he turned and charged.

Only the freshness of Mike's horse saved them from the murderous attack of slashing hoofs.

Mike almost lost his seat in the saddle, and in the milling confusion that followed, he dropped his loop and it caught in the brush. There was nothing to do but get down and clear it.

With tears in his eyes, he watched the mighty bounds of Flame as he raced on into the open range.

Mike remounted, and as he sat there watching Flame speed into the distance, he noticed that the stallion kept well clear of any place that might serve as a hiding place for another horse and rider. Mike knew then that Flame had learned his lesson well. If they ever attempted the same stunt again, Flame would head at once for open country where they wouldn't have a chance.

He told that to Trimble when he got back to the corral. "It's no use," he said. "We'll never catch him now." A slow smile came to his lips. "But I taught Flame a few more tricks. I think they might save him from others who want to try."

"You could still do it by hiring one of them windmill planes to chase him down," Trimble said, grinning at the tired boy.

"You mean helicopter," said Mike. "That might work all

right, if you didn't kill him first. But I couldn't do it. It wouldn't be fair. I—I matched wits with him and I lost, that's all."

Foreman Trimble stroked his chin thoughtfully. "Well, anyway, you caught his band." He looked at the horses milling in the corral. "You got some mighty fine mares in there."

There were some beauties, but at that moment Mike's attention was distracted by a shrill neighing from the ridge above. There, silhouetted against the sunset, standing proudly as if he owned the hills and the sky above him, Flame watched his imprisoned band below.

For a breathless moment, Mike watched. Slowly he went over to the corral gate and opened it wide. There was a thunder of hoofs and a choke of dust as the band streaked out.

"They're yours, Flame," Mike said thickly under his breath. "All yours. And so are the hills."

In his heart, he knew he was glad. These hills would always have their enchantment. And sometime, if he were lucky, he would hear the shrill neighing of Flame somewhere in the distance—Flame, wild and happy and free, in the hills where he belonged.

WILLIS LINDQUIST has loved adventure and horses since his boyhood spent on the Minnesota prairie. A resourceful and determined boy much like Mike in the story of "Flame," he earned spending money by tending bee hives and selling honey. For adventure, he and his friends built a raft with which they explored a lake near their home, imagining themselves engaged in all sorts of heroic exploits.

Though Lindquist chose a law career and eventually became a tax attorney for the Internal Revenue Service, he has never lost his taste for adventure. He has spent his vacations traveling in Europe as a photographer for *National Geographic Magazine*. At one point he traveled around the world for two years and visited more than thirty countries. At another time, he made a 102-day voyage, sailing from Denmark to Australia on an ancient four-masted bark. He is a member of the national law fraternity, and now lives and works in New York City.

The conquest of fear

Waif of the Jungle

BY NINA AMES FREY

1. ARANA

IT was early evening in a little village on the shore of one of the beautiful lakes in central Guatemala. The quick dark of the tropics had already fallen, and the mountains that rose in majesty behind the groups of adobe huts were black shadows against the dark sky. Inside one of the thatched-roof, windowless houses, an Indian boy sat on a mat and watched the smoke from the cooking fire rise and swirl out through the open doorway.

The firelight touched the face of the boy's mother, Maria, intent on her weaving. It cast shadows on the hunched forms of his grandfather and three men of the village. It flickered over a sleepy brown thrush in its cage on the wall and sent a gleam into the dreaming eyes of the boy, Arana. He was hardly aware of it, so absorbed was he in his thoughts.

"A wild horse," he was thinking to himself, intent on the sleek image in his mind, "as swift as the wind over Lake Atitlán." He sighed heavily and looked up at the small bird sitting so still in its cage, its head tucked under a wing. "Like you, little *cenzontle,*" he said gently. "A horse who will feed out of my hand and belong only to me." He chirped loudly at his pet.

Startled, the bird awoke. Its bright eyes fastened on the boy and a short lilting melody from one of its beautiful songs filled the room. Arana laughed and whistled back at him.

He was secretly very happy to be going into the forest with his father. At ten he had already learned to do the work of a man, and usually his days were spent in hoeing corn, picking coffee beans, or helping to cut down cedar and avocado trees to be made into the blunt-ended dugout canoes that were used on the lake. It was almost a holiday to be going on the mountain trails with his father. Might he not see a deer or a wildcat? Perhaps he would catch an iguana, the timid lizard that was so good to eat. He had not tasted iguana meat in a long time. Arana decided to take his rope noose and try to snare something to bring back to his mother for dinner.

He looked up at his father. "If we go into the far forest," he said, "perhaps we may see one of the wild horses."

"There are no wild horses," Maria said harshly. "Only on the plains, perhaps, there might be some. Certainly not in the forest. You dream too much, Arana."

"A mule we may have one day," José said kindly. "It eats little. If we had a mule, he would carry as much as I have in the *cacaste,* and then I could walk along with a load beside him. Or, if we had oxen and a cart, they could carry even more. But a horse . . ." he shook his head.

Maria was very practical. "We have no mule and no oxen," she said. "Yet we do well enough. I do not have shoes such as the *ladino* women wear in the cities." She paused and shook her pleated skirt and looked down at her bare toes. "I would not want them," she said. "Not even sandals do I want."

The old grandfather had been standing, listening quietly. "Beads for your neck and ribbons for your hair and perhaps a silver ring, though, you do want," he said gently.

"Well," Arana's mother said tossing her head. "A silver necklace, of course. Who would not?" But she smiled a little.

"Let the boy dream, then," the grandfather said. "Maybe he will find your necklace in the forest."

Arana was astonished. Necklaces in the forest? Sometimes he did not understand his grandfather.

They went back to the hut quickly, and José took down the machete, the long knife that was used for many purposes, and placed it in his belt. Arana retied his sandals, pulling the thongs closely around his ankles. Soon he would have to make himself another pair. These were worn and full of holes.

At last they were ready to go. They were starting out when the sun was high in the sky. It was hot in the village, even with the breeze that came off the lake. Perhaps on the forest paths it would be cooler. Often Arana had gone with his father to hunt in the very early morning. Walking along the narrow, well-worn pathways, his feet would be drenched with the dew from the grasses. He would see the stars wane with the coming of the sun, and even in the half light of the forest with its deep blue shadows he could feel the splendor of the dawn.

Abruptly they came to an open space, and the marsh was before them. Buzzards were hovering over one end of it, and a large pink heron stood calmly on one leg, looking for its dinner. A wild turkey was roosting on a branch nearby, and the tall grasses around the border of the swamp were moving as though an animal were wading carefully through them.

Suddenly a little creature about the size of a young fawn stepped through an opening and stood motionless before the man and the boy.

Arana stopped. "What is that?" he whispered to his father.

There was a silence. The little animal did not move, and José did not answer at once but looked intently at the small creature.

Arana saw that it was a young animal of a pale fawn color, covered with soft brown spots and white stripes that ran from its brown mane to its brief tail. He had never seen anything like it before. "What is it?" he asked softly again.

José motioned to him to be quiet. At that moment the late sun, slanting in over the trees onto the marsh, bathed the little creature in a stream of golden light. Its dark mane and strong head showed up clearly. Arana's breath caught in his throat.

"It looks like a small horse!" he said, his voice husky with excitement.

Arana and his father stood at the edge of the marsh and looked at the little animal. It was about three feet high and almost four feet long. It seemed to be blinking in the late afternoon sunlight, and it looked around the open space as though it were lost.

The boy stood completely still. He hardly dared breathe.

José shaded his eyes. "It must be . . ." he started to say. And then he said, "But no, it is too unlikely." He stood quietly beside Arana.

The small creature now came out of the underbrush completely and timidly ate a few mouthfuls of marsh grass.

"What is it?" Arana whispered again. "Can it be a sort of wild horse? Let me throw my noose around its neck."

"Without doubt the mother is near," his father said, "and we have no hours to waste. It is perhaps after all the animal I first thought it to be, called a danta. It is a somewhat similar creature to the horse. We do not often see the danta, as it is an animal of the night and generally sleeps by day. Our ancestors, the Mayas, carved it in stone and used the figure in so many ways that it was thought for a long time that the Maya people must have had horses. If you remember your grandfather's stories, however, the Mayas had never seen a horse until the Spaniard, Alvarado, and his men rode down from Mexico into Guatemala. The danta resembles the mule somewhat, too, but unlike the horse and the mule it lives near rivers and swims in them. That is why we sometimes call it the little river horse. It prefers the night, too, like the deer."

"Why have I never seen one before in the forest?" Arana asked. "I have seen the deer many times."

José started along the path again with a purposeful, fast walk. He did not look back, but Arana kept turning his head to watch the little animal at the edge of the marsh until they had entirely left the place. The danta was still there, standing and feeding quietly. It had not noticed them.

"Why is it . . . ?" Arana began again excitedly.

"You have never seen one," his father said, "because the danta's life is spent in the densest part of the forest. It lives, always, near water and runs into it if frightened. The priest once told me of these animals. They are gentle and easily trained. It is believed that at one time they lived in many parts of the world, but now they are found only in Guatemala and in one other place across the world from here."

"How large is the mother, if this animal we saw is only a young one?" Arana asked. "Is it as large as a horse? Could it be trained to carry a pack to market?"

José considered this carefully, while still keeping to his fast walk. "They do not grow quite as large as some horses," he said, "but the grown animal is large enough to carry a load and can be trained. It is brown, with a black mane, and it eats the leaves and berries and tender shoots of trees. In some forest villages the people hunt these animals for their flesh, which is supposed to be quite good, and for the hide which is used in making whips."

Arana walked on, so lost in thought that he did not see the fat iguana, hiding behind the glossy leaves and white flowers of the *madroño* tree. Even if he had looked directly at the lizard, he might not have seen him, so similar was the iguana to the color of the tree itself. The noose hung idly at the boy's belt. He saw nothing.

The forest was very thick and luxuriant here. The branches of the trees, the tall conacaste, the guayacan with its purple flowers, the *madre cacao* of delicate pink flowers and poisonous roots, the feathery palms and the straight pines all twined together over their heads, shutting out the light of the sun. But on the forest floor there was reflected a sort of liquid green color as though one were looking at it all through sea water.

Bees and butterflies in swarms were probing the many-colored blossoms of the forest orchids, and everywhere birds were gorging themselves on the juicy jungle fruits and berries, spitting out the seeds that pattered down with a sound as of light rain. The tall flowers and bushes that bordered the path brushed against Arana's face, they scratched his arms and legs, but he did not feel them. In his mind a plan was forming.

2. THE SEARCH

Arana awoke to the cry of a flock of *azacuán*, the falcon, whose flight to the north in the spring always meant the opening of the rainy season to the Quiché. There must be hundreds in the flock, the boy thought, from the sound of their beating wings and the harsh resonance of their cries. It meant that the rains would be plentiful and the crops abundant, and it seemed to Arana a good omen for his plans this morning. He got up quietly and threw off his blanket.

In the darkness he found his belt and searched with careful probing fingers for his knife. It would have to be sharpened on the road, there was no time now to look for a stone for that purpose. He picked up his sandals and his noose and went cautiously over to the cooking fire. Its embers were still warm, and on a flat baking dish there were a few tortillas left from the night before. Arana took some and placed them in a small fiber mesh bag which he hung from his belt.

Soundlessly the boy went around the sleeping forms of his father and mother, wrapped from head to foot in their blankets, and out the door with no more noise than the brush of a bird's wing. In spite of all his care, however, he stepped on a sleeping chicken. She gave an indignant gasp and rose up, flapping her wings with such suddenness that Arana nearly fell headlong over her. His heart almost stopped beating. Had they heard him? He listened, scarcely breathing, but there was no sound from the inside of the hut. Chickens' noises in the night were commonplace. Often the fowl slept inside on the floor companionably with the family.

Arana ran now, out through the patio and down the village street. At the church steps he stopped to sit down and tie his sandals. There he said a short prayer for a safe journey and a safe return.

"Go with God," the priest would have said to him, and seeing a candle lighted in the church, Arana hesitated. Should he go in and tell the good padre about his journey and his mission? He knew that the priest was often awake and at the altar at this hour. His kindness and understanding could be taken for granted, his advice might be valuable. However, since it was the duty of his grandfather to pray daily in the church for his people and as it was nearly time for that ceremony to take place, Arana decided to go on. He wanted more than anything to surprise his grandfather with his adventure.

The stars were beginning to fade from the sky now. It would not be long before the first pale fingers of morning light would creep over the mountain tops and splash gold upon their steep sides. When he had found the small danta and had captured him, providing that were possible, then he would display his prize to his grandfather and to the priest as well. He climbed the steep hill that led out of the village and soon found himself on the trading route which he had traveled the day before.

The branches of the low bushes beside the path bathed him in a ceaseless shower of dew, so that in a few minutes he was drenched and cold. He shivered a little and cut a short stick to beat at the branches in front of him and rid them of moisture. The result was that the gourdlike leaves above him emptied a quantity of water down the back of his neck, wetting him completely. He wished for a brief moment that he had waited until the sun was high and had dried out the forest. But then, if he had delayed, he might never have been allowed to come at all.

It was darker on the trail as he went along, not black like the night, but dim, as though he were looking at the trees through a fog. It was also exceedingly quiet. The birds, the monkeys, the parrots, the parakeets and the macaws, all the noisy voices of the forest were asleep. Only the owls hooted softly. The little rustlings of the leaves, the soft sighing noise the light wind made in the underbrush, now seemed almost loud and somewhat startling. Some hidden creature near Arana kept making a sort of small sneeze, sometimes almost beside him, sometimes a little distance away, but always unexpected. It made his heart beat faster.

After a while the boy became conscious of a kind of light rustling that seemed to go along with him. It stopped when he stopped and then started up again quietly when he went ahead. He held his breath and heard it distinctly.

Suddenly there was a small piercing scream, a shriek that was cut off in the middle with a long gasp. Then, complete silence.

Abruptly a fox darted across the path in front of Arana. It was carrying a small limp rabbit in its jaws. For one startled moment the fox looked at the boy, and then it was gone in an instant, leaving a trail of blood on the underbrush.

"Murderer!" Arana shouted, waving his stick. It caught on a branch and a small waterfall came down and drenched him completely. He rubbed his wet face with the sleeve of his *camisa*. For the first time he wished that his father's tall form strode ahead of him.

It was slightly lighter now. The stars had gone completely from the small patch of sky that Arana could see, and the miracle of a new day was taking place in the forest. The trees seemed to turn green at once, and the flowers returned to their brilliant color. The butterflies crawled out from under the leaves where they had spent the night and opened and shut their wings in swift motions like sails in the wind. The birds shook themselves, preened their feathers, and said cheerful good mornings to one another. A lark sang somewhere in a treetop, and a monkey came down, hand over hand, to look at Arana. It kept pace with him in the branches, swinging from limb to limb with careless ease.

Increasingly the upper forest was filled with a noisy activity. It sounded almost as though a large crowd had come suddenly into an empty room. Where there had been silence, broken only by a single bird call, now there were shrill alarms that resounded from the earth to the tree tops. Hundreds of tiny sharp eyes were watching Arana's progress.

The monkeys chattered, "There's a stranger in the forest. Beware! Beware!"

The parrots shouted, "The branch he carries at his side. Watch out for that!"

The birds shrilled, "Stay away. Away."

The excitement traveled. It reached the innermost parts of

the forest. The rabbits scampered to their certain hiding places. The weasels, the porcupines, and the armadillos hid themselves, each in his own fashion. All the hundreds of small animals near the path remained motionless, their sensitive noses sniffing the air. The deer stood up and trembled in their glades, their flanks close, their muscles taut, ready to spring in any direction. The jaguar and the mountain cat, the tapir and the wild boar were alerted. Their ears pricked, but they alone had no fear of an intrusion. They settled down again in their lairs. They slept. A small creature was in the forest. What of that?

It seemed an endless time before Arana reached the borders of the swamp. He approached the high grasses with caution and looked out first over the expanse of marsh from behind the trunk of a huge tree.

There was nothing to be seen this morning but a few small birds. The buzzards had gone. The heron had floated on graceful pink wings to another swamp, another feeding ground, for his breakfast.

The boy crept cautiously through the tall marsh grass, parting the rushes with the utmost care until he came to the place where he had seen the young danta the day before. There were the small footprints in the mud, still clear and distinct. But now there were others. They led to the far curve of the marsh. He followed them.

The water moccasins were sluggish this morning. The warmth of the sun had not yet loosened their muscles, and they moved through the water slowly. As Arana parted the branches of a small overhanging tree, a viper darted away, hissing.

The boy drew a long breath. A snake bite was something to fear. He could be bitten and die here alone in the forest. No one would know where to look for him.

"Where there are known snake places, walk confidently," his father had always told him. "Make noise with the feet. Snakes are cowards. They will run. All but the rattlesnake, perhaps, and he gives warning."

Arana did not feel confident, nor could he thrash his stick about or stamp on the mud. He did not want to frighten the danta, should it be near.

There was a foul smell here in this place and soon he came upon its source. A large creature lay on its side, its lolling head partly in the water. The stiff black mane was tangled in the bushes and the shaggy hide was ripped open, showing the bare flesh, stripped in places from the bone.

Arana did not have to look long to realize that this was the mother of the small creature he had seen the day before. The buzzards had been waiting for her to die and had feasted on the body already. He turned away. Had the little one died too? His heart was sick. Perhaps he had come all this way for nothing. He walked around the swamp to the other side. There was no sign of anything there. He sat down under a towering conacaste tree, discouraged and sad.

Something was moving in the bushes beside him! His heart stood still and his breath caught in his throat. With quiet caution he took the rope noose from his belt. Whatever it was, he would be ready.

Suddenly a shaft of brilliant sunlight came piercing through the branches of the trees. A head peered out of the low bushes. Without turning Arana could see the fawn-colored body with its white stripes and brown dots. The little creature was poised for flight. Quicker than thought the noose flew out of Arana's hand. It caught the startled little danta fairly around the neck and tightened on the small stiff mane. Bounding away with high agonized shrieks, it jumped high over the bushes into the forest.

Arana was unprepared for such strength. Holding the rope tightly, he was flung headlong into the base of a tree. His head hit the trunk with the force of a hammer, and he fell unconscious to the ground. The rope pulled through his nerveless fingers. The danta disappeared.

How long Arana lay at the base of the tree he did not know, but when finally he opened his eyes, the sun was high in the sky and for a moment dazzled him. A flock of birds was peering at him from above, two monkeys had come down to have a closer look, and a fat turkey cock with four hens was walking by, unconcerned and unalarmed.

At first Arana thought he was on the hard dirt floor of his own hut. He thought he could hear his mother grinding corn. It must be time to get up and bring in the morning wood. He sat up abruptly. His head ached. Where was he?

Gradually his eyes focused in the strong sunlight. He saw the marsh, his mind cleared, and the events of the morning came back to him. He remembered seeing the danta and throwing his noose around its neck. That was the last that he knew. The little creature must have leaped away. Time had gone by. By the look of the sun, several hours had passed and he had lost what he had come so far to find. If it had been possible for him to cry, he might have done so, but Arana never cried. Seldom, even as babies, do the Quiché Indians cry.

He clamped his jaws together and stood up. His legs were stiff and his head pounded, but that did not matter. What worried him most was the position of the sun in the sky. If he were to get back to his village before dark, he would have to start soon. Night closed in suddenly here in the forest. What should he do? Go back without the small creature he had so nearly captured?

Suddenly he had a thought.

"There should be tracks," he said aloud.

At the base of the large tree the boy knelt down on the soft moist earth and looked carefully around him. The sprawling footprints of the turkey cock and his hens were easy to recognize, but there were no footprints of the danta, so distinct, so different from all others. Arana sat back on his heels and looked about him. There, over on the other side of the tree, what was that? The bushes were broken down, leaves torn. The boy was exultant. He remembered now. The danta had taken a flying leap and had vaulted over the bushes away from the marsh.

Arana forced his way through the thick growth. Thorns tore at his face and ripped his *camisas,* but on the far side of the bushes he saw something. Four small hoof marks, clear and distinct! Four footprints deep in the soil! Wild excitement gripped him.

"He's here!" Arana shouted, and ran forward.

At once he had lost the trail. There were no more footprints. He forced himself to go back to the marsh, to start again at the big tree and go forward slowly and cautiously. The boy tried to be extremely quiet now. It would not do to frighten the small animal. Softly he parted each bush, examined the ground for footprints, and looked for broken branches. Finally he found another set of hoof marks. From there he followed the trail even more slowly. Here was a patch of hair clinging to a thorn. Beyond it, a few yards away, he found a shred of rope from the noose. At that place he lost the trail again in the dense undergrowth.

Arana stopped. He took out his knife from his belt and cut a cross in the tree trunk beside him, making a large white gash that would be easy to see. From there he walked in circles around the tree, keeping his eyes alternately on it and on the ground. He went in larger and larger circles until at last he found what he was looking for. On a hard bit of ground he saw two small imprints from the front hoofs. The little creature must be jumping and bounding about like a young deer. The boy pushed aside the heavy entangling vines and stumbled over roots he could not see. Now, however, he was going in the right direction. Soon he discovered another set of marks. Following them and other signs of the danta's flight, he was led finally into a sort of clearing far from the swamp. Tall pines spread their boughs high above the dark mossy ground. They made a thick canopy through which the sun hardly penetrated. It was a glade full of shadows.

Arana stopped for breath and leaned against the bark of a giant conacaste tree for a moment. The little danta was not here. He would have to look carefully for the trail out of this place. He rested his stick against the tree and felt the string bag at his belt slap against his thigh. He had forgotten the tortillas. There were five in his hand when he drew them out. Arana ate two and felt much better. He was about to start to eat the others when he hesitated. He might need more food later. He thought of his mother and of the village he had left that morning. It seemed a long way off. Would he be able to find his way back there? He looked anxiously toward the tops of the trees. It was difficult to tell here where the sun was in the sky, but he reasoned that there were several hours yet before darkness should creep over the forest. He took a long breath. Which way now?

Without warning two men appeared in the clearing. On the backs of each were huge bundles of split *pinabete* wood for the making of hand looms. They stopped short in astonishment when they saw Arana.

"Boy," one of them said finally, "are you lost here in the forest?"

Arana shook his head. "I came from the swamp," he said briefly, "near the *ceiba* trees."

The second man leaned on his staff heavily. The leather band that supported the heavy bundle of sticks pressed deeply into his forehead. He looked fierce, but when he spoke his voice was kind.

"I have a son such as you," he said slowly, "maybe taller and somewhat older perhaps. But he does not come alone into the depths of the forest. Have you no father?"

"My father weaves mats," Arana said. "We are from San Pedro La Laguna. I came from there this morning, alone," he said proudly, "before the stars had left the sky."

"There is a trail near here," the first man said, "but it is far from San Pedro. The stars will be in the sky again before you are there. Come with us to Santiago Atitlán. Tomorrow perhaps someone will be going by boat to San Pedro. That way you will reach home safely."

Arana hesitated. Should he go back like a small child with these two men? How would he feel tomorrow? He took a long breath and shook his head. Now that he had come so far, he must find the small danta. There was no other course. Nothing else could be considered.

"Thank you," he said to the man, "but I do not go with you to Santiago Atitlán. There is a small creature here in the forest that I have come all this way to find. Its mother is dead. It wanders alone, I think, and it must not be far from here. Already my noose is about its neck. When I have found the little animal I shall go back to the trail near the swamp. The trail is . . ." He hesitated. Where was the swamp? He pointed uncertainly. "Over there," he said.

The first man shrugged his shoulder. "With God," he said kindly but indifferently.

The second man scowled. His eyes looked fiercer than ever. He hesitated, started toward Arana as though to compel him to go with them. Then he stopped. "A child in the forest," he muttered. "Look well, little one. Go before the night has come." He seemed to be thinking for a moment. "There was an animal back a way by a great pine," he said slowly. "You can see the pine from here. It is not far. Perhaps it is the creature you follow. I did not look carefully, thinking it was a fawn. It had spots . . ."

"That's it!" Arana leaped to his feet with sudden energy. He turned to look for the pine where his fierce friend had pointed.

"Go with God," the man said.

"With God," Arana called back over his shoulder. The men had gone. He was alone again.

He could see the huge pine, but it was quite a long time before he was close to it. The trail the men had been following was faint and overgrown with vines. Great gray drifts of moss hung down from the branches here, and brilliant orchids covered the cypress and walnut trees. With every muscle tense, he pushed slowly through the brush that came to his waist and tangled his feet, making as little noise as possible. He must not startle the danta. It was his last chance. If the small creature escaped from him again and disappeared into the forest depths, there would be no time to follow him further and return to the trading route before night. His heart beat uncomfortably fast as he advanced step by step toward the pine. He held his breath and parted the bushes carefully and soundlessly. There was the danta!

All in one motion Arana jumped and caught the rope in his hands. The little animal gave a surprised desperate gasp, shot up with a high bound, and came down on four fiercely straining hoofs. The boy held on. He braced his feet and clung with iron fingers to the rope. The danta shook suddenly and violently all over and then abruptly stopped and stood still. Arana approached it with gentle hands. He patted the quivering sides softly.

"You are mine now, little one," he said. His voice was choked. He could hardly breathe, he was so excited. Finally he had a thought. He reached into the bag at his belt and brought out a tortilla. He crushed it with his fingers and held it out in his hand.

"It is good," he said softly. "Eat."

The little creature sniffed the corn cake, pawed the earth with its feet, and shuddered away. Arana held on to the rope, his fingers clamped around its end. The other hand still held the tortilla.

"Eat it," he said again. "We will be friends then." He offered the food a second time. The danta stood still. It stopped shaking. Its small ears close to its head went straight up. Its eyes were very soft and bright. This time it put its nose down on Arana's hand and licked the food from his fingers. The boy's heart overflowed with a sudden love. He patted the stiff mane with cautious hands. "No jaguar will get you now," he said.

NINA AMES FREY ("Waif of the Jungle") was born near Boston, grew up in New York, and now lives in a village in Southern Vermont near the Molly Stark Trail, named for one of her ancestors. She has always been intrigued by the exotic countries of South America and has made an intensive study of the ancient Mayan race of Central America, the remarkable Indians from whom the story's hero, Arana, is descended.

Mrs. Frey intended *The River Horse,* from which the selection in this volume was taken, to be a book that would acquaint her young daughter with the Indians of Guatemala. But she found herself so fascinated by the shy and beautiful danta that the little animal became a major character in the story. She reports that it resembles the horse of the primitive Eocene age. It still exists today, a nocturnal and seldom-seen creature, on the Malay peninsula as well as in Central and South America. Fossils indicate that the tiny horse also once roamed the Western Rockies of the United States.

The River Horse has been translated into many languages, and was made into a radio drama as well. It remains a favorite with American readers of all ages.

The mysterious pull of memory

Cristiano: A Horse

BY W. H. HUDSON

A GAUCHO of my acquaintance, when I lived on the pampas and was a very young man, owned a favorite riding horse which he had named Cristiano. To the gaucho "Christian" was simply another word for white man: he gave it that name because one of its eyes was a pale blue-gray, almost white—a color sometimes seen in the eyes of a white man, but never in an Indian. The other eye was normal, though of a much lighter brown than usual. Cristiano, however, could see equally well out of both eyes, nor was the blue eye on one side correlated with deafness, as in a white cat. His sense of hearing was quite remarkable. His color was a fine deep fawn, with black mane and tail, and altogether he was a handsome and a good, strong, sound animal. His owner was so much attached to him that he would seldom ride any other horse, and as a rule he had him saddled every day.

Now if it had only been the blue eye I should probably have forgotten Cristiano, as I made no notes about him, but I remember him vividly to this day on account of something arresting in his psychology. He was an example of the powerful effect of the conditions he had been reared in and of the persistence of habits acquired at an early period after they have ceased to be of any significance in a creature's life. Every time I was in my gaucho friend's company when his favorite Cristiano, along with other saddle horses, was standing at the *palenque,* or row of posts set up before the door of a native rancho for visitors to fasten their horses to, my attention would be attracted to his singular behavior. His master always tied him to the *palenque* with a long *cabresto,* or lariat, to give him plenty of space to move his head and whole body about quite freely. And that was just what he was always doing.

A more restless horse I had never seen. His head was always raised as high as he could raise it—like an ostrich, the gauchos would say—his gaze fixed excitedly on some far object; then presently he would wheel around and stare in another direction, pointing his ears forward to listen intently to some faint far sound which had touched his sense.

The sounds that excited him most were as a rule the alarm cries of lapwings, and the objects he gazed fixedly at with a great show of apprehension would usually turn out to be a horseman on the horizon; but the sounds and sights would for some time be inaudible and invisible to us on account of their distance. Occasionally, when the birds' alarm cries grew loud and the distant rider was found to be approaching, his excitement would increase until it would discharge itself in a resounding snort—the warning or alarm note of the wild horse.

One day I remarked to my gaucho friend that his blue-eyed Cristiano amused me more than any other horse I knew. He was just like a child, and when tired of the monotony of standing tethered to the *palenque* he would start playing sentinel. He would imagine it was wartime or that an invasion of Indians was expected, and every cry of a lapwing or other alarm-giving bird, or the sight of a horseman in the distance would cause him to give a warning. But the other horses would not join in the game; they let him keep watch and wheel about this way and that, spying or pretending to spy something and blowing his loud trumpet, without taking any notice. They simply dozed with heads down, occasionally switching off the flies with their tails or stamping a hoof to get them off their legs, or rubbing their tongues over the bits to make a rattling sound with the little iron rollers on the bridle-bar.

My friend laughed and said I was mistaken, that Cristiano was not amusing himself with a game he had invented. He was born wild and belonged to a district not many leagues away, where there was an extensive marshy area impracticable for hunting on horseback. Here a band of wild horses, a small remnant of an immense troop that had formerly existed in that part, had been able to keep their freedom down to recent years. As they were frequently hunted in dry seasons when the ground was not so bad, they had become exceedingly alert and cunning, and the sight of men on horseback would send them flying to the most inaccessible places in the marshes, where it was impossible to follow them.

Eventually plans were laid, and the troop driven from their stronghold out into the open country where the ground was firm, and most of them were captured. Cristiano was one of them, a colt about four or five months old, and my friend took possession of him, attracted by his blue eye and fine fawn color. In quite a short time the colt became perfectly tame, and when broken turned out an exceptionally good riding horse. But though so young when captured, the wild alert habit was never dropped. He could never be still: when out grazing with the other horses or when standing tied to the *palenque* he was perpetually on the watch, and the cry of a plover, the sound of galloping hoofs, the sight of a horseman, would startle him and cause him to trumpet his alarm.

It strikes me as rather curious that in spite of Cristiano's evident agitation at certain sounds and sights, it never went to the length of a panic; he never attempted to break loose and run away. He behaved just as if the plover's cry or the sounds of hoofs or the sight of mounted men had produced an illusion—that he was once more a wild hunted horse—yet he never acted on his "illusion." It was apparently nothing more than a memory and a habit.

WILLIAM HENRY HUDSON was born on a sheep farm in Argentina, of American parents, although he later became a British subject. In all his later writings he was strongly influenced by the years he spent in South America. *The Tales of the Pampas,* for example, is about the gauchos in the wild country that was typical of Argentina in the nineteenth century.

On the farm as a boy Hudson liked to talk to the animals and felt that he understood their thoughts. He was passionately fond of all birds and animals, bitterly opposed to hunting as a sport, and throughout his life would befriend all wounded creatures. Significantly, "Cristiano: A Horse" is from his *The Book of a Naturalist.*

Hudson's most famous novel was *Green Mansions.* It was written in Cornwall in 1904, after novelist Joseph Conrad had brought him to England. This haunting idyll of the South American rain forests, with its tragic ending, reflects Hudson's intense feeling for the world of nature and his poetic sensitivity to it. The book has been made into a motion picture, and is considered one of the great classics of English literature.

INDEX

to Authors' Biographies and Stories